BOOK SIX

FORGOTTEN RUIN

LEAD THE WAY

JASON ANSPACH
NICK COLE

WARGATE

An imprint of Galaxy's Edge Press
PO BOX 534
Puyallup, Washington 98371

ISBN: 978-1-949731-71-2

www.forgottenruin.com
www.jasonanspach.com
www.nickcolebooks.com
www.wargatebooks.com

TECHNICAL ADVISORS AND CREATIVE DESTRUCTION SPECIALISTS

Ranger Vic
Ranger David
Ranger Chris

Green Beret John "Doc" Spears

Rangers lead the way!

CHAPTER ONE

IN the windswept darkness the Rangers made ready for the sack of Sûstagul. In that moment, before it all went the way it did, in those moments just before dawn, late spring on the coast of North Africa, or what the Ruin now called the Lost Coast, they were like some army of ants, heedless of the cyclopean picnic of the gods they were about to ruin the day of.

Busy at war because that was life to them. And there was nothing else. Not to them.

This ruined stretch of sand and water, waves crashing, was the Gateway to the Land of Black Sleep. Empire of the Saur, foe of what remained of humanity. Kingdom of Sût the Undying himself.

It was cold in the dark as we stacked in ladders waiting to board choppers for the hit on the sleeping port city that had no idea we were coming for it. It was still out there, sleeping in the dark as it had for the last ten thousand years and the times before these times. When it had been other names in other times no one in the Ruin even remembered anymore.

The Rangers, ever scholars of war, told me it was once founded by Alexander the Great. And that he named it after himself. But he did that in a lot of other places too. That lost boy of total war who probably would have been

1

a Ranger, or conquered the rest of the world, the unknown part, if he'd had some of the known world left, or someone to show him where the rest of it was.

The story of the battle of Sûstagul is told, will be told, by me, in retrospect. A lot happened that day. Now you need to know the whole story, not just mine and what Talker got himself into, and out of, if was he lucky.

So, I start here…

In the dark with the wind coming off the coast and beating at our Crye Precisions and assault packs, you weren't cold. At least I wasn't that morning. All I was think-ing about as we loaded up for the hit, the choppers thun-dering off into the morning dark and all of us stacked in the chalks waiting for our turn to get it on good and proper with the enemy, was what I had to do today.

My responsibilities as Assistant Squad Leader.

You could smell the ocean in the darkness out there. The salt. The life breathing in and out of the emerald wa-ters that lay there beating out their hearts against the shore-line. To the east the sun wasn't even a rumor in the black between heavenly bodies that illuminate the sky during our days, and nights, of endless desert marching to get here.

Sun and moon.

Those silent lights were gone now, and so was even the cold starlight this close to morning. It was just Rangers in the darkness, waiting on the beach, waiting to play their games of misdirection and mayhem. Breaking and enter-ing. Putting the kill on the HVTs we needed to get rid of today. Leaving a flaming wreck of the enemy's plans, hopes, and dreams along our backtrail.

Then probably playing body-toss-the-losers for the high score on the other side of it all before we got the warning order for the next op.

Ready for the pump. The pump. Body-toss the losers. Do it again, Ranger. And again, and again, and again.

Games of misdirection and mayhem.

Or, as Chief Rapp chuckled and said to me one time when we were just beggars on the streets of the old, ruined desert ports the maps of the Ruin called Sûstagul, "You Rangers and your... '*Look that way! Ranger Smash!*' I love that 'bout runnin' with y'all. You boys never get tired of the smash. Good on ya."

This morning wasn't going to be so much a *look that way* misdirection as... *Suddenly, there were Rangers everywhere* for the enemy.

The HVTs in Sûstagul were about to have a very bad day, courtesy of Rangers.

We were facing a Bronze Age force of lizard warriors, their high priests, the local mercenary armies inside the city, the fanatics in the temple district, and yeah... the massive orc horde ranging out there in the sands to the south and along our own backtrail. Even the odds were against us getting it done this morning, but it had to get done. We needed those walls bad. But, in our favor, the enemy had no idea that helicopters would be putting us all over the chessboard before they could do anything about it.

Sûstagul might have been a down-and-out, flotsam-and-jetsam wreck of ancient sand-blasted buildings collecting along the worn-out coast of a fading empire of evil, but it did have impressive walls. And with the orc horde now estimating at ten to fifteen thousand... we needed those walls. Badly.

Most human cities in the Ruin do. Have walls, that is. Impressive walls, high and strong enough to keep out the monsters. Remember… there are more monsters and… let's call 'em *demi-humans*… than there are humans ten thousand years in the future. Human civilization hides behind walls and hugs coastlines purely for defensive purposes.

Humans are the minority in the Ruin ten thousand years since the last Starbucks served its final cold brew.

I mark time in coffee. Don't @ me.

Yes, the Rangers could have breached those ancient walls with explosives, and of course would have had a lot of fun doing so, but the enemy would still have had time to react. The labyrinthine port city of Sûstagul was built with a series of dead ends and defensive points where any of the factions, had they chosen to hastily collaborate, could have put up a defense effective enough to upset our time hacks for taking control of the city.

The choppers, on the other hand, negated the impressively high and thick walls and put us in control of three key areas fast, as the battle, a street brawl really, began this morning.

Three key points with Sniper Overwatch to boot. Game-changer for us.

As Captain Knife Hand laid out the mission, he'd put it this way, standing in front of an impressive sand table of the whole city the Ranger NCOs had labored over for days. "Sûstagul is being denied the enemy to the south, Mummy specifically, and it doesn't hurt our geopolitical goals that the Saur army has moved through the old port this week and boarded upwards of two hundred galleys anchored in and around the port. They're headed north across the Med to join enemy forces under the Nether King."

The Saurian army entering the city...

That had been a creepy sight for me. I was working intel with Freak Squad and the scouts inside the city as a translator, when it happened that their trumpets trumpeted, the cyclopean gates opened, and the city came out to watch a parade of demi-human lizard men in armor from a lost age. The Saur had once conquered, and enslaved, half the known Ruin. Standing in the shadows of an alley, dressed as a beggar, watching the impressive Saurian legions enter the city, wind their way to the port, and begin boarding the pirate fleet that had come up from the City of Thieves along the old Arabian Peninsula, was an experience to remember. As I have said, or written here, many times before, it was like watching something epic from a long ago of myth and fable, warriors and wizards and strange tales. Pipes and flutes, those rolling thudding and thundering drums we'd heard when we did the Lizard King at Tarragon. It was barbaric and beautiful in some otherworldly way I'd never anticipated it to be.

Yeah, they're the enemy. But I count myself lucky to have witnessed such a sight. The martial pomp and the wizardly fantasticness. The slaves and strange animals Kennedy said were magical creatures like small dragons. The Saur warriors dressed in shining armor, golden weapons, and white kilts. Their priests wearing headdresses like something from a pharaoh's tomb. Then along came squadrons of *cat people*, or what Vandahar told us are known as the *Katari*, assassins and guardians of the temples deep in the lands of Black Sleep. These came before the priests, swinging great censers of incense, silent and watching the crowds for assassins.

It was almost festive to watch. Until you remembered you were here, scouting, alone. And felt the wild and electric fear running through the crowd like even they knew the line between life and death, and some gateway to the afterworld was running in and among us all. I'll confess… at that moment, as I felt it, I found deeper shadows to hide in. Got closer to the walls. Slipped the ring on and hoped the invisibility was enough to evade the strange and dark magics that seemed to surround this army of tyrants from an elder age.

It's one thing to be among dangerous humans. It's another thing to be in the presence of things that aren't human. Dangerous *things*. Wild and inhuman things.

Word along the shadowy alleys and low taverns of the ancient port lying next to the Great Inner Sea we'd called the Med, a place that had seen such armies come and go through long millennia, was that the Saur were joining the Orcs of Umnoth, hordes of the Nether Sorcerer, in the north as the war in Tyranor, or what we'd once called Macedonia, Yugoslavia, maybe some of Hungary too—that general region—escalated. The tachometer of such things pegged large-scale global warfare for all the gathering armies.

"We're going to make sure they don't make it to the dance," the smaj had noted during the briefing. "Even if stuff goes seriously sideways in there… primary objective is to burn that fleet down to the waterline before they can get their sails up and goin'. We will deny them an opportunity to contribute to the war effort. Remember… never will you fail, Rangers."

We had a lot to do that day to make sure we did not fail.

The Rangers were taking Sûstagul with the help of two Accadion legions lying well offshore in Accadion Navy galleys. Once the city was under our control and the invasion fleet was destroyed, we would move to the next phase of our planning. Using the city as a base of operations, we would then wage war on Sût himself down in the mysterious Valley of Kings.

The source code of the Saur, as it were.

This was the epitome of a zero dark thirty operation. I'd been here before, but back then, those other times, I'd been so freaked out about getting everything right, I hadn't been able to step back and… I don't know if *enjoy* is the right word, but *experience* it maybe is better. *Experience the experience*, as it were.

It really is something to be participating in something like this. Stacked and laddered on the beach as the next choppers come in, beating the wind and waves, the pathfinder sergeants running the LZ. Another group heading into the hit.

I took a sip of my cold brew, held it in my mouth, and watched the whole thing get underway. Ready to do my part.

No fail.

No matter what.

A whole bunch of bad guys were about to get seriously rolled. When your enemies have no idea they're about to get whacked big time, there's an electricity in the air, an almost nervous giddy energy, that's wild and loose and feels both dangerous and weirdly fun. At least for me. Other Rangers and NCOs seemed to be either too busy getting us ready with last-minute checks, acting as pathfinders, already on the move out there in the dark, tasked and purposed into special teams, or just getting zoned for the mission.

Sergeant Thor had that stare. The killing meditation in his arctic-blue eyes as he watched the shadowy east where we were headed. He was going for big game that day and had an HVT all to himself and his spotter.

In the morning dark and wind, Task Force Pipe Hitter in motion and already rolling on all their objectives, it was like watching a trap unfold all at once. MH-6 Little Birds were already taking Third Platoon, led by the captain and Sergeant Chris, in toward the docks and jetty that protected the harbors.

There are two. West Harbor. East Harbor. The locals have different names for them. The sand table has its own and by those we navigate.

Third had the primary no-fail mission, really. Smoke the sleeping Saur navy in port. Everything we did was in support. If they failed, whatever it took, every Ranger knew it was their job to make sure that fleet never left port.

After dropping Third, the Little Birds would return to take the assaulters in Second toward the center of Sûstagul, the city between the desert and the waters where once other famous cities of antiquity had once stood in the sweeping sands, staring and daring the Mediterranean, as we'd once called that sea.

The Great Inner Sea, the Ruin names it on yellowing maps from here to Accadios.

But now, as each of us waited in the standard Ranger short halt patrol position, on one knee, staggered and every other person facing one direction while the guys next to you watch the opposite avenue of approach for danger, we knew what we had to do to get done what needed to get done. And then to get it done if it didn't get done.

Never shall you fail, Ranger.

I was facing east.

I could see the lights of the desert port city barely out there on the horizon. The lights in watch towers. The smell of morning smoke in the dark.

Maybe. Maybe it was just the downwash and exhaust of the choppers. Three Black Hawks were coming in.

Yeah, I'll tell you how we got aviation support here when we'd been humping assault packs and everything we could carry for more than a year now. Or was it longer? It's easy to lose track of time in the Ruin. Ask anyone. That's one of the weird things here.

A year ago, we arrived here. Fighting for our lives on Bag-of-Death Island. Taking the fortress atop the crag we now called FOB Hawthorne. Going out to give battle against the Lich lord. *Give battle*, that's a very Vandahar way of saying things if there ever was. My training in psionics with him rubs more and more of the old wizard off on me.

And I like him too.

In a world gone mad, he's the only sane one left, trying with all his quiet powers to get it back to where it should be.

I find myself becoming more and more like him in speech the more time I spend with him soaking up the lore of the Ruin. Learning how to use what the Ruin has revealed in me. Psionics.

Then the dragon we smoked.

And the loss, personal, and having nothing to do with the regiment, of Last of Autumn. Queen of the Shadow Elves.

The death of our own personal dream of escape.

And I'm done with that. Despite the fact that it still comes at me when I'm least expecting it. And so for today, on this day that the Rangers have been calling *No Easy Day* since we rolled out at two thirty this morning, I gotta ruck thoughts of her because there will be more than enough to do in the space of it all.

I got a job to do today. That's all that matters.

Never will you fail, Ranger.

Got it, Sergeant Major. I will not fail. No matter what.

I'm the assistant platoon leader for the combat patrol against our objective.

Yes, I'll break down everything for you, now that I'm writing this, everything that happened all across the city that day. The things I was part of, a very small part really, and the things I heard about and was tasked with putting down an account of for the official record. Everything.

We were hitting them by surprise but, yeah, it wasn't gonna be easy today. Hence… No Easy Day as it would be known in the record.

I'll tell you everything. But a lot of it I won't be a part of. First Platoon had a tough fight through the streets and we faced some hairy stuff, but we made it. Things went according to plan, other things didn't.

"That's how it goes, Talk," says Tanner whose skin is necrotizing where he's been wounded. The bones beneath the skin on one side of his face are starting to show. Muscle too. He's starting to look like that old heavy metal poster of the gunslinger with the sneering gritting teeth.

Some of the Rangers just call Tanner *Iron Maiden* now. He doesn't mind that.

That's not the worst thing that happened to us on that not easy day.

I don't know if we can call it a win yet, but there was definitely loss. Maybe you'll have to decide if it was a *win* or a *loss*. So I'll tell you everything now. Who lived. Who died.

Warts and all.

But that's how I remember that morning by the sea. Waiting as the Black Hawks came in and the Rangers acting as pathfinders running the LZ got us ready to load in for the hop into Sûstagul. I remember the sea, and the darkness, and the salt in the wind.

And I remember that at that moment... we were all alive.

Ask me now and I'll tell you that despite the things I'd lost before that, I'd tell you I had everything in that moment by the sea, in the wind and darkness. And now... now we have less.

"That's how it is, Talk."

But before I tell you that part, and I'm going to tell you in the next few paragraphs because I hate it when writers I used to read just dangle you with some big reveal and then bait and switch you at the end.

I may not be the best writer, but I'm probably one of the best here in the Ruin, due to the fact that all the other hack sci-fi and overheated literary authors died ten thousand years or so ago.

So, I win by attrition. Which is still a win as far as I'm concerned. I'm competitive that way.

Before I tell you the worst part. Let me tell you something good. Something noble.

Her name is Running Under the Moon. So of course, by that you can tell she's Shadow Elven. They got those weird names, almost like North American Indians. And this is her story with the Rangers in Sûstagul.

She's just a few feet away from me in the darkness that morning. Facing east too. Watching the city. And no, this is not another one of Talker's love interest stories where he meets another hot elf, or succubi like the ones in the djinni bottle in my ruck.

But I think she's beautiful all the same. She's plainly beautiful. She's wearing Ranger Crye Precisions that have been rolled and tightened just for her as best we could. She has a huge aid bag on her back.

And this is her story. Just a little good to get started before we get to all the suck and all the bad I have to put down here. I'm sorry. I didn't want to write it that way. We had other plans. It's just, things turn out that way.

I wish all stories were good stories in which everyone lived happily ever after.

But... Running Moon. She came with the sergeant major on the resupply galleys after the sergeant major and a few other Rangers took the surviving galley from the citadel and returned to Portugon to meet another Lost Boy supply column coming down from the FOB.

You'd have to have followed this whole account to have understood that last paragraph. It sounds... weird, even to me. But that's the Ruin.

As the sergeant major related to me over a cup of the best kind of dark magic, she was there with the Lost Boys when the galley made it back to Portugon. In her broken

English she pounded her clenched fist into her palm which means something in Shadow Elven and told the smaj, "My man… I go… to him. Now."

That's the only English she speaks. Or spoke at that moment. She's learned a few other words since then. The Rangers have learned some Tolkien Elvish phrases. Not all of it good. Not all of it appropriate.

She smiles and blushes when they use those phrases. She loves them.

The sergeant major of course said not just no but hell no, back there on the docks of Portugon. And long story short she just went anyway. It was either that or drown at Portugon when she threw herself into the water, pack and all, and began swimming after the sergeant major's resupply galley as it left port.

So they hauled her aboard and she slept on deck and said nothing. The sergeant major wasn't pleased, but what could he do. The Portugonians weren't pleased because women aren't supposed to be on their boats. Superstitions and all.

One day the sergeant major finally approaches her with some coffee which she takes once he convinces her it's not poison, and then drinks with two trembling alabaster hands in the cold wind on the deck as the galley beats into the east.

"Who is…" He laughs telling me this portion of the tale. *Tale*. Another Vandahar word. "… your… man?"

So apparently she doesn't know any English except what she's already used and one other word.

McGuire.

The sergeant I carried on the run through the werewolf scout infantry when the giant Cloodmoor was throwing indirect fire in the form of boulders at us.

The sergeant major swears, and the conversation ends right there until they link up with us for the resupply west of Sûstagul. Because neither of them speaks any language the other speaks. So really, nothing can be done.

The sergeant major did say he knew some Korean but most of it wasn't appropriate for feminine ears.

He's smoking mad by the time he reaches the beach along the Lost Coast for the resupply.

Once Talker the linguist is involved the story becomes clearer. In front of Captain Knife Hand, who is none too pleased either, the sergeant major, and Chief Rapp, and me. McGuire isn't even in the mix yet, but she keeps standing on her tippy toes trying to look at the Rangers and our patrol base. Trying to see her man. Trying to spot him.

"Find out what she wants, Talker, and tell her she can't have it," ordered the sergeant major. "We ain't bringin' camp hoochies on a hit. Then get her back on the boats and headed home."

I ask her what she wants. Or rather... what her story is. Which is really the best way to find out what someone wants.

"Running Moon. Your man is at war now. And our traditions forbid... um... you know... you being here. So... why are you here?"

Her face is earnest confusion. Many of the Rangers have gotten together with the Shadow Elven women back at the FOB, but that was almost four months ago. We've been on the move since then.

I wonder if it's even dawned on the Rangers that these women now consider themselves... a permanent fixture in these men's lives.

As she struggles to find the one she *loves*—she keeps telling me this fact in Tolkien Elven, and I feel bad for her. What if McGuire is a real jerk? What if he doesn't care about her after she's come all this way? What if—and oh yeah, Vandahar was there too, smoking his pipe and looking rather bemused by the entire thing—but what if McGuire's sweet words of love were just... you know... words?

"We're at war now, Running Moon. We're going into battle."

We call her Running Moon now. Her full name doesn't slip off the tongue. I have just noted it for the record. You know me, it's all about the record. And coffee. But you knew that was coming.

She nods, repeating, "I know I know I know," in Tolkien Elven like it's a prayer. Chanting it. She's like a mother cat with kittens and I'm starting to think, or rather fear, the worst.

"Please, Talker. Please..." she begs me, practically starting to cry. "You know what true love is. We know of you and our queen before... you know. I must... see him. He is my man now. I cannot lose him. I cannot lose... Sergeant McGuire. Or... I will be lost again."

And then it hits me that she's just flipped over to the unspeakable-to-non-Shadow-Elves Korean Elvish that she doesn't even know is Korean. A language not to be used with humans like Talker. And this is bad because I know where this is going and it's worse than what I'd imagined. Real worse.

I ignore the scab she just pulled back reminding me of Autumn 'cause I've got a Ranger tab and all, he lied in this account.

But it's bad. *Lost* as she uses it in Korean Shadow Elvish really means… kind of like a widow. But worse. Consumed by madness and grief really. In short, the word used to denote this state of grief and madness among the Shadow Elven women specifically is… *sobi*.

Okay, she's got it bad and it's worse than that. Autumn had told me the story. And it's not a good story.

"I go with you. I fight."

The captain interrupted because apparently he'd picked up enough Shadow Elven to figure out what she just said to me.

"PFC Talker…"

Oh yeah. They gave me my rank back after I rescued Sergeant Joe. Every time they say that—*rescued Sergeant Joe*—Joe looks like he wants to thunder-punch me. And the truth is… it was him that rescued me out there. But hey, I'm a PFC again.

They don't just give these things away.

But back to the captain. "PFC Talker, did she just say she wants to fight with us? Did I understand that correctly? Alongside us? Did I pick that up right?"

"Affirmative, sir."

He sighed and yes… that permanent look of indigestion was suddenly there. "Son, I have a lot to do today, and we don't have time for this. Tell her she's got to go back with the galleys."

"Sir," said the sergeant major. "She'll just jump in the water and swim back again. She's crazy for Sergeant Mc-

Guire and if he ain't feelin' the same, well... this is gonna get real awkward for all of us."

The captain might have sworn at that point which is something he really didn't do, contrary to pretty much every other Ranger.

Chief Rapp never swore. Which I never realized until I just wrote that down.

"Well, we'll tie her up and wait until they get back to Portugon."

The look on everyone's face when our commanding officer said, effectively, *Well let's just tie up one of our indigs* spoke volumes.

She could tell things weren't going her way as we spoke in another language. She fell to her knees and grabbed onto Captain Knife Hand's shirt as she began to sob and tell her story.

Her *sobi*.

All of it and fast, as she spoke rapidly, weeping hysterically, all of us standing there in this very awkward moment scroll-life had prepared none of us for. The captain clearly uncomfortable to the point of death.

So. This is the sad story of Running Under the Moon. Her *sobi*.

She was once a maiden of the Shadow Elves. Before they fell on hard times. Those times were good, and she dreamed, as girls do, of love, and family, and hearth. In time she was betrothed to a young knight in the Order of Ravens. One of their finest warriors. Storms of Winter. He was taken captive by orcs from out of Umnoth who had ranged deep into the Savage Lands on slaving raids.

They had two children, Running Under the Moon and Storms of Winter did. A beautiful daughter and a quiet son.

She left them when her man was taken in battle. She babbled hysterically as she told us leaving them to find her knight. Rescue him from the enemy when there seemed no way he would ever come home. The Shadow Elves were on the ropes in those days. They'd lost the fortress. I'd seen the visions of the centaur raids.

She left one morning with only a pack on her back. Following quiet roads and the ruin the orcs had left in their wake. Checking the dead to see if any one of them was the love of her life. The reason for her heartbeat.

She followed the orcs for months as they headed into the darkening east, whipping and herding their captives. Then beyond the Stone Lands she found him one evening, lying in the dust by the side of the road, his throat cut only hours earlier.

"I lost him, I lost him, I lost him," she murmured to me. I translated to the NCOs and officers. The looks on their faces were stone. But in each of them I read that they understood on some level. That Storms of Winter could have been one of them on some mission in the dark on the other side of the world we once knew. And that there was a name on each of their lips. The name of someone who would have come looking for them… and who would have been wrecked if they had not come home.

The pain was old, but you could still hear the wounds and freshness there in her tears and voice.

"When I came… back… the centaurs had come… taken my children and many others…"

For a long moment there was silence as she lowered her head, sobbing, her shoulders shaking before us.

No. No, I wasn't going to ask what happened to the children. The sorrow and shame in her shoulders told us everything there was to tell about that story.

She looked up at the captain and spoke English.

"He… good. Sergeant McGuire. He… see… me."

I remember Last of Autumn telling me that many of the Shadow Elven women had had similar experiences. Slain men. Lost children. Their shame in losing the ones they loved was so traumatic that they seldom spoke, and some never spoke ever again, the weight of their loss strangling them. In time they disappeared, leading lonely and mad existences in the forests, near the mass graves and among ancient ruins.

Grief fading from existence forever.

"They feel they are… invisible now… dead… in the world of the living," the Shadow Elven queen had once told me when we were in love and talked of such things. "They say no one sees them anymore and that it is… terrible and what they… deserve. They are *sobi*. Consumed."

Autumn, as their queen, had asked the fae to find these women and ask them to return to help the Shadow Elves now that the Rangers were here. For the honor of their people.

I remember when they suddenly started appearing at the FOB. Dark and beautiful women, haunted and silent. Collecting firewood. Carrying water.

And of course, no matter how hard they tried to become invisible, to be seen no more, the Rangers, men, saw them. Smiled. Tried words out badly. Made them laugh. Began something… new.

Men and women. Elves or humans. It's hardwired into us.

"Sir," I said, turning to the captain as she kneeled before us. "The only way I can see around this is… to let her see him. Maybe that will calm her down a little. Maybe Sergeant McGuire can tell her to go. Maybe she'll listen to him?"

Of course that didn't work and I felt like the whole command team held me responsible for that one. Sergeant McGuire was sent for and of course she gasped when she saw him, not bothering to even stand but crawling toward the Ranger like a woman dying of thirst in the desert.

We held our breath. This could go real bad. McGuire could…

But that didn't happen.

He ran to her, and got her on her feet, whispering to her in flawless Shadow Elven.

"I see you, Running Moon. I see you."

I translated and felt dirty for doing so. Like… it was something so beautiful I had no business eavesdropping. But that's sorta my job around here.

Captain Knife Hand swore again and the sergeant major did too, but then he laughed as the captain walked down to the shoreline.

"Sir, I got a plan for her," called the sergeant major to the captain once it was clear there was no way she was getting back on that galley. "We need more medics, sir. That's for sure. Chief, can you get her up to speed on pressure bandages and tourniquets?"

Chief Rapp laughed and slapped me on the back with one of his giant hands.

"With the help of Talker here I don't see a problem with that, Sergeant Major. That's what we Green Berets do. We teach the indigs. So ain't no problem there."

She was mumbling into McGuire's broad chest.

"I will never leave you, Sergeant McGuire. I will never leave you."

So Chief Rapp got her up to speed, and now, here in the darkness as we get ready to load onto the Black Hawks, she looks like a small, slender, tiny Ranger with an impossibly large ruck filled with first aid gear. She is watching the east. She is ready to do the job we have given her if it means that she is able to protect her man in some way.

He brought her back from a living death. She will die for him if she has to.

McGuire is with Third, hitting the port. That was gonna be way too busy to have her involved there. Plus, we need her in First.

"Talker, I will never leave McGuire," she tells me every time I see her. "Never, Talker."

Her English is getting better.

She is determined to do her job, the one we have given her. She will have it no other way.

Sua sponte. Of her own accord.

What took me so long to embrace, she did instantly. Of her own accord she has crossed the world over dangerous seas just to be next to her man. The price—she goes with us into battle to help the inevitable wounded we will acquire.

Sua sponte.

Of their own accord.

There's a lot of suck coming. A lot of awful. I'd had my own loss. My own *sobi*. Seeing her... what she did for love… it did something to me I can't quite articulate yet. But… something.

And now the bad. The worst part. At the height of our success that day, we were counterattacked from the southern trade routes by the Guzzim Hazadi. The Orcs of the Southern Deserts.

Two Rangers went to the Southern Gate and held them off so we could consolidate and ready a defense of the city. They faced odds in the hundreds and even upwards of a thousand.

We have the drone footage.

Of their own accord they threw themselves into the breach and stood their ground despite the unviable odds. And now they're dead. Not like Tanner, walking dead. An undead bounty hunter for my best friend.

And not like Brumm who got resurrected once.

I guess twice isn't an option.

Brumm and Kurtz killed in action at the Southern Gate.

The worst day ever.

This is their story if it's anyone's. Two brothers who became Rangers and wouldn't let the other one down even when they went Winchester on mags holding back an army of orcs at the Southern Gate.

They held the line of their own accord, and myself and the rest of us are alive because of what they did.

This is their story.

Sua sponte.

CHAPTER TWO

THE old Legion fortress at Sûstagul was the keystone to the whole operation the Rangers were pulling that No Easy Day. The ancient city lay near the mouth of the River of Black Sleep that led deep into the mysterious lands of the Saur and the Endless South beyond the southern gateways.

By zero dark thirty that morning the operation finally got underway, I'd already been into Sûstagul several times with small teams of Rangers masquerading as traders. This was scouting and recon work. Chief Rapp ran these operations with Sergeant Hardt because it was his area of expertise as this type of mission usually fell to Special Forces operational detachment alpha units or SOF-D, also known as Delta Force. These units excelled at clandestine operations among indigenous populations, often masquerading as those populations and mixing in and among them to develop actionable intel. Once there, hidden in plain sight, they fed the Rangers intel in preparation for when the time came for the Rangers to lower their particular hammer of doom. Or, as Chief Rapp liked to put it... *Hey, look over there... Ranger Smash!*

Once it got out that the Special Forces operator had summed up Ranger operations in that particular and succinct way, the younger Rangers started exclaiming, "*Ranger Smash!*" on everything from combatives to chow. NCOs like Kurtz and Hardt winced visibly and restrained themselves from PT-ing their charges to death for nothing more than GP. General Purpose. The phrase reached peak saturation when Jabba declared one hot and dusty afternoon he could, "Ranger Smash *bigga bigga* big Moon God Potion." This came after a particularly long march over broken and rocky hills along the coast to reach our patrol base before the hit on Sûstagul.

Under Chief Rapp's guidance the Ranger scouts, and some other specialized teams, began entering the old port city of Sûstagul in the last moments of daylight on random days, disguised in dark robes and leading camels we'd traded desert nomads precious Ranger valuables for.

Not anything from the Forge. No weapons or anything tactically valuable. But instead, things the Rangers owned. Personally. The strange, dwarven nomads we'd encountered in the desert wastes sought such strange and often useless items and murmured over them like those little weird guys who captured the droids in the first *Star Wars* movie. To me their language was gibberish, and even the Stone Kings Dwarves had never heard of these strange cousins.

The Stone Kings considered the southern lands evil and wasted and would have nothing to do with the darkly robed dwarven nomads. We encountered them along the desert coast after the last of the Atlantean Mountains and all the horrors we'd left behind were nothing more than grey sketches on the distant horizon. When I turned to look behind us on those long hot marches, if just to see how far we'd come that day and waiting for the galleys to show up someday with fresh resupplies, the lands to our rear where I'd almost died and had become who I was now seemed like another life, or dream, I barely remembered having.

But the lessons were real, and I implemented them in every new task I was given now that all the Ranger NCOs felt compelled to make sure I was worthy of Joe's tab on my left shoulder.

I expected that and challenged them by exceeding whatever I was given to do. No one said anything congratulatory. The win was that they silently accepted that I had earned it and was now expected to live it.

So I did.

Before I get deep into the infiltration of Sûstagul under Chief Rapp, now might be a pretty good time to tell you what happened right after the events in the desert with just Joe and me running from the Lost Elves and finding the djinn's worlds inside the bottle. After the battle at the pass.

But more about all that weirdness later. Remind me if I don't get it down because now, well, I'm carrying something really important, and highly dangerous, in my assault pack as we get ready to storm the city. It's more dangerous, in my unexpert opinion, than most of the explosives the Ranger master breachers are currently carrying.

The djinn bottle scares the hell out of me the more I think, and learn, about it.

Of course there are those two wishes I'm owed. There has been much discussion, by everyone, on the subject of those two fantastic things. Two actual wish-for-anything wishes in which, as I understand it, you can actually wish for anything. That's… more than I would have ever thought possible. To be honest I'm not a big and fantastical thinker who wishes for things. I don't daydream. I just went after what I wanted in life. I'm pretty grounded in reality if reality is coffee and languages and rando achievement points. Which it is. Fight me.

But back to the wishes. I thought they'd be easy to use. As in… *Talker wishes for all the coffee in the world.* C'mon… I'm me and all. What'd you think I was gonna wish for? The first wish had gotten us out of a really bad jam and nothing awful had happened as a result of me just wishing for what we needed at that moment. Which apparently is a thing with wishes. That often, really bad things can happen. I have been warned about this by the wizard Vandahar, the Ranger-wizard Kennedy, and even a few of the other Rangers who've taken me aside to tell me to be real careful. What I gathered from all this advice is that some of the Rangers are sitting around thinking up how they'd use my wishes. Let's just say… I have a pretty good idea what some of those wishes they'd wish are.

After a few of those conversations with the Rangers, I made the mistake of destroying my fantasy of wishing for never-ending coffee by telling PFC Kennedy what I had planned to actually wish for before the smaj or the captain could make me use it for something dumb. You know, something tactical and all that supported the mission.

I mean, isn't the Forge one big programmable genie already? So they've got their never-ending wish machine for all the weapons a Ranger can dream of using on his enemies. Whereas Talker would like a canteen of endless coffee. And… well…

When you think about it, it's really not too much to ask.

"Bad idea, Talker," Kennedy told me in his own morose way as I told him what I was thinking. "Wishes," he began, "at least in the game I used to play…"

I held up one dirty hand to stop his standard disclaimer of *game might not match real life*. We were cleaning weapons at the time. Really dirty weapons. The desert can get sand in anything and everything. And the RPDs we'd acquired from the lost Nam chopper whose owners the djinn would only speak of as, *They chose badly, Master...* these old Frankensteins got really *scrungy* in the desert. We were training the Accadion legionnaires to clean them, but even with constant attention the old Soviet weapons systems seemed to attract sand like no tomorrow out here in the endless desert wastes. And yet they still fired when you needed them to.

Dirty and all.

"Frankensteins FTW!" Sergeant Joe would crow every time they miraculously fired despite the conditions. Joe was a big fan and now had a small cult following of young Rangers who wanted to know all about the legends of MACV-SOG.

That's right, Joe now had two cults. There was crossover, but the original cult felt the new guys hadn't paid their dues. They didn't even quote Book of Joe. Who'd these guys think they were?

But all that, and by that I mean dirty RPDs, wasn't good enough for Kurtz. And so, after getting a class in how to clean them properly, one I'm sure I never passed as now Kurtz seethed without ever saying a word about me being tabbed and all, we were then required to teach the legionnaires. The happily fatalistic Italian male Accadion legionnaires who would not stop talking about the three beautiful succubi who lived with the djinn in the lamp. The legionnaires were always going on and on about their fantasies with each and every one of the beautiful girls… who might be demons.

That part didn't seem to bother them in the least. Beings of eternal damnation and all. To be fair, I understood. I'd had thoughts… and before you think you know what those were, I had this fantasy about one of them teaching me *Infernal*. The language of damnation. She liked to arch her back and stretch whenever she was around. Gossamer robin's-egg-blue silks that barely concealed her delicious curves. She had full pouty lips and I could only imagine the consonants those futon pillows would make.

I was pretty sure exactly how they'd use my wishes if the legionnaires, or the Rangers, could.

I had to remind them. "You touch one of those women… it's ten thousand years, *mi amico*."

My friend.

They all smiled and laughed, patting me on the back. Not listening to me in the least. The Rangers were wagering on which one of the Italians was going to get zapped into the djinn bottle for ten thousand years.

But as Corporal Chuzzo liked to remind me every time these encounters occurred, "To them, Ranger Talker, some women are worth ten thousand years in hell for, you know? But you would have to be an Accadion legionnaire to know that."

According to our resident wizard-slash-PFC, the three beauties that hang out with the djinn, the genie… they really are succubi. Which really are demonic entities. I knew the term—words, they're my thing, right after a good cold brew—but I didn't really know what a succubus was in the Kennedy's-game-which-was-now-my-life sense.

"What, exactly, is a succubus?" I asked as we scrubbed RPD springs.

Kennedy pushed his RPGs up his nose. It was getting hot in the late night as spring came on in the desert and we marched on Sûstagul over endless dunes and flinty hills where you could turn an ankle in a New York second. "They're female temptress demons. They want your soul, Talker. They'll trade you their... um... bodies... to get it."

I noted Kennedy got nervous when he said *bodies*.

I smiled but didn't say anything. I'd caught Kennedy, and pretty much every other Ranger, eyeing the hot demon-women whenever they showed up in the afternoons with Al Haraq, the genie.

My genie apparently, according to him. Al Haraq liked to check in with me each afternoon when he'd suddenly appear out of nowhere. It was unnerving.

"Do you need this, Master?" the Djinn would boom good-naturedly in his massive basso profundo voice, laughing deeply as he did so. His huge white teeth gleamed against his chocolate skin and his burning blue eyes seemed to have tiny fires in them. They were more like fantastic gems than eyes. Stroking his goatee, he'd stare down and studied me, waiting for me to give him a task or use my wishes. "Do you need *this thing* or *that thing*, Master?" he would ask. "Perhaps you are ready to make one of your wishes, Master? What shall it be? All the gold of Lost Ophir? The Cursed Gem of Aaolek? One of the girls as your concubine?"

The pretty demon girls arched their backs and stretched their shapely frames in their gossamer silks, distracting me and everyone else at the same time. Rangers and legionnaires dropped everything to get a good solid look at how much ten thousand years in hell might cost one. Everyone weighing how long ten thousand years really was, and if it was worth it.

"It's a long time, Talk," Tanner said with a smoke between his teeth one evening when we weren't even talking about them. He was cleaning weapons too. Not because Kurtz had ordered him to. But... he keeps his distance from most of the other Rangers now, and it has been noted.

The Ruin is revealing more and more day by day.

Not that anyone cares how Tanner looks. But I think *he* does. Half his face is rotting skin and muscle. Bone showing through beneath. To be honest the Rangers think he looks like a total operator. That half-rictus deathly smile.

"It's like a bitchin' tattoo," said one of the scouts to me one time.

I think Tanner is keeping his distance now that he's becoming, *the Ruin revealing,* or so it goes, some kind of undead Tanner bounty hunter. He keeps his distance, hangs with Kennedy and me, and watches the horizons now and then, and the crossroads when we come to them and when he thinks we're not watching.

Like he's in a trance and far away for a long moment at those quiet places.

"Thing about crossroads, Talk," he told me later after we passed one on another brutal twenty-five-mile march that day. "Here in the Ruin... that's where the dead wait. They tell you guys their stories as you pass by about where they've been, where they were going before they got dead. How they got robbed, murdered, hung, or just lost out there. I know you guys can't hear 'em like I can. All the stories are the same though. Different, you know, but still kinda the same."

But back to that cleaning-weapons day when Talker said ten thousand years is a long time.

"I wouldn't mind a dance or two from one o' them genie girls, Talk," he went on. "I'd do ten thousand easy for one of 'em. But… lookin' like I do I doubt even they'd want some of this. Plus, I seem to bother 'em whenever I stare at them, and not the way you guys do. One of 'em always rubs her bare shoulders when I watch her, Talk. Like… you know, someone just walked over her grave. Like she got suddenly cold and all. Or at least that's what my ma used to say happened when you get that shiver and ya ain't cold. A goose walked over your grave. She's got nice brown ones, that one. Shoulders, Talk. Bet they're soft. You could put your head down on those and just… sleep for a while. That'd be nice. I'd like that one last time."

Tanner doesn't sleep much anymore. I don't like that he says *one last time*. But I say nothing, imagining tomorrow will never come. Like you do when you're little and you never wanna grow up.

The Ruin is revealing.

He's still my friend. And… I feel like, yeah, maybe the Ruin is a bad place and all, full of some kind of new suck every day, and believe me, marching across the desert is no picnic. But I feel like I can take it as long as Tanner's still got my six somewhere out in it and all. A friend is a precious thing.

The desert we pass through was once called the Sahara, but now the old names are fading away even in our own minds. The new names we find… those are what things are called now.

The Land of Black Sleep, or so the maps mark it.

After the Atlantean Mountains and the battle at the pass, the Lost Elves fled into caves beneath those same cracked and broken mountains and the captain and the sergeant major both thought that was good enough and no need to go in there looking for them as they were not a part of the operation to hit the Jackpot, Mummy, after we took Sûstagul.

Sût the Undying.

So we let them go because the Lost Elves are not aligned with any factions we've so far met here in the Ruin and seem to be about their own strange dark quest that has no bearing that we can see on what we are here to accomplish.

Sergeant Chris did want to go back down to the caves and toss a few acetylene bottles down there in the dark and see if we could collapse the tunnels on them at least. But at that moment we had no acetylene as the resupply galleys had gone back to Portugon. So Chris said he'd come back and make it happen on his next TDY.

Those Lost Elves had some burritos coming their way as far as all the Rangers were concerned, and I had a feeling, I don't know if it was the psionics or just my gut, but I had a feeling we'd be meeting up with them again someday.

They seemed like troublemakers if there ever were.

Once we were deep in the desert, still along what the maps called the Lost Coast, the Accadions assured us this area was pretty much empty and abandoned. The eastern end of the No Man's Land. We could expect no help from any of the locals as they were mostly just hostile tribes of nomadic monsters. The main bunch was a loose collection of savage orc tribes known as the *Guzzim Hazadi*.

We'd tangled with them around the citadel, some of their more western tribes. The ones rumored to have four-armed giant orcs. But now we were entering their eastern reaches where they were rumored to be as numerous as the sands of the desert and under the leadership of a general. We sparred with them a few more times in running battles as we kept moving east, but the Rangers drove them off with what the orcs no doubt considered strange firepower. They shadowed us after that. We'd fought two engagements against these guys with our backs to the great Inner Sea, and I'll admit, to see them arrayed out there on the desert sands with flapping banners and war drums, filling the dunes in battle lines, gnashing their fangs and barking as they beat scimitars against copper shields and stomped their leather-booted feet, to me it looked like they would have pushed us hard at any moment.

But the Rangers were more than ready to oblige the fight and stack some skulls.

As was our new friend, the strange and mysterious gorilla samurai Otoro. As the Rangers formed their hasty fighting positions, the giant samurai in armor strode forward to the foremost position and announced he would fight with them there when the "slaves" came to die at his feet.

I asked Vandahar about Otoro's race and he merely blew smoke rings from his pipe and watched the blue sea that day. It seemed rough and storm-tossed, driven by some offshore tempest. I was drinking coffee because I had been reunited with my ruck so of course you knew that was going to happen.

"His people live far to the east, past the edges of the known world where it ends there along a sea without end. On tiny islands they live and fight their endless wars of honor and revenge. I have never been that far and so I know little beyond strange tales. And when I do not know a thing… I say little, Talker, for it is better to say nothing than to spread lies."

"And what about this… *Axe Grinder*… he's looking for. Seems he wants burritos?"

The wizard looked at me quizzically.

"I do not know this word *burritos*, Talker. What does it mean?"

I'd forgotten Vandadahar wasn't hip on Ranger slang. Lately burritos had been getting talked about a lot among the Rangers. We had dead from all our fights. People were gonna get burritoed.

"I meant to say, Vandahar, a duel. A… score. It seems Otoro wants a fight with this Axe Grinder… to the death, by the sound of it."

Vandahar waved that away and puffed at his pipe as he sat in the sand and watched the whitecaps out there in the dark blue waters of the Great Inner Sea.

"I do not know much of the before times you come from, young Talker. But the settling of debts here in the Ruin is a common thing. On any street in any of the greatest cities, or even settlements along the frontier, you'll find desperate men with debts and scores to settle in the muddy gutters outside any tavern. Even I, and I try to live peaceably with all races… even I have enemies among these. And then there are the darker folk beyond the walls, those who would seek to settle some wrong I have done them. All of the Crow's March would see me dragged through their dark and misty lands. And I won't disagree with them; my efforts on behalf of the council have made me many enemies in many lands.

"But I myself... I count none. Nor do I seek any. Gladly would I forgive my foes if they would but seek it. Sincerely, I might add. But that is me and I am a wizard and those are my ways, and they are not the ways of all. I understand that more than most: those are not the ways of all. This... samurai... his debts of honor are petty to my interests. I suspect he will die getting done what he seeks to get done. And as for Axe Grinder, this chap he seeks to engage in single combat... he sounds like an ogre of some infamous renown if there ever was by the given name of the ruffian. They like to go about suchly named."

I was asking all this because the smaj, before returning with the galley to Portugon, had tasked me to "Figure out what this monkey wants, PFC Talker. See if he's gonna be an asset or a problem."

Then the sergeant major gave me a look that said if the monkey was gonna be a problem, the *roughly retire* was gonna get discussed. And since the smaj had one hand and I still carried his threaded G19, well... apparently that's one of my jobs around here.

Never shall I fail. But honestly, I was hoping the monkey would be an asset. Like ya do.

So, have I got all that straight? We marched across the desert, me in spares from the Rangers because most of my gear was destroyed. Carrying my sword *Coldfire*. My ring that made me invisible. The cool shield. My carbine. The smaj's Glock. Assault pack filled with my coffee stash and Kungaloorian sugar. And a genie bottle with three demon girls and a djinn I didn't quite trust.

We marched on Sûstagul and the dark morning arrived when the operation we'd been preparing for finally began. A lot would be expected of me of that day. And of everyone. A little over a hundred Rangers to take an ancient city and pave the way for two Accadion legions to land on the shores to the east. Wizards, assassins, Saur, mercenaries, and a ranging orc horde looking to strike our rear at an opportune moment meant we had to do what needed to be done fast with surprise, and of course... much violence of action.

Never would I fail.

CHAPTER THREE

FIVE to midnight, six hours before the break of dawn, before the attack on slumbering Sûstagul, Operation Stranglehold began. Scouts led by Chief Rapp cleared the old Legion fortress just beyond the main gates that led into the old port city from the west.

The haunted old Legion fortress.

According to rumors and myths collected in the shadowy alleys and sometimes in candlelit hovels of bent scribes and enigmatic sages who were willing to work with the strange desert nomads who'd been showing up of late on the streets of Sûstagul, the old Legion fortress was where the Ninth Accadion Legion marched out from and never returned a hundred years or so ago. That was back during the heyday of the rising city-state in the years after the defeat of the Saur.

Corporal Chuzzo confirmed these stories for us from the official Legion history. But what happened to the Ninth… well, that remains a mystery no one has any solid clue about. All that is known is that they assembled one dark and stormy night and marched off into the deserts of the windswept south, leaving by the Gates of Death, or what we have tagged the Western Gate.

They were never heard from again.

There are three gates leading into Sûstagul, not counting the two harbors protected from the Great Inner Sea on the north end of the port city.

The Gates of Death to our east, where the Rangers will lead the way into the city for the two Accadion legions that are soon to land on the beaches nearby. No one uses those deathly gates, in Sûstagul that is, but the Rangers and legionnaires will, in order to storm the city early one dark spring morning right about now. They are called the Gates of Death because the great necropolis of Sûstagul spreads away from the haunted old Legion fortress near them. The tombs and burial yards surround the area east and south of the fortress, lying roughly between the abandoned fortress and the temple district to the south. The temple district is dominated by the Sanctuary of Pan. Or, as it is known locally, the Mad Piper's Palace. Apparently Pan, whoever that is, is some sort of local god that holds much political power and influence here among the *Sûstagulians*.

I don't even know if they call themselves that. Good guess, though.

In fact, now that I write that word I just made up down, it occurs to me that very few people refer to themselves as citizens of this desert port city on the southern edge of the known world. Everyone is always referred to by some other tribe, organization, or cult, here in the weeks I have spent with the scouts listening and gathering intel for Stranglehold. It is as though they, everyone on the streets and twisting alleys of this strange city, are just passing through on the way to somewhere that doesn't sit on the front doorstep of the Ruin's underworld.

The Land of Black Sleep. Empire of Sût the Undying.

What did Tanner say about crossroads on the march here? "That's where the dead wait, Talker. They wait there to tell you all their sad stories and all the wrongs that've been done to them. It's like listening to a squad that ain't got no weekend pass 'cause someone busted the DUI checkpoint and the smaj is looking for scalps."

The gate in that district, the temple district, is the most impressive and ornate of the three gates into Sûstagul. It is called the Gates of Eternity, and no one uses that gate much because it only leads into the south, ahem, the Land of the Black Sleep, and nothing good comes of going that way. Even if you go there by first going out by the Gates of Death like the lost Ninth Legion did.

The merchants near the Gates of Eternity are few and shops close early. That's where you find the weirder sages and mumbling scribes who prefer the cemetery quiet and shut their doors tight against the strange festivals of Pan that go on during full moons past midnight bell. It's a quiet district and not just because of the various walled sections of dusty old tombs and graveyards that turn the whole place into one vast spreading necropolis. It's a quiet that seems to come from the south, radiating like some haunting soundtrack in an old movie where the characters lose their minds in the desert, which was really some kind of hell.

That's my impression. Your mileage may vary.

The impressively carved and ornate gates are surmounted by two broken colossi, one of a human warrior, a legionnaire of Accadios, the other a Dragon Elf knight I recognize from having come across all those Ruins in the Savage Lands when we first arrived in the Ruin. The only reason I could figure for this is that the Savage Lands were once

Dragon Elf territory, and that this was once the forward mark on the map for those two empires at their zenith.

But they're all gone now. Still, the carvings are similar. Both statues are missing limbs and crumbling into the desert before the gate. The human statue's head has toppled off and lies half buried in the sand nearby.

Brumm remarked upon seeing them up close when he was on a scouting mission with a small team I was acting as linguist in, "Well hell, that's straight outta a *Lord o' the Rings* movie and all."

Vandahar later informed us those gates were guarded by the statues of "Accad the Reckless who founded Accadios long ago, and the other is Throm the Wanderer, first of the Elder Dragon knights who wandered far into the East Waystes and never returned from the Rifts. In those long-ago dark days both their armies joined in a desperate alliance at the River of Night and turned back the forces of the Saur in a terrible battle that marred the lands with great and dreadful magics. The battle was turned when Throm slew the great black dragon Revenanor, a most terrible foe if there ever was one, with his fabled blade.

"Thus they are called the Gates of Eternity, as the Royal Road the Saur pharaohs once used when they came into the City of Cobras, as ancient Sûstagul was once known in the Lost Years, begins there at the gates and leads down through the Valley of Priests and then into the Valley of Kings itself, where lies the Grand Pyramid of Sût himself." So says Vandahar.

The third gate, the Eastern Gate, is called the Gates of Mystery. Most likely because that's where the sorcerers' market that makes up the most active population center lies within the port city.

That's where First Platoon is going at dawn. Forty Rangers to make a major strike against the sorcerer chief, Ur-Yag. But that will begin in the first moments of daylight, once the Western Gate is under our control and the scouts under Chief Rapp have secured the haunted fortress.

Every step is a key in Operation Stranglehold, and so I'll lay it out now and recount how the scouts, Chief Rapp, and Tanner took the old Legion fortress to kick things off.

Step one started just before midnight as the rest of the Rangers moved into position near the LZs along the beach that the pathfinders had set up.

The Ranger scouts, working in small four-man teams, and surrounding the old fortress in the shadowy streets of Sûstagul, began their assault as the midnight bell rang forlornly within the city. They were carrying suppressed weapons, as this type of operation was definitely in the wheelhouse of Ranger *breaking and entering,* which was how they'd operated taking out high-value targets back in the sandbox ten thousand years ago.

Where it got unconventional is they were dealing with spirits and haunts inside the fortress. And suppressed weapons, for the most part, weren't going to work on... *ghosts.* Undaunted, the Rangers looked for other ways to attack the spirit world, because why not. Ranger gonna Ranger regardless of the negative material plane and the netherworld. And of course, a *Ghost Kill* was now as prestigious as a *Garotte Kill* in the *Ranger Killing Bad Guys Bucket List* constantly talked, and wistfully dreamed, about.

According to Kennedy, and later confirmed by Vandahar, the scouts were going to need magic weapons to effect the termination of these particular tangos. So the Rangers turned in their battlefield pickups and Vandahar schooled

Kennedy in the art of magical detection. Before long, the scouts had at least one magic weapon apiece to do the deeds needed to be done to take the fortress.

Three four-man scout teams hit the fortress at midnight beneath a waning moon. The night was hot and scudding clouds had drifted across the desert to diffuse the moonlight. Shadows deeper. The air stiller. All the things Rangers wanted for the quiet and deadly work that was coming in the hours before dawn.

They had three assets with each team. Chief Rapp as the Green Beret was already a combat multiplier in any given situation. But, as had become clear to us, and spelled out by Kennedy, the chief had also been *Ruin revealed* into, as what Kennedy's little game of strange dice, paper, and pencils called… *a cleric*.

Evidence:

He'd resurrected Brumm.

He'd *damned* an undead attack I'd personally witnessed during the battle against the Necromancer and the Army of the Undead. What is *damning*, you ask? Well lemme tell you this one 'cause it's crazy. Apparently there are types and even levels of undead. There's actually a pretty brutal hierarchy that works its way up from plain old skellies and zombies, or what we have taken to calling *zekes*, and on up to ghosts and ghouls, vampires, and even powerful liches which is what we're pretty sure this Sût is. Mummies too.

Anyway, sometimes a cleric of sufficient… *faith*, I guess—though Kennedy used the word *level* and then explained it as *power*. Then he had to explain that some more. In the end we got it. It was basically rank like in the Army. High enough rank and a cleric could damn the undead like a command sergeant major could smoke a whole battalion on payday PT to make sure no one got a DUI that weekend. Run everyone to death and maybe they're too tired to get into trouble. Clerics can also *turn* the undead, which means... make them run away. But Chief Rapp had damned them which meant... he'd effectively disintegrated them because he's such a stud of his own faith.

And there had also been other mystical, or dare I say *holy* occurrences that indicated the Ruin had turned Chief Rapp into some kind of holy warrior.

"He could be a paladin too, maybe," Kennedy had remarked. "But there are old rules about edged weapons, and remember guys, they may not even apply here. It's just..."

We knew.

But over time it was the chief's healing powers and ability to cure magical diseases by, as he called it, "asking God for a little help with this one or that one," that led us to believe he had become a cleric of some sort. That the Ruin had revealed him to be this.

Whatever it was... it was awesome.

Every Ranger wanted to be revealed. Mostly into some kind of killing machine like the captain or even Corporal Monroe who'd become a minotaur. Hopes were still high that this would happen among them, but we'd been here for a year now, so if it was gonna happen it probably would've already.

And remember... I have mind powers now. Psionics. No one wants those. They wanna be were-tigers or some version of the comic book character Wolverine.

I honestly don't even want psionics. I get a headache every time I use them.

Chavez in Scouts said to me one time, "Eh, no offense, Talker, but your superpowers are lame and all. You're like one of the lamer X-Men who can just shoot lights or something. You need to get good."

Then the Rangers started arguing about who was the coolest X-Man. Is that right? *X-Man*? What's the singular and why do I care? Whatever it was… in our developing version of *X-Men: Rangers* I was the equivalent of someone called Jubilee who wasn't very good and all.

Everyone at least agreed on that and for about three days I got called "Jubilee." And the best way to deal with that is just to say nothing, take it, and wait for a firefight or a sand kraken attack to change the discussion and in time… *Hey, Talker. Whaddup, Ranger?*

No more *Jubilee*.

Since there would be undead and actual evil spirits inside the old Haunted Legion Fortress—and believe me, that's a thing I thought I'd never say with a straight face—and since we had witnessed Chief Rapp actually destroy spirits, and the undead in general, with a mere wave of his hand, he'd be leading Team One into the gatehouse beyond which lay a courtyard full of graves.

Their job was to secure the access points, as the walls were too high and too unstable to support breach by ladder.

The city elders of Sûstagul had been burying criminals of the worst kind in there for hundreds of years in shallow graves at the height of the sun to avoid even remotely coming into contact with the angry dead that lurked there. It was considered, by the local denizens of Sûstagul, to be a very cursed place and so no one much stayed near the district haunted by rumors and other darker, more real, phantasms.

So of course, because of its isolation, height, and tactical value, Captain Knife Hand decided that would be our opening move for Stranglehold.

The chief would lead Team One in and clean the place. And by *clean* it was meant, whack the undead. The three Rangers surrounding him on Team One would keep the dead off him while he *damned* or *turned* them, or did whatever he did to secure the entry to the old fort.

Chief Rapp didn't even know what he was gonna do. But he had some ideas about how to give the restless dead their final repose. And of course, Vandahar had many conversations with the special operator advising him on what he personally had seen other fabled "clerics of great renown from the Golden Age" perform on the battlefield in epic wars of the past.

Team Two, led by Kennedy, would go for the fortress itself while Team One secured the entrance into the fortress grounds. And yes, PFC Kennedy was leading a fire team. The area they were headed into left the realm of kinetic CQB and got arcane. Here, he was better qualified than any Ranger to react to contact. So… he was tip of the spear on that one. Kitted up in plate carrier, FAST helmet, and all the Ranger gear and weapons he could strap. And the dragon-headed staff. Team Two would stack on the gate and then enter once the courtyard was secure.

Kennedy as the wizard was going in as extra firepower to confront what we suspected, via intel collection among the sages, lay within. The myths and legends I'd discovered by playing the part of wandering nomadic scholar and talking with the sages and scribes in the afternoons near the Gates of Mystery, was that there is a guardian who inhabits the main tower. Also, the sages insisted we drink small ibriks of dark rich coffee spiced with cardamon and cinnamon. That's not important to the story, though it sure was to me. Apparently a wizard who served the Legion long ago had created a spectral force that would retrieve the bodies of dead legionnaires and return them to the fortress in times of battle.

The guardian.

When the Legion and the wizard disappeared in their march to the south, the *March of No Return* as it is known, the specter remained in the main tower and is often seen to haunt the battlements late in the night. The districts nearby note that when a mercenary dies in a street battle between the various wizards in the market district, that mercenary's body often goes missing in the hours after the battle. One story even reported that the dead mercenary was laid out on a table at a local inn and his buddies were drinking all around him as a final sendoff when all the candles and the roaring fire were extinguished. Something cold and dark entered and dragged the body away, unmolested by the hard-bitten mercenaries who promptly departed the city the next day.

Legends say the specter, a hanged murderer the wizard used in order to make his magical creature, is this Collector of Corpses. Forever haunting the main fortress.

And because it's a magical creature and not an undead creature, Kennedy's job is to go in there and fireball that thing good and well.

Fire in the hole, as it were.

When the courtyard and the fortress were cleared, Tanner as Team Three leader was to enter the crypts with Team Three and deals with the Sisters of Death, if they actually exist. We aren't sure as this is just a boogeyman story told in the marketplace, but Captain Knife Hand insists we treat it as actionable intel. So Team Three goes down and clears the Sisters of Death. Witches, basically. There are rumored to be three of them, deep within the old Legion catacombs, cavorting with the dead and abducting the children of the marketplace for dark rituals and sale to the Saur in the south. Tanner's job is to make sure they either stay out of Ranger operations, or they get burned. He's been given the authority by Captain Knife Hand to make the decision on the ground.

Betting is heavy that he's gonna burn 'em.

Either way, securing the fortress at these three points is the key to getting the snipers in and taking control of the district. I wasn't part of the operation, but Tanner and I linked up later and he told me how it all went down.

So, I'll add this to the account in his own words.

It of course began at midnight because when else are you are going to hit a creepy old haunted fortress full of ghosts and the angry dead.

CHAPTER FOUR

"WE went in there hard, Talk," Tanner told me when he linked up with First as we hit the marketplace going for the tower of Ur-Yag. To the north, over the port district, black smoke billowed up in the early morning as Third Platoon under Sergeant Chris and Captain Knife Hand burned ships in the two ports to the waterline there.

They were already having their own hairy battle and I'd find out all about that later.

"Sergeant Hardt and his three guys were tip of the spear with Chief Rapp acting as the anchor. Team Two with Kennedy and my team with me, Hughes, Johnson, and Lee, were stacked on the right. Once the hit time went active, we came from three LP/OP points we'd set up in the district and converged on the objective. Team Three left the crossroads around ten and took up position in the dark near the Hanging Tree. Which, honestly, the wind wasn't up last night, Talk, coulda been a better choice for me. I'm seein' all these dead guys who hang around the tree, every convicted murder and mob justice victim for the last five hundred years whining about the unfairness of it all. All of 'em tellin' me they're innocent and all. Then again, some o' them are just plain crazy, know what I mean? Nothin' but nonsense, or at least you hope it is because some of the things they go on about are just plain *dark*. Plus, according to Lee, place smells like ripe death to the rest of the team. There's even two dead guys the wizards hung just last week. Two Tyranorian mercs the Cabal had a beef with for some reason or another."

Tyranor is where Greece used to be. Greece and parts north. It's sort of an area of continual warfare between the city-states and the orcs of Umnoth in the east under the Great Khan. Just adding color here.

Tanner continued. "So anyway, the chief goes in following his trick rifle and he's got Hard to his right on the wedge running security to keep the corpses off of him. That's when things get very weird. Did you guys feel that earthquake out there on the beach around the LZ? Because there was a big one right there in the district."

We did not. Even though everyone in the scouts reports feeling an earthquake at that moment just as Team One, Chief Rapp specifically, crossed under the old crumbling arch into the fortress courtyard where the broken gates of the fortress lay off in the weeds, none of the other elements in the detachment noted the phenomenon as we staged in and outside the city.

Just reporting the facts here.

"Corpses start pulling themselves out of the ground almost immediately, Talk. The place in there is a real wreck and if you were to ask me… that whole place should just get the torch. Pop some thermite and toss it in, one'll do the trick it's so dry and dead. Dust is hundreds of years thick. So anyway, we got night vision running, not thermal 'cause we got dead and as we've learned they don't throw no heat sig. Me… well I got the *Death Vision* now 'cause I'm dead and all. You know how I am, Talk."

I do.

"I'm feelin' it too and these ain't like the other dead. These are *screaming mad*. And you know, like… when you hear the ocean way far off? We all heard it, and I thought the op was blown as it got started. But when I called in to the captain as we stacked, if the other LP/OPs inside the city were hearing it, they all reported negative on noise. City was quiet at midnight. But things were weird *inside* the fort."

They definitely were at that.

"Hardt goes suppressed and starts dusting skellies and the zombies that are crawling out of the ground like warrior ants all at once. He's a good shooter so rotting skulls are exploding in bone spray and all. He's got Chavez and SpaghettiOs with him. It's that hot an' close, as those things just come out of all the shallow and badly marked dusty old graves that are everywhere. Drone feed didn't do that charnel house justice. It's a morgue in there and a badly run one at that. The city's been digging graves, but only barely, inside the old courtyard since the Legion went ghost."

Two points here. Talker's commentary.

The reason why the denizens of Sûstagul—sanctuary of Pan priests, wizards, and the various city elders—used the courtyard as a burial place is due to the tradition that the corpses that go there are the corpses of the murdered. Something about the disappearance of the Legion on the March of No Return makes them believe that corpses buried here can't return in spirit form to exact their revenge on those who likely had them killed. And the wizards, leaders, and temple seemed to have a lot of people killed as a matter of doing business. Apparently all these political and religious elements are burying their enemies and victims here for fear that some sort of netherworld retribution is possible.

Which, let's be honest, it probably is.

Point two is this. The Rangers call SpaghettiOs by that tag because he will trade anything he has for any MRE that comes even close to the fabled canned food. It is his coffee. I understand. I respect that. We can't all choose our addictions; they choose us when we are at our weakest. Lucky for SpaghettiOs, the Forge can even crank out old discontinued MREs that resemble this fabled product. Somewhat.

So among Rangers he is known as SpaghettiOs. Which is way better than the Jubilee round I dodged by being cool about it and all.

Back to Tanner.

"Rangers on suppressed and all is fine but it ain't doing squat at that moment because there are more dead than magazines. It goes hand-to-hand that fast because that whole place is filled with corpses, and more and more are coming out of the ground and the dried mud mausoleums that have been erected along the walls. Like I said, they shoulda just burned the whole place, Talk. Only way to be sure. It was like stepping on a nest of angry hornets if those hornets were dead guys. Angry dead guys. Then again, hornets are pretty angry to begin with so it's just like stepping on any nest of hornets. Anger's part of the package, know what I mean, Talk? It's the details. Like how you go on and on about coffee which no one else cares about and kinda pisses everyone off. Instead, you could get the details like hornets' nests being innately angry into your… is it *prose*… that the word, man, that what you call it? Let's just say writing and not be too fancy. You could do that instead of coffee which no one cares about it. You feel me?"

Tomato tomah-to.

Something I should have mentioned earlier: part of the magical weapon redistribution prior to the op involved my magical dented shield, the one I'd picked up in the rivers beneath the underground mountain where I'd gotten lost. Sergeant Hardt got it because it was believed he might need to use it to give the chief the time needed to do whatever Chief Rapp was gonna do to lay the smack down on the undead. I mention it now because Tanner's about to mention it then.

"Like I said, Talk," continued Tanner, "five-five-six is just goin' straight through these things if you can't plant your rounds in the head, and even the head shots sometimes don't do jack. First one of them things reaches Chavez of all people and grabs right onto him. He swears, pushes the thing off him, and shoots it a bunch for the effort. It's gettin' back up the whole time and coming straight for him again. Plus he's trippin' out as he shoots it like he just got drugged or somethin'. Talking about a world of the dead and all. Winter forever and all? But to Chavez's credit, he stays on mission and keeps blasting like ya do.

"SpaghettiOs takes that mace he got, the one the guy in Third says swings like an expensive golf club when it connects, real power hitter, and just starts laying into the zekes coming from the flanks. He's crushing skulls hard and keepin' 'em off the chief as Hardt switches to the shield and gets in front to absorb the attack. Like I said, if we weren't trying to do it quiet and all and keep the district *low fi*, then we coulda breached, banged, and cleared the hell out of that place like it was the Fourth of July. Honestly, the cleansing power of thermite woulda done the trick in an hour or less. I am a believer in that little cult. Entire place is one dry matchstick waiting to go up. Shoulda just done it that way, Talk."

Tanner tells me Chief Rapp is telling them to hold position when even some of the Rangers are starting to note the suddenly increasing and overwhelming odds that are rapidly developing and that it might be wise to pull back to the gate at least for a chokepoint to fight from. Plus, the support of the other two teams.

"Negative, Rangers. Hold position. He got this!" shouts Chief Rapp above the dead roar and the sounds of skulls being crushed. Then all of a sudden, an entire... I don't know... wing, Talk, or a phalanx of the dead just turns to dust all at once. Chief is holding out a cross like from one o' those old vampire movies, I kid you not. He shoves it one direction where they're concentrating and getting ready to push hard. Mind you, Hardt is doing everything with your shield, going all Captain America to keep them off the chief's front, using it like it's a weapon instead of, you know... armor. Zekes are just flyin' away from that thing, end over end, and ramming into the back ranks of the dead that are everywhere and pushing forward hard. To me, Talk, watching from the gate where we're stacked, and looking to contribute in a meaningfully kinetic way, know what I mean, Talk... all that still ain't enough."

"Sounds like it got close," I prompt Tanner when he goes all offline and *otherwhere* for a moment.

Then he says "Nothin'" to someone I can't see and continues with the story of the battle inside the courtyard. That happens more and more these days. Him going *otherwhere*.

"Next, Chief points that little silver cross he's got out like Kennedy's wicked fire staff. Bad guys on the flank turn and just run into the wall to get away from the Green Beret, collecting there like a rat pile. That was sick. Some of them even try to climb the wall just to get away from the chief's… *glare*. I mean, that ain't right, it wasn't the chief… it was that little cross that was freaking them out. I don't know if everyone could see it like I can—'cause you know, I'm one of 'em—but there were like rays of light coming out of it. Wasting them all and burning 'em. It wasn't good light, Talk. Not silver or gold or anything pure like that. It was like… if bronze were a light. But a light that rammed right into you and destroyed you. It started to hurt me just to look at it, man. Guess we didn't factor my condition into the battle plan and all. But I just sucked it up and held position 'cause I ain't important to what's going on right at that moment.

"So like I said, it was that light comin' outta the cross they were running from. Chief was pointing it like he was layin' the hate with a two-forty asking who wanted some next. Answer… none of them did, Talk, none of them wanted any of that, man. It was beautiful even though it hurt to look at. So by that time there's some serious death going on for the dead inside the courtyard. Ones that ain't burned is turned. But more and more of 'em are still coming out of the ground like there's a corpse pile ten miles deep under all the dead, dry dirt in that cursed place. When you think about it, there's a lotta dead over time. It probably goes back to before we jumped forward. Way back, Talk. Way back."

At that point, according to Tanner's account, Team Two pushed in to support Team One, going straight to hand weapons as they engaged the surging dead. There were ghosts in the mix now and Tanner doesn't do their description justice because that's his new normal, but the others on the teams say it was freaky. Like a CGI effect viewed through some kind of drug hallucination. The Rangers on Kennedy's team laid in with an axe, a sword, and a spear. Rangers gonna Ranger even if everything goes all cold and touch-of-death spirit world. But each of these three particular weapons had magical properties. The axe made things catch fire. That was instantly a bad idea as the corpses caught fire, were battered away from the hammer blows of the Ranger wielding the axe, and landed on other corpses that immediately caught fire as well due to their dried, desiccated, and sometimes badly mummified condition. Now there's not just dead dudes but *burning* dead dudes attacking Team One trailing smoldering black smoke like some smelly and ethereal snake.

"I don't know… I ain't you, Talker, that's what it looked like to me. So it's total chaos. Spear guy, Walters, he's just tagging zombies right in the skull with that thing and they're going fetal. Keeps chanting, *You're done, bro.* Then sticks another one. *You're done. You're done too. How 'bout you… you're done also.* Ghost chick, trailing blue light, she's some kind of Viking shield maiden, she comes at him and he just rams that spear right through her ghost belly and she disintegrates with a smile on her face. I think she was happy, man. Weird stuff.

"I got the lead on Team Three and I see where we can move into the room… I mean courtyard… and take up a position to support both teams. The death smoke doesn't bother my Death Vision any and I can see all that slaughter clear as day. But the night vision for the rest of my guys ain't handling it so well. So we hold for a second just to get the other teams anchored on each other."

Tanner lit a smoke and continued.

"Hardt domes this one zeke with the edge of the shield. Guy explodes in a spray of guts everywhere in response. Thankfully, that guy explodes *away* from the shield because suddenly there's maggots and blood spray everywhere, and the other zekes it lands on begin to smoke and die from the maggot blast. I don't know what that guy was but whatever he was he was some kinda undead IED, I don't know, know what I mean, man?"

No. No I absolutely do not. Is that a thing here? Dead Guy IEDs that spray you with maggots? Hard pass, Sergeant Major. I'll just go kill the gorilla if you don't mind. The one with the giant chopper sword that cuts dudes in half. I like those odds better than to have a dead guy explode in my face with maggots that kill even the already dead.

Hard pass.

Then I remember I am Rangering at the pro level now and if the smaj, or my fellow Rangers, need me to smoke some guy who might explode maggots and guts all over us… sign me up. Mission success is everything and you will do anything, and everything, to make sure we get the win.

In it to win it. Or…

Never shall I fail.

I am noting this for myself. Not for the record. It's important to remind myself how far I'll go now that I've come to realize who I am. And the answer to the question of *how far*… is always yes. All the way now.

After the desert… I'm all in.

Yeah, that may sound hardcore and all, maybe it doesn't. But to me, here's how I address this question every time something calls for me to Ranger as hard as I can. Three-day marches with no sleep. Running forward under heavy desert orc-nomad-massed arrow fire to get a downed Ranger to safety or get some ammo forward to support the push. Each time, I just ask myself: would I do this for coffee?

And the answer to that is of course always *yes*. I'd do anything for coffee. Anything. Period.

So that's how I Ranger now. If I'd do it for coffee, then… I'd do it to Ranger. Trust me, you can weaponize addiction. Ask me how. Thank you for attending my TED Talk.

"So then Hardt tells us to move in and support the left flank," continued Tanner. "We go in hard with hand weapons. I got this savage little sword that swings easy, man, so I lay into those dirtbags and carve some zeke forward, Talk. My team is hacking and slashing to link up right in line with SpaghettiOs and Hardt in front of the chief. By that time, we were all on-line and pushing the dead back a little. If they don't keep comin' outta the dirt we got this in the next few. 'Cept they do. They keep coming like the courtyard's a fountain of dead guys and ghosts.

"And that's when the chief takes a knee, bows his head, and it's clear he's askin', know what I mean, Talk? He's askin' for a little help. His… cleric thing. Somethin's about to happen, Talk. We all know it. And you know what happens, man… that wind comes up off the desert floor even though the night is hot and still. You guys feel that wind just a few minutes after the bell?"

We did. We missed the earthquake, but we felt the wind. We were on the sand of the beach to get close to the city. To the LZs where the choppers would come in and start ferrying us over the walls to secure key locations. The walls of Sûstagul are guarded and the gates are locked at night. So, at that time when the wind came rushing in, we were on the beach where the Legion would come ashore after first light.

I thought at first it was just the wind off the sea, but it came from the desert and it smelled… good. Like sandalwood. Clean and nice. And I'll just note here that it ain't the way the desert smells most of the time. Or at least since we left the shadows of the Atlantean Mountains. Mostly, the closer we got to the lands of the Saur, the whole desert, all the lands to the south that we kept off to our right as we marched here, they either smelled like orc horde, or something far worse. Not pleasant at all. Would highly not recommend. I'm honestly not sure what's worse, desert orc smell or bag-of-death dead orc island from when we first got here, which is a smell I cannot seem to erase from my olfactory memory even a year later.

So sometimes the desert smells like that. And you'd think that was bad. Unwashed orc smell. Then, at other times, it will smell like pure death. Like dead bodies out there rotting in the sands. Sweet and sickly. Believe me that's no picnic either. And you'd think that would be worse. You'd think those two would be the worst smell ever, right?

But you'd be wrong.

It's the third smell that comes out of the desert that's the worst of all. It's like… the smell of dust. Choking dust. But it's much, much more than I can even write down here. It's something else. It's the smell… and this was something Sergeant Kang once said and that guy doesn't say much on the whole, but he and I were on watch one night and he whispered, "It's the smell of forever out there. And it ain't a good forever you ever want to find yourself in."

After he said that I couldn't shake that line, that description, from my mind. Because he's right. He nailed it perfectly. It's the smell of not just years, or eons of dust, it's the smell of all the dust in a universe, or a dark side to the universe, that's forever. It's the smell of the loneliest level of hell.

I asked Vandahar about it one night, because you usually smelled it at night, and he had this to say. "That, my young Ranger, is the smell of the Saur. It is the smell of their dreams of their never-to-be-fulfilled avarice, greed, and lust for total power. It is the decay they dream of in their ancient tombs buried long beneath the sands in the times since you left the world you knew and came here. It is their plans. Their *hopes*. And it is what I wage my wars against. For if their dreams of dust become real, then there will never be light again. There will be nothing. And I cannot live in such a world. No one can, Talker. Not even them. It is the smell of madness rewarded."

And if that's not a weird enough explanation of the smell, I asked him *this* after that. 'Cause that's how I roll. I make things worse. Just 'cause. Talker for the win.

"Are they… the greatest *evil* here, Vandahar?"

Then, with no usual pleasant smile in his eyes, or kindliness on his lips, the old wizard looked down at me with all the reality I never thought existed and told me the answer I probably didn't want to hear. He was more serious than I'd ever seen him before. He stared *into* me and simply said, "No, Talker. That would be the Nether Sorcerer himself. A terrible being not of this… reality. And his dreams… his desires… are far more evil than theirs. Far, *far* more, Talker."

CHAPTER FIVE

"ALL them spooks were starting to flood the courtyard," continued Tanner as he unfolded the actions on the objective inside the courtyard of the haunted old fortress. "They're pushing the crawly dead aside, Talk, like you know, the skellies and the zekes. Slow movers. And hey, side note, in some cases, I think, man, I'm picking this up the way the other guys aren't, but there're ghosts and spirits starting to... y'know... *take over* those slow-crawler bone bags we can't dust fast enough and all."

I asked Tanner at this point to describe what this was like, watching the slow-moving dead get... *taken over...* and why he thought the other Rangers couldn't see this happening at the same time he was witnessing it.

"It was like I could see the ghosts just step right inside the dead and start workin' 'em like puppets. Once that happened, they got a lot smarter about how they were conducting the attack against our line right there at the front gate and all. Also, these, the *taken*, they had a strange blue glow in their eyes, or in the empty eye sockets where they once had eyes, know what I mean, man? Regular old crawly dead usually have this red glow and all, like there's some kind of low-grade fire, like an old oven or a burning coal burning inside that brain bucket. But when the blue glow takes over, that means the evil spirit, the disembodied dead, ghosts and spirits and all, have like, hijacked 'em now an' all. They're driving and they're, I don't know, not smarter, not… craftier… but they got like more… power, I guess? This is just my impression, Talk, and I don't even know how much of it's true and how much I'm just losing my mind as I become that other thing. But I know you want the details and all for the account. So… there's them. Put it down or don't.

"So I pick up on the ghost hijackers and run a check on something I think may or may not happen. This one zeke comes straight at me, missing its jaw, hair all stringy, skin thin and tight, like it's been buried for a long time and dried out like tough beef jerky that's about three years bad. Old mummy wraps and all hanging off it. It goes right over the top of the surge coming at us from all directions. Just like that. I got my Glock out and started banging away fast on it. Two shots, I'm pretty sure, right in its chest but of course that ain't gonna do much to the dead. I remember that at that moment, and it's so close I just try to put one in its thigh but the thing jerks at the last second and instead I blow off its knee. It goes down right in front of me. I holster the Glock quick, grab one of its arms and yank it back for a hold, except, I don't know… something inside me, Talk, tells me I can just snap this arm right off. So that's what I do. Right there. I snap the dead guy's arm off. I just disconnect its arm from its body and throw it off in another direction. Other arm, which is really nothing but a bony claw, goes for me anyway and I shift my boot and crush that one too, just to stop it from thrashing around like a crazy person. Now I got my knee down on its back and Lee asks me what the hell I think I'm doing and to be honest, at that very moment, I ain't real sure, Talk. But…

that me… the thing I've become… it wants answers from this dead guy underneath my boot…

"So I bend down and start talking to it."

"How?" I ask. Not what, but how. Because I'm a linguist, of course.

"Infernal. And yeah, I know: I don't know how to speak Infernal. Or I didn't know I know. But I knew. Like I said… it's weird and all, man."

I'm intrigued. Tanner has now gone from being able to *understand* the language of the damned, Infernal it's called, to *speaking* it. In crisis situations, anyway.

I need to learn this language *now*. Because reasons.

I ask him if he can teach me a word. Any word. A single verb. I'd kill for a noun. I know… I have problems.

"Can't, Talk. All I hear is English in my head when I speak it, but I know I'm speaking something else all the same. Here's what it's like. Put your headphones on full blast, hardcore metal, then ask someone standing next to you a question. You might be able to hear something, but… you gotta take the headphones off to get it clear. That's how I remember it now when I think about it. But… there's one word I know because it's always rattling around in my head lately."

Of course I'm gonna ask.

"*Numquam waar.*"

Except Tanner pronounces it as "*Num-qualm vare.*"

The Latin it must be leaps out at me because it's a common key in unlocking many languages. I can search around with it, often, and find where we're going. *Numquam* is *never*. For the second word he uses a Germanic *V* for *W* in the pronunciation and if I flirt with soft Dutch I get the word *where*. As in *where* are we going.

Never where.

This being the Ruin, many of the current functional languages are just mish-mashes of dead languages I would have once considered current. Well, Latin wasn't current. But the other dead languages are. Were.

I tell him what I think it may translate to.

"Does… *Never Where*… mean anything to you, Tanner?"

He goes all Tanner for just a moment, to the *otherwhere* he's been drifting off to lately in the middle of conversations. Now that's interesting. *Never where…* and he goes *otherwhere*. I didn't do that on purpose.

But he goes otherwhere when I ask, and when he comes back, he says no, it doesn't mean anything to him.

And what I feel next shocks me and even leaves me feeling a little colder, a little darker. I have a feeling he's not being totally truthful.

Not lying.

Maybe… a white lie. If there is such a thing.

"I just keep hearing her say it, Talk. *Never where*, if that's what it is, but in the language of the damned. And there's music I can't remember too. But it's like… it's like I'm surrounded by winter, or ice, and nothing lives there. And it's not terrible like it should be. It's beautiful… to me, Talk. It's like being happy about being alone, finally. Forever. And then this girl—I can't see her, but I know she's real beautiful—she just says those words over and over like it's a song. *Never where.*"

A cold shiver runs down my spine. And for some reason I'm thinking about Last of Autumn. Autumn. Just as it had been once.

"So, what did the thing you had pinned on the ground in the middle of the battle say to you? In Infernal," I ask, getting Tanner back to the story of the scouts' battle in the courtyard.

"First off, I asked it a question, Talk. I just knew to ask it specifically, like it was natural and all. Developing intel on the objective. Actions on it and all. But a little different, I guess. More like... pulling a raid back in the sandbox and trying to hunt down some bomb maker. You hit the first house, creep in while everyone's sleeping, and secure your bad guy. Then the interrogators, like you, if they're on scene, they come in and get some answers quick, then we get our next target location and we roll on that guy and just keep flippin' dudes till dawn. You feel me on that, Talker?

"So I just know to ask this guy I got pinned underneath me, who's turning the juice on. But all the words are in that dark language. See, all the undead, they got some kinda juice, you know, like power, coming from somewhere, from someone, or at least that's the way it's been with all the dead I've met so far. Technically that SEAL was undead, but I don't know... didn't vampires have to be made by other vampires? There's a question for everyone to get interested in: who made SEAL What's-His-Name? Man, I wish we could go back and smoke that dude again just for GP. General purpose and all. Know what I mean, Talk? You did that dude good and proper first time though. Shot him right in the eye. Left that bullet in his brain. Cool stuff. I'd like that on replay about twelve hundred times or so."

I shuddered at the memory of what had actually happened in the dark tower. That had been close. He could have killed me, and more importantly, he could have killed Autumn. Easily. Almost did.

Tanner noticed the goose that walked over my grave as I went to my own version of otherwise for a moment. He quickly continued.

"So I asked it who provided the juice for the fight. I mean, someone's powering up all these undead and makin' 'em come outta the dirt and the rotten woodwork all around the old dusty place. And it ain't random. It's clear from the fight they're all focused on getting Chief Rapp as their primary objective. He's their HVT, for sure about that. He has pissed them off good and proper. They want that dude dead. Sometimes they'll go flying right past one of the others who they could easily overrun and get down on the ground, because they got such a hate-on for the Green Beanie. And I know why, because I feel what they feel. He's life, Talk. He's the opposite of us. Them. They hate him and whoever's runnin' him. They hate the chief even more than the undead hajis can fathom in the world of the dead.

"At that moment, Hardt is working your shield like it's some kinda core ball and he's doing standing Russian Taps just to keep them back from the chief and his little silver cross. Sar'nt's just swinging it from side to side, cleaning up the dead whether they explode or not. The ones that don't go flying get cut in half and plain ruined by the magic in that shield of yours. Guy with the spear is just holding position and sticking the undead like he's skewering cocktail weenies at your sister's fancy wedding and he can't get enough. You know the kind with the little dough around them. With some mustard. *Bruh*, I could go for that and I ain't had much of an appetite since I died and all. But hey, them little hot dogs in dough, I could go for a plate of those right now for sure."

We all have our addictions, even at the gates of death. Great, and now I'm thinking about coffee.

"So who's powering 'em up?" I ask Tanner one more time to get him back on the narrative. I may be many awful things, but I've become a fanatic about getting the details down for the official account of what we did here.

Who knows, maybe we'll make it back and I can sell it as a science fiction story and maybe even a script to Hollywood. Then I make a million bucks and coast, driving around LA in my new Dodge Hellcat if that's a thing still, drinking hipster coffee with cute starlets trying to get their big break. Palm trees and the big Pacific Ocean. I could go for that now. Or probably DARPA and the Deep State come in and tell me it all never happened if I know what's good for me. And the whole story of the Ruin disappears.

In which case I'll publish it under a pseudonym that sounds like I made it up to sound like some tough guy private detective. Something stupid like… Nick Cole. Sounds like a real chungo.

Anyways…

"Yeah, Talk. Back on point. There's those sisters down in the basement spinning up the dead and the spirits too in this thing they call *the Kettle of Storms*. That's what this dead Dargonian swordsman is telling me I got pinned beneath me when I push him for some intel. Goin' on and on about selling his soul to them for a prophecy that his sister's family would have luck in their caravan business a hundred years ago. Yeah I know, makes no sense, most of the dead are half mad and trust me, ain't no picnic listening to them go on and on about their problems."

"What do you do?" I ask.

"I tell the assistant team leader I gotta shift position and link up with Hardt to let him know what's going on. He copies and I shift back to the dirty little blade, hacking my way through corpses who are just running past me to get at the chief. I slide in next to Hardt whose guns are tired from working that shield of yours and you know *that's* bad 'cause Sarge can PT like a beast. So. You know how it is in a fight with hands and feet and all, you get smoked real fast? Faster than you ever think it'll happen because you're in it and breathing heavy? That's how it is. I'm back-to-back with him and let him know what I got out of the dead guy and what I think we can do about it to get the dead shut down."

Tanner, as this all went down, him giving his account inside Sûstagul later that morning, lights another cigarette and hopes Kurtz doesn't catch him because Rangers don't smoke on mission. Dip, yes. But Tanner's a smoker and also… he's Tanner.

"See here, Talk, once the dead Dargonian swordsman told me—"

"How'd you know he was Dargonian?" I asked, because you know me. It's the details. And who knows what language live Dargonians speak. I love the Ruin. This place is full of languages. *And I bet they have some crazy coffee there in Dargon,* thought the junkie in me optimistically. What will really happen is, we'll end up out there in the middle of a desert hellhole the maps mark as Dargon, and they're all psychos. Psychopaths who drink tea. Like the British. Total lunatics.

No coffee for miles.

These are my darkest fears. Welcome to my world. Welcome inside my small and tiny terrified mind.

"He said his name was Khaiyam of Dargon. So... I did the math. You've seen Dargon on Vandahar's maps, that place out there in the Saudi Arabian peninsula, right? Though honestly, that map ain't got no grid squares, good luck finding anything without grid squares and azimuths and all. Besides which I flew over that desert once on my way into the Sandbox. Whole lotta nothin' out there, man. Anyway, dead guy says he's from there. So, can I go on?"

I'll allow it.

"I tell Hardt we gotta go down into the dirt where the dead are coming out and ice these sisters juicin' the whole bunch. And here's what's funny, Sarge looks at me like *How's that gonna happen, Tanner.* Then this skeleton with a spear comes rattling in, screamin' that ghost whisper and all and rams into the shield just as Hardt gets it up to keep it off the chief. Bones and dust go flying off in every direction.

"Hardt says we can barely push our way here, there's too many of 'em. 'Copy that, Sar'nt,' I say and tell him I got a plan. I lay it out, and Chief Rapp who's standing over and behind us, just blasting ghosts and spirits with his little cross, growling at 'em like he's burning belts on some holy crew-served weapon of eternal damnation, Chief Rapp says... *Let the man run his game, Sergeant Hardt. We got this! Make it happen, young man.*

"I take that as my cue. I race over to Lee and grab him and Chavez. Lee was carrying a rope coiled over his shoulder and waist. Like we always do just in case we're gonna rappel. Chavez keeps 'em off us and then I get Lee on belay, no Swiss seat ready to D-clip into so I just get the rope and go harnessless, getting the rope around my left leg then up over my right shoulder and controlling the descent with my left assault glove. Yeah, I know, it's gonna hurt, but I got super death powers and I don't feel things the way I used to. I tell Lee to anchor behind a piece of broken stone. I decide I'm just gonna plow through the spirits and dead guys and go down the side of the pit they're coming out of. It ain't gonna be pretty but it's gotta be done, know what I mean, Talk?

"And oh yeah, the pit. Did I already tell you about the pit? I didn't, did I?"

I assured him he hadn't.

"Sorry. Not that you're bothered by that I guess. I've noticed you don't have a problem with telling things all out of order. Kind of an affliction with you. Whatever comes to mind whenever it comes to mind, man. *Just get it down in the record*, that's what you told me more than once. *Warts and all*. I can dig that. Sometimes you just gotta hit the accelerator and go, don't matter where, long as you're moving.

"So anyway, the pit. I know exactly when it opened up. I didn't see it, but I *felt* it. Like… like someone finally remembered to turn the subwoofer on. It was like that. In the air, in your gut, all around you, like a thing that you didn't even know was missing until that moment. The sisters, Talk. Their juice. The pit had opened up and with it the sisters were… more present somehow. That's how I knew it wasn't just a pit, but a way *in*. A way to get to them. That, plus all the ghosts and such that suddenly came pouring forth into the courtyard. That pit was a route to the basement or catacombs or whatever was down there. To wherever the sisters were.

"So Chavez is just hacking away to keep them off us and he's getting tired. Chief blasts three shadows that come in and they all turn to ashes and dust in the night right there in front of us. Then I'm not running for the pit, but more… swinging side to side and stumbling forward just to reach it.

"That's when the Collector of Corpses we suspected might be inside the fortress shows up to get involved. He came from out of the main… *hold*? *Keep*? I'm still not up on all this fantasy architecture. *Huts and souks*, that's me. But this guy made up of body parts, and I don't mean that in the usual way, comes out of what we were tagging as the main building on the OBJ. He hits me with a body. Or at least part of one. One star, Talk. Would not recommend. He just tears off his shoulder and arm and flings them at me. And yeah, I can tell by the look on your face… that this is weird."

There was one sage who specialized in the old fortress and had told us much about its lost histories. My impression at the time, of the doddering old sage, was that he may have been slightly, how shall I put this… *crazy*. I mean, the things he was talking about were pure insanity, and I know, having been in the Ruin, that crazy stories like that should often be taken seriously, but his story of some sort of undead golem that could pick up corpses off the ground, or battlefields, and take them, or rather, make them part of itself… I mean, *c'mon*. Does that sound like it should be a thing?

No.

The answer to if there should be some kind of monster that kills you and then rips off pieces of your body to make them part of its own… is *no*. There should be no such thing as something horrible like that. Dragons, trolls, liches…

sure, okay. But a dead guy who throws someone else's rotting body parts at you is just wrong on so many levels.

And yet, there is such a thing. That particular abomination exists here in the Ruin.

Fun, huh.

So, it threw a body at Tanner and knocked him on his butt. There was some kind of magical kinetic effect with the tossed bodies. Kennedy suspects *rotting diseases* and *dark curses* too, but hypothesizes that Tanner's status as currently undead may have granted him some immunity to those effects.

The way I've heard this part of the story from others is that Tanner was trying to be a hero and go for the fatal strike against three dirt witches living down in the under-basement, only to get beaned by a dead body. The Rangers who have heard about this, even in the middle of the battle for Sûstagul, think that's hilarious. I have discussed their dark sense of humor and what they find funny. A Ranger going to a family function, my guess here, would be given explicit instructions by spouses regarding what topics are considered appropriate for polite conversation. With a specific admonishment against "funny death stories."

So—there's Tanner trying to get to the black hole pit, a gash in the dry dead dirt of this place that's vomiting up ghosts and corpses like some volcano of ancient death at the all-you-can-eat Chinese seafood buffet three days gone bad. He's on his butt. Knocked down by a flying limb from some dead guy.

"Even to me, Talk, and the smell of death never bothered me much when I was alive, and it sure don't bother me now, but that entire place reeked of bad, long-decomposing death and other foul… stuff. Know what I mean? And even with that odor all around me, the dead guy's arm that hit me was ripe in ways words can't describe. I wanted to hurl the MRE I'd eaten prior to the battle. And scrambled eggs and ham ain't good even when it ain't hurled back up."

I can imagine. But I prefer not to.

So what does Tanner do after getting hit by a corpse as he drags a rappelling rope forward with the intent of going down in a pit with only the weapons he's got on him? He gets up and pushes forward. Because Tanner may be a lot of things—I have yet to meet a Ranger NCO who will not hesitate to light Tanner up over everything to smoking to mouthing off—but no one has ever found him deficient in meeting the challenges presented to America's premier fighting force. Tanner's the first guy in the dark hole, on point, and ready to fight black on mags and down to sharp sticks and harsh words. He *Rangers*, man. And that's the best thing any of them ever want said about them.

In that, he's exactly like every one of them. And maybe that's enough to pay the rent on the scroll that day.

Stop. Time out.

I just used the word *them* to reference the Rangers. And even as I wrote it I heard Joe's voice. *Don't think you are something… know you're the real deal, Ranger.*

I'm one of *them*. They're depending on me to be one of *them*.

One of *us*.

So… correction.

In that, Tanner is exactly like every one of *us*.

Or like Morpheus said to Neo in that movie, *Stop trying to hit me… and hit me.*

Tanner gets up, two zekes slam into him. One a small dwarf who jumps on his back and tries to get him in a chokehold. The dwarf's eyes, according to Tanner, were gouged out, and as Tanner tried to fight the guy off, that was *disconcerting*, though Tanner chose other words to describe the situation. The other guy has got him around the waist like he's a linebacker trying to tackle a running back before he reaches the first and ten. Tanner jackhammers that second guy right in the brain and loses his sword as he makes the edge of the pit. The guy slips off and Tanner, without so much as a signal, with complete faith in Lee on belay, goes flying over the edge and down into the pit with the eyeless undead dwarf still on his back.

"I didn't action-hero it, Talk, like in the movies. I'd break both Lee's arms if I did that. Thinking back on it, I coulda just let go and fallen. I mean, what's gonna happen to me? I'll be *more* dead?"

"Well, you probably woulda broken your arms and legs," I said. "And now that you're dead and all, Tan, well that stuff wouldn't've healed because… you're dead. So you'd be a crippled dead guy."

"I dunno about that," said Talk. "What makes you think that? Maybe I got healing superpowers. Like Wolverine and all."

Like I told you, every Ranger wanted to be Wolverine.

I laid out my reasoning. "Well, here's the thing. All the dead guys, zekes and skellies we've met so far, they don't seem to heal much. If at all. Like the skellies? Their flesh is gone. Internal organs too. It hasn't come back. They're still walking around, but they haven't gotten new skin and livers and all. And then there's these dead guys who got hanged, or stabbed, or hacked, or chopped up. They're still missing limbs, or their necks are still broken, or whatever. The undead just don't seem to ever heal. That would be the problem with serious injury. Even if you are Undead Wolverine."

Tanner frowned. "I'll have to think about that, Talk."

He may still be thinking about it. But I did get the rest of the story out of him.

You're probably thinking at this point in the account, what about that Collector of Corpses? We knew he was some kind of heavy, and that's why we'd brought Kennedy along to deal with him. According to all my sources, not only the crazed sage but also some of the scouts and Kennedy, the thing looked like a giant hunchback of Notre Dame if that hunchback was made up of a bunch of dead guys' body parts.

Ranger Chavez swore the thing still had the rope it got hanged with around its neck. "He also had this one huge watering eye, Talk, that was running about all wild in his eye socket like it knew exactly what was going on. The rest of his body was like a serial killer from that one of them horror movies, all slow and all. Like it was a meat puppet. But that eye, it freaked me out, man. It was like whoever the dead guy was, that eye was the last thing in the body that was still him and it knew full well what was going on and couldn't do a damn thing about it."

"That freaked you out the worst?" I asked Chavez. "Not all the dead people parts it was flinging around?"

"Hells yeah. Creep show stuff, bruh."

Full disclosure: Chavez once won a game of Ranger bowling in which they took the heads off a bunch of dead orcs and started playing shuffleboard with them. I have no idea why they called it *bowling*, other than they were throwing the heads to knock the other heads off the "board," but it's their game and their rules and they get to name it so.

So, before I get to the Tanner in the Pit of Doom part, allow me to relate how they dealt with the Collector of Corpses, who was considered to be a game-changer because, big surprise, Chief Rapp couldn't *turn* or *damn* it.

The abomination came at them, pulling dead body parts off of itself and tossing them at the Rangers. It also had two tentacles that came out of its back, each with a massive rotting hand at the end. The tentacles would grab skeletons and zombies out of the crowd and just chuck them directly at the Rangers fighting to hold the courtyard. Some of the Rangers were trying to put it down, suppressed, on full auto. Hot smoking rounds tearing into its giant rotting body parts frame. And that weird knowing eye rolling around in terror.

Chief Rapp ordered Kennedy to smoke it.

"So what'd you do, Kennedy?" I asked our Ranger PFC wizard.

"Smoked it like a cheap cigar, Talker. That thing caught fire and didn't make it ten steps after I hit it with my fireball. Though I was amazed it did that much. Kept coming forward, I mean. The giant I hit with the fireball got blown right off the hill, remember that? But this thing took the fireball center mass and just kept walking straight at us, trying to grab more dead guys to throw before it went down. Wanna know something freaky, Talker?"

I already knew from talking to Chavez. But I let Kennedy tell me anyway, even though to be honest I really could have done without this detail a second time.

"The dead corpses in the thing's body, once it caught fire, they broke away from it, on fire, and tried to crawl or run away, like they were free from the curse it operated under now."

My jaw was open even upon hearing this for the second time.

"Is that thing, or anything even like it, in your game, Kennedy?"

"Hell no. But it is now, Talker. That's cool."

CHAPTER SIX

"I went down that fast-rope hard, Talk," continued Tanner as he related his account of the descent into the dark depths of the basement of the fortress. In seconds he went from the courtyard into the pit.

"Felt like I was going to tear both arms out of my sockets as I went down without any kind of harness. But hey… that's fast-roping. Shredded the assault glove I was usin' to control descent almost immediately. I saw my hand begin to smoke but like I said, pain man, it don't bother me the way it used to. Lee hung on though, and Chavez told me later he had to drop his sword in the dirt and get on the rope too because I was takin' Lee with me. His fingertips got all cut up too 'cause he's one of them that cuts the tips off to better manipulate his weapon. Bad move. I'm cool with cutting the trigger finger out—if you have to—but still, doin' what we do, Talk, you're gonna reach in some real nasty places along the way and all the coverage you can get is for the best. Keep as much covered as possible. In that, the smaj and I are one, Talk. But Chief taped up Lee's hand good and used some superglue on one of the bad slices."

As the story goes, Tanner descends into the pit, and to hear it the way he describes it… well, I don't think he does what happens next justice. He just says the layers of dirt he passes on the way down are full of rotting corpses just writhing around and stuck down there in the compacted earth of the sides of the pit. Also, that the pit is alive with more and more skeletons and zombies crawling up and over each other along the walls of the pit, surging out to make their defense against the Ranger attack. They're using the buried undead as ladders for handholds and stuff.

In Tanner's mind, he hears pure desperate rage and suffering coming from everything down there along the sides of the pit. But he pushes that away and gets ready to deal some death on whatever's unlucky enough to be waiting for him at the bottom.

"As I descend, I hear Kennedy deploy his fireball and smoke that corpse thing coming for the rest of the hit team. But by the time I'd landed on the floor of the dungeon down there in the old basement beneath the fort, tell you straight up… I was *in it*, man. That's what them guys who used to go into the tunnels in Nam musta felt like, 'cept I think that was a lot more claustrophobic."

From what he tells me next, he certainly was *in it* because it got weird fast.

But hey, that's the Ruin. Every day you wake up and think, *Well, yesterday was as weird as it gets*. Then the Ruin slaps you around and says, *That's where you're wrong, kiddo*.

So much so that the mortar team has taken to using their Sharpies to draw this stick figure guy with sunglasses who points both gun-fingers at something and then they just write *Kiddo* for shorthand to indicate some new and even more messed-up thing they've just dropped steel on.

It's their version of *Kilroy Was Here*.

Smaj has voiced that mortars have too much time on their hands and need more PT to cure them of this habit that seems to annoy only him.

"See, my first mistake was thinking that just because I came up with the plan, I was the right guy for the mission," continues the tale of Tanner in the underworld beneath the fort. "But that's just me, man."

Tanner will tell you that's what all the NCOs hate about him... "and why I ain't ever makin' it past corporal, if I even get that. I don't lead, man. I just get it done. Smart move woulda been to have Lee or Chavez go in and have me on belay. The intel I collected off the dead guy told me that the dead were susceptible to what the sisters had going on down there. I should have figured that out. But that's hindsight. See, if these three sisters could control the dead, then sendin' a dead guy in there... not the smartest move, see?"

That made sense to me. I'm not saying I would've picked up on it any faster than Tanner did. But he'd already evaluated his own actions, peer-reviewed himself, a big part of all Ranger ops, and conducted his own AAR. He immediately understood how he'd gotten himself deep into whatever was down there in the rank body pit beneath the old dungeon.

On hearing the whole story... I'm surprised it didn't go even more horribly than it did.

"It's dark down there, Talk. Real dark, man. But it's like a dark that's darker than... dark. Hey, I ain't you with words and all, Talker. But you feel me, man. It's super dark down there and all. Even for a dead guy with Death Vision. It was what the night thinks the color black feels like."

Then he went *otherwhere* for half an uncomfortable second.

And he started talking again while still staring out into that *otherwhere* he goes sometimes. Which feels like spoken-word creepiness. It makes me feel colder than I should when it happens. He started speaking that way, just holding that smoke between two fast-rope-wrecked fingers on his decaying hand. Thousand-yard stare.

Here's a question I thought I'd never ask in… ever. Can the dead get PTSD?

"I hear 'em before I see 'em, man. They're saying weird stuff… these three sisters."

"Like what?"

"*We come from the desert beyond the world, Revenant,*" hisses Tanner like he's imitating some old witch. Which—*ha ha*—he is. See what I did there?

He's imitating their voices and the effect is chilling to say the least.

"Another one starts speaking after that one," he continues. "Don't ask me how I know it's another… she sounds the same in my head, but different. And yeah, they're in my head and even though I'm dead and all, I feel real cold like I done screwed up big time and I'm about to pay in ways I never thought possible. Like when your sergeant shows up at the local jail and all that fun you got in trouble for comes to a record scratch moment. The next one says to me, *You're ours now, Revenant.* And then a third one pipes up, and I feel like she's the leader of 'em all. The older sister. Except… that word ain't right, Talk. More like… *elder* sister. But I ain't ever used that word in my life so I don't know if it's… what's the word… grammatically… technically… correct. But in some other part, the one that knows the languages of the dead and hell... it is. It's a word that feels right in a very wrong way, if you know what I mean. Listen, man, I know this stuff sounds witchy and all, but Rangers share critical intel 'cause mission depends on it. That elder sister says, *Ours to play with, sisters*. Then, *Yaaassss, my pretty Revenant. Ours to play with for a long, long time.*"

Like I said, at this moment in the story, Tanner's got a thousand-yard stare like he's right there back in it and all. Right there with those witches in black. Except these aren't speaking Spanish like that one the captain burned at the top of the pass as we escaped the orc hordes.

As I write that down I am reminded we have lived through some real stuff. Real stuff that makes you feel a little older than all the miles rucked and scars healing livid and angry.

Back to Tanner's account.

Right then and there, they try to take control of him. They start singing what he calls a creepy little girl nursery rhyme, but he can't remember the words and he tells me it's not like any nursery rhyme for children of the living, but instead for the souls in hell who never sleep and never rest. Make of that what you will, but those were the words used and when he told me that part, I felt that same cold he'd described run down my scalp and spine, and the desert morning air wasn't as warm as I needed it to be.

It was at that moment he felt, Tanner did, that he'd made a very big mistake going down there in the middle of the fight because they were reaching into his mind down there and figuring out what they could make him do, now that he was some kind of puppet for them.

In his defense, the Rangers at the pit were getting hit from every direction and there wasn't any indication the sisters weren't going to keep pushing the dead at them. They are Rangers, and the Green Beret, besides being a cleric who can ignite the dead and turn them to burnt ash, is both a giant and a stud in weapons combat, but… everyone has limits. If the dead were allowed to keep pushing, then they were probably going to win.

And Stranglehold depended on taking the old fortress before everything else got going. So this was mission-critical to our success there in Sûstagul.

One of the witches in the dungeon was whispering for Tanner to go back up the rope and "Kill yer friends, Revenant. Do us a trick and make 'em all die pretty, so they can join us down here. Forever."

"Yaassss," said the elder, and the other one stirred the giant black pot at their center. There were dead everywhere down there. Tanner described the floor as one giant Persian rug of maimed corpses.

"And I could tell, Talk, they weren't all dead. Many of them were undead now, but just lying there like that was their job from now until the heat death of the universe. They were just there to watch them witch sisters and all the evil they did down there in the dark.

"The more the three of them spoke, the more I began to see their world down there. Like I was shifting through some kind of thin bubble of reality, like the QST we came through to get here to the Ruin. Except it wasn't no basement, man. That faded away the more they talked. Where I was walking toward was some lonely… *moor*. Is that the right word? Again, I have no idea what that word means— well, I do, I can picture it and I know what a *moor* is, but trust me, man, I have never ever used it ever in my life. Imagine me runnin' my game on some chick at the club and using the word *moor* and car-crashing the whole pick-up. Too fancy. But a *moor*, this moor I'm walking into in their dream of death, because I've been there… it's like a swampy depression with bushes that are all low and twisted. The trees look dead, but they ain't. Sky is dead. The mud sucks at your boots. Place smells of death and there was a green storm in that death sky. Everything was grey and iridescent green like a snapped ChemLight. Really weird place to be in all of a sudden and maybe that was all just a trick on their part as I couldn't help myself walking closer and closer to the big black witches' pot they were all standing around. Laughing about what they were gonna do to me. *With* me. It was real bad, man. I knew that."

"So what'd you do?" I asked.

Because obviously you're here and you got out of it, Tanner. By that point, when he downloaded the story to me between actions on the patrol, he'd linked up with Second Platoon. Him and Kennedy. That was during our advance and attack on the market.

"Well, I'll tell ya, man."

He was back now from that *otherwhere* thousand-yard stare. His smoke had ashed out as he told me everything about that other world, that… *moor* where the witches lived beneath the basement, all grey storm clouds and green ChemLight.

"They were gonna use me to start killing, man. I could hear 'em in my head asking about how all my weapons worked, and then they got real interested in the grenades. They started mumbling and cackling to each other in another language I couldn't understand, but they were going on and on about how much fun that would be if I went back up there and just detted some grenades on the rest of the team. 'Wouldn't that be wicked,' they kept saying, and I knew at that point I was in trouble, man. But I also knew the mission and my fellow Rangers were in trouble too in ways they didn't understand yet. Those chicks were gonna turn me into an IED, man. You know how well that would *not* sit with the rest of the regiment? They'd be chapped, to put it mildly, that Ol' Tans blew 'em all up. Let's just say Kurtz would have thought more highly of that SEAL than me at that point. So…"

Tanner smiled wryly. And he was back in that instant. My friend. The guy who doesn't take it from anyone and always has a comment that'll get you through the incoming suck when it's raining down either verbally or kinesthetically. Pick your poison if you can.

I'll be honest, I felt like all the cold Tanner was describing, all that cold that was seeping into my soul hearing about the witches' basement moor beneath the dungeon, suddenly got blasted away in an instant by his smile and what he said next to me.

"I wasn't gonna let that happen to the team, man. I gotta rep. And I may be a lotta things but I ain't no witches' IED. Know what I mean? I got something for that. Something for them."

Solid copy, brother.

"There was lightning over the moor in there. Green lightning snapping across the sky. It had been in the distance as I walked toward the witches and their big black pit. But now, and as I stood there helpless as a baby, I'll admit I kept thinking, why wasn't I hearing the thunder that came with the lightning? Maybe I was, man. Maybe it was muted and all, like the lightning was striking way off and I was barely hearing the rumble that follows. It must have been like that, because when I listened for it, listened carefully, it was there. The thunder. And then I realized I was counting the seconds as the witches talked among themselves. Counting between strikes and distant rumbles. Just habit, you know? Marking the distance, like the scared kid brother in that movie where the little girl goes into the TV. Classic flick.

"But what I really realized... by which I mean, this is the important realization... was that I could control that. The act of counting. They didn't have the strings for that. It was mine. So... I just had a thought right there. I thought about the Uzi I was strapping. One of the ones you and Joe brought back from the deep desert. Been carrying that around. When they'd been asking about my weapons, they wanted to know what they did, and I *had* to answer them because they were pulling the strings and all. They asked about the carbine. *It shoots rounds*, I told 'em, and they seemed to understand what they saw in my mind. They didn't like that. They didn't like my knives either. 'Bah,' said one, 'too slow. We need the killing to be bigger.' Then they got to the grenades on my rig. That distracted them a whole bunch. But they hadn't arrived at the old MACV-SOG Nam weapon you guys brought back from the desert. I've been humping it the whole time just waiting to use it. So I said, I *thought* really, *Hey, witches... I got this thing for ya.*"

And they turned away from the big black bubbling pot and I felt them... *lose control for a second*. Like they greased out because they realized I could talk to them of my own free will. I could do that. And what they didn't know was I could also count the thunder after the strange green lightning on the dark skies out there over the moor. Man, that's weird."

Very.

"So they snap at me like they're real angry, but they wanna know what I got because… they're greedy.

"*Show us*," Tanner hissed, in imitation of the cruel hags. "*Show us now, Revenant,*" hissed another. "*What have ya gots for the killing work that needs to be done?*"

He paused.

"She said that. *The Eld.*"

Okay, full stop here for a second.

He said *Eld*. Side note, and I don't even know if I'll have a chance to get into this during the account of the battle, but it's intel and I'll put it down here right now so it's stamped into the permanent record of the Rangers in the Ruin. Last time I heard *Eld* used was Vandahar referencing "the Eld" of which Cloodmoor the rock-throwing Godzilla cloud giant was one of. One of the lesser, supposedly. Please don't let there be a greater. Come on, Ruin, cut the Rangers a break. For once. But to follow the thought for a second… my guess, following languages and what often ends up being intertwined with the speaking of words, is mythology. I'm guessing here, and I've thought about this previously, but I wonder if *the Eld* were some kind of Titans of the Ruin. Like in Greek mythology. The beings that preceded the Greek Pantheon. But here, right now in the middle of the account, Tanner, not recognizing what he was telling me, called the leader of the witches *the Eld*. Interesting. Noted. Will discuss with Vandahar later if we live.

Back to what happened next down there in the Hell Basement of Death that might be a gateway, or was, to another world or reality.

"So, the Eld sister," continues Tanner, "she tells me to give it here. The Micro Uzi the SOG used. And suddenly there's this terrific *snap* of thunder, and an instant after that a green ChemLight lightning strike right nearby. All of us are bathed in gamma green radiation like on the old Hulk show. Good show. I watched some episodes one of the Air Force guys still had on his iPad, and it kept makin' me think about the Ruin, you know, and how it *reveals*. Like, in a way, Dr. Banner was kinda going through what some of us are going through now. Becoming somethin' else and all. Something true. I thought about the captain, too.

"Anyway, this witch leader, she ordered me to pull the Uzi and show it to them right then and there. Like they freed up just a little, loosening the right strings to make it happen for a second. So I do. I pull it with my unhurt hand from under my right shoulder where I had it slung. I remember at that moment her greedy little snake's eyes went real wide because she either thought it was something powerful... or she figured out right at that second what Ol' Tans was *really* gonna do with the little bit of freedom he'd been given. Gimme an inch and I'll take a mile. Both exes will tell you that straight up, man. It was like she sensed what I was going to do just a second before my right hand came up, grabbed the Uzi's grip, finger in the trigger and thankfully that thing is open bolt, so I dusted her right there. Them Micros only got twenty-round mags, but at less than three feet, one-handed, collapsed stock and all tucked forward, I smoked her right on the spot. She didn't ragdoll or nothing like in the movies, or sometimes when you dome a guy. She just stood there as about twenty holes suddenly appeared in her. Maybe not that many but it was a bunch more than there had been a half second before.

You'd think that thing jumps. It don't, Talker. You just stick it out and ride it right into the target. That's what the Micro Uzi feels like. Or maybe I got super undead skill with guns now. That could be a thing, right? I don't know. My shooting was good in my humble opinion. She went down and I had another mag out and in when the second witch recoiled in horror beside the big black witches' pot. Witch number three points her finger at me and does something…"

Later Kennedy told me she most likely tried to curse Tanner right at that second.

"What would that have done?" I asked our PFC wizard.

"Don't know. And again, Talker…"

"I know, your game might be nothing like what we're facing here. But what might have been some possibilities if the witch had center-massed him with a hex?"

Kennedy took off his RPGs and rubbed the bridge of his nose.

"I don't know… she coulda turned him into a toad or hit him with a lightning bolt. Considering the description, I'd bet it was a curse of some sort, but she could have been calling lightning down on him and all. Witches are druidic in nature, so…"

Tanner says that at that very moment as she pointed her crooked finger at him, he felt a sudden wave of fatigue rush over him.

"It was like I was at the beach, just standing in the waves, and suddenly, Talk, a big one comes in and tries to knock ya down. But then you lean into it and make it through the force of piling water closing in on the sand and it hits the shore, and all the little kids run away from it and scream and laugh. Remember those days, Talker? Beach days. They were good. Real good. I'd like one more."

I do.

"He probably made his saving throw and defeated the curse. If it were the game, Talker," says Kennedy.

Kennedy says this after another warning that no such thing as *Saving Throws* has been verified to be operational in the *nano* voodoo of the Ruin. But he suspects Tanner made his saving throw "and the curse just bounced, Talker."

"Bounced?" I asked.

"Yeah. It must've bounced off him. Whatever happened, he fought it off and like he said… he just pushed through. That's probably the best evidence that there is something happening with the magic system in effect here."

"Magic system?"

Uncharacteristically, Kennedy imitated Vandahar. It wasn't bad. I was surprised. But it wasn't spot on. "The Ruin reveals, young Talker. The Ruin reveals," he said. He had spent enough time with the old wizard, learning his own skills, to have applied the Ranger gift for mimicry to the strange fellow.

As the account goes, Tanner then dusted that witch who tried to hex him with the next mag, or at least most of it. Then he spent some hate on the witch screeching and clinging to the boiling cauldron.

"I could smell her skin cooking as she tried to grab on to that big boiling pot, man. And I can't smell much. But that was pretty bad. I got another mag in and worked her over 'cause I wanted them good and dead. Know what I mean? Only way to be sure and all."

That action right there, Tanner smoking the trio of witches, stopped the attack in the courtyard above on the rest of the team. After he filled their scarecrow frames with blazing nine-mill, all the undead went back to being just rotting corpses and bones, and, according to Tanner, "That moor down in the basement… the sky suddenly rolled away, and it was all gone and then I was just down there with all the remains of the corpses in what looked like some ruined jail. I got outta there, linked up with the hit teams, and reported what happened to the chief and Sar'nt Hardt. Then we called for the snipers."

Sergeant Hardt commo'd with the sniper section via the drone over the city at that point, and gave the all-clear for the snipers to come over the wall.

At one in the morning, while the desert turned silver by the bare moonlight, with the orc hordes like dark shapes moving around in the dunes, looking for some angle of attack, or just menacing the rest of us Rangers hunkered near the LZ, the snipers dressed as Bedouins camping near the wall went over and into the city.

Two snipers, graduates of assault climber school, as all Ranger snipers must be, easily free-climbed the rough exterior of the small squat tower they'd camped under and executed the watch with suppressed sidearms. Ropes were lowered and the rest of the snipers and spotters came up with ammo and gear.

As I have said, that district is quiet because of the many necropolises and walled-off sections of other fading and overgrown cemeteries. Even the streets are lined with graves because there is little business here. The haunted fortress is considered enough of a deterrent to invaders or thieves just on superstition alone. But there is a city watch at the Gates of Death farther along the wall, and at every tower including the squat little ruined tower the Rangers took.

The snipers crossed through the quiet cemeteries, reached the old Legion fortress, and went up into the battlements of the old fort to identify their shooting positions and prepare for the attack at dawn. Sergeant Thor went into the old commander's tower, found a wide window, and laid *Mjölnir* down on the dry creaking wood amid the shattered and desert-rotted debris. He set up his shooting platform at the back of the room he'd selected with a perfect view of the Temple of Pan in the next walled district to the east.

In a few hours, his target would appear ceremonially. But by that time, the fight at the port would be well underway and the smoke of burning galleys would be drifting over the suddenly war-torn city of Sûstagul as Operation Stranglehold got underway in full.

CHAPTER SEVEN

IN the hours before the coming of the night when Stranglehold got underway, a hulking minotaur sat on a flea-infested bed in the early morning quiet of a low-rent inn near the Sûstagul port district known as Dockside. The hulking monster was busy performing primary maintenance on the M60E4 SF mod light machine gun he'd carry into a long battle that day, now just hours from kicking off. But there was still work to do for the Ranger detachment's lone reconnaissance team operator in the port district.

A few hours before dawn, Rangers would be crossing the line of departure to hit Sûstagul from two directions while maintaining a beachhead outside the city menaced by the nomadic orc hordes of the Guzzim Hazadi, while holding the Gates of Death at the western edge of the rotting old port city there next to the sea. The map marked this city as a vital point on the map just a few miles east of the silt-laden basin that fed the River of Night. Or, as it was known in the world we'd come from... the Nile.

Now Sergeant Monroe, formerly Corporal Monroe and just recently promoted, was acting as the sole member of the Ranger recon team on the ground in Dockside during the hours of darkness leading up to the mission. In the early moments before, as it began, and then during the fighting, Sergeant Monroe would be the Ranger eyes and ears on the other side of the line of battle.

Dockside, where he'd been undercover and feeding intel to Chief Rapp's network inside the city, was a long narrow isthmus that connected the outer hammerhead peninsula to the main walled port of Sûstagul on the edge of the desert. It was a rough area of sailors, shipwright-type merchants, short-term warehouses, taverns with at least a murder a night to claim their status by, and small strange orphans who seemed to live in the shadows and among the constant throng of citizens when they weren't in the water, selling fruit to the moored galleys riding at anchor.

We thought they were orphans or street urchins of some sort.

Once the assault on Sûstagul started, Sergeant Monroe would have vital tasks he needed to perform as the battle developed. The Ranger who'd been revealed to be a beast that seemed so much like that maze-dwelling killing machine from Greek antiquity would be calling out conditions on the ground as the Rangers took key areas and engaged the enemy beyond the port district at the Lighthouse of Thunderos. Meanwhile, small teams would move into areas to set up mines and high-ex to channelize the enemy when the inevitable counterattack came to open the road onto the hammerhead peninsula and retake the lighthouse and open the bay.

Sergeant Monroe would also be reporting on the status of the civilian population and enemy movements during the battle in the port district as the teams of Rangers came in to perform a classic Ranger operation: airfield seizure. Except this time, instead of taking a modern airfield littered with anti-aircraft, special guard units, and civilian and military aircraft deep in enemy-held territory, they'd be taking a Bronze Age port filled with the war galleys of a building Saurian advance force, powered by slaves chained to the rowing benches below decks.

Weather conditions would be updated also. And there was one other mission: Sergeant Monroe would be tasked with liberating the slaves aboard the warships almost singlehandedly.

There were over one hundred galleys waiting out there in the middle of the night darkness, the gentle swell entering the bay making the ropes creak, the hulls groan, and the many chains shift for comfort in the cold dark. The slaves were one of the biggest problems with this op, and had come to the forefront of planning almost near the end of the training phase we'd been endlessly stuck in, going over our tasks and static loads to get ready for taking Sûstagul one dark morning.

That dark morning was now.

The war galleys had sailed into the port two weeks prior to our attack. I was on the ground then, acting as a wandering scholar who liked to move about the city accompanied by the "strange desert nomads" who'd shown up in Sûstagul of late. The city was that kind of crossroads civilization of the Ruin where there was always some new strange lot to be wary of. The "nomads" wore black cloaks that covered their thick, muscled, PT'd frames regardless of the grueling wastes we'd just passed through. The heavy dark robes also concealed rifles and gear. The disguise was topped off with the classic desert Bedouin turban.

The Ranger scouting teams moving among the ancient stall-laden streets of Sûstagul and under the shadows of high walls and strong towers where a hundred languages were shouted, cried, laughed, and cursed, observed and reported with little notice. We did here chatter regarding us, overheard in our various teams of "beggars," "nomads," or wandering "scholars," but it amounted to little more than the observation that there was something new and strange in Sûstagul, as the fishwives like to murmur in a patois of Italian, Arabic, and some Chinese. *The strange nomads. Hope they're bringing in gold from the desert and leaving just as quickly as they came.*

It helped that we maintained a "caravan camp" of nomads near the walls under the tower the snipers would take just moments into the operation. We even had camels.

At other times, especially when working with Chief Rapp, we were just down-and-out drunken sailors who couldn't work anymore and were considered invisible by the locals running their guilds and trades. In these roles of unwanted castaways, we wandered the streets with an invisibility that nearly matched that of my ring, drifting through the shadowy alleys of the docks during the morning and the thronging mercenary-overwatched marketplaces in the brutal afternoons, passing under high, sunbaked brick walls and staying in the cool blue shadows cast on ancient stones below. Never settling anywhere, always moving. Always observing. Always reporting. Measuring and recording distances while studying the various defensive structures of the entire city. Developing the new map we'd need to take the city and make it the new Ranger base of operations against the Saur in the south.

That was Captain Knife Hand's plan. We'd take the city. And now that the 160th Special Operations Aviation Regiment (Airborne) was involved in the game after rescuing Sergeant Joe and me out in the desert, along with the

Accadion legionnaires, we could do that by just hopping right into the battle via helicopter transport instead of battling our way through a medieval city filled with dead ends and small fortress-type bunkers we'd have to fight our way through just to get into the market.

There was nothing we could do about the market district. It had a heavy presence of mercenary-run security for the ever-paranoid wizards who'd made small fortress towers within which to conduct their research into the dark and arcane secrets of the sorceries buried beneath the southern sands. But that district was where we needed to go to dominate the city. I'll get into that later, and also how the 160th ended up here and in contact with us, supporting the mission to take the city. I know that's a big story, and as Kennedy, who read much of this account while I was considered MIA in the desert, puts it, "You go on a lotta tangents in your writing, Talker. Did you ever take any classes, or study how to write... you know... books?"

And the answer is... *no*. This mess is all me, buddy.

Taking that advice though, I will try to stick to the story and the focus of the first moves of the Ranger battle for Sûstagul. Now that the old haunted Legion fortress was under our control as of just after midnight, and the first of the MH-6 Little Birds were inbound on the beach LZ the Ranger pathfinder sergeants had set up to grab Third and put them in control of the port, I will tell you how this plan came into being, and how it got altered now that the new development of the Saur advance force had boarded the slave galleys.

Or mainly the problem of the slaves, Sergeant Monroe's solution, and the irregulars that would assist him in doing the impossible that day.

"You have to understand maps, PFC," grunted Kurtz to me as our team got some time on the sand table prior to the attack out in our desert camp near the shore as we got ready for the pump. I'd been to the planning briefings with the command team because those involved the dwarves and they still needed help understanding our concepts and words. And there were the Accadions and the giant gorilla samurai Otoro. So I'd been busy doing that linguist thang. Now with Kurtz, who'd be leading the augmented weapons team into the market in support of Second under Sergeant Joe and Chief Rapp running the battle there, we were getting walked through what we'd be doing once the battle for the port was underway.

I know… action movies have all kinds of things happening on the fly and battles every ten seconds. But that's ten thousand years ago—and it's movies—and what I've learned is you plan, train, and wait a lot for what amounts to a very short period of intense life-and-death fighting.

All that planning, training, and waiting pays dividends like you wouldn't believe. Rangers don't believe in fair fights.

"You in a fair fight, son, you done something wrong." So sayeth Joe from the Book of.

"You have to understand maps to understand how a battle is going to go down, Talker," lectured Kurtz as he bent down on one knee, taking notes on the small notebook every Ranger carried. The whole team was with him, but I could tell that Kurtz was already there, in the city. Weeks before we'd walk one step of that plan in real time, he was there seeing every building, every corner, every street fight where the team would need to move and set up.

"Every LT's got some fancy plan about how he wants to run the fight, you see. Problem is nine times outta ten, geography is going to tell you exactly what's gonna happen regardless of anyone's plans."

So sayeth Sergeant Kurtz with little eloquence and much blunt-force truth. Such are his ways. Attend and know wisdom.

Now that I have the tab, I realize how much I don't know. And so, I attend and know wisdom. I know nothing. Teach me more of your killing ways, Ranger sergeants. Listen, I don't say this stuff out loud. I'd be the new Kennedy. But I think it as I try to learn and absorb everything they know about explosives, CQB, and war. And a bunch of other stuff.

As I have said, the weapons team, along with Second, would need to smoke the powerful wizard Ur-Yag who basically ran the show in the market and most likely passively controlled much of the city through dark powers and influence on the trade networks. I was on that team going into the market in a leadership role. Everything I didn't know was going to cost someone. And I'd learned from Monroe what the real burden of leadership was. And that... that changed me and it's what these next sections are about in the lead-up to the street battles that were about to go down.

Also... Ur-Yag had to have some kind of relationship with the Saur. We had no hard intel on that, but the connection seemed obvious. We couldn't take any chances he was an ally, now that we were going to strangle the Saur's ability to leave the southern deserts and join in the greater fight against the Cities of Men. So Ur-Yag was tagged as a jackpot with a smoke-on-sight greenlight from the captain.

Sorry, more about that operation later too. This is what happens when you get me focusing on that narrative of the story.

So, the slaves...

The captain had said, during the briefings I'd attended along with everyone in a command position and the dwarves and others, "The port is the key to the battle. The Saur have been moving in from the south in small- to medium-sized company elements for three days now. We think there's about four thousand of them now, all loaded on the galleys according to our scouts on the ground who're moving about the city. The Saur have had little interaction with the locals and stayed on the ships for the most part. We've moved the hit time for Stranglehold up three days because word on the street, according to our linguist, is they're going to depart soon. Hitting them now denies their contribution to the war effort."

Hey, that's me!

We were now officially involved with the larger war. Captain Rechs had returned to Accadios and was on his way back with two legions and a formal alliance with the Cities of Men under the Accadion banner.

But back to me.

This is how I found out about the slaves aboard the galleys and the plan for the Saur to depart soon, upping our timetable. One day I was doing my usual eavesdropping among the sages who spend much of their time in a small coffeehouse—and yes, there is such a thing here in fabled Sûstagul. Winner me. I found it, and I won't lie to you about how I did so. It's on the Street of Imps. Or, as it's known in the local language, the *Sharie al'Sshbah*. I smelled it when we were scouting. Observing and reporting. I smelled that beautiful dark temptress of coffee brewing and so, acting the part of wandering scholar that day, moving with a team of scouts acting in the desert nomad role as my security team, I... *observed and reported*. Sergeant Hardt was the team leader on that one. I smelled the coffee as we passed from the great gates that guarded the main road through the city and bisected the walled district of the market, entering the long isthmus of the port known as Dockside.

There, amid the swarming press of unwashed bodies, savory spiced meats cooking on the street, rank camels and other strange animals, fresh sweet fruits stacked in stalls, and wafting lotus rolled in thick dark leaves and smoked by old men watching from the shadowed stoops of shops and residences, I smelled *coffee*.

And believe me, none of the scouts smelled it. Heathens. So, it's probably some kind of *Ruin reveals* superpower my psionics have given me, right guys? *Detect Coffee*?

Or at least that's what I'm thinking.

Of course I had to investigate. So I hand-signaled, subtly, the team leader that I was moving into this low shop from which stretched old multicolored faded ailing cloth like some kind of awning over the whole front half of the crumbling shamble where the aroma of coffee came from. *Aroma* is a better word than *smell*. See, Kennedy, I don't need writing classes. I improve as I go. Hardt closed with me as we had done before to interface on a plan of action and find out what I was up to... then he smelled it too. The aroma.

The coffee. Oh joy, me!

"Oh, c'mon, Talker!" he hissed as he got close to me without trying to seem like we knew each other on a street filled with busy merchants, strange travelers, and the residents of the district and city.

"Listen, Sar'nt," I began. "Chief said I had to investigate everything of interest. This is definitely *of interest*. To us. Honest."

"To *you*, PFC. We all get it. You like coffee more than anyone. And I get that's saying something among NCOs. But…"

"Solid copy, Sar'nt." We were talking in hushed tones near a high wall of that sunbaked, almost squashed brick that sectioned off every road and district within the strange old port. "But here's the deal about coffee. Here in the Ruin, which you gotta admit is kinda like the oldy-olden days before our time, Sar'nt, a place that serves coffee has got to be like an open comm line we can tap into for local chatter. There's intel there, Sar'nt. I can smell it."

"You're smelling the coffee, PFC."

"*And* the intel, Sar'nt. Trust me. Coffee, for addicts like me, and I bet there's a bunch of us, them, those guys, in there, it makes us real chatty. Especially if we need to keep hovering around however it is they brew it up and serve it in there. So, me going in… *gold mine* for what's going on for us. Gold. Mine. *Way* better than wandering around trying to pick up half a conversation on the streets. Trust me, Sar'nt. There's useful stuff in there and it's worth a cup and a little time."

Hardt's eyes narrowed. That was all I could see of his face. But the message was pretty clear.

He leaned close and grabbed my chest through my wandering scholar's robe disguise. "*One* cup, PFC."

"Affirmative, Sar'nt. One cup and if there's nothing worth listening to, I'm back on the street quick."

He nodded.

"Can I get a cup to go if it's a dead end, Sar'nt?"

The look I received after that one told me that when we got back to the camp there was going to be some serious PT in my future.

Who cares, I thought as I entered the dark establishment and saw many, many travelers sitting around ornate low brass tables sipping rough clay cups of… oh my… coffee!

Many were turbaned. Many were clearly merchants. Long and pointed beards, hooked noses, gold rings, earrings. Dark skin and burning eyes. Quick darting looks here and there. Others seemed intent on their palaver, a Vandahar word if there ever was one, as they talked with some other like friend who waved and gestured about goings-on in this city or that land. All of it fueled by the glorious dark coffee whose scent—aroma—hung heavy in the air beneath the striped and faded sailcloth.

I listened to everything as I went straight for the coffee because me and all. Shout out if you knew that was coming. And this was a pro brewing setup I needed to watch. An old man worked the bed of hot sand that the brass *ebriks* filled with hot water, fine ground coffee, and spices were placed into. As an official coffee pro, I knew there were hot stones and a small furnace beneath that burning sand. Next to the old man, who was bent and slight, a dark-eyed girl, curvy and showing some generous wares, worked at grinding the coffee and placing the spices in the *ebriks* as the old man worked the hot sand, measured the fine ground coffee beans, then placed the *ebrik* in and out of the scalding sand. Bringing each beautiful brass *ebrik* to a boil three times and then pouring the fragrant brew into a rough ceramic cup ready for consumption. Another girl, who seemed the twin of the beauty working the hand-crank grinder, carried the cups to tables as merchants eyed her flesh appraisingly and tipped soft pats to her shapely rear undulating beneath a rough cotton dress. Her taut belly was exposed and clad in a pearl chain that tried to dazzle the eyes as much as her brown skin revealed did. Large bangles of many precious metals danced on her wrists as merchants gave her soft strokes on her tan arms and pressed silver coins into her palms, trying to hold her gaze for just a moment. She smiled kindly, flirtingly with some, and worked them all like a pro.

She was their queen. The coffee their communion. This place their temple.

And then I realized I was standing in front of the bent old man and the girl working the grinder.

"Yes," she said in Arabic. "What do you want?"

She was younger than the one working the floor of the coffeehouse. But beautiful in a way her tawdry doppelganger wasn't. She was serious and her voice was deep and husky.

I looked into dark brown eyes, smelled coffee brewing, and was pretty sure I'd done something right and ended up in someone's heaven. Mine. I was surrounded by all the languages I'd ever want to decipher for the rest of my life.

"Coffee..." I croaked, my voice dry from the desert heat on the crowded streets and the salt of the nearby sea. The days were getting hotter every day and if we didn't attack Sûstagul soon and make our move on Jackpot Mummy, we'd be fighting in the desert during the height of summer. And no one thought that would be a picnic worth attending. But we'd go. We'd make them pay for ever being interested in us enough to try and smoke us from the moment we arrived.

Burritos. Yeah, there were tentative alliances now. But for the Rangers, as Joe had held forth at night, this was about *burritos.* And everyone from the captain and the smaj down to Kennedy knew it. They'd messed with us, now they'd find out.

"Sit down, stranger," said the dark-eyed beauty working the grinder. "My sister Aaila will see to your needs."

I stuttered because I'm smooth like that, "I like to w-watch… the coffee… brewing. M-may I?"

Me Thag. Want thing. Girl nice.

She gave me a look. I don't know what it was. But if I had to guess now, it was something like… *Well, that's a new one here in the city.*

"I'm a stranger…" I said, feeling like my cover was blown for no reason I could think of. This girl had a strange… power. She made me nervous. Like she was some human lie detector and for a second I wondered if my psionics were picking something up about her. "… from a strange land. We have no… coffee. Where… me… I mean… me, er, I… come from."

She watched me and I could tell, and this was weird, but I could tell she knew I was lying. But she nodded and muttered something in a language I didn't know to the old man at the stones.

The only thing I caught was the Chinese word for Papa. *Bàba.*

"Interesting," I said, recovering smoothly and pretending I actually had. Listen, you've read this account. I got game. But she was jamming my *chi* for some reason.

Then she began to tell me everything about how they did their business. About the making of coffee. And I was entranced with everything she said. The whole thing. And of course… really it was her. But she was adding coffee to the lust I seemed to have for her instantly. I thought to myself… this must be how Caligula felt. Except with coffee.

Hey, been a long time in the desert, buddy.

And the tempting djinn girls ain't making things easy. In fact, their game seems to be… making things… more difficult… for all involved.

"This is how we brew our recipe…" she began, and proceeded to explain everything in detail, as though she was proud of what they did. I knew it all. But I luxuriated in every described moment of it. She explained the grinding. "It must be very fine, stranger from a strange land." Then she taught me the spices as though I'd just arrived from the moon.

In the absence of marketing pros and the internet videos of influencers ten thousand years running from the out-of-control nanoplague… she was doing marketing exactly as they had, except Ruin Bronze Age style. She taught me, informed me, and I knew it all already, but I was bewitched by every revelation.

Ròuguì. Which is Chinese for cinnamon.

Cardamom. Which is Portugonian for… cardamom.

Cīnī. Hindi for sugar.

She had no idea what these languages she used were. They were just part of her speech.

Finally, "From the spice markets of Kungaloor," she said proudly as she spooned a small amount of cīnī up from an ornate silver box using a pearl-handled spoon. Fine brown raw sugar. She was very careful with this ingredient. Proudest of it more than the others.

Like this was her gift to the world. The spell, or prayer, she truly believed in.

They were making Turkish coffee. One of my favorites and absolute must-haves back in the world we came from whenever I could find it. To the point that when I went to some new city to study a new language, I'd usually try to locate Middle Eastern markets to frequent on those days when the coffee shops closed early and there was still much studying to be done.

A small cup of Turkish and a baklava, or a date mamul, and I could study all night. Especially if the coffee didn't stop and the shop didn't close.

When my cup was prepared, she took it from the old man and handed it to me. For a moment time stopped for the two of them and they stopped their constant machine of preparing, brewing, and serving, to watch me taste what they had made. Crafted.

I smelled it first. *Cupping* is what pros call inhaling the aroma of coffee, and then I sipped. It was dark, and rich, and smelled of strange foreign lands with exotic spices your mind translates in images and things you never knew before and want to go to now. It hit hard and any fatigue from the desert and the heat faded away as I felt at home under the sailcloth, shielded from the relentless glare of the desert sun.

I'd closed my eyes during the sip, and when I looked up, they both were smiling at me. The bent old man and the dark-haired, dark-eyed, curvy beauty who seriously worked the grinder and believed in what she was doing. Because I was too. Smiling. Smiling at what they had made. What I had tasted. Where it had taken me.

The old man danced back and forth on both of his feet for a second, patting his daughter and murmuring something in their strange patois.

I caught a little that time.

"It is good we came here, Amira. I still have the magic to seduce. Things will be different here now. Things will be good."

She nodded at him, lowered her head, and returned to her grinding work.

"My father says it is good," she said to me simply.

I nodded.

"What is his name?"

"Sandoman of Parvaim."

"And you?" I asked. Because of course. She was beautiful.

She came up from her endless work, huge dark eyes studying me and looking for the lie I would surely tell her. Sure there was one.

"Amira."

CHAPTER EIGHT

SLAVES. Remember the narrative is slaves and I know there's a lot of moving parts to this battle. The attack on the market to smoke Ur-Yag. The Rangers taking and holding the Lighthouse of Thunderos which was the key to taking the port and channeling all the Saur into the Rangers' killing zone. And then there's Sergeant Thor Yahtzee-ing the High Priest of Pan only to have to go in and smoke their actual god on foot. Again, I'll get to that. There was a lot going on, go figure it was a battle and it wasn't just *This is what Talker saw and did.* Other people have lives too.

And of course… what happened at the Gates of Eternity with Brumm and Kurtz holding the line.

But, at this moment prior to the battle, the slaves on the galleys became a real problem two weeks out from the hit. The Rangers' plan had been to initially go in and just burn the galleys with incendiaries and high explosives. Or gun runs from the Little Birds spooling out thirty-millimeter explosive death with their chain guns and sinking them in the harbor. From the coffeehouse, we gained intel that the galleys were crewed by pirates from Skeletos and that the galleys were slave-powered. And that threw a wrench in our plan of total murder and mayhem rained down from above.

Because the operational plan to take the city, and eventually use it as a base of operations against the Saur in the south, consisted of winning the hearts and minds of the city and doing as little collateral damage to them as possible so we could stay here for some time as the spring and summer war season got underway.

That was critical. We needed to win the hearts and minds of the people who lived here. Excluding the strange wizards who made dark deals with the Saur in the south. Or the Temple of Pan which seemed to be well loved but much feared. Rumors of child sacrifice abounded.

So yes, the Rangers could do shock and awesome. That was a given. But that would result in a lot of collateral damage happening among the civilian population. Especially in the market district which is where we expected the fighting to be intense as we actually needed to perform a movement to contact. No ambushes. No *Surprise… Ranger Smash!* We actually had to go in there and kill the enemy with them already knowing we were coming.

It had the making of a fair fight, and the Rangers didn't like that. A tough fight wasn't a problem for them. But a fair fight meant they hadn't done their homework. So yeah, we had some surprises, and that caused a general sense of comfort to abound as we cleaned our weapons and tightened our gear and loads we'd be taking in to pull our particular brand of mayhem.

Ranger Smash in effect.

And then there was the wizard.

"I may be of use with that problem," mused Vandahar behind a cloud of smoke rings during one of the command briefings regarding the attack on the market.

"And how would that be?" asked the sergeant major. "From what we've seen of your… capabilities… on the battlefield you seem on the same level of destruction as mortars or a Carl G. We're concerned about the damage we might cause in there to the civilian population."

The wizard blew a smoke ring and looked off out into the desert beneath the flaps of the tent where the briefing was taking place. Then some thought seemed to come to him, and he smiled happily. He straightened his robe, relit his pipe with a spark from his long finger, and said, "Yes, I may be a *magical Carl G,* as you call it. But… there is business between Ur-Yag and myself. Which is why I will go with you and use some *illusions* to convince the populace there to stay clear of your attacks through the streets of that cursed den of foul sorceries. And to be frank… the battle between Ur-Yag and myself will go a long way to make that point to them, as it should be very public. So there is that to aid you in convincing them to clear the way for Rangers."

That had been the plan. Minimize damage and involvement to the civilian population of Sûstagul. The Rangers could do that, and maybe Vandahar could too. But to be honest, here in the Ruin we hadn't had to factor in much of that kind of consideration in many of our previous conflicts. A lot of the times it had been, just as Chief Rapp put it, *Hey look that way… Ranger Smash!* Now we needed to take care because we'd be using the battlefield, the city, to operate from after this. You wouldn't win many minds or hearts among sprays of blown-out sunbaked brick that was once someone's home or business.

But… it was obvious that the wizards, and the Temple of Pan, weren't well loved here in Sûstagul. A lot of that intel was thanks to Amira and the coffeehouse. I was hitting that place two or three afternoons a week. For the intel. As for the Saur... they were downright the stuff of nightmares. The citizens wanted to have as little to do with a marching army of lizard men straight from the pyramids to the south as possible. So, getting rid of these three elements... Saur, wizards, and Temple... would result in us being seen as...

"Don't say it, Talk," Tanner had warned me when I went back to the weapons section and told him what was going on with the planning and development of Stranglehold.

"Say what?"

"*Seen as liberators.* Been in long enough to know that they never see it that way. Best you can hope for with a civvy pop is that they fear you more than the last guys, and that you're gonna get outta their hair real quick when the biz is done. Which is what armies are supposed to do. Ain't s'posed to play cop. That's a hangover from the Deep State days and it's one I hope we didn't bring with us to the Ruin."

So we wouldn't be seen as liberators. But we'd remove *our* problems—wizards, Saur, and Temple—and hopefully that would, at a minimum, buy us a little bit of goodwill among the local *civvy pop*.

"It won't," replied Kurtz who was listening in on us. But he didn't explain any further.

"He's right," said Tanner after Kurtz left the tent to go ruin someone else's life with his presence. Jabba, who was nearby, nodded in agreement. He nodded along with anything Tanner said lately. Like some dog who'd learned an almost human trick.

"He does that," said Tanner, regarding the little goblin who'd seemed to have acquired more and more of the Rangers' dented gear, "'cause I let him hit my dip. But—get this—he just chews it and then swallows it. Then smiles real weird. I hope that Moon God Potion shows up with the galleys. *Rip It* on this one would be good. But the gob is tearin' through my dip like it's Joe's beef jerky. I ain't got that much to keep up at this rate."

Ranger problems.

Or as Tanner put it, "Can't think about goin' dry before resupply, Talk. That's an unforgivable sin."

So the plan, as I was saying, was to minimize damage and hope that would buy us some goodwill for the time we needed to operate out of here against the south and the campaign against Sût the Undying.

The temple battle didn't have a lot of civilian interaction problems we could foresee, as the district was pretty much just the temple and, again, word on the ground was they were not well loved.

Vandahar could help us with, as Tanner put it, "civil affairs" in the market.

And the port was really just about smoking the Saur on the ships as they tried to dislodge Third at the lighthouse. Plus, the battle at Dockside was going to telegraph enough to the local population that those who wanted to get out of the way had time to do so. If they wanted to. Otherwise they'd picked a side as far as the Rangers were concerned.

Then one afternoon the mood was serious in the city because the Saur had just moved their biggest force yet in through the Gates of Eternity at the southern walls and marched straight to the port where they loaded onto the war galleys. That was all the talk in the coffeehouse that day. And that was when Amira said something I hadn't heard in any of our planning and briefings. Something I thought important enough for me to leave right then and there, get out of the city, and report to the smaj.

So I did.

"Your contact says those galleys are filled with slaves from all along the coast north of here running up to what we used to call Turkey?" asked the sergeant major upon hearing what I'd learned.

"Yes, Sergeant Major. They call it the *Sorrab* now, along the border of the Eastern Waystes. The Skelotos pirates raid those areas for their galley slaves. It's… a thing for them. A bad thing."

"What do you mean, *a bad thing*, PFC Talker?"

"I mean… it's why the locals hate the pirates, the Saur, and pretty much everyone involved in the slave trade. Sûstagul is a crossroads city, Sergeant Major. They all have contacts in other regions, including the Sorrab. Which means everyone's had someone they know end up as a galley slave. Someone they care about. It's said the Saur eat their slaves down in the Desert of Black Sleep. That's the rumor anyway. Unconfirmed as far as we're concerned, but they're lizard people so… why not. Makes sense.

"What I'm getting at, Sergeant Major, is that, if we could rescue those slaves… well, maybe this is the psionics detecting something the locals are broadcasting, but I'd bet rescuing those slaves will buy us a *lot* of goodwill here on the other side of the fight. A lot. And… I know I'm selling it, Sergeant Major, but… also, it's the right thing to do."

The sergeant major stared at me over the canteen cup of coffee he was drinking.

Then, "You'd bet?" he muttered, considering what I'd reported and my assessment of it. It was a question. But it wasn't asked like I needed to give an answer.

"Well, how we gonna do that, PFC?" Again, the senior enlisted man wasn't asking for a plan. He seemed to be talking it through to himself as I listened along. But I answered anyway.

"I don't know, Sergeant Major. We're stretched thin as it is."

"And it makes the whole port job a helluva lot harder. Hell, impossible really."

Silence.

I was probably going to get cast away from the smaj's blue percolator for what I was about to say next, but I said it anyway.

"That's what we Rangers do, Sergeant Major. We do the impossible."

Those grey eyes of the sergeant major, who'd seen more combat in more places around the world than any of us, were like shark's eyes. More impossible done than any of us would ever imagine. Then he snorted and said what he said next.

"You got that right, Ranger."

We drank coffee and everything was okay after that. I was still near the percolator. I had not been cast out from its presence. So how bad could things really be?

We all have our metrics for success.

I have mine.

Don't judge me.

CHAPTER NINE

THE story of what happened in the port, the battle there, is Sergeant Monroe's story. Sorry, I know you like to hear what happened to me in this or that. Or maybe you don't and you're just sticking around to see how badly it goes for me. It probably will. As Sergeant Joe says, "Some people get away with everything until one day… they don't." True, his lesson was on burritos, but I feel it has other philosophical and practical uses.

But I couldn't be everywhere that day of the Battle for Sûstagul. And important, and very brave things, happened that day at many actions. Just like Tanner's account of the taking of the Haunted Legion Fortress, the story of the port is Sergeant Monroe's, and this is how he told it to me when the time came for me to hear it.

"I always thought, Talker, that bein' a sergeant was my big goal in life as a Ranger. First make it through RASP. Learn to pay the rent in the regiment. Get Ranger qualified. Find my job as an NCO and be better than any other Ranger at it. That ain't just bein' the undisputed squat king back at the batts. Beast mode for life is how I went at all of those steps I'd decided, and been taught, were the path to becoming the Ranger I wanted to be."

Tanner thinks the reason Monroe was revealed to be a beastman like a minotaur is because his whole life approach to being a Ranger was beast mode.

Truth? Who knows? I don't. The Ruin reveals, and the revealed wonder why.

"That morning, sitting in the dark," continued the minotaur Ranger, "the pig cleaned and ready to rock, I could only think about one thing. My first time out, as a sergeant, and I'd screwed up the first thing I'd been told not to do about being a sergeant. My... troops... were in it out there in the dark doing the intel work for me as a battle that was about to go all hurricane got ready to go live. And all I could think about was that I needed to protect them from what was about to happen, and to tell you the truth, I had no idea how to. I thought I did. But there in the dark, three in the morning, all you can do is think about all the things that are gonna hang you and the ones you got charge of, up. How everyone is gonna get killed because of what you didn't get done. I'll tell you... when you and the old man came to give me my mission and tell me what needed to happen, that was... all I could think about. Going beast mode and gettin' it done, man. I didn't think about my... can we call 'em *my troops*? Can we call 'em that? Whatever they are. They were mine that morning. And, in the dark, sittin' in that rat- and flea-infested inn, it was dark and quiet and suddenly all my plans, and what was expected of me acting as RT there in the port... that went out the door and all I could think about was little Muhara and the rest of them.

"I've had leadership roles before, Talker. But them stripes, and something that was once told to me about what you do, what's expected when you wear 'em, it found me there in the dark. I had… screwed up. It was gonna get hot in there and I had no plan… for them. I mean… they're really just kids, man. That's all, whatever they are, that's all they are. That's what I was feeling right then."

So, let me explain what Sergeant Monroe meant by his "troops" just being kids. And this isn't a tangent and it's not the coffee I've been brewing all night trying to get this account down in the aftermath of the battle as the city still burns. In places.

There are many, what Kennedy would call *demi-humans*, in the port city. What's a demi-human, you ask? Well, without causing anyone who reads this to go fetal and get into some argument about the nature of what it means to be human, in Kennedy's game demi-humans are dwarves, elves, even some really ugly suckers we've seen in the city who we're pretty sure got some orc in 'em down in the old blood line and all. Other races can be demi-humans too. Anything humanoid, two hands, two feet, bipedal, some sort of tribal organization.

Humans have tribes.

Animals have herds.

There's the difference.

So technically, a minotaur is a demi-human. And because they're big and strong, not really members of the local guilds and private armies the wizards have in the marketplace, they're outsiders. And therefore, these types, we noticed, tended to gravitate toward hard labor. Which, in a city, is a kind of invisibility. Porters. Diggers. Stevedores in the port. Laborers doing relentless labor have a tendency to become unnoticed. Invisible.

We'd seen the orc types. And the dwarves. Some with a bit of ogre or even giant in them. Misshapen, haunted creatures. Digging ditches, hauling immense chains. We saw a guy who was easily ten feet tall pulling the breaker chain that acts as a boom to guard the entrance to the harbor. The Lighthouse of Thunderos is basically the giant winch for the chain that keeps enemies out of the bay. Or in, if that's where you want them.

But more about that later.

That poor blind dude works there on the edge of the hammerhead peninsula hauling the chain in beneath the lighthouse during the mornings and in case of an attack from the sea.

Or so we suspect.

We had used Monroe the minotaur as part of Freak Squad to move among enemies because he was more likely to be taken as OPFOR than as a member of our side. The Freak Squad was an ad hoc team that got thrown together, usually for special scouts into enemy territory, every so often and based on mission needs. Kind of like a long-range patrol, and we'd done it three times before in crossing the No Man's Land.

Tanner and Monroe were always on it. Me and Kennedy because of our powers. A couple of others who were changing. Being revealed. The captain was an obvious choice but he was in charge of everything and unless it was a battlefield scout, his time was better spent elsewhere running the whole show rather than assuming his other form.

The sergeant major didn't like the term *Freak Squad*. He preferred *Goon Squad*.

I asked Tanner why the smaj had made such a small distinction. Tanner told me that, "Every commander has a goon squad. Basically, it's an off-books group of pipe hitters who get all the stuff done for you, that you as a combat leader can't legally get done. They might get called Garbage Men. Even Trash Collectors. Sometimes it's just keeping the Kennedy types, before he became our valuable wizard, tight and all. Sometimes it's payback on the enemy with no records kept. It ranges. But it means they trust you to get it done and keep your mouth shut."

There were a couple of other Rangers who were *becoming*, or revealing, and they were getting tried out for the Freak Squad.

Now, as we tried to develop the plan to seize the port, it occurred to someone that we needed a Ranger recon team inside the port well in advance of the operation. And that was difficult because if you look at the map, Dockside is just a narrow isthmus that has a lot of buildings squashed and squeezed together and all of them are pretty busy with ship loading and unloading. Dockside has always got someone somewhere doing something. You can't put a Ranger recon team on a roof because everyone will see them. The nomad act only worked if we kept moving, didn't engage, and were outside with our camel "beards" by nightfall because everyone knows nomads don't like sleeping inside city walls. *Duh*.

But a minotaur, working as a stevedore on the docks, gave us all the intel and access we needed regarding that area of the operation. And on the morning of the attack, with commo, he could tell us in real time what was going on just in case we lost drone feed, which, at this range from the Air Force crew, was starting to happen more and more often. And the wizards we'd encountered before had been able to identify and knock out drones in previous fights.

So putting an RRT on the scene in Dockside was vital. As anyone will tell you who's worked with a Ranger recon team. Monroe went in alone after getting promoted to sergeant, and every day either Hardt or myself would link up with him at one of three locations in Dockside, grab a piece of paper he left, and return with the intel to the CP in our camp outside the city.

He loaded ships all day, watched and observed. As the zero hour got close we smuggled in Sergeant Monroe's gear. Special plate carrier. Special chest rig. Assault pack. One Carl G with three rounds. One Special Forces M-60 with laser targeting system that helped him acquire due to the ungainly nature of his revealed hulking minotaur body. Grenades and flashbangs. IR strobe. Comm. Three claymores. Some other useful stuff.

Lately he'd taken to carrying a battle axe that never went dull. It took off the limbs of enemies like they were butter. Kennedy had identified it as magical under the tutelage of Vandahar and said it was the *Axe of Skaarvang the Blood Dealer*. "A mighty Frost Giant warrior from Dire Frost in the long-ago ages when those savage tribes came south to attack the Cities of Men." Kennedy was sounding more and more like Vandahar in the way he talked. Or trying to.

To watch that Ranger work, that axe made you wonder why he'd even bother with the sixty. But we were gonna be in it that day and it was best, since he'd be in there alone, right in what we were hoping was a channelized attack from the Saur, that he be armed for bear.

"Sucks to be the bear," said the sergeant major when I humped in the sixty in a special bag the dwarves had constructed of finely worked leather. It slung over Monroe's shoulder, and it was really just a cover to keep the sixty camouflaged and looking like the kind of heavy tool bag—mattocks, picks, shovels—a working-class minotaur in the Cities of Men might have as he went about his business.

Note: demi-humans are rarely tolerated in the other Cities of Men, according to Vandahar. "Monsters are considered horrible foes, even if they are the offspring of matings between their own kind and the forces of darkness. These are often killed with little cause. But Sûstagul is a strange and mysterious city, and truly the oldest of all the Cities of Men, though it was not always a City of Men. The Saur once called it the City of Pythons. But that was long ago when they ruled the known world and held all in the sway of their ancient claws."

So that was how Sergeant Monroe came to be operating as a scout inside the city for some time before our attack. Now to his troops. Here's how Monroe tells it.

"They call them the *Flotsam*, Talker. That's what the sailors and everyone who lives in Dockside calls 'em when they're being polite. From what I can understand. Like I said, my Arabic ain't great, but two in the sandbox and I get by, know what I mean?"

I do, actually. You can learn languages if you're around 'em and just make the effort. Most people don't wanna try, is my take on why they don't learn.

"Usually they have curse words for 'em," continued Monroe, "or they call them *the Children of the Sea Whores*. You know what they're like, man. Years ago I watched this doc on orphan kids of soldiers from Vietnam. People called 'em *Dust Children*. They had a hard time of it. Hard for them to immigrate too. People in that country hated them because the kids reminded them of the war. No one wanted them. Rough bein' a kid like that.

"So I saw 'em, saw these Flotsam everywhere among the docks. People call 'em thieves when things go missing. I figure they're probably a little gang or something. Survival. But when I'm working loading a ship, they're out there selling fruit to the galleys in small canoes. Except they don't ride in the canoes. They swim alongside. And… they got gills, man. I've seen 'em dive. They can stay under longer than anyone ever can hold their breath. But they look just like us."

I did some recon among the sages once Sergeant Monroe related this to me and found out the legend of the Whores of the Sea. There's a beach not far from here and on full moons mermaids, or at least that's how it was described to me, come ashore and *mate* with men from the port. Sailors passing through. I don't know if that's true. But apparently these children are the unwanted results of these unions. In Sûstagul, according to the sages, the children are considered to be nuisances and a problem, but they are allowed to exist. Because killing them invites some kind of curse, according to local lore. The mermaids will come in and get you, they say.

Back to Sergeant Monroe's story.

"So one of 'em, this little girl, on one hot afternoon when I'm lying in some nets because I've just offloaded an entire shipment of wine jars from Tyranor, and it's tough being careful with those heavy clay jars that make walking gangplanks and up and down through holds brutal and all. So I'm recovering until the next ship comes in, lying there in these nets, and I doze off because the sun is nice and hey, who's gonna mess with a minotaur who's got a wicked axe and all? I hear the sea birds and the creak of the tackle and the sounds of the ships and…" He practically sighs in satisfaction. "I'm tellin' you, Talker, I never thought I'd love those sounds as much as I've come to love working down there. I like it here, man. In the Ruin. It's cool and all. Don't tell anyone that. I'm in it to win it with the Rangers. All the way to take Sût's skull and whoever else we get point and kill on. I'm down. But you know, Talker, and I bet you do, there's other experiences here in the Ruin. And sometimes they sneak up on you and whisper something in your ear about other ways to go when you're not looking. When you let down your guard a little. All that stuff Thor keeps jawin' about around his little fires and the cult he's got going on over in snipers.

"Okay, so I wake up and there's this little girl, tan, blond hair. Blue eyes. But like she's mixed race. Eyes like the shallows of the sea where it's aquamarine to almost green. Tan skin like she lives in the water under the sun all day. She's only… six, maybe? But who knows, here. Them elves are all way older than us. She looks six though. And she's just sitting there, get this… *petting* my minotaur fur. Like I'm a dog. And you know what, Talker? *I am*. It feels good in some way that's gotta be part of the Ruin revealing. It ain't like any of the Rangers have petted me. First off, I'd kill 'em. Second… that's weird. And I ain't taking a chance with those hotties you got in your bottle. That's ten thousand, I ain't interested.

"So no one, since I… revealed… has done this to me. And now… well, now I know what it's like to be a dog that gets petted. Feels like… feels like you *belong right where you're at*. I know… super dumb. Do *not* tell anyone this, Talker."

"I won't," I lied.

But here I am putting it in the account because it is intel.

"She speaks enough of the port Arabic that I ask her what her name is, and she says, Muhara."

Muhara means *shell* in Arabic. Like seashell. Linguist working here, folks. Pro-level stuff. Stand back. I don't want anyone getting hurt.

"So there we are, and she's just petting my fur and sometimes tracing my horns with her tiny finger, and this real dirtbag dude named Mamamo who's the right-hand guy of the guy that runs everyone that loads down there comes by and hisses '*Nifaya*' at her. Which, from my time in the sandbox, I know means *trash*. Then he throws some fruit he'd finished with right at her. She scampers away and leaps into the water behind the nets and she's gone."

Sergeant Monroe's huge minotaur traps suddenly bunch and flex as he tells me all this. His massive leathery hands form fists. Opening and closing.

"I walk over to this dude, and he's like laughing and telling me how they're a problem in the port and they're nothing but *dirty little thieves* in this nasal little carpet-seller con man voice he's got. I already did not like this dude…"

Sergeant Monroe is silent for a moment before he tells me what happened next.

"I knocked him into next week, man. One punch right in the gut and he actually flew through the air and crashed into coiled rope on the other side of the dock."

"What happened to him?" I asked in the silence that followed.

"Uh… he's dead, Talker."

Well, that could've blown the whole op, but I agree with the correction that dude deserved. He just didn't survive the lesson.

"Problems with the… Bronze Age teamsters after that?" I asked.

"Yeah. They were butthurt. But then they said, 'Beast Man load good. Load Mamamo's work and no problem with coin.' That's what they told me."

According to Monroe, what happens after that is that the kids in the port, the orphans who can dive and sell fruit and seem to be everywhere in the shadows, they see him as a friend. A kind of protector. Because of course they're always everywhere, in the shadows, the alleys, the docks, underneath the docks in the water, watching and seeing everything. They saw what happened with Muhara.

And in time the brother of Muhara, or we think that's who he is, makes contact with Monroe and relays the message that they will *watch for him*. We're not sure what that means, but intel passes back and forth between the minotaur and the command team, and with some coaching from Chief Rapp, in about half a week Sergeant Monroe has his own squad of intel gatherers. We give them some missions about finding out what and who's on certain ships we haven't gotten close to. What the forces around the lighthouse and the smaller lighthouse on the other side of the harbor where the boom chain connects, are. They are forged, vaguely, into assisting the minotaur in his recon mission as the battle approaches.

When asked if they want something they simply shake their heads. The six of them that meet with me and Monroe seem to represent the rest.

The only thing the leader, Aija, says, is: "We saw from the water what he do for Muhara. He take care of us. We take care of each other. He *us*... now."

They speak another language they won't speak around us. Their Arabic port patois is rough. But that's how it comes out. On the morning of the attack, once they get the signal from Monroe, they're going to board the ships the Saur have hopefully disembarked from, and free the slaves. Lead them to jump overboard and swim for the areas away from the main fights. They are thieves. That's how they survive. They know how to pick locks and release chains. They can swim underwater because they're amphibians of some sort. They will do this because someone, a minotaur stevedore, sleeping in the nets one hot afternoon, saw them and demanded, in the way of the Ruin, that they be treated as humans. Respect and the right to be.

And now to what Sergeant Monroe told me about being a sergeant and getting it all wrong on his first time out. Sitting there in the dark and knowing his troops needed to be protected as much as the mission needed to be accomplished.

Everyone knows the story of Alwyn Cashe. A sergeant who went into a burning fighting vehicle covered in gas to save his troops. There are other stories about how sergeants come to understand what Cashe knew to do in that instant moment of final decisions. Knew what was expected of him as the greedy flames tried to take his troops.

These stories are passed down. So that you know.

"When they gave me my stripes and did the promotion ceremony, Talker, I was pretty excited. Scared too because now you gotta live up to that position and find your job and earn it here in the Rangers. Just like you pay rent on that scroll. Every day. Promotion comes with a lot more than just some rank and what you think you do… but you don't. So I was juiced to show them what I can do, know what I mean?"

Why yes. I am a little acquainted with validation by accomplishment, said the guy who has several degrees in doctoral levels of language studies that defy most academic explanation. I always got a thrill out of blowing someone's mind who thought they knew a lot. Showing them what I can do. I am acquainted with this.

I am a small, weak person. I may tell other lies to accomplish the mission. But here, in this record… I am fatally honest. Warts and all.

"So this one sergeant I respect a lot," continues Monroe, "and I'm not gonna tell you his name because you're probably putting everything I say in the account even though I told you not to, but I understand… it all goes in. I get that. It's gotta go somewhere, right? But this is his story and maybe… I don't know. Maybe it's the story of all NCOs. The secret story they tell you, or something like it, when you get in the club. And then you realize it's all about something way more different than you thought it was on the way there. Anyway, this guy tells me about being in the sandbox way back in the day. They were running down some POWs who took a wrong turn and got ambushed. One survivor. The rest… didn't make it and they got buried in a shallow grave outside some location.

"Rangers ran it down and figured out where the bodies were buried. Those bodies, our guys, US Army soldiers, guys and girls, they'd been lying in the sand in the desert for a couple of weeks. The NCOs knew it was gonna be bad digging them up. Real bad. So there I am with my new stripes and everyone congratulating me, feeling good, and then this sergeant takes me aside to tell me what those Ranger NCOs did on that day when they found the shallow graves of our own guys and needed to get it done."

The big minotaur Ranger paused, cleared his throat. I could tell that whatever he got told, it weighed on him like a heavy burden and would for the rest of his life. And for once I felt, just for a brief moment, like I didn't want to hear it. Like I wasn't ready. Like it would change me.

Someone once wrote on the internet, a thing that was back where we came from, that once, a long time ago, when you were a little kid, your mom called you home as the streetlights came on one day turning to twilight, and that was the last time you ever played with those friends you'd played with as a child. You weren't a child anymore. You'd grown up, and you never knew it.

What I was about to hear... had that feeling.

"The NCOs knew the younger soldiers, the new Rangers, couldn't handle what they were about to dig up to get those bodies out of there. Get 'em home. So they put them all on perimeter security, facing outward... and the NCOs did the digging. And it was bad, man. Real bad."

We sat there in the silence of his fleabag room at the inn. Everything smelled of bad fish and smoke. Some drunken singing going on in the main room below. But there between us, as he told me this... it was the silence that is the very universe.

"That's what the sergeant I want to be like told me had happened to him when he was a young Ranger. Just a kid. And that's what it means to be an NCO, Talker. You protect them, Talker, from the bad as much as you can for as long as you can. That's what you do as an NCO. And that's what I was thinking about that morning in the dark, knowing the kids were out there in the water, waiting for my signal."

CHAPTER TEN

"GUNFIGHTER to Lead Wharf Rat… we are inbound with Pipe Hitter on Circus."

Wharf Rat was Sergeant Monroe on the ground in Dockside just thirty minutes from dawn as the opening moves of Stranglehold got under way. The black MH-6 Little Birds along with two fully loaded Black Hawks from the 160th SOAR had just departed the LZ on the beach where the teams that were going in by air were stacked in chalks and waiting to load. Scouts and snipers were busy taking out guards along the walls and keeping an eye on the roving orc nomads ranging through the dunes south of the city.

The Lighthouse of Thunderos was the objective we'd tagged as *Circus*. The impressive structure watched over the approach of the harbor along the easternmost anchor of the hammerhead isthmus that connected to the narrow peninsula of sleeping Dockside. There were bets among the Rangers that the lighthouse was probably considered one of the ancient wonders of the Ruin. It was a narrow ziggurat topped by four strange men with long drooping mustaches. The statues were giant, and each stood in front of a crystalline shield that could reflect light in any direction if the proper fires were lit inside the lighthouse itself.

From a distance it was pretty amazing.

I was still on the dark beach at the LZ. The surf was starting to slow roll across the sand as the day neared. First Platoon and the snipers had already secured the gates and the old fort. Third Platoon was the main element of Pipe Hitter and led by the captain and Sergeant Chris. They'd take the lighthouse, then split up into elements to take smaller locations along the isthmus to secure the harbor and prevent the war galleys from moving into the open sea to escape or oppose the landing of allied galleys bringing in the Accadion legions onto the long beaches nearby.

In the moments before Sergeant Monroe would get the two-minute warning that the first Rangers were "hopping" right into the enemy's rear and taking the hammerhead isthmus and the tactically important lighthouse, I had my NVGs on and was watching the static electricity flinging itself around the tips of the spinning blades of the Little Birds on the beach near our position as our chalk waited for the next ride into the battle.

I had butterflies in ways I hadn't in other fights. I was ready to get into it. But also ready for it to be over. If asked myself, and I didn't at the time because I knew I wasn't going to like the answer, I would've told you I felt like I was going to be sick to my stomach. I chalked that up to nerves being in a leadership role. I'd been in other fights. Other battles. This one felt different though. Bigger. Larger scale. The room for error higher. The losses more final.

But I'd be lying to you if I didn't tell you it was one of those moments you live for. Like you're at some heavy metal concert and everything's about to go down in the darkness as the crowd in the dark all around you feels alive, electric, and dangerous. But it's a good kind of danger. The electricity was loose and running wild there on the beach and the Rangers in Second were stacked in the chalks in the soft sand farther up the beach. And yeah, we were fist-tapping and making last-minute checks. We'd humped a lot of Ruin; now we were getting a ride right into the middle of a battle, and the enemies waiting in the market had no idea what was about to happen to them. We'd have surprise, and if we kept up the roll, we'd keep it.

So yeah, I was pumped.

Sergeant Joe walked by and handed me a piece of his beef jerky and nodded toward our new medic just a few troopers away from me. Her face was serious as she watched the dark to the east we were about to head into. I could see her lips moving silently. She was watching the disappeared Little Birds carrying McGuire into the battle with Third ahead of our entry into the fight.

Wordlessly, Joe was reminding me to keep an eye on her. She wasn't a Ranger. She was here because she felt some duty out of love. She wasn't gonna lose another husband. So she'd be supporting the weapons team as a medic.

I stuck the jerky Joe offered in my mouth and tried to chew, but my jaws hurt from the tension and the chin strap on my FAST. I tapped my helmet twice and nodded, letting him know I had her covered.

On it, Sar'nt.

We still had some time to go before the birds returned and we loaded, made the short trip along the coast flying nap-of-the-earth, gained some quick altitude, and came over the walls fast and hard, gunners suppressing any groups of Saurs or the clusters of mercenaries that might come out to fight us off. Down, on an LZ near Market, we would enter in force and smoke Ur-Yag the Sorcerer.

Market had been the hardest area in the city to penetrate and develop intel on. Much of what would be going on in there would be recon by fire. We knew where the wizard's tower was. We'd identified some danger areas. We'd shoot, move, and communicate, calling targets as we advanced. We weren't even going to breach the tower. We'd just bring it down with explosives and try to get back to the fort or call for the birds to pull us out. We did not have the numbers to fight all the private armies and assassins we suspected were in there. But, if we came in fast, smoked the biggest problem in the district, and pulled back, then… we could leave anyone who wasn't interested in getting along with us a way out through the east. Through the Gates of Mystery.

"Always leave your enemies a way out," the sergeant major had said when reviewing the plan. "Nine times outta ten they don't the want fight so bad after you've shown 'em just how committed you are to ending their lives. A nice exit and a lot of them will *didi mao*."

But right now, inside the city and on the ground, as Sergeant Monroe got the word from Gunfighter Three about the inbound Rangers heading for objective Circus, I and everyone on the beach was ready to finally get this done and over.

Except for Moon in the sand nearby. That's what we call her. Running Moon, our medic. Running Under the Moon. Her name keeps getting shorter. Now we just call her Moon. And she always smiles like we're saying something kind to her. She's a… grateful person. I don't know why. That word to describe her just always leaps out at me when I observe her. She's grateful. And she reminds me, even in the middle of a raid and capture, to be more like her. More grateful.

I've been grumbling to no one, because that is not what Rangers do, about some of the hands I've been dealt recently. Last of Autumn. But I'll be honest, warts and all remember, that, yeah… I've grumbled to *me*. And… sometimes to Jabba when no one's around. Because he has no idea what I'm talking about. But he is a good listener especially if he thinks you've got some Moon God Potion you're holding back. I've been grumbling where no one can hear. Where it doesn't *count*. Except it does. It always counts. Maybe especially when no one else is around.

I'm going to try to be more like Moon.

Here in the dark on the shore as our go-time approaches, she's watching the east and saying prayers for her man. Grateful for him. Thankful she out-stubborned the sergeant major and threw herself into the water in Portugon and swam after the departing galley. She's grateful for the one who sees her. McGuire. And I also suspect she's running through all the things we've tried to cram into her elven brain about rendering combat medicine.

"She's a quick learner," Chief Rapp had noted to me. "Given more time I could teach her some of the more advanced techniques we learn in the SOCOM medical course. The only thing I'm concerned with is her using the nasopharyngeal tubes. She's a bit squeamish and seems hesitant in getting it done. Gotta be definite with those. And you Rangers are physically stronger than her. If they fight her, which people do when they're hit and thinkin' they're gonna die, she might need some help with that. Watch for that PFC, Talker."

I told the SF medic I would.

I reminded myself that there was a time when Autumn had seen me. And that... I'd rather have had that. Than never have had it at all.

I'm really awful at being a combat leader. Moments to action and I'm working on my own problems. I let it go. I'm grateful. Time to lead, fight, and get everyone through this.

I had a lot to do as assistant team leader. I'd prepared for all of it in the typical Ranger fashion of determining to be better than anyone else out there on the battlefield today at what I did. Every Ranger ran through everything chanting that same thought in everything they did to prepare for the killing work that was imminent. Don't believe me? Two-forty gunners check every linked round to make sure it's going to feed and fire efficiently. What we needed to do today needed to happen so fast that the city had no idea what was going on until they were reacting as we wanted them to all the way to total control.

Yeah, it was Ranger Smash. But we couldn't hit and fade. We had to own the walls by dark. We were too far downrange, beyond the support of the Forge. We needed some *walls*. And today, we were going to take them away from someone else.

Third would quietly take control of the isthmus in the opening moments. City guards out there on the hammer-head isthmus, and a small Saurian platoon that had started patrolling the lighthouse, were all about to die from suppressed MK18 carbines as the birds came in, dropped the Rangers, and returned to get Second waiting on the beach.

By dawn the Rangers would be in control of a major chokepoint and setting up defenses and ambushes they were going to get pushed on pretty fast if the Saur reacted as we thought they might.

"Rangers," asked the sergeant major at the final briefing. "What am I gonna say?"

Sergeant Kang answered. "No plan survives contact with the enemy."

"Damn straight, Sergeant. But you know the commander's intent. Divide the enemy and kill them at every opportunity you find and can create. Minimize civilian casualties. Control the walls by dusk and if the orcs outside surge for the walls, mortars rain hell on them and the drone operator'll dump her AGMs. Get those Legion boys on the wall and be prepared to hold for three days."

Once the Rangers had control of the isthmus, they'd set off explosions to breach the lighthouse and raise the boom chain in order to let the enemy know they were trapped in the harbor with their war fleet, and they'd need to retake the lighthouse to get clear of the *X*.

Snipers would engage the pirate crews at will to deny the enemy freedom of movement in the harbor and prevent them from deviating from the channelized avenues of approach to retake the lighthouse.

"We are a small element," said the captain from the shadows beyond the light of the briefing projector. "By creating initial confusion and sowing chaos throughout the battle, effecting this by taking out leaders, we want to encourage the enemy to do something they think is, at the time, effective. And then we want to be there to meet them with massed outgoing fire and high explosives. Sergeant Monroe as the RRT will be the first to strike at command and structure as we set down on Circus."

The plan for that opening move went like this…

As Saurian leadership tried to recover from the mortal blow Sergeant Monroe was tasked with delivering, Chief Rapp as warfare doctrine planner theorized the Saur would rally troops on the ships to march up the peninsula and try to take the isthmus and wipe out the Rangers engaged in combat there.

"Except at that point more of these strange, what they might only guess are some sort of flying griffins, I imagine," said Chief Rapp from the darkness, "these will be our birds, coming in again to put more troops behind them for the attack on Market. This should cause them to attempt to divide in order to respond, thus taking the pressure off Third defending Circus."

We were hoping their command team would split their forces and attempt to protect their rear while we went for the kill shot on Ur-Yag in Market as fast as we could. Bleeding the Saur at small ambush points within the city and along Dockside as they tried to penetrate the city, and at the same time attack the Ranger-held hammerhead isthmus, would see the galleys free of guards and forces and allow Sergeant Monroe's irregulars to liberate the slaves belowdecks.

The objectives were one, a dead Ur-Yag, and two, a Saur force confused and unorganized attacking two separate kill zones and being whittled down by attrition through ambush. And then there was the Temple of Pan standing down, as their high priest lay on the front portico with his head blown off courtesy of Sergeant Thor, at just after the dawn ceremony where we'd observed them making their offering every morning.

Sniper fire from the Haunted Legion Fortress would support smaller missions within the port, mainly the ambushes against the Saur force turning into the city to support the local head honchos we'd determined needed to die for us to take complete control.

Outside the city, one squad from First would hold the gates as mortars set up outside. The Accadion galleys would beach, and the two full legions would hit the sands, eight thousand men under the command of Captain Tyrus. They'd enter the city, interface with the sergeant major, and take control of the walls while the Rangers continued to eliminate resistance within the city, rolling in teams on hits as they developed.

By nightfall, before the orc hordes of the Guzzim Hazadi could figure out we'd made our move and attacked the city, we'd actually be in charge of it behind high walls and supported by two legions and a navy just offshore.

Bold gamble? Yes.

Impossible? Maybe.

But we were Rangers. This is what we do.

The orcs in the dunes and rough hills weren't armed for siege warfare. An open wall and they could, and would, flood through, unless someone stopped them. Otherwise they needed to get us on open ground where they could surround and mass arrow fire once we were pinned down. With our backs to the sea and using optimal terrain features along the march here, we had been able to defeat, outmaneuver, and fend them off.

And someone, two someones, would hold the line on that breach. I will tell that story. But not yet. I will tell it if I can. And right now, I'm so tired of writing, drinking, and brewing coffee as grey smoke drifts over the city in the late night turning to early morning, I just might be able to.

I'm still in shock, though.

Yes…

Yes… I am.

I need a smoke.

Okay, in the morning dark, in the quiet of Dockside, with choppers full of Rangers about to ruin someone's day as the battle got ready to get underway, Sergeant Monroe stepped out of the quiet inn along a deserted street. The business on the main street of Dockside would be different than it was most days. Today it was the killing trade. And tomorrow, if things were done right, the merchants would open their stalls and clean the blood off the streets and by noon, when it was time for coffee, the fight would be a distant thing that had happened long ago. But now, the shadows were deep and dark here in the early morning after the moon had gone down and the sun was just a few minutes off. It was quiet. A perfect quiet.

No birds even yet.

Sergeant Monroe as a minotaur can see quite well in the dark.

The sixty was strapped and covered at his side. Easy and ready to use at a moment's notice. The Carl launcher slung over his back, as was the battle axe underneath that. He wore a rough tunic one of the fishwives had sewn him made of sailcloth and faded sacking. This was to cover the plate carrier. He had one belt of seven-six-two loaded and ready to rock and roll. Another over his thick neck.

"Wharf Rat, this is Gunfighter Lead… we are inbound with Pipe Hitter on the Circus."

Monroe tapped his throat mic to speak and gave the pilots in the stick a weather report and status of enemies on the ground as of that moment.

"Gunfighter… skies are clear and twenty-two over Circus. Winds out of the northeast at six. Chickens are asleep. Cleared to insert Warlord at this time, Gunfighter. Wharf Rat moving to start the show. Rat out."

Then the hulking minotaur moved the dwarven leather cover off the sixty, gave the fat silencer at the end of the barrel a small turn to make sure it was snug and ready for the suppressed work of CQB, and set off for the guard post up the street from the merchant's house that the Saurian general had made his CP inside Dockside.

Ranger Smash was underway.

CHAPTER ELEVEN

"I rolled up on the lizards at the checkpoint and hosed 'em," explained Sergeant Monroe the Ranger minotaur with little fanfare. "It was dawn. They were cold, and like our intel indicated, perfect time to ice 'em. They had a fire they were standing around. The count was the same as it'd been every night. Four. All they saw was the local minotaur cargo loader heading down to the docks and taking the way he always did when he went that way."

Sergeant Monroe would break it all down for me, step by step. Telling me about his secondary tasks as even at that moment the inbound helos could probably be heard in the distance as he opened fire with the SF mod sixty and killed the cluster of elite Saur guards who'd let their guard down when they needed it most.

The sixty is a weapon US troops have called "the pig" since the Vietnam war. It's an effective medium machine gun. Very effective. And like the animal, it's very present in almost any metric you want to think about it. Heavy. Nothing for a swole minotaur. Loud and obnoxious. Relentless, yes. The fat silencer suppresses as much as it can and no one in Dockside has probably ever heard anything like gunfire in their lives. There is only the constant sound of the galleys riding at anchor. The tackle clanging. The ropes creaking.

Death is dealt in a long burst that ensures the Saur on the street are good and dead and now the battle has begun.

I think all wars, all battles, start with one unremarkable engagement in the unexpected quiet. Then things spin up and everyone gets involved with everything they have to throw at the other side. Because of course… it's a fight for survival. And nothing can be spared if you want to see tomorrow.

We'd seen four Saur guards there at the checkpoint, holding long spears, their hooked swords on their glittering gem-and-gold woven belts. The Saur were always wrapped in heavy cloaks during the nights and early mornings, and they maintained a small fire right there in the middle of the street as they guarded their general. After they'd come into the city in that triumphal march up from the Gates of Death, past the Haunted Legion Fortress into Dockside and onto the war galleys, they'd blocked off an area in the harbor a local merchant had built his home in near the two galleys docked on the water he operated. It was a tall, leaning affair of a mansion, as most of the houses in Dockside were. Everything in Sûstagul was made of mostly stone. Not a lot of easily accessible timber nearby, and what came into the city was usually used for roofs. So the general had a small fort near the docks and the Saur presence had been heavy in the previous weeks. But in the last week it had lessened. And Captain Knife Hand had cleared the minotaur for a decap operation against enemy command and control.

The reason Captain Knife Hand had decided to hit their general at dawn is that would be when the Saur would be their weakest. With the coming of the sun, their cold blood, they being lizards and all, would start to warm. They'd get more active as the day wore on, which also served the overall battle plan. This is what we wanted. Rangers do not have the fight they don't want. That ain't how they do things. They do not believe in fair fights. They want every advantage, and they will go to great lengths to get them. We wanted our enemies to get excited and active and throw themselves into the meat-grinder ambushes the Rangers had set up to channelize the enemy as the sun began to rise and it was clear they were under attack by us.

An attack just after dark on the other hand, or in the middle of the night, and the Saurian commanders might have decided to hold position and figure out what was going on, giving them a few hours to get it together.

We didn't want that. We wanted chaos from the start. Chaos we were in control of as we managed their decimation and, finally, their destruction.

Sergeant Monroe fired at the Saur as he came out of the pre-dawn darkness along the street. And as the lizard-men guards were bleeding out in the street, the minotaur proceeded on up the street toward the merchant's house the Saur were using as a command post.

There was no finesse here. We needed to take out the CP before the battle started. We knew where the ground force commander for the Saur was, thanks to weeks of intel development and the Saur practically making that section of Dockside a no-go zone as soon as they entered the city. At first there had been more patrols and a heavier presence, now they'd practically left it wide open.

Still, one heavily armed man, or minotaur, even if he was a Ranger, wouldn't have made it. A fire team would have been needed at least. Except that the minotaur, thanks to being a stevedore, was accepted as background. Just another local. Plus, chatter on the streets indicated the Saurian fleet was ready to haul anchor soon and beat for the exit of the port, and the windy seas beyond. The patrols had stopped, and we figured those troops had been moved aboard the war galleys in preparation for departure in the days to come.

But not the general and his staff. Life aboard a ship is not easy. Rank has its privileges.

The Rangers would take advantage of that too.

We weren't sure how much of the staff we'd get in Sergeant Monroe's hit, but the captain and chief were fairly confident, via the developed intel, they'd get the Saurian GFC at the least and create enough chaos to cause troop mismanagement from the get-go of Operation Stranglehold.

For the record, the now-dead Saur ground force commander was officially known as General Xol of the Temples of Soth. He was a huge scaly green Saur with a broad chest sheathed in a fantastic breastplate that looked to be covered in shimmering mother-of-pearl.

"That's probably magical armor," contributed PFC Kennedy.

The sergeant major tensed his jaw visibly. Make of that what you will. Maybe he resented that Kennedy had magicked his way into everyone's hearts as a never-ending font of nerd lore and tactical advantage gained when really the smaj had intended to disappear the wayward un-Ranger-like PFC into a shallow grave somewhere along the way.

Or it was just how he let Kennedy know that he still expected Ranger out of him despite his ability to cast fireballs and do strange things with that fantastic staff.

"It may be a real hippy walk through this never-ending road to the Emerald City and the Wizard of Oz…" said the sergeant major to Sergeant Joe one time. "But I'll be damned, Sergeant, if that kid's not gonna breach and clear with the best of the assaulters like a Ranger do."

General Xol wore a headdress like some Egyptian pharaoh of old, carried a massive spear, and was attended in the streets by a squadron of some of the most swole Saurian warriors we'd ever seen in the field. These dudes weren't just gym rat adjacent, each one was Conan actual. We also noticed that the shifty Katari assassins were always shadowing the general on the streets and on the rooftops whenever he moved about.

The Katari are cat-like humanoids that guard the Valleys of Kings and Priests in the Lands of the Black Sleep. They are effectively assassins, and we'd tangled with them before. In the streets, they made hits on HVTs impossible. So the one time to get the general was right now as it all went down in the sleeping dark. And instead of using a squad of Rangers, or even a fire team—remember we were stretched thin for a company-sized element; we were three platoons and barely a hundred Rangers supported by twelve dwarves and a giant gorilla samurai—Sergeant Monroe was going to do it all on his own. Because one, the Saur had provided the opportunity, and two, Ranger Smash in effect.

We were going to take every chance we could get to own the walls by nightfall.

Sergeant Monroe moving fast and humping a ton of gear and weapons, easily, he would tell me, breached the merchant's house there in Dockside as he stepped over the cooling bodies of the bleeding-out Saur.

"I think my heart and cardio have increased significantly, Talker. I mean, I was also juiced because this was a straight-up bucket list killing spree if there ever was one and I was out there in front all by myself. Take that, Third!"

Note: he did have sniper overwatch. The Ranger sniper and spotter on the northern edge of the fortress had range and field of fire to cover if he got into it. But yeah, humping a smoking pig, six dead already, four guards at the post, two at the door, for Sergeant Monroe the action was indeed the juice, and he was rushing on his run to capitalize on the momentum he'd just acquired.

He planted his massive, booted foot on the merchant's door, a door the orphans had assured us was barred, and smashed it open with one savage kick. He'd breached. And what happened next cost him the rest of the belt fed into the light machine gun he was strapping.

"What happened next?" I asked.

"The choppers were over the city and heading across the bay to circle in and make the LZ out there by the lighthouse. I heard that just as the front door shattered, and I put my shoulder into it and just shoved in to get through. Three tangos immediately reacted to the breach, and I opened fire on them. Even suppressed, it was still loud in there because that house is all stone and it's got a mosaiced floor on the bottom floor. But I had EarPro on so it wasn't bad, and I had amplification active under thirty decibels for anything nearby.

"First lizard dude hit takes a burst in the chest and his green blood paints wall and a tapestry of fishes and gods and, you know, typical stuff. Not my jam. He goes down behind a wide desk spread with maps and feathered pens.

There are two guards in there and they go for me with the short swords. The... what's Kennedy say they are?"

"Khopesh."

"Yeah, those sick things. I dust both with drag and fire and they die on the carpet. I hit the main room and see the general getting up from that ivory throne we saw them bring through the streets when they did their initial parade."

It had been the typical conqueror's parade you would expect out of such a Bronze Age army. Caged animals. Leopards pulling chariots. Dancers. Human and lizard women, which was interesting. And the ranks and ranks of marching Saur in their finest armor tramping through the dusty streets of the desert port. It was actually pretty impressive. Or at least it was to me.

"Oh, and by the way..." continues Sergeant Monroe with his actions on the objective, "not that it's important and all, but right at that moment I figure out pretty quick why we never saw the merchant, his family, and the staff, after they made that location the CP. The guy and his staff officers ate them, or at least that's what it looked like on the floor all around. I don't know, but what was left of the meal they'd had the night before, and were still having when I started shooting, was spitted and roasting in a big fireplace."

Well, that's just horrible.

"There's about six of them in there and there are golden... I don't know if *flagon* is the right word, but... more like vases? Slender at the top, and fat and wide down below. They were everywhere. On every surface. Like beer cans in the barracks on Saturday night and all. It's a real drunken mess. Bones and blood like they butchered them right there in the room too. The merchant and his family, that is. It's pretty sick. But I fought through an open field morgue one time in the sandbox, so… I don't rattle easily.

"So then the stupid general stumbles drunkenly for that big spear we think is magical and I have a second to waste two staff officers who don't seem as drunk as the rest. These guys go for knives out, and I tear them to pieces with the sixty in seconds. Killing spree in effect, man. I got thirteen dead and I ain't even half a belt or two minutes into this. Some of the others run from the room but according to plan that's okay. We need squirters to start telling the story and creating the chaos."

He's right. The plan was to do what Rangers do and decapitate command and control early on. But to do that effectively in the Bronze Age world of war that is the Ruin, because these primitives don't have commo or phones, we had to let some runners squirt from the hit so they could spread it around and freak everyone out.

We're assuming lizard men freak out.

"I got more dead lizard staff officers dying as I work them over, and the general turns with the spear and instead of hurling it right at me, he raises it into a guard position and mutters something. He's either slurring or that's lizard talk. Who knows? I guess you do. But hey, I just work the pig for big prizes. And you know what happens next… the bastard flashbangs me."

Later I'd ask Kennedy what he thought happened.

"Sounds like the high-level spell *Sunburst*. If it were the game—and…"

"Don't say it. We know, Kennedy."

PFC Wizard sighed and continued on with the spell description. "He'd need to make a con save or go blind and take some damage if it was *Sunburst*."

"Con?"

"Constitution. How strong and hardy you are. They don't call Sar'nt Monroe the Squat King for nothin', Talker. So my guess, he saved and wasted that dude, amirite?"

Kennedy was right. More or less. The spear's flashbang effect went off and it did blind Sergeant Monroe for a second.

"I could see negative images seconds later after the world went all *Hey don't look at the sun, idiot*. Everything was black and white but... reversed for a second. Felt weird and I puked on the sixty. That vision I see in the dark is crazy. It's ain't like the Predator vision in the movie. It's more like... radar meets fifth-gen night vision. So whatever that spear did, it jacked me for a second and I felt like was gonna puke, which I did, but... I've been thinking about this... I am a minotaur. Right?"

Yes.

"Okay... so according to myths and stuff, I dig mazes and especially things that confuse people and they get lost in my maze and all. I should be lost in there in the dark and all where it's confusing too... but... that's the kind of trap minotaurs would set, right? Mazes. Confusion and disorientation. So maybe I got a special skill that makes me un-vulnerable to those things?"

"*In*vulnerable. I see what you're saying, Sar'nt. Again, Kennedy's explanation of why objects may appear closer in the mirror, and the Ruin ain't necessarily his game, may apply. But in order to understand what you can do... your *minotaur powers*..."

"Superpowers, man. Like I'm an Avenger or something. But jacked and all. I'd probably beat the crap out of the Hulk. Easy. But that's 'cause I'm a Ranger, just bein' a minotaur helps and all, know what I mean? Superpowers. We gotta understand those better."

Sure. I don't think minotaurs have superpowers. But I don't say that to him. Now... *psionics*? Totally superpower for sure.

"So yeah," I continue, "your superpowers might have gotten messed with by the flash but somehow your... maze-finding-your-way-around abilities... I guess... rebooted pretty fast."

"They did. I heard him coming for me once he thought he'd knocked my vision out. Heard him even though I couldn't see him. Heard him move that staff from guard position to attack. He's huge and he lunged, and I could feel the displacement of the volume of air in the room as he rushed toward me. I went to one knee for no reason I can figure out and unloaded in the general direction I thought he was coming from. That's *gotta* be superpowers, man. I had no idea at that moment if I engaged and rang steel, but when my vision returned, he was splattered all over the floor. I popped thermite, threw it into a shelf of leather books and ledgers for some kindling, and let it burn. Then I left out the side door of the residence according to plan."

Just like that, Sergeant Monroe had terminated the Saurian ground force commander and shifted the decision-making capabilities of how the fight would go for the next few hours until the Saur reestablished some kind of chain of command.

The smaj had called this "dealing out their GFC." Later, and this was bold of me to ask, but I wanted to know the phrase origin "for purposes of the account." That last part was not totally the truth. Or not at all. A new Ranger phrase from back in the Hard Old Days was like some vein of gold for me for reasons I don't even know. Talker, coffee junkie linguist, just wants to know the origin of said cold-as-ice murder phrase. But I framed it as needed for the account, concerned the sergeant major might not have taken the time to explain after the murder look he gave me over his canteen cup of very hot coffee, not bothering to blow the steam off as he took a drink.

Which is pretty hard.

"Pure voodoo warfare, Talker. My guys back in the day would have called icing the primary leader *Dealing Out*. Like poker and all… you have a great hand, and you know you're beating the others at the table. But like then, in this situation now, with their GFC dealt outta the cards, the decision tree goes from the trunk to the branches and someone in those limbs might have been waiting to take their shot at being lead. And you gotta consider they might be real good at it. So back to the cards analogy. You could go for the next card and be dealt out at the table because someone else got what they needed instead. Of course, saying you *dealt out* the GFC isn't as cool as some of the operator speak you boys go on with, but it was a really easy way to explain to new Rangers back in the day what was going on using cards 'cause that's all we had to kill time. Now you all got your damned iPhones, Xboxes, and whatnot. Maybe that's how it fell outta use. World may change, but that don't mean it gets better."

Then he picked up his Kindle and resumed the Chapter of whatever book he was reading. I just note that for the record and I hope he doesn't read this account.

The Rangers would use *dealing out* the enemy ground force commander to capitalize on a series of bad decisions made by the enemy, and it's good they did as the Saur began to deploy powerful mages against our lines. A battle that was decisively in our favor quickly started trending toward desperate. The power of magic in the battle was one where the Rangers did not have a significant advantage, and we could even be considered at a loss.

The Rangers' tenacity and ingenuity would become the deciding factor in many street-level engagements.

"I moved to the next position up the street," continued Sergeant Monroe's account. "Then faded into an alley and watched their CP burn as it started to get light in the sky. Five minutes later the helos were back in the air and heading west along the coast to grab Second. That was when the Saur began to come off the ships and into the streets all around me."

CHAPTER TWELVE

THE helos were back on the beach, chopping hard at the air and throwing static electricity at the LZ as our chalks advanced to load. The weapons team was on one of the Black Hawks. I'll be honest, I really wanted to hang off the skids on one of the Little Birds all cool-guy style because... wouldn't you?

Strapped and ready to roll on the oh-bee-jay.

But I have not unlocked that achievement yet, as of this account. So I will Ranger harder until that cool happens and I can award myself the sick little thrill I live for of been there, done that, got the scars to prove it.

Of which I'm collecting quite a few.

Sergeant Joe loaded in with the weapons team and I caught this funny exchange between the pilots and our platoon sergeant. It felt good to hear, if just to shake the nerves I had. Or maybe it was the static electricity mixing with the air pressure changes of the birds on the LZ, but I did feel like I wanted to throw up a little for no good reason I could figure out. In hindsight, I was nervous about the battle. I'd been in enough fights to be smart enough to know what was coming and what needed to be done to get to the other side of it.

"You guys any good?" asked Joe as we started strapping in.

"You got the best available on a Saturday morning, Sergeant," quipped the co-pilot who was watching the load in and the spinning blades for clearance issues. Then the pilot managing the throttle keeping the bird on the ground while watching the dancing instruments added, "On short notice, Ranger."

Joe laughed and growled, "Wouldn't have it any other way, Nightstalkers. Just get us to the LZ and I'll bring you back a t-shirt, or a goblin skull."

Then we were pushing off the ground and climbing to turn to the intercept course, inbound on Market to join the attack.

I was pretty pumped. This was the first time I'd actually been in a helicopter. I know, hard to believe after all this. But remember, before joining the Rangers at Fifty-One, I'd been in training for the better part of a year. I'd been to Airborne School, but you don't jump out of helicopters there. So, going into battle for the first time in a chopper with actual door gunners, and loaded to the gills with Rangers ready to get their kill on, I'll be honest and make a confession. Please don't think less of me.

Coffee… for a moment I forgot all about you when we were inbound on the LZ at Market to get our kill on.

I beg for forgiveness, Dark Mistress.

There are two moments you will feel more alive than you ever have. When the bird lifts off and you're headed into the storm. Everything is done. All the waiting is over. This is the "nowest" moment in your life and you know it. And also, going high cycle on a medium machine gun.

Few experiences compare.

And no, there's no Fortunate Son toggle switch up in the cockpit. But there doesn't need to be because in about six minutes we'd be over a battle underway, giving the surging Saur a good look at us going in right behind them. Hopefully, that would cause them to split forces from Dockside and water down any attacks they were intent on.

So. Right now it's time to tell you the story of the 160th Special Operations Aviation Regiment (Airborne) and how it ended up in the Ruin hauling us into the fight we'd just picked at Dockside.

The 160th is the primary rotary-wing support to all Department of Defense special operations forces. They are highly trained in what they do, and not only do they fly the most advanced aircraft the military can buy, they fly them like stunt pilots into some of the tightest situations no sane pilot would consider flying into. Often under heavy ground fire from the enemy, on dark and stormy nights with suspect clearance on an LZ that someone who won't be flying has determined to be the best spot for Rangers and other special operations forces to suddenly be where they aren't supposed to be and pull their own version of *Ranger Smash!* Not only all that, they are also trained to fight and survive on the ground through intensive combat courses and the dreaded escape and evasion school where apparently waterboardings are a thing. They're tough monkeys and they have a pretty cool tag.

Nightstalkers.

Okay, if I was some dude on the ground with an AK and a bowl of rice tasked with ambushing or guarding, and I knew these guys were coming in with stealth-rigged choppers, high surveillance gear, electronic warfare, full-spectrum night and thermal imaging, two door gunners with miniguns, the pilots sometimes having rocket pods and chain guns, carrying in America's premier tip-of-the-spear fighting forces who do not view failure as an option… and they're called *Nightstalkers*…

Pass. I'm out.

Too bad the Saur and the Ruin had no idea what all that meant and what was coming for them. Otherwise a lot of them might have not died trying to be unfriendly to the newcomers there to liberate their city.

Since they'd arrived in the Ruin, the 160th Nightstalker element that had been assigned to go forward in time back at Area 51, had managed to survive some pretty hairy tangles. As one does in this ten-thousand-year future version of Kennedy's game, allowing for the usual caveats. Almost from the get-go they were in it as deep as we were.

Then one of their birds picked up Joe's radio traffic on the old Vietnam-era PRC-77 we'd found inside the djinn's world inside that old Chinook. From there the Nightstalkers had been able to locate the main body of our force, manage some communication, and begin the first steps of coordination of forces.

The MH-6 Little Bird that had saved our bacon back on the side of the blood-red cliffs as all the psycho Deep Elves in the Ruin streamed away from the desert pass the fortress the Rangers were overrunning had guarded, that Little Bird and single pilot had had just enough fuel for the gun runs it provided to pull us out of the fire. Then it was bingo fuel and needed to head back across the desert to reach the 160th's mobile base on the edge of the coast of what we would have once called West Africa.

That was their entry point into the freak show that is the Ruin. They'd come out the QST on the other side of the mysterious Atlantean Rift on the Atlantic coast of Africa. Those areas are murky and dark as far as any maps or intel we could find in Portugon; even the sailors wouldn't go there, saying it was a land filled with strange monsters and that sometimes pirates went there to hide and never returned.

Now go with me for a moment back to those last days of the world we came from. When the nano-plague was eating the world alive. When suddenly, PFC Talker found himself among Rangers, running around the giant hot airfield of the enigmatic Area 51 base with Kurtz doing his best to try and kill me before we even jumped through time to get here.

Before the briefing where they laid out how dire everything was, and their plan to fix it all. Or survive it all. Spoiler... it didn't work.

Back at that briefing there were fifty special operations teams. The big brain scientists, Deep Staters, and pained generals with medals on every available space of their uniform, basically let us know we were going just two years forward in time to restart the world after the out-of-control nano-plague destroyed everything we knew.

Ate all technology. Anything modern. And turned people... into monsters. Think about it.

But we didn't have all the info then about the Ruin revealing, and what we were being told was unbelievable. But true. And ultimately, truer than we thought even possible. By the looks of the Ruin, the entire world *was* destroyed, then remade again... as the Ruin. Part Tolkien novel for reasons that aren't immediately clear because so much of the world's history was consumed in a long dark age, then an age of Saurian slavery, and there was a lot of war, destruction, and survival along the way. Books get moldy, and they may not even be true in the first place. Might get written in a language by a tribe of werewolves, or minotaurs, or dwarves, or even orcs who get wiped out and the book, unreadable to the conquerors, gets used for fuel that next harsh winter. All we know is what we found on the other side of the QST, and it was a world full of goblins and elves and a lot of jacked-up stuff that will try its best to kill you every day. Like Kennedy's Collector of Corpses. Things like that are a thing here. Seriously.

So, like I was saying, there were fifty special operations teams, like the Rangers, going through the quantum singularity tachyon gate. SEAL teams... well, we know what happened there. Remember, McCluskey was right there in that briefing, just like me, and Tanner, and all the rest, hearing how it was *do or die* in order to save the world. Green Beret A and B Teams went through. MARSOC. Off-book teams. Support teams. Groups of Deep State secret squirrels. We're pretty sure the Delta Kings who took over most of Western Europe about eight thousand years ago were one of the special operations groups in the briefing that day.

Combat applications group also commonly known as Delta Force.

The SEALs showed up twenty years before we did even though they left the same day. All the aircraft were on the runway that day, lined up with us loaded in and waiting to go through. Though... the SEALs were the test group and they went through a day before, now that I think of it. That's the story if you believe McCluskey. If he was a vampire, and therefore... immortal-ish... he could've been lying about their arrival time. But let's say twenty years was accurate.

As for the rest... we just don't know.

Captain Knife Hand and the Air Force crew who brought us through the QST, they figured somehow the math was all bad for the transit through time, and seconds of difference in when you entered the gate might mean tens of years or even hundreds on the other side. Or just seconds. Also, the concept of *quantum* is involved here. Which movie people back in the day used to use for all kinds of nonsense to make their scripts work. But in a nutshell… if you know where a quantum particle is… it's not there. That's the rule. Now go nuts thinking about it, or just accept it means something to someone with a big brain and endless time to obsess over the possibility it might be true.

The QST monkeyed around with quantum entanglement for purposes of time travel, forward only please, and all the scientists, Deep State funded, back where we came from, were certain to the point they were willing to gamble our lives on it that they could measure and calculate the arrival times of travel forward through time. Spoiler again…

They got it wrong.

Massively.

The Baroness, who's still back at FOB Hawthorne, though not her specialty, and frankly I'm not sure what her specialty is other than her being brainy sexy, acknowledged that the initial computations to fling us into the future might not have been "as ironclad as everyone hoped for."

We were sold "absolute certainty" when really they meant… "we hope so."

I'm cool with it. I love the Ruin. I do. But it's best to be honest about these things. And now we're going forward again. In real-time, I mean. Building something here, I think. And as we do that, we should make sure words mean what they mean. Going forward. We should avoid the mistakes of the past.

True, during the briefing they did indicate the science wasn't spot-on, but their confidently stated margin of error was *three years variation* on arrival time... as in, the various groups going through the gate would arrive anywhere between two and five years forward in time. Not *up to ten thousand years later, at least eight thousand years apart, and all across the world*. I mean the Ruin. Effectively making any contributions we could make to mutual survival null and void, and giving that plan to restart civilization no possible chance of success.

Man, Deep State would have been so let down once he found out how all over the place, and time, we got scattered about. There would have been nothing for him to organize and ruin.

Deep State.

Yup. That guy.

So, and oh wait... did they send the president through? Makes ya wonder how "all in" on that plan to save the future they went. They probably knew things were going to get really bad. They wanted the military units to go through and make it safe for them to shoot through to the other side with some kind of Green Zone and air conditioning. Have a mineral water, sir, while we push the orcs back from the wire. Steaks at five and then volleyball if the harpies aren't out.

But there was no way to know. Because no one knew. Guessing was all anyone had.

But if they *did* go through... if they took a leap of faith into the dark of quantum entanglement and go forward, thinking we'd somehow made it ahead of them...?

Boy, if Deep State's breakfast was ruined by the orc horde that tried to annihilate us in week one, then theirs, those government types who didn't have Rangers, or SF, was probably flat-out burnt toast and runny eggs. Maybe one day down the line we'll find some mural, or hieroglyph, that shows the Presidential Seal. Or a crude drawing of someone who looks like the president getting eaten by the Saur. Could've happened. A long time is a long time. Could have happened at any time. The Ruin is hard on strangers and newcomers.

It's best to be hard right back at it.

Oh my gosh, that could have come right out of Kurtz's mouth. What's wrong with me? But it is the truth. Whether I like it or not. It is what it is.

But, okay, the 160th. Someone, in planning this whole mess, decided that all the cool guy special operations teams were going to need air support and transportation in the phenomenally bad guess of two to five years to a Mad Max future and then we'd install Western Civilization once again.

I won't write how much I started laughing once I wrote that down and read it back to myself. I haven't laughed so much since… well, you probably have to be in a dark place to find humor in getting told the equivalent of *Hey why don't you run down to the deli for a sandwich* and ending up in ancient China where you don't speak the language and everyone's trying to kill you. A lot. Oh yeah and all the Chinese are orcs and some of them are giants and others can shoot fireballs. And other magic stuff. And demons. And undead. And I have a genie bottle and a ring that can turn me invisible and my best friend is some sort of undead bounty hunter.

It's been real fun. But I just popped out for a Hot Italian and all.

So, the 160th Special Operations Aviation Regiment (Airborne) formed a small detachment to fulfill that mission thinking they were going to the deli for a sammie and instead ended up in Africa with lion people trying to kill them. The Ruin's fun that way. Good times. Supported by a C-5 Galaxy, the largest transport aircraft in the US military arsenal, five MH-6 Little Birds and five Black Hawks, in tight formation, flew the deck of the desert back in Area 51 with the C-5 right on their tail in the last seconds to nail that totally *absolutely certain* lie that someone knew what they hell they were doing.

They didn't stick the two-to-five-year window either. They missed it even more than we did. But just by a little. Here's a thought. When dealing with quantum entanglement, close is like a hand grenade. It's gonna make a mess wherever it lands. Accuracy isn't really important.

Apparently, the timing caused some real pucker factor among the pilots and crews of the 160th. Helicopters had to time it just right to be in front of the low-and-slow C-5 Galaxy with gears and flaps out so they could all of them hit the QST within a tight window that would *absolutely certainly* guarantee their arrival in roughly the same time and space.

And it worked, sorta.

But that makes a few of the Rangers wonder how much the big brains planning all this really knew at the time.

Or as Tanner put it, "They knew enough that they knew those Nightstalkers needed to almost get themselves killed trying to play gay chicken with a Galaxy coming down the runway on their tail. I'm cool with gunfire and explosives and low-altitude jumps into rocky terrain, Talk, but flying in front of a heavy lifter to jump through time in a chopper seems downright dumb to me. Pilots are almost as crazy as SEALs in my book, man."

It does make one wonder how much the deciders knew back as this all went down. But again... *absolutely certain*.

And like I said, at least a little bit of the plan apparently worked out for the Nightstalkers and the supporting Air Force crew in the C-5. They all came through at the same moment. That part, the brains got right. But the two-to-five-years-later part... not so much.

You're probably asking—if you're not some orc who bashed my skull in at the Rangers' last stand and is now tearing pages of this journal out to feed the cookpot you've got us in—why the Galaxy? As in, why did the 160th need a massive aircraft in support? Why not just send the helos through? Right on. Very smart question. The C-5 had mechanics and parts and, more importantly, a storage tank for fuel that the onboard Forge could crank out to keep the helos flying with a refueling pump that had been installed.

In other words, the C-5 is a flying giant gas station with a garage.

That's why they had to pull the flying circus trick to get the Nightstalkers through at the same time.

In summary.

The Nightstalkers left on the same day we did, though we're not sure at exactly what time. They leap forward through time and arrive not that long after us. They've been here two months.

Which naturally has us wondering. Other air units may have gone through on prior or follow-on days. Again, the military, and especially when Deep State derps are involved, is all *need-to-know*. Secrecy is their weapon and how they control everyone and stay in power. For whatever that's worth. Which ain't much when Ugluk the Orc and ten thousand of his ugly friends decide they want your stuff.

Or, as Tanner put it when Kennedy and I were figuring it all out over cleaning the Legion's RPDs one day…

Side note: the Accadion legionnaires do not understand the concept of a clean weapon. No armorer worth his salt would let them turn in their weapons in the condition they think is *acceptable*.

"It's-a clean, Talk-ir," Corporal Chuzzo would say, trying to argue each of his legionnaires' weapons through inspection.

Not. Even. By. Half.

"That?!" he would exclaim when we drew his attention to some buildup that needed to be removed from the chamber. "It came-ah that way!"

Back to the 160th Nightstalkers. As Tanner put it, "Secrecy's cancer, man. They killed us with it back there. If there's one reason I'm glad to be in the Ruin now, it's hard to have secrets here. Truth gonna truth just as much as Ranger gonna Ranger. You can't make up what you want about these monsters we fight here. Not if you wanna go on livin'. These things'll kill you dead if you don't believe in 'em and what they can do to you. Feel me, Talker? Truth. It just is. So-crates said that, I think."

"Socrates," I corrected.

Tanner snorted.

"I know. You just ain't never seen *Bill and Ted*. Then you'd know."

My life is less lived.

The helos peeled off in every direction as the Night-stalkers exited the quantum singularity tachyon gate because they had to get out of the way of the incoming C-5 busting through hot on their tails. It's a good thing they're all half stunt pilot, half high-speed military aviator. Even so I guarantee they weren't sure that C-5 was gonna miss 'em. But it does. Barely. It takes off into the sky adding max power to climb because when they come out of the gate, they're just over the deck of a coast like few of them have ever seen.

Utterly desolate. Blasted. Huge circular ruins in the distance that span hundreds of miles in salt flats and strange colors you've never seen in a desert. Like some huge crater from a meteor strike has created walls and towers within the lava flow as the fractured crust turns to butter under intense heat and pressure. Then someone built a city in it all. Except the city was dead and old. That was what one of the gunners told me who'd come in on the first contact in person between the Rangers and the Nightstalkers here in the Ruin.

I had to get their story for the account, so I started with the door gunners because they were chatty and… they had coffee. It wasn't great coffee. *But I ain't fancy*, as Tanner says when needs must.

The Nightstalkers were able to make it to the city, flying over a dune sea that went off in every direction. The helos were getting low on fuel, but they could put down anywhere. The problem was the giant C-5 Galaxy. It could land on rough surfaces, but basically it needed some kind of airstrip. Even a dirt one. Which wasn't optimal. As they neared the vast ruined city, a city hundreds, and as the gunner said, "I mean *hundreds* of miles wide, man."

Think about that. There are no modern cities where we came from that are that large. Los Angeles, which is spread out over the whole basin, isn't really even much bigger than twenty miles. You can count the supporting suburbs and call it fifty or even a hundred if you want to be generous… but not *hundreds*, plural, of miles.

This city was megalithic fantastic.

Concentric circles, walls formed by lava and melted earth, turned into perfect defensive fortifications with strange towers carved from the rock. The city got lower and lower toward the center and the Nightstalkers never even made it there. The outer rings were so blasted by the heat of the ancient comet strike that the ground, or what had once been desert sand, had turned to burnt, smooth, hard glass. This must have happened when "the stars fell, and the Nether Sorcerer and the dragons came to the Ruin," as Vandahar would say.

The C-5 was able to put down with some damage just inside the first ring, and the Nightstalkers came in around it. Immediately they set up a perimeter, and even though they thought they'd come in close to the wall and the towers, they were actually miles from it.

"It was a really strange place," the door gunner told me. "Really strange. Quietest place I've ever been. It was like everything was smothered in a blanket and the heat was off the chart."

What happened next defies explanation. First off, some of the 160th started to go missing in the days they tried to figure out everything we'd tried to figure out.

Where are we?

What's going on?

Why are orcs trying to kill us?

Except in the case of the Nightstalkers it wasn't orcs. It was lions. Or to be more specific… humanoid lions.

In the intense quiet of the days that followed, small DAGRE teams—Deployed Aircraft Ground Response Element, basically the SF of the Air Force—started to make forays into the strange city to see what intel could be gained. Even with drone recon much of the city was inaccessible due to its vast mind-numbing distances. But from what they could see, it seemed totally deserted.

And yet members of the element were going missing.

Then one day, every wall of the two rings they'd set down between was filled with these strange lion-men, and even other types of cat-men too, as in leopards and cheetahs. No tigers though. For hours the cat people, all dressed in skins and rude armor like African tribes, watched the 160th.

The ground force commander started to get nervous and decided it was time to go. Problem was the task force was facing a couple of problems.

Again, they have a Forge, so fuel and parts aren't a problem. The problem, or at least the biggest problem, is the C-5 itself. The smaller problems are the fact that the helos have nowhere near the range of the Galaxy and the Galaxy is not equipped for in-flight refueling. They can only ground refuel, and as I said, the C-5 needs something close to an actual runway.

According to the gunner, the dustoff from their initial insertion into the Ruin was hot and close. Toward late afternoon the sky turned red, a dust storm came up, and before they knew it the ten thousand cat warriors were silently moving forward on them from all sides, using the sudden storm as cover.

Note, their weather guy, a combat weather forecaster known as a special operations weather technician, didn't even predict the freak storm that came up to cover the lion people's assault. Cat people. Cat-men. We have no idea what they're called. All Vandahar would say was "I have heard vague rumors of the mysterious south. And what I have heard, I have not liked to experience."

Believe me… weather is really important for battle-planning and warfighting, and you might need to know a bit more than "winds will be out of the southwest with a light chill in the air and you should put on a light jacket" as the bullets start flying. So the SOWT, the combat weatherman, getting caught with his pants down was a little more concerning than the local weather guy ten thousand years ago getting the weekend forecast wrong.

And now the Little Birds were making gun runs to keep the "runway" clear of the cats.

"I kid you not, Ranger," said the door gunner. "Skin of our teeth. That's how close it was."

They flew north and eventually found another place to set down. The C-5 busted a gear but had the mechanics and the Forge to get her working again with a lot of ingenuity and sweat. Just in time. The cat people showed up and attacked again. This time in the middle of the night.

"You think desert ops are brutal in a sandstorm. Trying suppressing an LZ with tracer fire going off from every minigun in the detachment, orbiting the combat zone and trying not to hit the flying gas station that keeps everyone supplied and therefore alive. That one sent me to the Forge tech the next time we set down asking for him to crank me out a carton of smokes. He said I was the third guy to ask that morning."

So basically, they kept leapfrogging across the Atlantean Rift, or the ruined Sahara Desert as we once knew it, and arrived in our neck of the woods. By that time the Little Birds were scouting ahead for landing zones for the Galaxy and that was how Joe and I got found running and gunning across the desert.

Good thing for us. And them.

Now the C-5 is west of our position along the coast on a landing zone the dwarves easily cleared and built once they understood what was needed.

Sadly, many Rangers were forced to dig that day.

Once we take the city the C-5 can redeploy forward, and we will have another Forge.

And that is how the Nightstalkers got involved with the Rangers.

CHAPTER THIRTEEN

THE Rangers had about an hour to get ready for the incoming counterattack as the Saur began to figure out, by reports of runners running to and from the various junior commanders streaming off the ships, and of course the black smoke boiling out of the smoked command post in Dockside where the Ranger choice to deal out the GFC had just gone down, that they were under attack within their own controlled space.

Two galleys pushed off from their mooring points as signals were exchanged and tried to make for the boom chain. The snipers made short work of the crew sending shots at the helmsman and then the replacements that were sent aft to take control of the wheel. Eventually we guessed people stopped volunteering to steer the ship from the place where people's heads kept turning to red mist.

Within minutes, both galleys were caught up in each other's oar banks and adrift within the harbor waters among the other moored war galleys. A fire started on one and the order to abandon both ships seemed, according to the spotters, to be given as Saur slipped into the water easily, sans weapons and armor. The remaining sailors fought the spreading fires and eventually abandoned, leaving the slaves belowdecks to go down with the ship.

In seconds three Flotsam orphans were aboard, coming out of the water in ways a Navy SEAL would have envied just a little. Small and dripping wet, knives out, the urchins headed belowdecks and a few moments later ragged prisoners now freed were streaming out of the dark holds and leaping into the water to clutch oars, if they could not swim, or swimming away from the port and toward the eastern arm of the harbor, aiming for a strand of sandy beach called Little Pharos. It was a long swim across the harbor, but that had been the designated point for the rescued to shelter out of harm's way as both forces did battle inside the city to see who got the say-so regarding all things going forward.

The Rangers had decided it would be them.

If you would have asked me, it seemed we were already off to a great start with the assassination of the enemy GFC and getting the first two boatloads of slaves to safety. But of course, in every game, including games of death, the enemy gets to make their moves and what the sergeant major had said about every plan never surviving contact with the enemy started to earn its reputation as being true way more often than not.

Sergeant Monroe was now staged in the alleys between the north end of Dockside and the hammerhead isthmus where the Rangers were wasting Saur patrols as they swept in. Gunfire was not suppressed at this time because we wanted the population to get nervous and get out of Dodgeistan before the gunfight at the Ruin Corral really started up.

Within minutes, First Squad, under command of the captain, was storming the fabled Lighthouse of Thunderos with breaching explosives that shattered the morning quiet across the bay. Out there, the city was beginning to realize today would be no ordinary day. A massive charge breached the marble walls on the isthmus, and for a moment in the fading thunder of the blast resounding out across the galley-laden harbor and the still quiet city, a small pause fell over the soundscape of battle. Snipers were waiting for the next galleys to push off and try for the isthmus and flank the Rangers emplacing there. In the quiet, Sergeant Monroe told me he felt the whole city, or at least Dockside around him, hold its breath as though finally coming to the realization this was going to happen now. And then, on cue, out there in the lighthouse's main building, the Ranger assaulters pushed into the breach and began double-tapping every guard and Saur defending the fantastic Lighthouse of Thunderos.

The shooting was cacophonic, and as I said, it was staged to be so. The Saur, just by listening to the battle, would realize they were imminently threatened from that direction, and that if they were to fulfill their mission—a mission we could only imagine had come from the Lich Pharoah himself—they would need to retake that lighthouse in order to control the harbor boom chain guarding the exit. More explosions rocked the isthmus as grenades were detonated and Rangers continued their violent assault through the objective.

Meanwhile Second and Third Squads, led by Sergeant Chris, were emplacing their medium machine guns, explosives, squad designated marksmen, and reaction forces to hold the small road leading from Dockside out onto the isthmus. Fourth was still sweeping and taking out small outposts of Saur guards who watched out toward the Great Inner Sea for the approach of Accadion sails. This work of clearing the isthmus was going on with suppressed weapons under the leadership of one of our last platoon leader officers, First Lieutenant Barreras, along with Sergeant McGuire.

Now as the Saur began to mass, kitted in armor, spears, and swords, it would be Sergeant Monroe's job forward of the line of battle to report on developing enemy movement in the streets. Within minutes, the Saur were sending troops and running to and fro across Dockside. Then the shrieking bronze horns rang out in calls to form up and advance as the sun began to rise over the galleys in the harbor and then the desert port city itself. Squads of lighter-armed, more slender Saurian archers advanced in columns and wedges where they could, arrows nocked and ready for targets to engage. Walls within the main port city turned from blue silhouettes into golden temples and towers, bronze roofs burning in the morning sunlight as the enemy prepared to respond.

Back on the beach LZ west of the city, it was our turn for the hop into the fight. The sun continued to rise just over the horizon, and as Second Platoon loaded onto the choppers, the walls in the city shifted to sunblasted cream, creating long cool shadows in the deep alleys between the buildings in the harbor district and the city itself, east of the ruined fortress where the snipers were beginning to take out more helmsmen and captains aboard the galleys. Dead pirates lay in pools of blood as the Saur delinked from the war galleys they'd intended to take into the northern waters of the Great Inner Sea to do battle against the Cities of Men.

At that point the Saur leadership that had survived the assassination of the GFC presented a new opportunity in the developing chaos the Rangers were intent on capitalizing on as much as possible. With forces advancing up the lighthouse road to retake the isthmus, a small clutch of high-ranking commanders literally gathered in the streets down from Sergeant Monroe's observation post in the deeps of an alley. He'd gone up onto the second story of a warehouse building and was watching as Dockside residents tried to make their way south out of the battle and into the desert city of Sûstagul itself. He spotted what had to be a Saurian command team assessing the assassination he'd just committed against their commander. They were standing just outside the building that had been their general's CP, where flames were beginning to leap through the first- and second-floor windows as more and more dark smoke bloomed and blossomed through the roof above, debating what to do next. Some Dockside residents tried to start a fire brigade, but the Saur hissed at them, and their troops formed a line and drove the civilians back away from the unplanned funeral pyre of their general.

Via radio, Sergeant Monroe apprised the captain, who had just taken control of the lighthouse, that some kind of command team was busy trying to regroup forces and was providing a target of opportunity.

"Wharf Rat, can you confirm lizard sixes?" As in, how did the Ranger know these were actual leader types.

"Warlord... I spot six headdresses of the type worn by their leaders. Pharaoh gear. Lotsa shiny gear and fancy golden jewelry. Clear security teams and giving orders to push the civvies back from the area. Permission to neutralize?"

The captain asked how the minotaur Ranger planned to knock out the entire enemy command team that had formed in the absence of their general just outside the place where he'd gotten smoked. The opportunity was a good one, but was it worth exposing the lone member of the RRT?

Knife Hand got a one-sentence reply from the minotaur Ranger beyond the wire.

"Warlord Actual. Carl G does not care at this time."

There was a brief pause in the channel. Old Man Sims was running around telling everyone about this exchange after the battle because he was the ground force commander's radio man for the operation. So that was how I heard this detail and why I'm adding it to the account now.

The captain's reply after that was short.

"Warlord Actual to Wharf Rat... send it. Warlord out."

Less than thirty seconds later, Sergeant Monroe had the M4 84mm Carl Gustaf recoilless rifle deployed and ready to engage. Of the three rounds he was carrying he had one in the tube, and he doubted he was going to need two to get the job done. He'd pop and fire, then fade back into the network of tight and dirty alleys he'd spent his evenings as an off-work minotaur scouting. He'd get them in one shot and had no intention of even sweeping the kill zone with the sixty.

If Rangers can hurt a target mortally, and then disappear like ghosts that were never there... that's like frosting on a cupcake for them.

A cupcake of extreme violence, that is.

Sergeant Monroe edged out of the alley and depressed the firing trigger on the Carl G, sending the rocket right into the center of the adorned gaggle of Saurian officers lamenting the death of their fabled commander, or more likely vying for a new leadership position.

The concussive effects of the weapon wouldn't bother Sergeant Monroe's massive bull's skull, but the optic was a hassle with his horn. He adjusted, overcame, and fired.

Sergeant Monroe spent one of his two ADM rounds—area denial munitions—on the developing Saurian command team. This round effectively turned the recoilless rifle into a shotgun as the canister round sent eleven hundred steel flechettes hurtling into the enemy command cluster. They were ruined in horrible ways that defy description. The minotaur Ranger didn't stick around to find out who survived. He knew he'd executed a perfect *Ranger Smash!*

In other words, the enemy, distracted, had become absorbed by a problem the Ranger had initially created for them to get distracted by. Then he'd attacked them from another angle by *Surprise, losers!* when their focus was absorbed, and they were clustered in a nice tight group for the normally anti-tank weapon to devastate the group with a bold new munitions choice. The horrible ADM round. Behind the slaughtered lizard men, the former CP reeked of burning lizard skin ripe in the sea-breeze morning air.

Sergeant Monroe faded, tossed the spent shell into the alleys, and none of the Saur even came north of that position on the street as none who survived had most likely even seen the 84mm rocket attack originate from there.

For now, everything was unmanaged chaos, and at this point, one would think the battle was easily ours as the plan was mostly still intact, and contact with the enemy had been achieved.

Twenty minutes later more Saurian troops entered the streets, mustering off the war galleys en masse along the docks and surging into the streets of Dockside to support the first attacks against the Ranger-held isthmus. The second wave was formed up by younger Saurian officers, less adorned by golden torcs and other ceremonial trappings. Junior war leaders. Most likely small-unit commanders, who pushed everything they had all at once toward the hammerhead isthmus as fast as they could and… *all at once.*

The *everything they had* would prove to be the bonus they needed to become combat-effective against the surprise Ranger attack in the desperate moment facing their forces. I'll explain in a moment.

More explosions from the Lighthouse of Thunderos and the raising of the boom chain had convinced the Saur they were under attack and locked in now. They would need to fight their way out or die inside the city. Whoever was in charge right now had at least the common sense to figure that much out pretty quickly. Frankly, we'd planned for them to take longer to arrive at that conclusion, probe in other directions, and water down any kind of major and effective attack against any one of our separate elements. Again, we were stretched thin. Getting pushed hard anywhere specific by four thousand Saur, estimated, was going to, to put it mildly, place a strain on that portion of our line.

"Wharf Rat to Warlord… eyes on at least five hundred in the street and pushing on your position now. Looks like they're sending the whole tribe outta the docks straight at you. Expect second and third waves."

"Six wants to know if you are covered at this time, Wharf Rat?" replied Sims for Knife Hand.

"Solid stone on all sides and I'm off the axis of advance. Standing by to pick up any HVTs that enter the game. Rat out," growled the minotaur.

Thirty seconds later the first Saur, at the double, three ranks deep, got ate up by the outgoing fire of Third's two-forty gunner and AG. Specialist Rico, now Sergeant Rico who'd originally been part of Kurtz's weapons team, savaged the Saur in six- to eight-round bursts of plunging fire from his elevated position on the top of a seagrass-covered small rise that lay at the top of a narrow road the Saur were using to reach the lighthouse. The isthmus, unlike the city, was relatively desolate and had two low rises that ran through the center of it. Then the dunes and the small fort that guarded the seaward beach. The Rangers had already tossed flashbangs and grenades and entered firing, ruining the small force guarding the beach from the fortress.

As the Saur advanced, seven-six-two greeted them violently, streaking away and mixed with tracers at twenty-four hundred feet per second. Hot, huge rounds tore into Saurian breastplates worked with silver twining serpents and strange stamped hieroglyphs in turquoise and gold plate. Shining leaf-bladed spears shattered. Swords raised and ready to charge were cast into the sand and dust along the road as their wielders got holed by huge rounds that occasionally looked like hot streaks of fire.

And then one of their wizards threw up some kind of shimmering defensive barrier around the follow-on ranks of Saurian foot advancing against the Rangers' first positions. Fast-moving rounds glanced off the gleaming barrier and shot skyward or off into the nearby port waters. The Saur rallied on the bodies of their dead and slogged forward once more under fire. Lobbed spears and arrow fire from the flanks began to fall among the Rangers, centering on the gun team.

"Weapons team leader reported ineffective fire at that point as the barrier just batted away all our outgoing," Sims related to me later. "Then the snipers had eyes on a wizard

Saur with long flowing white robes, pushing just behind the infantry. He wasn't himself inside the barrier, too far removed from the action I guess, so they took the shot and put him down. But by that time, and this is according to Kennedy 'cause I never played any of those stupid games, hockey was my thing, but their wizard got off a spell of sleep, or something, and knocked out Rico and the AG. They were like dead to the world when Sergeant Chris and the QRF shifted up the hill from their position and got the two-forty back in action just in time. They were literally firing point-blank into the Saur by that point and one of them got a spear right in the gut below the carrier. They moved that guy off to the beach, but he died. I think it was Gertz."

We were inbound on the helos over the city now, Second Platoon strike team on Market, courtesy of the 160th. I saw the Saur massing out of Dockside below as the chopper turned hard and fast, and there were way more than five hundred at that point pushing on the Rangers, with more developing in the streets.

That it looked crowded was an understatement. But you could see outgoing fire from the two-forty rocking the front lines pushing forward like rats trying to get off a ship. A line of mines went off and ripped a flanking force to shreds in a series of savage explosions. One of the older warehouses collapsed suddenly.

Joe and Kurtz were calling out the LZ as we approached the area we'd insert into the battle on. It was some kind of garbage debris heap right there in the city between the docks and Market. Bronze Age cities don't care about planning in the same way Carl G don't care.

I would say, at that moment, with the morning sunlight flooding through the open doors of the beating chopper, I was seeing at least close to two thousand Saurian infantry, supported by archers and mages, pushing off the galleys and heading into the streets of Dockside to take the isthmus in the north on the thin shore of the Great Inner Sea. We'd crippled their leadership, but the small-unit leaders knew they were in a trap, and they were going to take the isthmus because they didn't want to die there. Then they'd secure the lighthouse and figure out what to do next. It was like watching a giant live-action sand table fight itself in real time.

I saw a fireball streak upward, and it was definitely magical in nature. It shot up into the sky from the city streets, aimed at one of the choppers to our rear as we turned hard for final on the LZ. It missed, but it was that close to hitting the Ranger-laden bird.

The door gunners on the first LZ were already opening up, suppressing the LZ as a troop of mercenaries from the market ran to assist the battle in the docks. The mercs were torn to pieces as the ground erupted around them from outgoing rounds striking the garbage-strewn road.

And that was all I saw of the battle as we set down for the attack on Market and rushed off the choppers, pushing through stinking garbage to start the day and the battle. I followed Kurtz and Soprano, as Kurtz directed the gunner into an overwatch position atop a small pile of refuse. Jabba came struggling along with more belts than you'd think possible, clutching as many cans as he could, muttering his *Big Bigga* speak. The field of view from the position the team sergeant had selected was perfect to annihilate anything coming from our twelve out of the imposing gates of the market we were about to breach.

Nothing attacked us immediately. I had imagined some opposed beachhead and fighting for our lives as soon as we were off the birds. Instead, medieval garbage rose and fluttered in the manmade winds of the departing choppers. As the sun rose higher over the city, the smoke from Dockside, carried inland by the ocean breeze, drifted over the city and filtered down into the city streets we were surrounded by beyond the small "park" of the desert port city's garbage.

Park. Yeah, right. One star. Would not recommend.

If you think modern garbage once smelled bad, Bronze Age garbage is the hands-down winner. "Where-a the burn pits, *Sergente?*" erupted Soprano in his Mario voice. Then in normal wiseguy, "Gotta be burn pits nearby, man. Who planned the insert point to be a garbage pile?"

By that time the choppers of the 160th SOAR were in the air and headed back to the LZ for refuel. The breaching team already had ten pounds of C4 on the solid wooden- and bronze-bound gates that guarded the market we needed to enter. We suspected there were magical wards on them, so we weren't taking any chances with the amount of explosives we were using on a wooden door.

The market was a viper's nest of magic-user types.

A moment later, the signal to fire the demo was given over the comm and we all ducked as there was going to be a lotta flying shrap from the wooden gates suddenly coming apart. Splinters and stuff.

The gates exploded and we entered fast in teams just as we'd rehearsed forever to get to this moment. The fighting started almost immediately.

Whatever nerves I'd had were gone. I had a job to do, and I was going to do it better than anyone else that day.

CHAPTER FOURTEEN

AS Second Platoon began making early gains in our attack on Market, small teams of local mercenaries—dirty, hard-eyed swordslingers—came out to face modern warfighters armed with medium machine guns, explosives, and other fun kinetic toys. And meanwhile the battle line at the hammerhead isthmus began to go seriously south.

The Saur had rallied from the devastating loss of their general and were now pushing all available forces in the harbor forward at Third Platoon holding the isthmus. Intuitively one of their battlefield commanders had sensed the anchor of the attack was Sergeant Rico's two-forty bravo team and began pushing troops right at them regardless of the hate being laid. Medics had Sergeant Rico and the assistant gunner back in action, but the calls for support by fire from First and Third Squads were getting urgent as Sergeant Chris rallied Rangers around the enveloped gun team, directed fire, and dropped 40mm grenades using the M320 danger-close all over the three-pronged attack hitting the hill.

From Sergeant Monroe's RRT position deep in the network of dark and slimy seaside alleys formed by the shipping warehouses along the western edge of the narrow peninsula, marching troops of lizard men were streaming forward, undaunted by the effective coordinated fire the Rangers were laying from their positions.

The order had been given to spare as much of Dockside as possible in order to gain favor with the locals on the other side of all this. Therefore, the mortars at the gate weren't being brought into play. The dwarves had fortified the gate and had thrown themselves into building defensive positions around the mortar teams—much to the delight of Sergeant Raines, the mortar team leader. The Rangers, whenever the dwarves were around, didn't have to do any digging, and as has been said before… Rangers hate to dig.

Troops of Saurian archers—lithe, armored in sleek leather stamped with strange glyph-like symbols of hawks, carrying longbows—sent massed indirect artillery fire into the Rangers from areas where they could engage. They fired fast and shifted, and that was smart. This was discussed during the AAR and it showed a mobility in warfare the Saur excelled at. One sniper team on the fortress was re-tasked with spotting indirect commanders and eliminating them when possible.

The Rangers began to *Yahtzee* Saurian archers at every possible chance. The range, smoke, and obstructions in Dockside didn't make for easy shots, though several dead archer commanders were found in the streets later. But even with this support by fire, the archers attacked the line on the isthmus with consequences. Some of the Rangers were hit and many recorded bounced or shattered arrows off plate carriers and FAST helmets. Some were wounded but kept fighting anyway, either leaving the arrows in until the medics could make decisions, or just snapping the shafts off and continuing the principles of good marksmanship at close range while more arrows rained down and strange Saurian magics coursed through the hot morning air, generating malevolent damage all along the line. The Rangers needed to address this new style of magical warfare, adapt to it fast, and overcome as the battle developed, pressing to see who would take the advantage and run with it in the next few moments.

Right now, the Saur had momentum and weren't wasting it.

Saurian casters, wielders of their ancient, deep dark magic, part sorcery and part necromancy, moved in to support the massive attack hitting the Rangers along the isthmus.

And a brief note on that attack. It was so unexpected that Captain Knife Hand and the planners couldn't be blamed for the reaction the Saur had launched to deal with our trap. Despite losing their commander, they had committed to a breakout before we could pull them in two directions. That was the flaw, and as the sergeant major said later when he made the rounds passing out MREs and the smoke drifted through the twilight streets, Ranger faces dark with blood and soot, "You corner a rat, best give 'em a way out. I shoulda seen that. Was my fault."

The sergeant major was arranging hot chow with some of the local merchants. We could trust them thanks to my contacts with the coffeehouse and Amira.

In near total darkness there was a quick after-action conducted and it was brief because of the events that transpired after the battle. But it was needed.

Even then we were still in it.

The AAR revealed the Saur had fought ferociously and with focus. Our plans to split them and control the battle hadn't gone as planning had initially intended. But what came of the AAR regarding the Saurian Infantry we faced, boiled down to this comment…

"Stands to reason," suggested Sergeant Kang when the floor was opened to provide critical feedback, "that these were advance troops, sir. So they should have been considered more… elite. Like us, they would have planning and communication skills beyond what is normally expected of the troops we've engaged and defeated so far. Just as we would, they considered violence of action a primary option to deal with an ambush. Their only way out of the trap was for all of them to push in one direction, at all costs, hoping the overwhelming violence would change the position of the enemy and make us react."

Everyone agreed with that assessment. The Saur that day hadn't flinched in the face of our gunfire, nor in the aftermath of the death of their commander, and even the subsequent *Ranger Smash* of their command team.

But it was another Ranger who offered this thought…

"Might be more to it than that. There was, from our position, a feeling that they were more afraid of not doing what they were told, which was to attack, than anything else. The way they threw themselves at us indicated their hearts weren't in it."

Finally, Kennedy offered this, and again, it's amazing how the PFC wizard now holds so much sway over the Rangers.

"Sir," said Kennedy to Captain Knife Hand, presiding over the AAR as the day ended and a cold wind came off the sea, blowing more of the burning building smoke through the quick AAR before we were sent to the walls. "You can't discount magic here. There are spells like mass hypnosis, or mass suggestion, other things too… that would have taken their free will from them and forced them to overrun our positions even though they were being cut to shreds by Rico. Sar'nt Rico, sir."

Like I said, I was busy in the market by the time the situation in Dockside began to get desperate. But I do buy the mass hypnosis thing because of one of the things Sergeant Monroe noted in his account to me later.

As the Saur pushed hard on the gun team, Sergeant Monroe was hunkering in the shadows behind a stone warehouse near the old harbor which was on the western side of the peninsula that formed Dockside. The volume of outgoing fire, though centered and plunging down into the front rank, was sending strays and ricochets down into the edge of Dockside, so it was best for the looming beast man to lay low and maintain cover.

The captain had him on short notice to redeploy for any targets of opportunity that presented themselves.

"Chance of getting hit by friendly fire was real as it gets down in there, bro," the minotaur Ranger told me later. "Some of our rounds are going through all the construction down there, blowing out windows, shattering doors, tearing off the roof tiles. The dogs are coming out to tear apart the dead Saur lying in the streets and fight over who gets the tastier parts. I'm laying low and looking for the lizard wizards comin' into play because I can hear the chatter and something weird's up back on the line and I'm just itching to get into it. Arrows of fire and acid hitting our guys up there on the hill and it sounds wild. Combat's fun when you get used to it, man. Ain't nothing like it and it's nothin' like what you thought it was gonna be. But it's fun. Or at least it is for me. Then there's that chain lightning that almost killed those three guys over in First Squad with the captain when he tried to flank the main thrust and the Saur just hosed them with magic fire and lightning."

That was close. Captain Knife Hand barely got First out of there and they fell back throwing grenades to disrupt the push.

"Rico's AG," continues Sergeant Monroe, "says the lizards got so close, one of them grabbed the SAW gunner on perimeter security with flaming hands and burned him bad right there on the spot. Gunner kicked him and hosed that unlucky gecko up close and personal. Gunner kept on fighting even though all his tats are black peeling flesh now. Chief got him wrapped in gel and bandages. That's a lotta ink money gone right there. But hey… you're alive. Chief even said a prayer for Gunner and he said that actually seemed to make things better from a pain management standpoint. Or so he says. You know Gunner. He's all about the show.

"So here's the deal, Talker. We know as the push really develops that the Saur voodoo is the game-changer out there. So I'm looking, Talker. Lookin' for one of them lizard wizards to drop the hammer on. Big time. Lo and behold, in marches a troop of lizards with what looks like a bunch of gear they're pulling on a small cart. First thing that bothers me about this bunch is they're not hissing. I mean they're breathing and that's kind of a hiss, standard for them, but not their usual communication orders and answers and such. Nothing like what you'd expect from a group of normal soldiers working together. NCOs barking, privates bitching. They're, the ones that have come in with the cart, they're like zombies except they're alive. They ain't dead. Or undead. I've wasted enough of those in the short time we've had here to know the difference."

He paused, thoughtful. "Or maybe that's a minotaur superpower? *Detect Undead*? I'll ask Kennedy but I bet that's a thing. Anyway," he continued, "they start setting up a small catapult and a group of them gets some kinda... I don't know but it feels like *Greek fire* to me... they get it going in a pot. I've studied that kind of warfare, Talker. The Byzantines used Greek fire to ruin Greeks with. I always thought it was like napalm, but that stuff, Greek fire, used to burn in the water. And if this stuff is anything like that... then that's gonna make our defense out there a lot harder with everything on fire and all that massed arrow fire and infantry pushing in using the actual principle of mass to try to ruin our gun team.

"Anyway, it's clear they're gonna start dropping their version of incendiary mortar fire all over us, and with all that foliage out on the island, and our guys nowhere to fall back to, again... I'm pretty sure this ain't good. So I decide I'm gonna do 'em because those guys don't need that on their plate right now. And just as I'm getting ready to smoke 'em, this tall Saur walks into the alley where they're all just standing there like dummies in a store window. The wizard lizard hisses some orders and I'm pretty sure this one's the real deal—like *actual* lizard wizard, man. They start getting ready to arm and fire their tiny catapult."

He looks at me. "So I smoke 'em all right there."

"The sixty?" I ask.

"Negative, young Ranger. Work smarter not harder. I just tossed a grenade right into their center and let it go bang. They had no idea what it was. They really didn't even see it. No one covered. No one moved. They stood there like store window dummies and took the blast at close range. I'll say this... that wasn't easy for me."

At first I think he means using a fragmentary explosive on others. I have seen those effects. I have created those effects. They may not have been humans, or what remains of them, but… it's pretty messy.

But he doesn't mean that.

He holds up his leathery and dark minotaur hands, which are huge. "Couldn't pull the pin, man, because my fingers are way too big. Look at 'em. They're huge. So they continue loading their Greek fire round and it's now or never to get them done and I'm literally fumbling with a frag I can't arm. Imagine that. I actually thought about using my teeth, but… that didn't work. So I improvise."

Sergeant Monroe smiles.

But he is a minotaur now, and let's just say… it's kinda unsettling.

"I pull the pin with the tip of my horn, Talker. Pop the spoon, toss it in there at them, cover. It annihilates the entire bunch. I didn't want to use gunfire here because out there on the main street are battalion-sized elements of Saur marching forward from the docks. And I only got one belt left for break-glass-in-case-of-emergencies stuff, know what I mean? Yeah, I'm an X-Man for sure, but… those odds are stupid even for Colossus."

Makes sense to me. I just write all this stuff down.

"Magneto could have handled all of 'em," Tanner says later when I relate all this. "And you're more like Professor X, Talker. You could just dust 'em with your brain I bet if you practice more and all. But Kurtz got you on team lead and he's gonna ride everyone to peer assess the hell outta you. So… you got that to look forward to, brother."

Meanwhile Sergeant Monroe's narrative continues.

"When I pop from cover and check the effects of that frag I tossed… I see most of them are dusted straight up because they made it easy and stayed in close proximity to each other. It ain't total carnage, but there ain't a lot of 'em moving on the other side of bang. Some. But the wizard, the real deal, was far enough away that he ain't dead outright. He got knocked on his butt for sure, probably missing a few fingers… or claws. I'm guessing he has a mild concussion of some sort. But he's getting up anyway, and he spots me and says a *strange word* right at me."

Of course I immediately want to know what that strange word is. Why? Because me.

"What'd it sound like?"

Monroe shrugs. "I dunno, like one of their words, Talker. All hisses and strangling chokes to get it out. Hurts to listen to if you ask me. But I heard it clear as day right there in the aftermath of the blast because… it *echoed* off the walls of the alley square where this all went down. The strange Saur word sounded louder than their boots and gear out there on the cobblestones and the trumpets and gunfire farther off. Word was… I don't know… *grrabchoc-chh*… maybe? That's what it sounded like. Weird. Very… resonant though. So that was my first clue some magic was going down. Well, that's not totally accurate, the lizard mortar guys in a trance seemed pretty sketchy right before I blew them all up. Then this wizard lizard dude enters, and they get to work getting ready to drop Greek fire all over our line.

"Here's what's crazy. Of the ones that ain't dead, one of them, he's even missing an arm… the guy gets up and starts trying to fire the small catapult again like someone told him to get back to work regardless of the detonated grenade and the fact he's a lefty now. So I know I gotta move fast to get this whole thing shut down."

"What'd you do?"

"In a minute, Talk. The lizard wizard first. He says that word… *grrabchocchh*… and you ain't gonna believe this but I swear it happened right there. A giant ghostly lizard claw, bigger than me, just *appears* right in front of him. It's all ghost-y and green slime like the ghosts in the original *Ghostbusters* movie, except it ain't funny. And it shoots right toward me like a Javelin missile. This thing speeds down that alley, straight past the dead lizard parts on the ground and the lefty in a trance trying to get the catapult operational again… and decks me with a solid punch right in the gut."

I laughed.

"It's funny *now*, Talker. Wasn't then. Trust me. That ghost claw just straight up *mollywhomps* me good right into the back of the dirty alley that was my LP/OP. I'd set the pig down on the bipod to deploy the grenade and now I'm nowhere near it. So when this thing knocks me into next week—and it was a solid blow, I won't lie to you. It felt like I shoulda been down for the count. But… super minotaur powers, amirite? Can I get a *whoop whoop*? I just charge the dude without even thinking twice.

"And bro… I got that Raging Hunter in .454 Casull with the modified trigger guard so I can work it. Coulda smoked that dude right there with a big old hole in what was left of his head. Big old bang to boot 'cause that .454 is pure *thunder*. But, get this… *doesn't even cross my mind*. I'm enraged by the smackdown I just got from the ghost hand. It's like I can see how mad I am, and how the other me, the minotaur part, is in full beast mode now. And I'm like, *Dayum*. Out of the corner of my vision, I see the ghost claw coming around to knock the tar outta me again, and without even thinking I pull the battle axe and fling it right at the wizard like it was some core hammer you flip and bang onto a truck to work your obliques."

Sergeant Monroe pauses, seeing it all go down once more in his mind. DVR'ing the violence for a lifetime of viewing pleasure. Like a true Ranger, he is amazed at the kill. And also, at what comes next.

"I'll tell you right now, Talker... and this can go in because I think it's common. Put it down in your account if it means anything. First time I ever smoked a haji in the sandbox, it was at range like most combat is. Way out there and you're shooting at pop-ups. Even though it ain't and it's real and you know all that. And even though I'd been through all the ranges at Benning, there was a part of me where my finger was hovering over the trigger way back then that first time and knowing it was time to pull on a real live pop-up. And I was like... *I don't know, man. This is real. This is a line.* I was asking myself if I was really going to cross this line, finally. Smoke an enemy. The enemy. Situation was legit. But still... you know? First time you have all those thoughts."

I do.

"Then you cross that line and you're never that guy anymore. This axe throw... it was the opposite of that. Pure beast mode. My mind and body just connected with the haft of the axe as it came over my shoulder and I hurled, not flung it, not threw it, I *hurled* it right through... did you hear me?... right *through* this lizard wizard. My axe went into the wooden door the guy was standing in front

191

of when it came out the other side of his guts. Pure. Beast. Mode.

"Lizard wizard grabbed his guts where the axe had just went through a half second before… then he fell over dead."

Silence.

"It was beautiful, man."

Ranger gonna Ranger.

CHAPTER FIFTEEN

DESPITE Sergeant Monroe's success behind enemy lines, the Rangers holding the top of the road and protecting the Lighthouse of Thunderos were in it and getting pushed hard from all sides forward of the line of battle. The magic started to fly up there in every direction no matter how much the Rangers held the line and refused to give an inch to the Legion of Saur throwing themselves into the teeth of the Ranger front.

According to Kennedy, after listening to Old Man Sims's retelling, the lizard wizards began to throw *sleep*, *charm*, and *hold person* spells all over the Rangers as they got close to the lines, shielded by their dying infantry getting ventilated by the extreme volume of outgoing fire the Rangers were dumping just to hold the line.

I have no idea what those spells actually are, but I can guess *sleep* puts you to *sleep*. Linguist for the win. Sergeant Rico and his AG had been hit with that one, but the medics and the Rangers who'd been qualified in the infantry medic program slot Chief Rapp had instituted had been able to get them back to combat-effective and alert with atropine injections and an IV bag to hydrate. Guys were actually fighting with IV bags taped to their FAST helmets.

Then, according to Kennedy, First Squad on the right flank, holding the western edge of the isthmus, got hit by a black glowing orb of death that came right from behind the ranks of lizard men getting cut down by fire, blown to pieces by lobbed grenades, and shot to death at near point-blank range.

The Rangers were working their carbines with fire and movement, calling out mag changes and targets in a blurry dance of death to coordinate effective fire against the small pushes now trying to exploit that flank.

"I mean, I don't think it was an actual Sphere of Annihilation…" Kennedy laughed to himself and pushed his RPGs up on the bridge of his nose as he explained what he thinks might have happened. "That's like a high-level artifact. But these Saur seem to be magic treasure hoarders, and if that *is* a thing here, then… it's something I should brief everyone on. It could be a problem if we run into one of those."

"And what would the briefing be?" I asked Kennedy.

"Oh. Run away. Do not touch it no matter what. That's save versus death. It's bad. Ask anyone who's ever tried to go through Tomb of Horrors. But I don't think this was that artifact. My guess… it was a Circle of Death. Lower level but enough to do the job in these circumstances."

According to the guys in First Squad, the Circle of Death hit them and the first thing they all felt was extreme anxiety. Big-time. Fear, really. Which is saying something for Rangers. So… this was almost alien to them and that bothered them from the get-go, but being Rangers with automatic weapons and explosives, they've dealt with their anxiety, and fear, by just spitting in its face and getting done what needs to get done.

It's not that Rangers aren't afraid of stuff. It's just that they train to do stuff that comes with a natural fear factor, and they do it anyway. Fear is part of the job. They saw the orb come rolling through the front ranks of lizard men they were fighting, and by this point the tall grass that lay before the two hills the Rangers were holding was littered with torn-apart and shot-to-pieces lizard bodies. The orb came from the second or third rank where some magic user lizard wizard was probably hiding out and cast the spell while trying to avoid getting his head blown off by outgoing fire. It rolled through the front rank and just, according to Deacon, the Ranger from First who gave me the story, just "sucked the life right out of those lizards in front of us." They withered, went fetal, and looked like warmed-over death.

Sergeant Ross, who was running First, shouted, "Gimme the Goose!"

Goose is another name for the Carl G. He was going to fire a round danger-close right into the thing. But the Circle of Death moved in so fast and exploded all over the squad's fighting positions, and the Carl couldn't be deployed in time.

"I felt death, man," Deacon told me. "And… it wasn't like I've seen it before. I mean I've seen some guys die—and what I was feeling like didn't feel like that. Felt more like… a severe hangover and having done something really bad during said severe hangover. Not that I have done anything like that that I'll admit to. But… ever have a dream, Talker? A nightmare really, where you murdered someone… or re-enlisted even though you said you weren't gonna do it again? But you have in the dream and now you're locked in for another four? And you had plans for back on the block? That's a nightmare."

He paused and looked at me, trying to see if I under-stood his metaphor. I did. It wasn't great. It wasn't Ray-mond Chandler. But, meaning conveyed. Because every-one tells me their stories, I have found it helps if I just act like I understand what they're saying at the time even if my limited experiences don't match theirs.

Don't stop the roll of the story is a rule I have devel-oped in my role as Ranger Detachment Keeper of Records. Ask follow-up questions later as they occur or don't get an-swered along the way of the telling of the story.

"So… everyone gets all… worked up," continues Dea-con. "They get all Hudson in *Aliens* when he goes out a hero. Best scene ever. That's how I wanna go. Except it'll be ugly orcs and ogres instead of them aliens. But guys are literally coming out of their fighting positions, mag dump-ing up close and personal, and using some pretty harsh lan-guage to boot, even for Rangers, man. Like they're all just instantly pissed it's gone this way for them. They're going on, me too, about what we're going to do to these scaly bastards if they keep coming for us. Jones pulls his knife and just guts a lizard all savage that came in fast behind the ball. Swears and just sticks this lizard warrior through the abdomen and then rams the blade right up into the thing's lungs. Pushes that dude off, and I swear, spits in this dy-ing lizard guy's face and goes straight after another without taking a breath. Our line is breaking up because we're so freaked out and dealing with it… you know… the way we do. Violently."

Or, as Kennedy would analyze the whole attack on First later, "The lizards cast some kind of *fear* spell on the Rang-ers in First. If I had a roleplaying game, Talker, where you could play Rangers and fight monsters… and believe me that would be some awesomeness right there, I wouldn't even want to DM it, I'd want to play, but... none of my guys are ready to DM in my world yet so I have to and all."

My guys. I note that. Even Kennedy knows he is a cult leader now. He is the most powerful PFC the Rangers have ever seen and they can't even wrap their minds around it. He lives rent-free in the Rangers' heads now and it's amazing when you see it. So instead... they have embraced him. Amazing to see what a year and a magic dragon-headed staff can do.

"The lizards cast fear on Rangers," continues Kennedy's analysis, "and *in my game* Rangers would presumably have massive saves against it, when you think about it. It's part of the selection process of becoming a Ranger. Not saying they don't have fear, Talker, but even me... I mean, you do some Ranger stuff, and you start getting addicted to the edge. You pass dealing with fear as part of the job and move on to looking for it where you can find it because that's where the edge is. And you learn... fastest way to find an edge to get into is to smell fear. Weird... never thought about it that way.

"So, bad move on the lizards' part. Cast *fear* on Rangers, easy save for them in game terms. Get ferocity in return. In other words... they got *buffed* by having *fear* cast on them. That would be my guess. And remember, Talker, this may have nothing to do with a game that existed ten thousand years ago."

"Buffed?" I break my cardinal rule of not interrupting. But, because of my superpower, it might be important. I was always looking for ways to make it more powerful to help the Rangers. Help us.

And of course, also because I'm an achievement junkie. I'm sick, I know. That has been admitted to in this account. Don't @ me unless you've walked a mile in my combat boots.

"Yeah, *buffed*. It's more of an MMO term. But… think of it like this. They drank a magic potion, and it suddenly gave them superpowers for a few minutes. The Rangers metabolized fear into violence and started ruining lizard dudes in bulk."

Which is actually what happened. First got so carried away with their out-of-control savagery that they almost lost cohesion with the line of fire as they suddenly started advancing on the enemy, taking arrow fire, and slaughtering every single lizard they could shoot, stab, or strangle.

Yeah, strangle. *All* of First got garrote kills.

Their mags went dry and without going into their assault packs for spares, they started using their personals, then the pickups they were carrying, and then their combat knives, in a frenzy of death.

Note, knives have a tendency to get stuck in guys who run away after you try to hack them to pieces, so garrotes came next. As the flank freaked out and tried to fall back—or in some cases just stood there, amazed in their own Saurian minds that their overwhelming attack was suddenly getting countered by even more overwhelm coming back at them—the Rangers strangled them in the tall grass.

Captain Knife Hand had to run from the battle at the center to get them back into shape, literally changing into were-tiger form and roaring at them on the field to fall back to the line of battle and link up.

"It was… amazing," said Deacon. "We went berserk. If not for the captain we probably would've killed our way right into them until we were right in front of friendly fire or too deep and strung out to get back to the line without getting hacked to pieces by the lizards. Then Captain Were-Tiger comes in and that's… something. You've seen it."

I have. It is something.

Deacon spit dip as he finished his account, staring off at the walls we were holding. The savage drums beyond them that night.

"It was like we lost our minds, Talker. Crazy."

CHAPTER SIXTEEN

THE situation was getting progressively worse when the captain broke in over the comm with a call for fire mission and added the words that make any infantrymen exposed without cover shudder: "Danger close."

Meaning the coordinates to start dropping steel are as tight as they can get, and have been checked and re-checked with a seriousness that matches some girl showing up at the first sergeant's office with your dog tags and other cut-the-blue-wire situations because the lives of your men, and yourself, really depend on this one.

Danger close means the enemy is inside the perimeter.

There are a lot of dead infantry lieutenants who got shiny medals and weren't around for the award ceremony whose last transmission in these situations when the enemy was as close as it gets, was basically, "Send it," when apprised the rounds would land right on top of their position.

That's how bad, and how quickly it turned as the Rangers faced a developing force of four thousand Saur trying to get off the docks and push on the isthmus.

We were well into the situation in Market and by that time Sergeant Thor had shot the high priest on the massive red sandstone steps of the Temple of Pan in that district and was now dealing with the developing fallout there that had just gotten much more weird. Don't worry… I'll explain. Meanwhile the smaj was sitrepping from the Gates of Death that the Guzzim Hazadi, the orc hordes of the desert who'd been shadowing us since leaving the deep shadows of the Atlantean Mountains, had sensed our plans to take the city and were looking to take advantage of it. Long-range sniper arrow fire from the fantastic orc archers was going after the mortar platoon just outside the gates, but the hastily erected dwarven defenses of sand berms, hauled carved stones, and whatever other salvaged building materials the industrious dwarven combat engineers conjured from nowhere I could see and finally combined with their endless tirelessness for digging like moles, protected the Ranger mortar men who prepared to employ the hundred-twenty millimeters in order to drop steel on demand.

Lately Sergeant Chris had been spending time teaching them, the dwarves, explosives. They nodded, murmured, and were eager to employ high-ex both for fun and construction. They were rarely eager about anything more than beer and defense, so their curious interest in high-ex was amusing to the Ranger NCO, who gladly taught them that "Destruction is construction, boys, if you do it right."

The first mortar rounds went out, arched over Dockside, and fell earthward as shots were bracketed and adjusted for range and target. The pause on the radios was ominous as Sergeant Raines alerted the Rangers on the isthmus with a not melodramatic, "Shot out."

Then the rounds landed, position noted, fire adjusted. Bracketing for the final "Fire for effect" in which all batteries would open fire and drop everything they had as fast as they could.

If that didn't slow the Saurian advance...

According to Sergeant Monroe, when he followed one of the alleys north toward the battle the sound of Ranger gunfire had become muted as the sound of the marching lizard man army—boots, horns, hissing like a parched man strangling—overwhelmed the soundscape. When the sergeant arrived at a place where he should have been able to see the line of battle, the Rangers had pulled back to the far side of the hill, and he saw none of the Ranger elements there fighting the spears of the enemies swarming upslope and pushing over the crest. Third Platoon was now fighting a reverse slope defense along the beach on the backside of the hill. Fire teams had broken down line cohesion and were dusting fast-moving Saurian archers trying to flank between elements and roll up the sides with suicide light spear attacks. Saur heavy troops massed below the small hill just as the first mortars found their range after destroying one of the outbuildings in Dockside.

The Rangers had more wounded, but no KIAs as of yet other than Ranger Gertz, who died on the beach after being pulled back.

Gunner, the SAW gunner for the Third weapons team, held forward of all friendlies as the two-forty got pushed between barrel changes, and the decision was made to fall back and establish a new line on the other side of the hill. The captain, his Crye Precisions ripped and torn, chest rig flapping because now in were-tiger form he was too massive for his gear, stalked the hill just below the fight as the Rangers pulled back and the weapons team got ready to run a line of traversing fire along the crest for anything that survived the imminent mortar strike.

Old Man Sims picks up the story from there.

"I was right behind him as he adjusted fire below the hill they were staging in, and so was Sergeant Chris. Dude was working the carbine and keeping the first heavies to come up off us with some pro-level shooting. They surge and make it past all their dead in the grass and Sar'nt just shootin' 'em dead as fast as he can. Captain likes the final shot the mortars drop and tells them to elevate fifty and send it 'cause we got no time left. They're coming.

"He turns to tell me and the platoon sergeant to get off the hill and get down, and this Saur in a scaled kilt, massive chest covered in breastplate that was so shiny it blinded me as the sun caught it, this sucker comes up hissing like a cobra. He'd kept low in the grass and then popped up with a trident and tried to run the captain through. The thing spits a spray of poison, but the morning wind grabs it and it goes off away from the captain. Knife Hand's got his MK18 in his off hand and he just slashes with his free claw right across the lizard's throat and green bloody spray flies in that wind and the guy goes down in the grass and he's done. Then Captain calls out over the radio, 'Send it, Sergeant Raines, send it now!'"

Old Man Sims, who's only twenty-three years old, is still, actually, a very young guy. Stuff still amazes him in that way it does young people. He's still got that youthful… excitement I'd call it, of a young man going to his first rock concert. Your first time out in the world lasts longer than you think it does. The older you get the easier it is to see. But physically, he's an old man. Because of the curse. And so, both of these factors combine, and it makes him seem like some crazy old man who sleeps in the alley behind the liquor store and cooks over an open fire late at night and talks about hopping a train for Mexico and running off with some woman named Rita.

I don't know. That's a lot of… description. I'm just trying to convey how *disconcerting* the curse he's under is. He is a *young* old man and that makes him seem… *squirrely* for looking so old. You constantly have to remind yourself he's just some kid who joined the army, got into the Rangers, and now looks like some broken old ruck hump line infantry sergeant who's smoked too many cigarettes and rucked more miles than you can imagine. High-interest car loans, ex-stripper wives, Uniform Code of Military Justice actions, and all those field exercises mostly in the cold and rain. Radio watches and smokes all through the night. Sometimes in the desert and all that relentless heat it can throw at you with more to spare. All of it makes you old fast, older than you should be. Older than you ever thought you'd get.

Tanner calls it, "The me starter pack."

Your mileage may vary. That's just my two cents. Go read someone else's account of what happened to us in the Ruin. Oh… no one else wrote one. So, I guess you're stuck with me.

Coffee, anyone?

So the captain, according to Sims, just slashes the throat out of one of the Conan Actual lizard praetorian guards that are now leading the charge onto the hill to overrun the Rangers on the isthmus and retake the Lighthouse of Thunderos. Sims, under arrow fire, along with Sergeant Chris and the captain, are running downslope on the other side of the hill when the first mortar rounds start to fall.

"He's called it right on top of where we were, man," says Old Man Sims who smokes cigarettes regardless of the constant corrections of the Ranger NCOs and their hatred of lit tobacco and worship of cut chew. I believe Sims's reasoning is that most of his life has been stolen by the witch's curse when we were back on Bag-of-Death Dead Orc Island and now he takes what mean pleasures he can find in lit tobacco. I further believe the NCOs pity him and allow this even though they cannot help themselves from enforcing Ranger standards with a fanaticism people in cults would find *inspiring*. And with no little resentment, when corrected, Old Man Sims returns their furious Ranger fervor and also sullen pity for a cursed dying man by smoking right back at them, coughing as he does so.

"I'm dying, man," he always says afterward as the NCO disappears to go enforce and correct standards somewhere else. "It'll be funny," says Sims in their wake, "when I'm the last Ranger and everyone else is dead and I have to dig our graves, hacking up my lungs the whole time. I hope I make it. I really do because some days I just live for that and nothing else, man. Nothing else."

And in that... Sims is one hundred percent Ranger. Throwing dirt on all the NCOs that gave him a hard time for smoking is his "burritos."

Some days I just live for that and nothing else, man. Nothing else.

It's savage, in a sort of pitiful, death's door kind of way, but the younger, or younger-looking anyway, Rangers hold him in high esteem for sticking it to the NCOs like he does. In the face of death by old age because to them, these young Rangers, it's impossible to believe you'll ever be that old.

And the NCOs allow this veneration of Old Man Sims because young Rangers need to challenge stuff. Not be beaten into submission. Then they wouldn't be Rangers. That's what makes them tip-of-the-spear killers who come for bad guys like ghosts in the night. Challenging stuff gets them ready for the Spartan mercilessness that is Ranger culture. Best they learn that skill now, they'll need it later.

Sergeant Chris told me one time the NCOs get worried if a new Ranger doesn't challenge them at some point along the path of development as a Ranger.

"What about me?" I asked. "I wasn't a big challenger."

"Well, you got busted to private for basically doing the right thing. And also the thing you should never do, at the same time. You did both at once. You disobeyed orders and left your squad hanging. So, yeah, we considered that a challenge—though there were those who wanted to either kill you and bury you in a shallow grave or just give you to the Air Force and pretend we never knew you. But we knew you had it in you. We were just waiting for you to figure it out."

I wondered who wanted to kill me and bury me in a shallow grave outside FOB Hawthorn.

"Kurtz?"

Sergeant Chris shrugged. "Him too."

Incoming begins to fall all over the hill Third Platoon has ceded to the enemy and the area between the north end of Dockside. I've seen the aftermath of the mortar strike… it was brutal. The Saur pushing and staging there got wrecked. Limbs and body parts. Stuff you don't wanna see even if it is a lizard man. Or once was.

And by wrecked, I mean torn to shreds. Not to put too fine a point on it. Or as Tanner put it, "There ain't nothin' left but hamburger and slag up there."

Still, the mortars weren't enough. The Saur had reached, and this was from Captain Knife Hand during the AAR when we discussed the failure of the plan to lure them into splitting forces and attacking the elements in Market, but the Saur had reached a decision point in which they had to go through the mortars because there really was no other choice for them.

Note: Sergeant Kang and a team had set up mines and one gun team had been redesignated to hold the only gate in the wall that separated Dockside from the main city. Through attrition and the chokepoint, we'd planned to devastate their forces as they split to deal with Second's attack on Market. There were other ways into Sûstagul, but the main gate to take out Second's attack would have been through the Gate of Blue Dolphins as it was known. But between the gun team and the mines that should have been more than enough to devastate their numbers.

As Captain Knife Hand put it during the AAR, "The Saurians were on 'death ground,' Rangers. Sun Tzu put it this way: *'On death ground, fight.'* Meaning, there are certain situations you have no good choices available to you. I'm sure many of you have been in that very situation. I know I have. You just have to fight like hell and hope you make it through. Which, as Sergeant Kang has aptly stated… is exactly what we'd do if we were in their situation. That was a command failure to see this coming and I take responsibility for it. Learn from it, Rangers, and don't make the mistakes I made when it comes time for you to make the calls."

Again, I'll pause here to say… I've worked for people in the civilian world, been in academia, lotsa places. I have never seen the level of brutal honesty you find in the Rangers. Especially regarding their self-evaluation process. They are merciless on their enemies, but they're harder on themselves. *We* are, I mean. We have to be. It's the only way to win out here. And, as we say, Rangers are in it to win it. Even when we lose. We're gonna learn from that so we can kill you better next time we meet. So… you got that goin' for you, lizard people. Every Ranger now knows more about how you fight, and you best believe they are going to stay up late applying that knowledge to kill you better the next time we tangle.

Rangers have a reputation. And it's well deserved. I only live to be worthy of it now. And I'll be honest: it consumes me on levels I haven't made clear here yet. I learned the creed in RASP. Sure. But now, when I go over it, having learned it and survived in the Ruin alongside the Rangers, and becoming one along the way, I realize I never really knew the Creed. I'd just memorized it and *learned* it as best my limited experience would allow me to. I know it now better than I ever did, because I've seen it applied, and lived it. And here's something further: I will know it even better tomorrow by the things I do today, and tomorrow.

A in the Ranger creed puts it this way…

Acknowledging the fact that a Ranger is a more elite soldier who arrives at the cutting edge of battle by land, sea, or air, I accept the fact that as a Ranger my country expects me to move further, faster, and fight harder than any other soldier.

I think about this now and after the AAR. I think about it a lot and understand, now more than I did, what it means. It's what the captain was saying to his Rangers. Learn from my error and move further, faster, and fight harder than any other soldier. Because they're all trying to kill you.

There are no second prizes out here. None. It's winner take all.

And that's why you gotta be better than any other soldier.

"What happened then?" I asked Old Man Sims.

"What happened?" he says, lit smoke between his lined fingers. Wrinkled eyes staring out at the big emerald Inner Sea and seeing it all once again. What he'd lived along the way to surviving. Back there in that moment again and probably for many days until the end of his life. Yeah, he's still just a kid. In an old man's body. But he's lived some serious stuff. And maybe in that, he's the perfect version of every soldier there ever was. You do this stuff, and you get that look. Been there. Done that. Got the scars.

And the memories.

"Sergeant Chris getting the ACE report on the beach," says Sims after a moment. "Medics are pulling the wounded back into the water. Captain's gone up the hill, I went with him. They're coming again and at that moment it don't look so good for us despite the mortar strike. He turns to me and tells me to get the Legion commander on the horn fast. He's already down the hill, moving fast, and looking for one of the Rangers that was in Third strike force."

"Who?"

"Guy who got bit by the mermaid."

CHAPTER SEVENTEEN

BACK at the citadel, Specialist Commons straight-up Rangered when he got bit by a mermaid. That was when we took the Tower of the Mermaids on the assault against the citadel we'd suddenly been forced to conduct. If you remember, the singing sea babes had lured us out into the water right in the middle of a pretty serious fight. Even Thor got suckered on that one, and I'd be lying to you if I told you it didn't make him think a little bit more about carving off on his own and trying out all the extreme sports the Ruin had to offer. I mean, he *did* think about it more. In fact, it convinced him more and more that he wanted those experiences. He'd probably have been cool getting turned into what Specialist Commons did. But during that ambush by sea hoochies, my psionics kicked in and I smoked one and that was just enough to break their spell and for us, more importantly, to break free of their… embrace.

Commons had already gotten bit though. Two were trying to drag him under and down into that watery netherworld out in the deeps of the Great Inner Sea I'd seen inside their hungry minds. Commons stabbed them both, freaked out, and ran on shore screaming, "I got bit!"

It was not uncommon for other Rangers to shout, "Got bit!" whenever Commons passed by on some task with a purpose. Like a smart Ranger he endured it and, in the end, put in a request for the Forge to crank out a PVC patch for his carrier that showed a hot manga mermaid with big vampire teeth and the phrase by which he had become famous among Rangers. In the end, he made it his own.

"Got bit!"

Three days after the bite though, he started getting real sick. By then Joe and I were lost in the desert. The battle with the medusa at the citadel was over, her genie exploded in the waters of the Mouth of Madness, her army fleeing into the lost lands beyond the edge of the map, her citadel burning in the hellish red afternoon.

Side note about the queen medusa that I wasn't present for, because I'd jumped into the angry waters of the Mouth and gotten sucked under the Atlantean Mountains...

After the Rangers took the citadel, she came out and surrendered to them through a brief negotiation, because after all, her citadel was on fire and she needed to get out of there. What happened next is the captain proved we weren't in Kansas anymore. That the old rules of where we'd come from didn't apply anymore. The Ruin was a rough and mean place, and we were going to show it what those words really mean when applied by Rangers. With a sack over her face she was led out in chains by her own servants. Blind orcs and other captured races of the desert. She had blinded them in order for them to serve as her slaves, and now her own slaves delivered her to the Rangers. Because the translator—that's me—wasn't around, communication with her was rough, but she indicated she'd been paid by the "Dark Forces from the East" to use her fire djinn to suck, specifically us, into the Rift and destroy us by either drowning or murder.

The command team was at a loss with what to do with her next as her forces scattered into the desert and the Rangers put the citadel to the torch. But what to do with the queen of the medusae was the next big question as we were now facing a forced march through the Atlantean Mountains and then on Sûstagul. Fighting the whole way. The galleys under the command of the sergeant major were sailing back to Portugon for more weapons and gear brought down by the Lost Boys and Rangers who'd remained at FOB Hawthorn.

When asked for a promise of never interfering in the affairs of the Rangers, the medusa queen shook her covered head in the negative that she could not make such promises.

"Why can't she?" asked the captain.

One of the surviving Portugonian sailors, along with a lot of Rangers contributing what they'd picked up in their travels across the world going exciting places and killing interesting people, were doing a rough, *very* rough, job of translating the negotiations for unconditional surrender. I both shudder as a linguist at how awful this was, and grind my teeth because this would have been a very useful situation in which to have me around, employing the special amazing thing I can do with regard to knowing a lot of languages.

But that's the shallow seeking-constant-approval-through-achievement old me. I'm different now. Sorta.

"I took blood debt in silver of Caspia to destroy you and your men," she rattled and hissed through the sack over her head. "I have failed... *for now*. Leave me alive, and

I will see every Ranger dead. That is a promise from the Lady of Serpents. And I will destroy also those that gave aid and comfort to my enemies. I am the last queen of the medusae. To fail would make me not queen anymore. And I would have it no other way. The stars may as well go dark, Ranger," she spat at the captain and assembled company.

This was told to me by Thor, the whole exchange. And I'm glad Thor told me because he caught it all in that savage, overdramatic, purity of reality he seems to crave out there in the Ruin.

He's an excellent storyteller and it would be an interesting read if he wrote part of this account. His face and voice just suck you in and make you think you're right there seeing what he saw, experiencing what he experienced. He nails the details and the dramatic tone.

Now you're thinking… Oh, I'd like Thor to write this and get rid of Talker's annoying habits of coffee and tangents.

Well, coffee anyone?

As I was saying…

"Sergeant Major and the Green Beanie start talking it over off to the side as her tower burns in the background," continues Sergeant Thor. "She's kneeling and when she says that part about being *queen of the medusae* and the stars might as well go dark… I totally believe her, man. She is a real live queen by the way she carries herself right then and there. Even though her empire is burning down around her because she made the mistake of bothering us on our way to a kill, she's still every inch a monarch from some age that happened way before we started strapping the scroll. Her forces are slaughtered and running for the desert. She's in chains. She's kneeling in front of the captain like he's some Mongol khan, some savage warlord. And there's us, dirty, shot, bloody, sweaty, and tired, counting our dead, we thought you and Joe were among them at that point. It was all, everything, how it must've been for the entire history of ancient warfare before politicians started using it all for their own selfish gains. Stupid. What we were witnessing was so pure and so brutal…

"I'll tell you right there, Talker, the Ruin was calling to my blood, and it wasn't just calling, whispering… it was screaming. This place is a kind of truth we've never known before. I want to go out there and experience all of it once we put this Sût dude down good and final. I want to know. I gotta go there. Even if I have to ETS myself from the regiment when the time comes."

Then he tells me what happens next back there at the citadel when everyone thought Joe and I were dead and gone.

"Like I said, even with that rough sack over her head, she tells the captain she'll be our enemy forever. No matter what. No questions asked. No quarter given. Ever. She doesn't beg because that's not how leaders do it here. Here… they tell you what they're gonna do no matter what situation they're in because their rep… it's like credit at the bank for them. Without it, they're broke.

"Then the captain says, quiet but totally… *him,* y'know… he says to her, 'Tell her… I understand as a sovereign that that is the choice you must make. I respect you as a leader that you would prize your word over your own life. We Rangers, we do the same. But my duty is to the men and the mission. Rangers leave no enemies alive along their backtrail. I'll execute you myself and I will be quick, and it will be painless out of respect for you. Ask her if she has any last words to say before I carry out my judgment."

Thor nods at me in the dark as he tells me this.

My judgment. That's what time it is, I tell myself, or hear some voice in my head say. And then another, something maybe connected to the psionics whispers, *And it's later than you think, Talk-ir.*

A goose walks over my grave.

"Straight up, man," says Thor. "That's what he said to her right there beneath the burning citadel. That's how the captain rolls."

"What does she do?"

"She holds her head up high, and I swear, and I was close enough to hear, I heard her sob… *just once.* Like she couldn't lock it down and it just suddenly jumped out of her. And for a long moment she was just quiet kneeling there in the dust and blood. Then she said, 'I have one… last… thing to say to… the skies, *Ranger.*' Captain says not to take her sack off. He picks up a sword that had been dropped in the dirt and he walks toward her. It's gonna happen. Man, it's like the most savage barbarian moment I have ever experienced. Even I'm just rooted right to the spot there because I know… Knife Hand's right, Talker. The world the way it was… it ain't that way anymore. It's this way now. And so, it has to be… *this way.* So, she says, once we tell her we can't take the sack off because she'd try one last time to turn us to stone and we knew it, she says she understands.

"Then she holds her head up and shouts to all of us… but really, she was shouting to the skies… 'The first medusa, she was just a woman like me. A beautiful woman who had been a slave. Hurt. Abused. Hunted by men. Cruel men. She was just a woman like me. She wove the snakes into her hair to keep all away from her. Made alliance with the serpents to protect her so she may live in peace. That was all she ever wanted. Peace. I made my kingdom at the edge of the Ruin. I too just wanted peace. They called me a queen. I became one… along the way. Out of need. For peace, I told myself. But now, I am just… a mortal… who has done wrong. I hope there is some other world better than this one. One that saw my heart, and never my hideous face. These are the last words of the last queen of the medusae. Bury me and mark my grave not as a queen… but as a sinner mortal… begging the one who sees. Do what you must… Rangers. Do it now… and make Sût himself take you into the Lands of Black Sleep.'

"She spat that last part out. *Rangers*, she hissed. Like we were a curse just like the one Sims got. Her curse. I get that. War is hard. There are those that ever regret hearing the word *Ranger*."

"Then what happened?" I asked, thinking to myself, *surely… something different than what must.*

"Knife Hand grabbed her head through the sack, grabbed the snakes, yanked 'em back hard, and sliced her head off right there clean and cruel in just one stroke. It was brutal, man. Utterly brutal."

My mouth was hanging open.

"But that's how it is here, Talker, now. This is the Ruin, this is what it is, and… we can't lie to ourselves. There are only the living and the dead here. The captain voted for us. I and every Ranger would too."

So that's what happened to the Medusa of the Citadel, and I only note that for the record.

But back to Specialist Commons who would begin to get sick three days after being bit by one of the vampiric mermaids in the surf close to the shore as that battle got started and ended with the medusa's curse on us all.

The captain called for Commons as the Saurian trumpets to attack began to trill out on the other side of the low hill just beyond the north end of Dockside. More arrows came arching across the sky, falling in the surf the Ranger medics were trying to keep the wounded alive in as the waves washed up on the small beach.

See, Commons got sick. Then, he got better. Once they figured out why he was strangling to death and turning purple and unable to process oxygen normally, they figured it out. The first clue came when Commons started to grow gills and his feet started to web over. His skin is only vaguely scaly along his feet, legs, and abdomen. It's almost golden and he thinks it's pretty cool. Now. *Now* he thinks that. At first he freaked out. Or so I'm told.

Commons has a tendency to freak out. Then he gets it together. Understandable in his case.

But it was the gills. That, combined with the wound from the mermaid attack, a bite to be specific, led the chief to his diagnosis. "I do believe that the Ruin… has *revealed*. Although Specialist Commons has come by it in another way than just the aftereffects of the nano-plague having its way with us for reasons that are not altogether clear. Just like Chief McCluskey became a vampire… I'm thinking Specialist Commons is about to become… a mermaid."

It is widely reported that Commons groaned and gasped at that moment, "Please let there be such a thing as a mer*man*?"

Wizard PFC says there is.

The chief tested this theory by carrying Commons down to the ocean and soaking, then immersing him in sea water. Ranger SDMs went down to make sure the trollop mermaids didn't show up and do their seducing and biting thing. And yeah, after a minute or so the color began to come back into Commons and he could breathe, both in water and out.

Through trial and experimentation, he can now do both. But still, every seventy-two hours or so he needs to be in water. Since we traveled along the coast this wasn't a problem, and he was in the water most every day now that he was being taught by the chief, an SF combat diver, and the other Rangers who've been trained in combat swim and dive. Commons was in the snipers before this happened. Now he's on the path to becoming our very own SEAL. But better.

Commons reported to the captain there on the beach as the next push from the Saur got underway and the Rangers swapped and distributed mags and grenades, making a hasty plan to weather the next push.

"Need you to get out in the water and clear the beach, figure out any obstacles," ordered Captain Knife Hand. "We're requesting the Legion come ashore here to support. We need that beach ready to handle the beaching of the galleys."

Two minutes later Commons was down to his Ranger panties and slipping into the surface of the choppy ocean, disappearing beneath the waves. Offshore, the first galleys of the Legion were under full sail and aimed straight at the beach the Rangers were determined to hold. Behind the Rangers, the Saur were coming over the hill, kinetic hate already outgoing in high doses and full effect.

The Rangers had determined themselves not to budge.

Captain Tyrus and the first legionnaires stormed the beach fifteen desperate minutes later and from that point on, the battle for Dockside turned for the Rangers.

CHAPTER EIGHTEEN

WHAT happened next in the battle for Dockside as an entire Saurian legion tried to push out of the war galleys in the harbor, the orphans meanwhile setting the rowers free as fast as possible under the deadly overwatch of the snipers, was pure battle royale slugfest on the beach the Rangers were holding.

The problems facing the Saur commanders at this point were, one, they had a host of troops and only one narrow lane to push them, and two, the Rangers were masters of channelization, high explosives, fire team CQB, and with their backs to sea… they had no other choice but to hold.

The first of the ten Accadion heavy war triremes rowing hard for the shore saw Rangers tossing grenades, creating interlocking fields of fire erupting in deadly bursts from tight groups of Rangers covering as much as they could, and Captain Knife Hand directing fire from the two-forty bravo team left of center.

The Saur hit this kill zone with everything they could, which wasn't everything due to the limited lane they had to push within, and Sergeant Chris with one other Ranger kept the flanks free by managing chains of explosives, MPIMs, and basic claymores that constantly checked the Saurian heavy foot and archer elements seeking to either flank the Rangers at the beach or push on toward the Lighthouse of Thunderos. The Saurians learned the hard way, as massive strings of explosions denied them access, not to try these avenues again.

Remember, they have no idea what we're using on them. High-ex might as well be extreme juju, and Sergeant Chris, moving fast and laying explosives along the hill's tall grass and twisted coastal trees, was like some kind of deadly new wizard they'd never before encountered, and were getting leery of getting to know in any detail. The dwarves had started to call him "the Boom Wizard" lately, and they knew by these explosions, as they attempted a QRF through Dockside, that their new master and friend was hard at work practicing his magic.

The Saurian commanders made a conscious choice, we surmise, that they would destroy our center and work from there.

Fifteen bloody minutes counted down as white sails on the sea grew larger and the rowers pulled hard for the sand. Then the first trireme, following Specialist Commons in the water, signaling the sailors at the bow where to bring their ships in closest to shore, stowed her oars and glided onto the inner sandbar like some leviathan coming to rest. Nets came down, and the legionnaires in full kit—breastplates, tasseled kilts, and horsehair plumes—shouted in unison, dropped in, and waded through the surf, surging right into the ranks of the Saur without hesitation as the battle began its second phase.

Captain Tyrus was first into the water, first on the beach, and took the blow of one of the Conan-Actual Saurian praetorians who tried to ram the captain's circular shield with a heavy spear. According to Corporal Chuzzo, the captain crouched, took the blow, and leaned into the strike. He waited for the solid *snap* as the heavy spear shattered, then flung his shield to the left and stepped forward through the sand to deliver a brutal slash to the huge Saurian war leader in the first moments of the Legion's battle on the sands. The savage cut of the blade disemboweled the *diabolus*, a Chuzzo word. Translated from Accadion, or Latin pidgin Italian among other various languages, it means *devil*.

"The diabolus... he went-ah down, Talk-ir. Captain Tyrus... he hammer him with-ah the gladius after that. But... see by that time we all on the beach and tryna form-ah the front rank to follow the *capitano* into the fight. It was much fun."

What the corporal of the Legion called *fun*, the Rangers did also in their own way. They were low on mags and now that the battle was hand-to-hand, their magical pickups came out—the strange and sometimes enigmatic magical weapons the Rangers had managed to loot from the dragon horde and undead army along the way to the moment of that battle on the sands—and the Rangers went hard at the enemy hammer and tongs.

Sergeant Chris would tell me later that the Rangers still had a lot to learn about this kind of warfare and that in reality, his guys just fell in with the Legion and started swinging swords and tomahawks like untrained savages looking to stack skulls.

"They're used to the combatives pits. But out came those tomahawks..." snorted Chris, who's an avowed knife devotee. "Those are for the purists, you know that, right, Talker? They're not very good weapons."

I have no official position. I just tell it as it was told to me. The purists will tell you they love the tomahawk for practical reasons and then teach you how to split skulls, break arms, and slash your enemy's throat. "Plus, you can do other things and they're cool" is usually what follows this defense.

The knife people have the same arguments and same defense. And same "they're cool" justification.

I have *Coldfire*. In the kingdom of hand-to-hand weapons... this thing murders. Trust me.

And yeah. It's cool.

The battle got bloody at that point, and while the Legion thought it was fun, the Rangers, especially the berserkers in First, went straight nuts fast. Meaning they got real tired pretty quick as the battle lines between Saur and Legion got ready to brawl in earnest and settled the minor skirmishes for position on the field. As the Legion formed their three-deep lines of shields, spears, and final rank waiting to rotate in, the Saur formed their own while strays from both sides, and those caught in the center, continued to swing and hack at one another.

Legion NCOs beat the rankers into shape and managed the chaos as the calls to position and battle rang out. The Rangers went where they were told by these NCOs, and the young legionnaires told their new allies they were in for some real fun now once it got started.

The Rangers may or may not have understood this from the smiling and eager dark-eyed and olive-skinned Accadions who were ready to rumble Bronze Age style.

Then the Saurian drum orders to *march forward* rolled out over the beach and the lizard men hissed and gnashed their fangs like the waves of the ocean as they came out against the Ranger/Legion line in a massive battle wedge. Saurian archers shot at the front ranks of the Legion from the flanks, when in truth, if they'd managed to gain the hill the Saurian heavy foot was currently occupying, they could have shot right down into the second and third ranks of the Legion lines.

The Accadion legionnaires on the flank caught the incoming direct arrow fire with their massive shields and covered the Ranger NCOs who began to either lob their remaining grenades out onto the flanks to keep the archers back, or, using their 320s, land 40mm grenades out there that devastated these close-knit, lightly armed squads of archers seeking to get close and fire into the Accadion Legion lines.

Both sides slammed into each other moments later as the Legion advanced to meet the incoming Saurians. Shields held by legionnaires, and some Rangers, were held hard against the sudden impact of hundreds of heavy Saurian spears thrusting out in unison at some hissed command by their war leaders. Then the shields of both lines crashed into one another a second after that and it was knives out for everyone. The Legion hacked over and beside their shields with their *gladi* while the spears in the second rank rammed forward and jabbed into Saurian flesh as the shields there were smashed aside, shattered on impact, or cut away from the claws holding them. Saurians hissed and died, run through by the sudden appearance of the Accadion spears from the shield line, and the Legion pushed forward hacking and spearing while the Rangers taking positions in the ranks and began to learn this type of warfare up close and on the fly.

Small battles broke out along the line as the shield walls lost cohesion here and there, and the Rangers went in swinging their battlefield pickups, tactical tomahawks, or knives, of which they had many in abundance. The Saur did not flinch as the Rangers chopped and hacked at them like breathless madmen, new to this type of war. But though the lizard men cut, slashed, and hacked back, they lacked the ferocity of these aggressive newcomers.

Random gunfire went off as the Rangers threw that surprise into the mix of the wild battle erupting along the sand of the beach. Either from what remained of their sidearms and rifles, or from their personals they'd brought along for the ride ten thousand years into the future. The Saur were shot down, gutted, and stabbed as the Rangers fell back from these sudden brawls, shouting curses and other epitaphs for the dead, then reformed the lines with the Accadions. Meanwhile the NCOs in the Legion screamed, beat, and kicked everyone, including the Rangers, into the battle lines they wanted for the next push forward. Rotating the tired out, throwing a fresh legionnaire or Ranger from the third line suddenly forward to take up a shield or grasp a heavy spear in the front ranks.

At first the Rangers chafed at this—being pulled out of the fight, yelled at, then shoved around to be where they should be according to these tiny, scarred, and yet still hulking Legion sergeants. But the Accadion lower enlisted smiled and used their awful English to explain to the Rangers that this was how they fought. The lower enlisted Rangers who were cruising on rage and their coveted one-each -in-case-of-dire-emergency Rip It they'd smashed just moments before the fight, saw their sergeants adapting to the Legion, serving on the line where they were told, and followed the example quickly, understanding that in this type of warfare, with the heat, and the breathlessness of real live hand-to-hand combat, and the length the battle might go, that the rest, rotation, and management the Legion NCOs enforced… was absolutely vital in this type of fighting.

As one of the Rangers put it to me later, "It became like a football game, Talker. Once we learned their commands, it was like their sergeants would see some gap in the line, point toward one of us… and in we'd go for a few. Stacking skulls and pushing for a few more yards to make a down. After a while it was like… Put me in, Coach."

In other words, as I have come to understand it, it's like two evolving fronts, or teams, constantly rotating players in to take advantage of plays on the line, gaps, or sudden skirmishes that were constantly erupting in the battle. Behind all this, the leaders of both sides looked for vulnerabilities and pushed their NCOs to take advantage of these moments with trumpeting horns, fast-running messengers, and sheer thunder in their voices to make themselves heard over the clash of arms and shields, and the hissing and screams of the dying and wounded.

Captain Were-Tiger and the Legion's Captain Tyrus fought from the front, but took small "breaks" to assess the lines and redeploy men to take sudden advantage of some opportunity. They dove in where needed, stabbing, spearing, hauling away the dying and the dead, or suddenly finding themselves in a furious fight surrounded by wicked lizard men stabbing and spearing, all the while constantly trying to reestablish the moving shield wall.

At the same time, the netcalls going out to the rest of us across the battle for Sûstagul seemed frantic and dire from the beach. Much of that can be blamed on Sims. He seemed a little wild over the net. Still, it sounded, from all accounts, like a real fight.

Meanwhile back at the Gates of Death, the sergeant major was leading the mortar teams and perimeter security squad to defend the access point into the city. The dwarves had done all they could do regarding improving defenses and had asked to form a QRF and move to hit the rear of Dockside. Guzzim Hazadi cavalry, orcs riding war camels, were surging out of the desert under indirect fire from the mortar section. Huge sprays of sand from impact strikes went up among the smooth dunes as a ragged line of orc archers atop the strange, armored camels came sweeping out of the desert with their ululating war cries.

The sergeant major had to hold the Gates of Death open so the other half of the troops aboard the Legion war galleys beaching at the original insertion point could run a mile and get in that way. The smaj's bet was that he could still hold and allow the dwarves to QRF, so he allowed their request. And just as they departed, the enigmatic gorilla samurai Otoro stated, "I will hold the gates, Rangers. Axe Grinder must be among these now, and we have an appointment to keep. My honor will not fail you."

This was translated for the sergeant major by Ranger Sakoda, who is Japanese-American.

I feel like I'm becoming more and more useless as we go along.

The dwarves fought their way through the city, hit the Saur from behind, and started carving into their command structure while the dark Saurian spell casters sent arcane magics into the battle to aid the Saurian strike against the Rangers. Sergeant Monroe would tell me what happened next as he went to link up with the incoming QRF and guide them into the battle.

CHAPTER NINETEEN

"I got the call from the smaj while I was running around in my alley maze, taking shots when I could," the minotaur Ranger related to me later. "The QRF from the dwarves was coming in to relieve pressure on Third, and I was to provide assistance if I could. I was down to two rounds for the Carl, half a belt for the pig, and my axe."

"What about the four-fifty-four?" I asked. Just making sure I got the details and all. Hey, I'm me. If he got into more scrapes than he'd told me, I wanted to know how and when. This record is a reflection on me, and I want it to be total and accurate.

"I'll be honest about the Raging Hunter, Talker. Reloads are a hassle. I really have to take my time because my fingers are so much bigger now that I am what I am. Maybe if I grow some long fingernails, which would look wicked sick because my nails are black and all... but still, in a fight, reloading a revolver with bull fingers ain't smooth and easy. Until the Forge way back at the FOB can crank me out some speed reloaders, it's best not to rely on that weapon more than what's in the cylinders. Though I did here and there. Got heavy in there for a few. Had to smoke a few geckos up close and personal. Boy were they surprised. Like they're lizards and they're thinking... oh hell, is that a minotaur? And why does the minotaur have a hand cannon?

Then again… they have no idea what a Raging Hunter is. Probably thought it was a magic wand, amirite? Well, it is. One that makes big holes in you, LOL. It's a magic death wand. Man, Talker, I love this place."

Meanwhile…

The dwarves, according to Max the Hammer, get into the city in their typical Amish-biker-gang-about-to-ruin-your-day pattern. King Wulfhard at the leading tip of their wedge, Max to his left in the position of honor and defense, they enter the city and make for Dockside to relieve the Rangers there.

They aren't stopped initially because again, the Saur are centered around the docks and the mercs are buttoned up and dealing with Second's attack on Market. They make the Gate of Dolphins and run into the vanguard of the Saur there. These are led by a Conan-Actual praetorian-type lizard man, but the rest are normal troops. The dwarves are outnumbered at three-to-one, but the Saur have most likely never fought dwarves and so they think, because they are taller, they have the advantage.

They think wrong.

The dwarves, who have been fighting the Orcs of Umnoth, large, aggressive, and very violent orcs in large numbers apparently, are not at a disadvantage. In fact, this is how they fight all the time. It's Tuesday for them.

In less than a minute the Saurian vanguard is dying in the dust of the gate, and the dwarves are advancing against the Saurian command section, surrounded by Conan Actuals and supported by lizard wizards, as Sergeant Monroe calls them. Battle horns ring out, and as Max tells me later…

"Most likely, Talker, zhat vas ze call to defend zheir leaders. Zhey knew zhey vere in trouble ven our king sounded der Horn of Zhad. So… zhey sent everything zey had to stop us. Ve taught zhem gut, then. Very gut did zhey learn zheir last lesson."

At that point Sergeant Monroe made the rear of the Saurian line midway up Dockside near where he'd smoked the head general. What Sergeant Monroe saw were the dwarves being attacked from three sides with more coming in for the rear.

"At first I thought they were in big trouble, but as I got close, I could hear them calling out to one another as they wailed on every lizard coming close to them. I'm pretty sure… and I don't know numbers in their language, that's your job, Talker, but if I had to guess… they were counting out to one another how many they had killed, and laughing, as they did so. I didn't understand it all, but that was the sense I was getting of what they were at while they were laying waste to everything that crossed their path."

I could imagine that. The dwarves, all in their big floppy leather hats, swole like prison bikers, every ounce of gear on their backs and strapped to their unending amounts of heavy armor, swinging their great runed axes, maces, and hammers, crushing and smashing the Saurians who tried to come at them in lines and form assaults against them in the mazes of streets and small alleys that form Dockside. I've seen them fight, the dwarves. They're like a well-organized, moving hurricane of chaos that laughs at anything you intend to do to it. And like a hurricane, you can't stop it, you can't even predict it. That's exactly how they fight.

"They were hard to follow, Talker," continued Sergeant Monroe. "I mean I only picked up their trail in Dockside because of all the bodies they left in their wake. When I got close, I could hear them laughing as the lizards hissed and tried to kill them. See, every time the lizard wizards would try to use a spell on them, if it didn't bounce right off their armor and all those charms and runes they got all over everything, then King Wulfhard would bellow something and they'd simply go hacking and slashing off in another direction down an alley and into a chokepoint to get away from the lizard wizards. One time they went right through a building, fighting their way in and defending it as they went through, making the lizards pay for every step, then out the back door as they set it on fire and left, muttering at each other and laughing as they went. They're a well-oiled fire team, moving and hacking, laughing and calling their kills. They didn't need my help, man."

But then they did apparently.

The Saur got wise to the rolling attack of the dwarves, redeployed their wizards, and set up a trap to stop all movement from reaching the Rangers at the beach. Monroe, shadowing their move up Dockside, saw the ambush go down just seconds after the dwarves got into it.

First the lizard wizards hit them with magical webs. Giant sticky sprays of enchanted webbing erupted away from the three wizards in conical hats and white robes who'd lain in wait for the dwarves to try that particular street to reach the battle. In seconds the dwarves were stuck and busy trying to cut themselves free with little success. At the same time, Saurian praetorians using heavy bows flooded from a side alley across the way, formed a line, and were ready to fire into the prone dwarves stuck within the magical webbing.

That was when the minotaur joined the battle.

Monroe opened up with the sixty, ruining the line of archers with heavy bows. Advancing down the body-littered street, he worked the pig and burned the belt. And when the belt was dead, he tossed the sixty, grabbed his battle axe, and advanced on the three wizards.

"I dumped the pig because it was dry and there was no ammo resupply in my future. I'd come back and get it later… if there was a later. But the QRF needed rescuing now, so I advanced with the axe."

He destroyed the three wizards, but it wasn't easy.

I asked him to slow down in his account and tell me exactly what happened. Initially he just said, "So I wasted all three of the lizard wizards and got the little guys outta there and back in action." But I wanted to know how. Because there was a lot that happened in that little sentence, I could tell. And for purposes of the account, I needed to know. Plus… it was pretty badass.

"You want the play-by-play, Talker?"

I do.

"Okay." He paused, remembering. "Okay, I toss the pig and get my battle axe off my back, and I'm already running… but that ain't the right word. That's not what I do now, man… know what I mean?"

I don't. I ask for clarification.

"Well… I *charge* now, man. I'm a bull. I guess that's what I do. So I'm *charging*. But I got that battle axe in one hand, and I just jerk it back into a two-handed hold, like a baseball bat, and right as I passed the first wizard, this tall guy with a leathery old snout, missing teeth, one eye, and some kind of python wrapped around his neck and glaring at me… I just sweep the battle axe forward as I charge past and gut him in half in one savage cut. It's all oblique work, man. That's why I do so many landmines with the weights, or any bar I can get a hold of. Obliques let you explode in core movement and hand-to-hand is all about the core. I fire the axe as I pass, and the guy goes down and now I'm on number two like white on rice.

"This guy has two asps, but they're made of gold, and they're alive, wrapped around his scaly old wrists. I think they're asps. We didn't get to handle asps in Ranger school. Mainly water snakes. He's missing one eye too. But where the other guy had an ornate patch in the form of a gold and jeweled scarab over that eye, this guy's just got an open old scarred socket. Anyway my axe is down and to the left from the sweeping cut I just dealt on Lizard Wizard Number One, so I stop on both feet, planting them you know, and jerk the axe straight back to the right as hard as I can like I'm jerking kettlebells in the gym. It takes his head clean off, and that's when Lizard Wizard Number Three fires a green ray at me from a ring on his finger. I'm guessing that was a magic ring, obvious guess, and after I killed him, I went and looked at it. But then I understood why the other two guys were missing an eye and then I didn't want it so much or think it was the kind of thing we should have around."

I didn't understand. I told Sergeant Monroe so.

"The eyes man, his two... I don't know what the word is... *apprentices*? The first two I'd killed had to be his apprentices. And I think this guy, the master or whatever, had taken an eye from each of 'em and turned it into rings he kept on his claws. And this part is crazy. Even though I'd gored the guy and he was dead, and so were the other guys, both of their eyes, each in one bronze ring, were *still roving around and looking at me.* Weirdest thing I'll ever see, I will tell you that right now."

Wait, you gored the last guy?

"Yeah, man. The green ray destroyed my magic axe, which sucks by the way, great axe, so... I lowered my horns and ran him straight through, then arched my back and flipped him off my horns. He went end over end and I heard his back snap real loud when he hit a cart and folded across it the wrong way your back doesn't want to go. It was sick, man. Minotaur superpowers. I'm telling ya, Talker. Minotaurs got superpowers for the win. Every time. All day, all night. The minotaur PT train don't stop for the station. Make it hurt, drill sergeant, make it hurt."

Then he high-fived me.

CHAPTER TWENTY

THE high priest's head exploded. Bone matter and brains painted the mesmerizing carved red sandstone steps as the brief morning breeze passed by the celebration of death that always took place during this time of the morning in front of the Temple of Pan.

The shooter had accounted for the wind and distance at just the right moment to land the shot right from the fifty-caliber anti-materiel rifle known as *Mjölnir*.

Sergeant Thor did not shout or even mutter "Yahtzee" as other Ranger snipers might have done when dusting a target at distance in conditions such as the spotter had noted in the last seconds before the shot was taken. But Thor's spotter did mutter the standard Ranger phrase as he observed the perfect shot, the red mist drifting and disappearing as suddenly as it had appeared. He whispered the epitaph, or insult, take it as you will, then added... "Domed him, bro."

Thor said nothing and instead inspected the next chambered massive fifty-caliber round before returning to the scope and watching the whole wild scene take place below on the temple steps.

They were deep inside the room. The old fortress's eagle's nest. Back in the shadows, elevated by makeshift debris, and watching the steps of the temple and the spreading pandemonium.

Recoil on a Barrett was nothing to joke about. But for the jacked sniper it was nothing to be bothered with. He used the weapon in CQB sometimes, going full rapid-fire savage at close range. When needed.

The doming of the priest had been the finale of something so savage and tribal that even the Ranger snipers tasked with supporting this phase of Operation Stranglehold had found themselves watching in utter grim fascination. A bewitching that verged on staring at pure horror.

The scene had been no cheap roadside carnie show below. It had been something primal and raw, pomp and circumstance mixed with fervor and magic. Danger was in the air like downed power lines on a snowy night when the roads are ice and everything is frozen. Except it's already boiling in the desert and sweat was dripping into the shooter's and spotter's eyes as they waited for just the right moment to pull the trigger past its final break and unleash the sudden thunder of *Mjölnir*.

Now, shot taken, target down, all was utter chaos as the worshippers, junior priests, onlookers, and all involved, struggled to understand what had just happened to everything they navigated the compasses of their lives by.

Faith.

Trade.

Eternity.

Evil.

Red mist and a headless corpse that was once the High Priest of the Grand Temple of Pan. Leader of the Children.

Two things to note here. One, the reason for the elimination of the high priest. Two, the religion of Pan.

I will endeavor to explain it all.

Possibly both were the reason for the legendary Ranger sniper's silence as he waited for chaos's next move to show him who else needed to die this morning to complete the mission.

The Rangers needed chaos now. Division. Opportunists seeking to consolidate the loose power on the ground down there emanating from center mass of the body of a dead evil cleric of high order.

The Rangers needed this bunch paralyzed and rudderless for the moment in order to keep nailing the other two objectives to complete Operation Stranglehold and for Sûstagul to lie within their grasp by the end of the day.

The spotter was calling in the kill to the smaj, who was currently running radio traffic as the captain and Third Squad got real busy fighting for their lives on the beach. We were just getting into it in Second over at Market, and I only caught, "Jackpot Gacy is KIA. Confirmed. Jackpot Gacy is off the table at this time."

So, that went as planned, I thought as we pushed on the tower of Ur-Yag. *At least we don't have to worry about that insane bunch over at the temple.*

Foolish me. This is the Ruin. This is the beginning of the End War, as Vandahar calls it. A lotta moving parts and rogue pieces. Anything can happen. A lot of strange things *are* happening, and Thor was about to enter the mythic world of the Ruin to ensure the Temple of Pan did not enter the battle until we had full control of the city with the rest of the landing forces of the two Accadion legions on the wall and watching the desert sands south of the city.

So let me tell you about why we needed to do it this way. Why Sergeant Thor had been assigned to nail the high priest of the Temple of Pan. Why that murderous thug and real living nightmare of children needed to die at first light.

There are three enemy elements in this battle, Operation Stranglehold. The Saur, who were currently being dealt with at Dockside. The wizards in the market under the leadership of the "Grand Vizier Ur-Yag," as he was known far and wide in the lands of the south. That was our job in Second. Get Ur-Yag.

And then there was the Temple of Pan.

The temple is the newest and grandest construction inside the ancient desert port city. It's beautiful. I won't lie to you there. On par with what the Temple of Athena must have looked like once and long ago, except all carved in swirling red sandstone like something you'd find in pulp fiction books about the lost cities of Mars. Not even approaching the size of the ancient Greek wonder of the world, but it feels like that when you see it up close or looming over the city. Immense. Epic.

And frightening, if you believe the rumors about what's going on inside.

You should.

It lies within the southern walled district of the city, near the Gates of Eternity. When the Saur came through, they passed right by and the temple had nothing to do with them as though some truce had been arranged in advance through dark meetings late in the night or dark arts centering around seeing stones and crystals that reach across vast distances for viewing and communication. Either way, when the geckos came marching through, the temple's entire force was out in full and surrounding the temple.

Holy warriors with merciless sneers.

Quiet guardians deciding who lives and who dies.

Saffron-robed monks with bloody wrapped fists willing to fight to the death for their singing god.

Worshippers seeking desperate salvation from death and damnation and willing to do any evil to avoid the judgments.

We got a look at all that going on in the weeks and days that led up to Stranglehold, and we realized we didn't have enough ammo to deal with them, the Temple of Pan, if they decided to throw in with one or the other factions and go to war against us as we suddenly smashed their city. We aren't sure what their relationship with the wizards in the market is, but we suspect, or at least I do from my intel gathering on the ground, that there is some competition between the two groups. No love, surely, and much mistrust and suspicion abounds. The merchants and denizens of the market did not like the Pan worshippers who flocked to the city from across the Ruin to participate in strange and dark ceremonies that made the nights seem hot and uneasy.

A dark heaviness fell over the city during the festivals that came and went with no rhyme or reason.

"Cultists," the people of the market would hiss in whatever language I was listening in on with. Then invariably they'd spit in the dust and make some sign with their hands as though indicating they wanted nothing to do with that bunch over there in the "new temple."

Side note: the *new temple* is two hundred years old. But in recent years it's become much more active, much more secretive, and almost everyone senses something "unclean" going on over there, as I would often overhear.

When I asked Amira, over my third cup of coffee one breezy afternoon—Hi, Talker here. Have we met? I enjoy coffee—what the temple was all about, all she could tell me was, "We are new to the city. My father, sister, and myself have come from the Sorrab and so what is known of this city is still new to us. But I can tell you this…"

She leaned forward and placed a cool and slender hand atop mine, and I felt… something I needed in that. She's like her sister, with an innate raw sexuality that emits from her like some perfume that makes the desert smell better, but she is more earnest, honest-seeming, as opposed to her sister's use of the trait as tawdry marketing for the coffee shop.

"But I must tell you this, Talk-ir," she continued with a seriousness I found intoxicating. "As strangers in many cities, we have learned to feel the temperatures of the locals. That is how we learn to survive in a new place once again…"

Her voice is dark and husky, rich with secrets I want to know.

So, she has a story. Oh, help me… here I go again. On my own. Another Autumn? Or the dead girl from Portugon who thought I'd be her savior. Maybe it's best I just…

"… they are worried about the Temple of Pan, Talk-ir. The citizens of Sûstagul do not like that place at all, or the smiling priest least of it. They think there is great evil there, Talk-ir. It is none of our business here in the shop, but it is noted, and we hope for the best. Such evil… never ends well for people like us."

So, reason number one as far as the command team was concerned for wasting the high priest in the early moments of the battle was that we could not deal with the temple warrior priests, of which there are two kinds we have observed. Plus the followers who dress in saffron robes and sleep all through the district, and even sometimes in the necropolis, and attend the ceremonies that go on at the temple. There are literally thousands of these worshippers surrounding the temple at dawn, and again in the evening when the great brass bells ring and incense fills the air through the night, drifting off over the walls and into the desert wastes.

But… ominous note here… there are few *children* observed among the throngs. And fewer the more you look every day. The cute one with the curly hair you noticed the day before, held by a mother whose eyes are wild with the ecstasy of the priests' slaughtering of goats and sprinkling over a desperate throng chanting holy texts and sounding like some important football crowd at the game on which the entire season was riding… you look the next day just to confirm your suspicions and the child, who was singular, is missing. But the mother… she is alone with that same seeking-salvation look in her eyes, weeping tears of joy as the high priest slaughters more goats and thunders out his answers to the holy chanting.

It's like some opera. Some dark opera with a chorus thousands strong that makes you feel uncomfortable in the hearing and haunts your sleep. You wake through the night swearing you're hearing it out there in the Ranger "nomad" camp. But it's only the moaning wind crossing the desert night. Going from here to there.

There is an otherness to the whole thing. And you wish… you wish this wasn't part of the story.

So, as the sergeant major put it during the run-up to the operation, "We deal that high priest fellow out there first thing and the temple goes into chaos and maybe that buys us a few hours to consolidate on the objective, get the Legion in here for crowd control to deal with all them followers, and get on those walls and let them orcs *know* we got the walls, and if they come, we'll fling 'em off with cut throats and gut shot just to prove what bastards we are."

Chief Rapp concurred with the wasting of the high priest.

"Organizations like that—cults—always gonna have second- and third-in-commands looking to promote themselves first opportunity," said the chief in his Mississippi Mud matter-of-fact accent. "They'll stall any kinda involvement in what's goin' down at Market and Dockside in order not to lose control of the people under their sway. If we could get PFC Talker in there, we might find out what the politics are, exactly. Then see if we can divide 'em up by smoking the priest and paying attention to who steps up to grab the horns next. We don't like the way it goes, the snipers put the hit on that one too. We need the guy who's gonna use the fear to get those followers into the temple and under his total control. The guy who's gonna use them to put his competitors down pretty quick. Accuse them of that bad juju that caused the death of the Old Boss. The snipers do it fast, staying down, that's important—no one from this age knows what a gunshot wound to the head is, so to them it's a sign from their god—and the opportunists will use that 'cause all they smell is the vacuum power creates and their desire to fill it with themselves."

PFC Talker did go in. Twice as a scholar, I did. Once with the ring on even. It's madness in there and it makes no sense. But yeah, something dark is going on in there and I'll get to all that when I explain point number two of why Thor needed to dome the high priest as Stranglehold went down.

Technically he didn't *need* to dome the "grand poo-bah"—sergeant major word he'd used extensively during training walkthroughs for the pump—but when I asked him about the shot later Thor simply said, "Point of professional pride, Talker. I could make that head shot and I needed to. For me. Always train your skills to the razor's edge and then don't be afraid to go there when it's real-deal time. Otherwise, how do you even know if you got 'em? Paper target and steel is one thing. A priest flinging goat blood and gyrating like a wacky wild inflatable fun guy at some car lot in winds coming off the ocean just after first light… It ain't what separates the pros from the hobbyists, Talker. It's what artists do when they make art and stuff. It's something more."

Art. Please explain, savage warrior poet.

"One time I was on leave, and I met this chick who made pottery. That was my time, Talker."

I didn't understand what he meant at first.

"Like you in Portugon," he clarified.

Then he said nothing, and I knew he knew about what had happened at the Purple Abyss and the girl the city guards found in the mud flats. The time I almost walked away from my brothers. From the Rangers who'd led me to join them and become one. The time I was most ashamed of. Am most ashamed of.

She deserved better.

"I'd just gotten back from South Am doing some stuff no one knows about," Thor continued. "Other wars that don't get the press some do because the power brokers are getting some action on the back end, never mind dead Rangers. Bad wars, man. I took thirty days and went to surf out in California. I was at a crossroads. There were big swells and lots of rain that year. Met this girl named Coco in a college. She majored in pottery, and we hung for a while. One night, late, like when you can only hear the trains and dogs, I asked her what made art... *art*. I was at that crossroads, Talker. The one where the road goes off in another direction. One you start thinking about taking. She was silent for a long time as we lay there and then she told me this...

"*Art is the thing you have to get right first time out. You have to because you only get one shot with each piece. No one gives a book or a movie a second chance. Every piece I throw... it's got to be the best because I know I'm only going to get one chance to make it. One chance for the observer to see it and... feel something.*

"I asked her, how do you do that? How do you make great art in one go. One pass. One shot. She told me, *I put everything into it no matter what it is. Big or small. I throw my heart over the bar, and I follow it right into the piece. I put me into it.*"

And *I* asked... because you're wondering what this has to do with Sergeant Thor doming some high priest ten thousand years later in a world gone all monsters and magic on the red sandstone steps of a Temple of Evil right in the middle of our operation... well, I asked that. I asked what this had to do with the situation here. Now.

He laughed in the darkness as we talked around his fire. We were waiting to go to the walls. No one would sleep tonight. Or sleep well.

Brumm and Kurtz were dead at the Gates of Eternity.

"I liked her a lot, Talker. She was a cool chick. Whole scene there, whole time in the bars and going to her friends' hippy art shows and drinking coffee and beers in the late night and just talking under lights in weird places, whole time I'd been thinking in the days leading up to that late-night lesson she was giving me, that maybe... maybe I could make art there in Long Beach and just... become something else, y'know? But then I realized everything she was saying about *putting you into it*, all of it, betting the whole house on your talent, skills, and what you're putting into it, that was being a warrior. For me. I told her that. And after, we lay there in the dark for a long time and she cried for a little while and I asked her why."

He paused. Going back to that honest moment in the dark. Sidra and I had those.

I waited silently. Because Thor, this dude can tell a story. We don't have Netflix here in the Ruin. Listening to Thor is about as close to the movies as you're gonna get.

And if I remember movies at the end... Thor's stories are a whole lot better. If I ever get back, I'm going to Hollywood and I'm gonna sell the script for *Rangers in the Ruin*. Any studio who picks it up will print money and I'll just buy a Ferrari and drive from coffeehouse to coffeehouse.

But I have said that before. Dare to dream, Talker.

"She said she was crying because she knew I was leaving," answered Thor. "That I had to go back to my art. War. After a while she fell asleep and I left as the sun was coming up and the fog lay over everything like some blanket that tells you it'll be okay wherever you're going to next. And that it will cover up the traces of the fact that you were ever there."

Sergeant Thor and I sat there for a moment as I tried to digest it all. Then he said, "I wonder whatever happened to her."

I don't know, man. That was all ten thousand years ago. Even though it only seems like yesterday. Some days I feel older than I should be. Tanner says that's common for being a Ranger and half the reason he screws up and gets busted is just to remind them all he's only twenty-four. He's just a kid.

But I think it's something more than that. We are older. Ten thousand years was a long time ago.

Or maybe Tanner's just right. Soldiers live and wonder why.

Reason number two for smoking the high priest came with the worship of Pan itself. The religion of Pan doesn't seem to be local to the desert port. In fact, the desert port of Sûstagul, because it was once the primary port of the Imperial Saur when their empire stretched over most of the known Ruin, is filled with many strange chimeric statues, cracked, broken in half, missing noses or arms or even heads here and there, throughout the dry dusty city streets of the city and the port.

Forgotten relics of lost ages that still make the locals uneasy. It's as if… even though they are there, the locals prefer not to see them. For reasons.

I know the feeling.

These statues often front old buildings, buildings that might have once been temples but are now something else. They look strangely like the pharaohs and deities of the ancient Egyptian pantheon. They can even be found in small alleys or out-of-the-way corners one never goes unless they make a wrong turn thinking they were getting a shortcut and instead come face to face with some serene half-Saur half-cat god looming in the darkness of the old side street.

Staring at you.

Around them, I have always had the vague feeling I was being watched.

Furthermore, in such a wild crossroads city like Sûstagul, different than all the Cites of Men out there clinging to the edges of the Great Inner Sea, you would think these statues would have been torn down or even defaced as new gods inevitably came and the city changed hands, whether from the Saur or the various empires of men and elves that have come and gone for ten thousand years in the Ruin.

You'd think.

Sûstagul was once home to pirate kings and the hangout of that famous male medusa pirate that Vandahar told us about during the intel gathering for the hit on the dragon. So… it's seen a lot of *come and go*. And though these statues are clearly Saurian in nature, no one has seen fit, or felt brave enough, to remove them. The chimeras of hawk, human, lion, asp, cat, are always there, everywhere if you look close in this city. But so are the Saurian scales, claws, and lizard eyes staring out from behind the animal humanoid fusions carved in granite. Most of them with Egyptian kilts, sandals, staffs, and hooks of office. Scarabs and diadems of power. They are clearly ancient pharaohs of the Saur, or even the gods of the pharaohs themselves.

They are unsettling. And best unseen if the mind can do you a solid and pretend they're not there.

The scribes, though, know less than they wish to, and during my time with them I heard strange myths and sometimes clues about the origins of the Saur going back to even the times before the Great Dark Age just after we jumped forward ten thousand years to avoid the nanoplague and its destruction of everything we knew.

Cocos and Sidras.

Vandahar only speaks of these subjects when I query him on them. "Their ways are too corrupt, young Talker. And when one looks close enough at the Ruin, one can see the claws of the Saur in the very foundations themselves. I wish it were not so, but it is. And it's best to know less of the ways of the Saur... for to know more has trapped better wizards than myself, and many have gone down into their midnight tombs, never to return."

But this part of the account is not about the Saur. This is about the Children of Pan, as they call themselves. The intel I was able to develop is that the Children are all over the Med... I mean Great Inner Sea. You'll find them in every port, though given time, they will wear out their welcome and be persecuted, driven out from those cities.

And for good reason apparently.

Their ceremonies involve child sacrifice in exchange for promises of immortality. This becomes a problem wherever they go, not surprisingly. As you've been reading this account, you've probably figured out there are still more monsters out there beyond the limits and edges of the civilization the Ruin calls the Cities of Men. And so, in any human civ here in the Ruin, it's all hands on deck. Including children. They contribute to the very survival of any settlement, village, or city. They *are* the survival of the group, in a forward-looking sense. Valued and protected in the Cities of Men.

So if a religion comes along, starting under the guise of being about music and greeting the dawn of a new day for favor and luck with crops and rain, or against war and disease, and after a while the little children start to go missing... well... it's not too long before it's pitchforks and torches in all the cities from Accadios to Portugon.

It's said to be allowed in Caspia, according to Vanda-har. But as he says, "That nation of witches will get up to any abomination if there's some power to be gained with their sugars and syrups. They seek fellowship with Azmod the Fiend himself."

Their ceremony began that morning of our surprise attack, with all of its wild ecstasy of goats' blood offerings at dawn, strange and haunting music coming from the temple deeps within, and disembodied flutes calling the worshippers to an eternal night of the soul if they would but just surrender… everything.

I'd previously observed the ceremony from afar, and even on a couple of days saw it up close dressed as a follower, moving among the dazed crowds gassed by something narcotic, sensing the priests' spells in the air to hypnotize, coerce, and weaken the will. Fortunately I had modified my psionics on the fly as their dark sorceries came for me and my will, using Vandahar's *blind seeing* trick, the one I'd used to deceive the medusa back at Tarragon. It provided some defense. But even so I still felt the call of the thing known as Pan.

Later, I'd understand it wasn't just a call. Later I'd understand I'd picked up valuable intel as the chants drummed on and the flutes battered my mind. As the priests prayed and cast their spells. Later… I'd understand. And since the account of what happened to us in the Ruin is my own little AAR, After-Action Review of Talker's actions in review… then allow me to fess up.

I failed there. I'd gotten a taste of the intel we needed for what happened next. I just hadn't recognized it.

Deep within the commander's fortress tower, just moments before taking the shot, Sergeant Thor made last-second adjustments to the scope. To windage and elevation.

The priest came running out of the temple, holding the head of a goat. Carrying the hasty mummy of that night's child.

It was hard to sense, to feel, the wind there in the back of the room of the old tower.

The spotter cross-checked the black book the snipers kept during their observations of goings-on with the target. Comings and goings. Times. Personalities to note. Wind and temperature shifts at the shooting moment.

Thirty seconds to go and the priest cast the goat head into the crowd, clutching the mummy to his bare chest like he was cradling that dead child.

Thor felt the wind, watched the small scrap of cloth they'd placed near the window. Saw it pick up in the breeze. Saw it begin to flutter.

A stronger breeze.

At ten seconds he adjusted windage one last time.

The spotter confirmed the shot and as the priest held the dead mummified child high, turning toward the grand red sandstone entrance to the temple, beckoning to the thing within that the rites and offerings had been made, he lowered his head, back to the crowd.

Perfect sight picture.

Thor fired and blew out the front of his skull, sending the contents within over the steps of the great temple.

As the crowd began to grow silent at first in disbelief at what had just happened, the spotter whispered the confirmation of the kill, and everyone held their breath.

Then the crowd, in ones and twos, groups and clusters, began to scream in disbelief.

They had been rejected.

Their faith was not enough.

Worried priests cast eyes at one another. Temple warriors' leather-gloved hands went to the hilts of their swords. Monks began to slash and cut themselves with small flint knives, sending blood all over their saffron robes, whirling in anger and rage, attempting to reverse time by their fury. Or create a whirlwind that would see the destruction of everything in the city with fire, rage, and total chaos.

Then the temple began to shake.

Stones exploded outward from the fat scalloped multi-ton bloody sandstone blocks. Spraying out into the crowd and crushing some.

The Rangers held their breath.

"What the..." muttered Thor when the thing called Pan stormed from the massive, cracked front of the grand temple.

CHAPTER TWENTY-ONE

THE thing called Pan was a satyr. Except a giant and bigger than any troll or war ogre we'd faced yet. It wasn't Cloodmoor big. But it was hill giant big, just like the one Brumm had smoked with the Carl G back in the river when we first got here and the orcs pushed us and overran the weapons team.

It was a giant goat-legged biped with a hairy torso and the face of a horned leering devil. With goat horns that twisted and curled. It came out on the main temple steps, huge hooves crashing against the stone and sending up sparks as it danced first forward and then side to side like some impossible animatron that should never be able to do anything remotely like that.

It leered around at the crowd, then searched the roof-tops and taller buildings in the district. Scanning for who had dared disturb its tribute. Its pomp. Its circumstance.

The worship it so craved and demanded.

The Pan thing wore scale mail short pants made of thousands of bronze coins punched and linked together. Two huge bracers of gold grasped its brawny forearms, limbs that hung and swung like the arms of some circus gorilla capering for the circus tent crowd. In one hand it held a massive silver flute, in the other a rough circular shield the size of a small school bus. On the face of the shield was painted a green-eyed and leering hydra from some elder age of Titans.

Or what did they call them here in the Ruin? The Eld?

I still wonder if this Pan thing was one of them. The Eld. Hiding out after whatever in the Ruin, Vandahar and his clan, had wiped them out. Or fought them to a standstill. *The Old Agreements* the wizard had declared Cloodmoor must abide by when we first met him on the other side of the river. After the Cloodmoor Mile.

My quads still feel that one a year later.

The Rangers gave various utterances of disbelief at the sudden turn of events, swearing and ready to lay some hate on command. Thor held them as he weighed the new development. What was happening was happening because none of the intel indicated we had a bigger player involved than the now-dead formerly very powerful high priest.

Thank you me for failing to detect the presence of the Pan thing. The flutes and their otherworldly call had been clear indicators that something bigger was lurking within the battlespace.

But who would have guessed it was a minor god? And that it was pissed we'd just whacked its high priest?

If the Rangers were bothered by that, it didn't show. They were ready to waste it regardless of its status within the divine order.

Ranger snipers gonna Yahtzee.

As I have said, up to this point Stranglehold had involved selecting for the most ambitious high priest, via sniper fire, who would then turtle the temple populace and keep them out of things while we got our kill on. On the other side of it all, we'd deal with them from a position of power. Indications indicated... there is no more military planning and intel phrase than that one... or so I imagine in my limited experience... but conditions, let's say it that way... *conditions* indicated the Temple of Pan wanted no part of anything other than to run their death cult and be left alone.

We were gonna leave them alone. But we'd kill anyone they could ally with and then burn them out once the walls were secure and the orcs had gotten the message and disappeared off to some other side of the Desert of Black Sleep.

Now the spotter was on the comm with the smaj, letting him know what was going on with the plan. Which was basically, the plan was trainwrecked and now we had to deal with the actual god of the temple itself.

Kennedy would note later that it might not have been the god Pan, the thing the worshippers venerated as some kind of divine being, and that instead it might have been merely an avatar of that being, or just some minor powerful servant who ran things. But the Rangers were happy to accept the Pan thing was a god, after the battle, because they'd killed it and they thought that was pretty cool.

"Thor smoked some god. That was pretty cool," a Ranger said in the most understated way. As in, *Hear that new song from so and so? It's cool.* I heard that while picking up MREs in the dark by ChemLight for the section after the battle. After the AAR. As night fell and fires still burned out of control and I tried not to think about what had happened at the Gates of Eternity.

And tried not to think of the djinn bottle in my assault pack and what it could do for me.

As chaos began to reign among the worshippers below, the Pan thing screeched and howled horribly, making a pantomime show of stunned disbelief as it stared down and pointed with one of its massive, crooked, dirty, hairy fingers at the dead high priest on the temple steps. Brains blown out courtesy of Sergeant Thor.

That'll teach ya to strangle and mummify children so you can fleece their parents.

"Say again, Reaper," barked the sergeant major over the chaos of battle at the Gates of Death. He had problems of his own right at that moment. The Guzzim Hazadi were harassing as the other legion, the one that had stayed aboard the war galleys and maintained course for the primary insertion point on the nearby beach, came ashore and marched at the double for the Gates of Death while orc raiding parties made sorties close in and fired volleys of arrows. The sergeant major needed to hold the gates open and keep the desert orcs back until the legion was through. Mortar teams were now switching to primaries to hold the gates and ominous talk of *final protective fire* was beginning to be discussed.

As a non-infantryman who'd had to develop all his CQB in real time with the Rangers here in the Ruin, Tanner had explained *final protective fire* to me. It was the infantry version of *danger close* when calling for fire. Or, as Tanner put it, "If you hear that go out on the net from command, to 'fire the FPF'... then you know for damn sure things have gone to hell in a handbasket and you better be right with God."

But we weren't there yet. The sergeant major was moving among the Rangers, walking through arrow fire like he couldn't be hit and blazing away with his sidearm.

One of the mortarmen told me later he heard the sergeant major mutter after blowing an orc off a camel at close range, "It's Texas wherever I set my boot, and you bastards are gonna find out it's the Alamo if I get pushed. You want it… come get some."

Now the orcs who rode in close to fire at the mortar teams died in heaps, many of them crushed by their camels. Bodies worked by good and steady marksmanship as the Rangers determined to hold the gates until the legion hustled through.

"We got Pan Actual in play, Doghouse," updated Thor's spotter as the scene began to get wild in the temple.

One of the snipers was cursing whoever decided they didn't need to lug in a Carl to hold the old fort.

"You always need a goose, man. If just for GP."

At about that moment the Pan thing spotted the snipers in the tower, and no one knows how it did so. It just sensed them. Its huge ugly nostrils scenting the wind and finding them among the towers of the old fortress. Smelling them in their hides. Its cruel eyes scanned the crumbling battlements and dark eye-socket windows no living being had looked out from over the hundred years since the Ninth Accadion Legion had disappeared into the desert never to return. Then it pointed that massive, crooked, dirty, hairy finger, and gave a blood-curdling war cry that shattered the ear drums of many of the worshippers who'd fallen to their bellies and were crawling toward it, seeking to touch its very being.

"Reaper," said the sergeant major with some difficulty as he performed a one-handed reload on my Glock while orc camels thundered across the sands, hooves drumming, their riders firing arrows close and dangerous. "You tellin' me you got some kinda low-level *god* comin' out to play bad guy against you all at the fort?"

Silence.

The Pan thing was busy playing its flute now, and everyone in the sniper positions was starting to feel hotter than they ever had in any desert they'd ever served in. Not on-fire hot. Dry. Dry like the moisture was being sucked right out of their skin. They began to itch. They stopped sweating almost instantly.

Some were already shucking out of their armor as it became unbearable to wear. Priests were running among the people, pointing toward the fortress. Temple warriors were forming small squads to move quickly for the wall and old gate that separated the fortress from the temple. Monks ran like dancers, twirling, flinging blood, knives out, crazed singing, as they sought the murderer of their deity.

"Affirmative on god, Doghouse. No idea if major or minor but we are starting to feel it may be making some kind of magical attack against us."

The sergeant major came back a moment later.

"Reaper… smoke it regardless. I got things to do here. Doghouse out."

Thor heard the command to engage and fired the massive anti-materiel rifle again at the twisted, leering giant whose grotesque bulbous eyes fluttered as he trilled the flute. The music, according to the snipers, was like being hit by some sonic weapon DARPA had sold to the Third World to control crowds. The kind of weapon that caused your skin to sizzle, but with sound. The Pan thing, it moved quickly for being so large, jerked at the last second, and Thor's shot, aiming for the head, nailed it right in the shoulder instead, blowing out chunks of hairy flesh and blood across the high temple wall. The shoulder was connected to the arm holding the shield the size of a school bus.

And still the perverse beast continued to play the damn flute, sending out waves of pain and heat, and shortly calling new magics to aid it.

Thor fired again and the Pan thing, quick as lightning, jerked the shield up even with its wounded arm, blocking with the shield, and rewarding the soundscape with a loud *DWAAAANG* that resonated over the screaming temple crowd now spiraling out of control and threatening to spill out into the streets where we were fighting in Market. Torches were springing to life as much as the wailing and gnashing of teeth.

"No penetration," shouted the spotter on Thor's next shot. Other snipers were beginning to reposition to take out the giant thing now looming over the walls of the temple district, leering at them and furiously playing its mad silver flute.

As we advanced through Market, I heard the flute above the sounds of the fighting we were engaged in by then. And also, the savage disconcerting cries of the thing as it roared out things we couldn't understand. Things that drove the guardians of the temple into action, and the worshippers into violent ecstasy that seemed a madness all its own. But by that time the two-forty was working and we had, like the smaj, problems of our own to be concerned about.

Within a minute, shots from the snipers were disintegrating in midair. The three-oh-eight rounds and fifty-cals the snipers used were suddenly unable to hit the huge, twisted satyr. Spotters were calling "no joy" and "failure to penetrate." Snipers swore and declared they weren't even getting started as they reached for their special rounds. Thor was rapid-firing into the shield, but it was clear the

Pan thing had begun to employ strange magics against the sniper rounds used against it.

For instance, and I collected this very quickly from the snipers… sometimes small, strange ghosts would suddenly appear right in front of the rounds streaking toward target… and the specialized munitions would explode in ghostly bony sprays, the bullet *disappearing from the prime material plane* as Kennedy would explain to us later.

In other words… the Pan thing was summoning negative plane spirits to intercept incoming sniper rounds and destroy them. Contact with that plane caused objects to explode.

"Matter, meet anti-matter," muttered Kennedy. "Poof. Be glad, it could have set off some kinda massive nuclear explosion if you listen to some physicists. But then again, those guys are all dead ten thousand years ago, so who knows. Maybe the game got it right. Maybe the whole *place* is my game."

Or, as the smaj summed it up during the AAR… "Damn thing threw up a magical air defense system. That's what that is."

But *Magical Air Defense Artillery from Negative Plane Spirit World…* man the Ruin is weird… wasn't all the Pan thing could do. It cast more spells using the notes and songs of its flute. Or so we theorize.

That's a thing here—flute magic—and we now know it's an attack. Next time something like this tries this schtick on us we will *kill it better*.

Shimmering light sprays began to cross the field of vision between the snipers and the minor god they were trying to put rounds-on-target in. The snipers were losing the ability to acquire as the lights and sounds messed with their ears and eyes. When shots did get through the ghostly air defense system, the massive shield attracted the rounds and they rang out with that same metallic *DWAAAANG* on impact.

The snipers' mouths were getting cottony as all the moisture left their bodies. Their heart rates were increasing. Some were beginning to feel sick. The air was getting heavy and thick and felt like, according to one of them, like you were stuck in the exact concussive moment after a Carl G fires.

That's not good.

And still, that wasn't all the twisted giant satyr could do. The music of the Pan thing, the silver flute it was playing, danced and shrieked out notes like some mad Hammond B3 organ gyrating in the final passages of some strange acid rock band's final psychedelic performance of the night.

The snipers' heads were pounding, and they were losing the ability to communicate.

"I knew what I wanted to say," said one. "I just couldn't think of how to make the words. And as soon as I had that thought… I thought… what if I can't fire… and then I forgot *what* it was I was gonna fire. I knew the word: *rifle*. But I couldn't… *think* it at that moment. The music was everything. It was everywhere. And it always would be until it was the only thing. Seriously messed up, Talker. It was pure hell, man. I mean not Ranger school bad… but pretty bad. Close. But not that bad. No way."

Thor got out of his hide, shirtless and sweating, muscles ripped, set *Mjölnir* down, crossed the room to his assault pack, stumbling as he did so, and pulled out his smartphone and selected some song to play over his OpsCore headset.

"Which song?" I asked when Thor told me all this. Because that's what's important here. Knowing what song Thor was listening to when he wasted a demi-god. That's information we need in the record. It's definitely not just because Talker must know.

"Any song. I just needed to block out the noise that thing was making with its flute. It wasn't just driving me mad, Talker, it was like my brain had turned into a merry-go-round and it was spinning apart. I was stumbling, I'd lost my equilibrium, and I couldn't even remember my own name. But something told me if I could block out the sound… then maybe we could do something about that bad boy."

Which song? I asked again. Because, come on.

"Beach Boys at first. 'Good Vibrations.' Reminded me of surfing and I'd been playing it every night when I went down to the beach to watch the waves. Liked that one a lot. But then it went on to this Cream song I got off one of the scouts. 'Tales of Brave Ulysses.' Weird… that made what happened next feel… epic. Even to me. I know, I got this reputation for being—and I say this with no ego, Talker—for being *a legend,* whatever the hell that means. But that song was… it made it all feel… like I *was,* man. I went out there to kill that thing, maybe not like a legend, but at least like some… hero. And I knew it. And it's all I want now. Those kinds of experiences. I ain't long for this, man. What happened out there… cursed me… in a way like Sims, but different. I'm different now. I feel like I'm gone already. But I'll see this through. Then… gotta bounce. Gotta find that girl in the song."

"So what happened?" I asked to get him back on track.

"Tried to reacquire with my rifle, once my brain stopped spinning, but the lights out there were blinding me. They weren't sound, but you could *see* the sound and it was the weirdest thing I've ever… seen. But for the moment, at least the music blocked out most of the flute and I could do something. I had action, Talker. Dumped another mag on that thing anyway but still no penetration. And I could tell, it wasn't gonna work."

"So what'd you do?"

What happened next is the stuff of legends. Legend. It's what makes Sergeant Thor… Sergeant Thor.

"Grabbed that chunk of steel I'd been using for hand-to-hand and went in to kill it up close and personal. That was the only thing I could see that was gonna get it done. Otherwise, it was gonna cook our brains."

CHAPTER TWENTY-TWO

I added this to the account later. After I was able to interview all involved and get a clear picture of what happened in the battle with the Pan thing. At the time, Thor just told me *I took the Bastard and went out to kill it.* Then added, "Got it done and got outta there. Job done. Back on sniper support."

That was the really bad Cliff Notes version of the epic takedown that followed what happened as the minor god tried to use a magical death flute to lay the smackdown on the Ranger snipers holding the old haunted Legion fortress.

A lot had happened after that moment when he grabbed his bastard sword—he calls it *the Bastard*—and ran for the temple to engage the giant demon god.

A bastard sword. What's a bastard sword as opposed to a long sword or even the massive German *Zweihänder*? It's a sword of indeterminate, in nature, design, and capable of multi-role use. Meaning it can be used one-handed, off-handed, or even two-handed to go all Conan the Barbarian.

It's a brutal chunk of steel. I prefer the light dance of *Coldfire* to the Bastard's heft and volume, which feels like much more than it should. And believe me I've gotten jacked since I entered the Ruin. Humping the two-forty in Ranger school, and everything along the way on foot, remember, and this catches me by surprise every now and again sometimes… but we haven't traveled by vehicle for over a year and a half now. We've walked everywhere.

Even as Rangers, where we came from, vehicles are standard for every day. You get cut walking everywhere like we didn't where we came from.

Well, we did get that one-day galley ride before we got sucked into North Africa, or the Atlantean Rift, by the awesome magical powers of the dead medusa queen's also-deceased djinn. But other than that, it's all been by foot to get anywhere.

The Bastard, as opposed to *Coldfire,* which feels more like an elegant and deftly balanced weapon, is brutal and mean and it ain't pretty. *Coldfire* catches the light and turns it cold. Sometimes it glows faintly, ghostly blue, and I can't figure out why. The Bastard feels like some cartoon bruiser's baseball bat. Thor wields it like it's as light as a feather though. Until it connects. Then it just crushes the target. Hard. Thor, or the magic inside? It *is* magical. But that's all we know. And it's not light, he's just that swole. You can feel the wind displace when he swings it around his back and comes at the target, putting all of its relativistic weight into a savage chop or a brutal slash.

Since the citadel, we've been training three times a week with our pickups. The dwarves have become our weapon masters. They've forgotten more about weapons combat of all kinds, with any weapon, than we'll probably ever know. You have to be honest about these things. The dwarves live and breathe weapons all day long. They carry them when they do anything. There is never a time when they don't have at least three on them.

Having said that, many Rangers told the dwarves to hold their beer, which said dwarves will gladly do, and accepted the challenge to master their pickups at the pro level. But that's just Ranger standard. They know their lives depend on their weapons. A Ranger will master his carbine, sidearm, holdout, various knives, feet and fists, teeth and head, elbows, and anything else he can get his hands on.

There are no second prizes in a fight. The Rangers understand that, and as they will say at any time during any endeavor... they are *in it to win it.*

So Thor went down through the haunted old fortress as fast as he could, running through the shafts of blood-red light that filtered into the gloom through the cracks and rents in the falling-apart old pile. He made the ground floor, crossed into the necropolis beyond the rotting walls, and raced for the old gate that led into the temple district.

The pandemonium in the temple was swelling, and it was like running toward some mad rock concert that had turned into a mass casualty event.

At this point I asked Sergeant Thor to tell me, and this was later and that's why I've gone back in and added this to the account, what exactly happened as he fought the Pan god in the temple district.

These are his words, and I have faithfully transcribed them.

"First group I met were temple warriors coming out in a fire team of four. Two guys with swords. One hammer. One spear. They see me coming and I charge to engage because the ground I'm on is not good. Lotsa open graves. Lotsa shifted and unstable dirt. Bad footing for a fight even if the odds are good, and already they ain't. This is not where I want to fight."

Grave-robbing is big business in Sûstagul. We have no idea why. Vandahar has unrhetorically commented, using our own lingo: "You don't want to know." Then makes his eyes wide and keeps moving. Some subjects bother him and it's interesting to note his responses. Necromancy is one.

Back to Thor's account.

"Spear guy is lighter, lighter armored than the rest that is, and he runs with the spear at me as the others get ready to flank. Spear guy stops short and thrusts with the spear that's got a hook below the point. I spin to avoid the thrust, start swinging as I come around, and aim the Bastard high. I catch him in the side of the head when I finish the swing and connect."

"Did it come off?" I ask, imagining a lopped head flying away like in some movie.

As I said, we know the Bastard is magical, we just don't know what, exactly, it does. It has an edge, but not a sharp one, and despite all sharpening attempts, it defies the effort to make it any keener. Thor took it off a psycho elf back in the desert fortress at the top of the pass. It was unlike any of their other weapons and the wielder seemed to be one of their elite warriors. After a few swings, Thor decided to keep it and has been working with it ever since.

"Negative on the decap, Talker," answers Thor. As in *negative on the decapitation* I have envisioned.

"Cut from his jaw up through the top of the skull. He went crashing over into a grave and his spear hung there for a second. I grabbed it and flung it at one of them. One of the sword guys. Missed but made him duck. I'm worried about breathing too hard but right there I'm not even feeling winded as it gets going in earnest. Hammer guy comes in, raises it up to crush my skull, and I throw the Bastard up to block and disarm with a sweep just like Max showed me. That executes and I hear the guy's wrists break, both of them, as he tries to hold on to his hammer. He steps back looking at them… his wrists."

"Is he a human?" I ask. Details.

"Yeah. Same as we spotted on the temple grounds. Hard boys just like the mercenaries over in the market. Pros with scars and tattoos. I follow the disarm with a thrust and run the Bastard right under his breastplate, getting low and pushing upward as I insert the tip of the blade. Comes out his back and at that moment I'm thinking, *Hell, hope this thing doesn't get stuck.* I was worried about that, so I take time to put my knee in his chest and yank the blade back like I'm ripping a pull start on an outboard motor. Blade comes out fine. But I'll tell you this… I'm freaking out because there are two guys ready to do me in and I can't hear them through the music. I have no idea where they are right at that moment. I need to hear, but I can't. Because of the Pan god music.

"But again, I ain't winded. And everything feels… not *slow*, but… but perfect. Like everything we've learned in order to fight this way… it's all coming together, man. It's fun. It's perfect and I'm enjoying it."

Four-on-one combat with sharp sticks for keeps is *fun*. Noted. I have not experienced it that way. Every fight for me has felt oddly lucky that it even swung my way. Four-to-one odds feels… very *unlucky*.

"Both swords are charging me when I get my head up and back in the battle. Hammer is gurgling on the ground, but still on his knees looking at me, or up at the sky, as blood runs out of his mouth in torrents. He's done. I take a wild swing with the Bastard and bat away the first sword to take a cut at me. That guy parries and spins, then down-chops where I was. I shuffle back, keeping my left boot on the ground and allowing that to find the terrain. I take one hand off the Bastard and shove dying Hammer Guy into the path of his friend's sword. That guy's blade connects and sinks into his buddy. It didn't get stuck, but it took a bad bounce on the guy's armor and that jammed that dude's chi for a second. Since I was in the guard position, I could have lunged on him, but the other sword comes in on my right and I trade two blows with him and then get serious as I strike right at his hand with the Bastard. I think he lost some fingers on my cheap shot, then he shouted, stepping back, and fell into an open grave. After he crawled out, with one hand after the battle, I bashed his skull in with the hammer. But now the other sword guy has gotten it together from the bad bounce off his buddy's armor and he starts making sweeping cuts, advancing, and stamping the ground trying to drive me back. I'm lighter because I don't have all the gear they do and so I stay away from his cuts, then see an opening too small to make a cut and just ram into him with my shoulder. I'm bigger. I knock him down into a pile of dirt and then jam the edge of the blade up, right into his throat because he had nothing guarding it. I push hard and I think it's a decap, but not the head flying off kind. I just pushed until the throat disconnected from the head. So… technically I got one, Talker. Then, like I said, I grabbed the hammer off the ground and bashed in the skull of the guy with the missing fingers trying to climb out of the grave."

I think my mouth was hanging open when Thor finished relating his first engagement with pickup weapons.

Hand weapons. It was violent and horrifying in its brutal bluntness. But it was a matter-of-fact account, and when he'd finished that part he simply stated, "Once that was done, I got myself together and ran for the gate to the temple."

That was incredible. But true.

"I made the temple courtyard," he continued, "and everything was chaos. The people, the ordinary people, the worshipper types, they were screaming and crying, running here and there. One guy was repeatedly head-desking himself into a statue of their god near the steps. Like I said, chaos. The troops didn't see me as anything other than some guy with a sword, and they had bigger problems right then. The priests were trying to rally monks and warriors to them. Or some were. One priest was being hacked to death by temple guardians. I didn't know if someone thought he was a threat to the new leadership, or some old score was getting settled as the deck got reshuffled. All I knew was I was going for the Pan thing regardless of everyone's personal drama. So I charged it there on the steps."

Okay, so here's Sergeant Thor standing six-six, and this thing has got to be twelve to fifteen feet high. And he charges it. "Like ya do," as Tanner says about any incredible choice a Ranger would make that no sane or rational normal human being would even consider.

Ranger gonna Ranger.

"What does it do? Does it react? Does it see you coming?" I'm thinking it says the goat-god equivalent of *Puny mortal... how dare you attack my personage. Can't you see I'm a god?*

But it doesn't say that. It runs from the madman charging at it with a chunk of sharp steel.

"It falls back inside the temple, keeping the shield between me and it," says Sergeant Thor. "I hammer the shield, driving it back, and I'm thinking—"

Let Talker interrupt here a bit. Sorry. We've fought a lot of strange things so far but, to my knowledge, we have not fought a god of any kind. So… this is a first. And if it were me, I'd be thinking, *Holy hell, I'm fighting a god. And I'm winning. Achievement Talker. Take that, Sidra. I did make something of my life.* And then I'd go get a coffee as a reward for doing something incredible. But to be fair… I'd get a coffee even for doing something not incredible. I'd just get one no matter what.

Coffee.

But not Thor. He just states, and I quote: "I hammer the shield, driving it back, and I'm thinking, 'If I can get it off balance and knock it on its butt then I can get on top of it and see if it's got a heart I can run the Bastard through.'"

To quote Tanner again: *Like ya do.*

"But that doesn't happen. It gives ground and keeps the shield between us and there's not much I can do about that. It's bigger than me… but here's the thing I've found, Talker. Some dude's big… he probably ain't a good fighter. I am, but I had to force myself to be. People don't want to fight big guys, so big guys have to make sure they don't get by on just being big and not knowing what the hell they're doing in a scramble. Know what I mean?"

I could see the logic of that.

"Now little guys. Nine times outta ten, littlest guy in the squad is the best in the pit. That dude's been getting picked on his entire life. He's a fighter. You gotta watch out for those guys. They know what the hell they're doing because they've been doing it their whole life."

Makes sense.

"So, let's say you're a god. You've probably been getting by on the big-guy-nobody-mess-with-me thing. Last time you've been in a real fight? Never. And then we take into account this whole messed-up cult is based on murdering children… as I think about that now that it's all done and in the dirt… and so of course he fell back into the temple when I came for him. A bully would. A bully's a coward and nothing more. Punch a tough guy and you're gonna find out one of two things: that guy can either fight, or he's just a bully and he'll back down.

"I smelled bully and I knew it as he tried to get away from me, keeping the shield between me and him, still playing that flute as hard as he could because he doesn't know what ear pods and noise cancellation are. Now I got some Mötley Crüe on and it's playing 'Dr. Feelgood' which is one of my workout songs when I want to do hardcore HIITs. Hardcore and fast. And no, I ain't pickin' songs. Phone's on shuffle. So if 'The Piña Colada Song' comes up, and I got that on there and don't ask me why 'cause I ain't telling your account and you can go take a flying leap into a dragon's mouth, but if that song comes up in the playlist, I'm screwed."

Now I really wanna know why he's got "Escape" on there, which is the official name of what most people call "The Piña Colada Song." By Rupert Holmes. I know some things besides languages. But mostly they're random and weird. I've told you I'm an authority on crows. For no reason in particular.

"I make three attacks," continues Thor, "and I'm screaming Viking war cries like I learned to make when I was convincing the battalion I'd converted so I could change my name and get my operator beard because… *chicks*. Okay, so I'm putting everything into it, just hammering this dude's shield and driving him back, and I feel that he's now just trying to get away from me."

I sense Thor's got a plan. But I say nothing because professional log keeper working here, folks. And like I've said, this dude can flat-out tell a tale. This is the best Netflix I've had in a year.

"I let him get away. Let him back off enough and then I pull a frag… we're in the temple now. It's huge in there. There's soft red light and red mist and it seems larger inside than on the outside. Huge columns, smooth and made of that same swirling red sandstone—that stuff's beautiful— and these columns climb up high into the ceiling and I can barely see up there.

"Then these beautiful… let's call 'em harem girls… come running past us in saffron robes as we fight. One falls right between us, and I don't even think about it because I got a red mist vision going and I want this thing dead. I toss the grenade at the thing once it's backed up a good twenty meters, and as it leaves my hand, I see the harem girl in this flimsy saffron silk… *robe*? I don't know what it's called. *Dress*, maybe, but there ain't much of it whatever it is, and she's pretty sweet for the chicks around here. She falls on the stones of the temple floor and I realize she's gonna take the blast from the grenade if I don't get her to cover. I spring for her, grab her, and get between her and the blast as I'm counting seconds too fast. I'm almost to the column when the grenade dets just under the Pan god's shield. I caught some frag but it's just another cut. Just another scar. I get more every day here."

Okay… now Thor's not only fighting one-on-one with a giant mythological satyr god, he's picking up chicks in the middle of it?

Listen. Rangers live fantastic lives of adventure and danger. More than ordinary people will ever know. Even when not in the Ruin. Tip of the spear wherever it's going down around a very dangerous world. Flinging yourself out of aircraft at speed and all that stuff and the high explosives and the gunfire. Very exciting.

Then there's what we do here in the Ruin, and you've read this far.

But then there's Sergeant Thor. He's just that guy. He's a legend. Sometimes, around soldiers… there are such studs. I've read the accounts, seen the plaques. There are some guys that are just… extra.

So I'm *sure* she presses full pouty lips against his as they both weather the blast behind the column in the Temple of Ever Doom or whatever this movie is called.

"You kissed her, didn't you, man?"

Thor makes a face.

"No, man. She slaps me. She's insane with fear. She's hot. Sure. But she's probably been a slave in there and I'm sure that hasn't been a great life. She's got a chance to flee, and she starts hitting me and manages to land a good one on my ear that leaves it ringing. If she'd hit me open-palmed, she would have busted my eardrum and I would have lost my balance. But she doesn't and she breaks free. Blast over, I let her go and she runs shrieking toward the exit. I don't blame her."

Then what happened?

"I come around the column, still got the Bastard in one hand. The god's down on the floor prone. Shield is wrecked and lying in the middle of the floor between the massive columns rising up into the red mist. That flute is lying off to the side. I approach slowly and see the god thing is struggling to get up. I don't think it's dead, but overpressure rung its bell for sure. I shuck my sidearm and start shooting it in the head. Off hand. My aim's not great. Pistol's dancing all over the place but I'm putting rounds in its skull and it's just watching me as I do. Its mouth is working, twisting like it's some kind of deaf person try-ing to speak. That big silver flute is lying off, out of reach, smoking. Or something. I'll tell you about that in a second. Nah... I'll tell you now. It turned into a giant python and slithered away deeper into the temple.

"So I empty the mag in the god's fat skull as I approach and skin the Glock when it's dry. My muscles are shaking. It's bleeding out all over the floor. Its head is down, lying back now. It's dying and I feel all the adrenaline fading from my body because I know it's over now."

For a long moment as he told me this, Sergeant Thor was quiet. Just watching that whole moment again. He's telling the story, performing it even though he doesn't know he does. He's a gifted storyteller. What did they call them in the old times, the medieval times... the Viking age?

Bards. Skalds, I seem to remember. Maybe he's one of those. Maybe it's not even the Ruin revealing. Maybe he just is. But I know if I asked if he was, a skald or a bard, he'd just shake his head and whisper in his deep bass voice...

"No, Talker. Ain't one of those. I'm pure savage, brother."

Kennedy tells me those are called *barbarians* in his game. If Sergeant Thor wanted to be revealed as anything, it would be that. I'm sure of that. And maybe... maybe because he's special without trying to be special... he just *is…* maybe the Ruin must bow to him and accept what he has chosen to be.

Weren't those the terms of the deal when I first met him? He'd forced the Rangers to accept him as a Nordic pagan even though he wasn't one. He just wanted to play the part so he could live the way he had defined himself.

He's Sergeant Thor. He is other than the rest of us whether we like it or not. That doesn't even seem to be a consideration to him. The Rangers revere him because even in his greatness as a Ranger's Ranger, a sniper, a warrior, a stud… he is humble in that he is intent on being fully who he conceives himself to be and living the truth of that journey.

He's honest even if he is slightly nuts. Or maybe we are. Hard to say.

Yeah, I'd cast him as the Warrior Skald. But he has decided to be a warrior. A swordsman without peer. A barbarian coming in from the howling wastes of ten thousand years ago… to explore the Ruin of now. To sift it and judge it and find it wanting by the ways of a true man. A noble savage finding truth in battle.

That's my epigram for this section.

Your mileage may vary.

Then I asked him what happened next—to the dying god on the temple floor.

"It was dying, and I needed to make sure it was dead. And that it would stay dead."

So what did you do, Sergeant Thor?

Maybe it was psionics, maybe it was just the way a good story must go. I wanted to be him, but I knew I never would be. And I was glad for that. Glad he was in my life. I hoped he wouldn't leave us anytime soon. I needed him as much as I need my dead friend Tanner. I need them all. Brumm and Kurtz too.

I need my dad.

But death had something else to say. And so, Talker has learned… *cherish what you have now.* Nothing lasts forever. Though I thought it would. I wished it did.

The Cities of Men. The dream of us. Thank you, Autumn. I am glad you are not here in the bloody opening moments of this war.

All the criticisms of me and my account are true. I make it about me. And it isn't.

But in my defense, I love these characters in this story in which I am but a small player. To me… they were like gods and heroes. And I knew I would think about them until the day I died, someday, even if they are no longer there. Even if they have gone on by then and I am old. They will come and stand around me.

And that will not be a bad thing.

So what did you do then, Sergeant Thor, as the Pan god lay dying at your feet?

"I climbed on top of him… and cut his head off, Talker."

True story.

The spotter reported that Sergeant Thor emerged from the red sandstone temple dragging the bloody head of the dead Pan god. The worshippers screamed and wailed, their world ended. The temple guards ran, as did the priests. The game was over. And the Temple of Pan was done here in Sûstagul.

They would not play a factor in the rest of the mission. They scattered into the desert, leaving by the Gates of Mystery, and in the days that followed, there was little trace of them to be found.

CHAPTER TWENTY-THREE

"FIRING, firing, firing!" declared Sergeant Kang over the net as the main gates to Market blew wide open on the ten pounds of C4's demand that they do so immediately.

"Looks that kill!" declared Sergeant Joe, who was running Second Platoon and the op to smoke Ur-Yag, the chief wizard here in the district. "Eyes on corners and blind spots. Everyone's a shooter here. First Team, move now to position one."

"Looks that kill" had been Sergeant Joe's constant refrain during a very important part of the run-up to this particular section of the pump.

The *rehearse, rehearse, rehearse* part. Rangers do this until you can do what's gonna get done... blind, in your sleep, and under fire.

"Looks that kill" was his reminder that we use our eyes to evaluate everything and everyone we were going to come into contact with. It would be tight and busy and there was going to be a lot of dark magic going off—which is the Ruin's version of high-ex, but weirder—so we had to use our eyes.

"Looks that Kill, Rangers. Everywhere and everyone."

That was the cue for First Squad, under Sergeant Kang, to move into the street leading into the market, sweep to the right, and take up an immediate overwatch position from the corner of the first major sturdy stone building.

First would cover our entrance from this point.

We knew all of this. Thanks to rehearse, rehearse, rehearse. But we'd also reconned the hell out of this district and we knew each and every building by the rocks, plastic sporks, too-small pencils, dry Sharpies, and anything else we could use to develop our sand table. We knew every dance of this operation and Joe was just calling the moves now and getting ready to react and deploy us at anything unexpected or any target of opportunity dumb enough to get interested in what we were doing there.

This mission was simple. Which meant it was probably going to be hard. And I've been running with the Rangers long enough to know the tougher something is, the better it is to keep the operation simple.

Pity the solo HVT who ain't that big in the grand scheme of things and the Rangers have a few extra minutes to get creative and they're in the mood to see if something can get done just to see if they can pull it off.

We had to smoke three wizards on the way into the objective. The objective, as I have said, was the very powerful, according to Vandahar, high-value target sorcerer Ur-Yag.

He's a real bad dude.

But there were also tons of minor and major wizards here in the district. This was the largest area in Sûstagul, and it wasn't just walled, it was walled within walls and fortified towers watching everything in the dark streets, tight alleys, and dead-end ambushes. The place with filled with not just towers with mercenaries and crossbows, but also quick reaction forces of hard-bitten brawlers who had made their living fighting with the same types of weapons we were now only getting good with.

Which was why we were rolling thunder in there and weren't stopping to tangle. If you got in our way, the plan was to rock you hard, starting with the two-forty. If you didn't die like we needed you to—and the way we needed you to die was *fast*—then you go with grenades or even the Carl.

Hand-to-hand weapon combat was not our game to-day. We were playing hit and fade. We weren't good enough to go in and fight our way to objective with axes and swords. And to be honest, that would have been quieter. But, as Joe said, "The boom lets 'em know we're serious and in town to party. Since these guys are all high ASVAB winners like PFC Kennedy, they're gonna want to assess what the hell these Rangers are doing running amok where they shouldn't be, and bonus round of nachos… why all their guys get so dead so fast. We will take advantage of that pause to think and roll on each target until we smoke the big bad. Then we pull back and let them deal with the fallout. Command is hoping that means they sit the rest of the day out. If not, there are two Reapers on station from the Air Force back at the FOB and if the connection's good, they can drop all over anyone who gets uppity. But we risk civilian casualties and that won't play well now that this is our new home for the purpose of killing Mummy. So we do this dance loud, but not AC/DC. Copy?"

We copied, heads in our notebooks writing down all the commander's intentions and committing them to headline every action up to, and on, and departing the objective.

And remember, Talker's in a leadership position. So I'm wired tight and trying not to let coffee come in and tell me sweet little lies about being everything.

We were ready for weapons combat. Everything gets done with firepower on this one. No time for anything else.

Unless you're Thor and Monroe. Those two had already gone back to the Nacho Weapons All-You-Can-Eat Bar for seconds and thirds in extreme weapons combat. And I had *Coldfire* on my back, but only because I needed it there.

"They got weapons, they get dead," Joe said in the run-up to the op. "We ain't doin' line dancin' today. Mag dump to keep 'em back, keep 'em off the gun and the medics too. Flashbang everyone, give the civvies a way to go, opposite direction preferable, and anyone who doesn't avail themselves of our courteousness gets hole-punched. A lot."

Those were the commandments as *rehearse, rehearse, rehearse* went down until I was dreaming of the market and this day long before it ever went down.

"First down and covering the street," announced Sergeant Kang over the comm once they'd entered Market.

Without being told, Second was already on the move to their position inside the main walls. Second Team, or squad, though Joe preferred to call us *teams*, moved quickly in to take their position.

I should note that Sergeant Joe had been talking to Chief Rapp too much lately and word was the chief was whispering the sweet lies of SF to Joe and intended to train him up as a doc, or what we'd've called ten thousand years ago… an 18 Delta. Whether Joe was going to do this or not was unknown. He played his cards close to his chest. But the Rangers felt he was settling for less if he did so. Well… maybe that's not really true. Just inter-service rivalry. SF 18 Deltas are highly trained and some of the things they have to do with regard to combat medicine verge on the incredible. Plus, another Delta would take the pressure off Chief Rapp as detachment surgeon and primary health care provider for the Rangers.

Still, the younger Rangers felt both awe at this, and betrayed in the same moment, though they never said so aloud. Maybe I could just pick it up, what they were feeling, with the psionics. Or maybe I don't read people all that well because I'm some kinda narcissistic sociopath who makes an entire account of what we're doing here about himself, when all this legendary-heroic stuff I've been focusing on more in the Battle of Sûstagul and what happened here to us has been going on all along. While I've been just surviving and getting my mind around Rangering at the pro level… they've been doing it all along. That needs to be said and it's something I've been critical of myself lately regarding it.

In my defense… I haven't had coffee since before stacking on the LZ for the ride in. Poor me. Talker need coffee. There, got that out of my system. I'm weak and small. Tomorrow I will purge my weak-willed self and I will be something, someone else. You'll find me different if I'm not dead and Tanner's taken over and is probably doing way better. If it's Thor writing this tomorrow… I'm screwed. Thoughts and prayers me.

And now, as you're about to find out, we got into the weirdest, most magical battle ever. Who woulda thought? After all, we were just going in to smoke four guys who'd practiced the dark and magical arts at the pro level for most of their lives. Magic to them was like dip to a Ranger. Ain't much you do without a pinch under your lip. Sorry, family members who invited your Ranger to someone's princess wedding—that dip lip is gonna be there in the picture you paid fifty thousand dollars for.

Ranger gonna Ranger.

And yeah, I have been known to hit the dip now and then. I blame the tab.

Kang, as master breacher, had applied the charges, blown the gates off their hinges, and fell back to First Squad as Second stacked left and right of the breach, covered, and tried to pick up any immediate targets by pie-ing what they could see from the blown-in doors and the rough rubble along the main gate walls. All clear, First had moved in, swept right, and taken up overwatch.

Second under Joe moved in and swept left, taking up the opposite side of the street.

No contact yet.

Now it was our turn.

My turn to do my job in a leadership position. My heart is beating way too fast.

The weapons team, Third Squad, now pushed into the breach. Sergeant Kurtz directed the gun where he wanted it, facing forward in the twelve-o'clock position with max coverage of the street. Then radioed that we were down and in overwatch.

Now I was on, as assistant weapons team leader. My peer review had been ongoing from every Ranger from the moment I'd gotten assigned the position, and I couldn't tell whether they were serious or just riding me hard and messing with me. So I took every task my job required as heart-attack serious and made it happen, constantly chanting my requirements as ASL, assistant squad leader, over and over in my head.

The squad, or weapons team, consisted of Sergeant Kurtz as the squad leader, Specialist Soprano as the gunner, and Jabba, who had been given no rank. He was only known as *the Jabba*, or *that Jabba*, or *the gob*, which was a kind of a rank all in itself. Sometimes the little gob would joke and swagger around when he'd had too much Moon God Potion and point toward his bare upper chest right above where sergeant's stripes would go and then gaggle-crow in goblin pidgin-American, his imitation of Sergeant Kurtz, "Me big bigga big Saar'nttt. Me Saaar'ntt Gob. Bigga do say Jabba Big. Bigga do or you gonna pay. Bigga biggie big."

When he did this, often unexpectedly, Soprano almost died of laughter and could not be brought back to life and mobility until Jabba stopped performing as goblin-Kurtz. When Jabba finished, he had a huge toothy—or what teeth he had—grin, and his eyes were wide and mischievous.

Other squads of Rangers would give him Moon God Potion or MRE coffee sugar, which he gladly and greedily accepted, if he would do the imitation for them. But of course, only when Kurtz wasn't around.

So we had Kurtz, and then Soprano and Jabba on the gun. Then came Brumm as the SAW gunner to pick up slack during barrel changes and pull flank security. Tanner was on rear security. Then myself in the ASL making sure Kurtz's will was implemented and all information during long and short halts got disseminated. Also, I had to take care of our medic, Moon. Finally, Kennedy and Vandahar came along as… indirect magical support. Though there would be a ton of direct-fire action.

Tanner would say, "It's like having two tanks with infantry. You gotta watch 'em and protect them, but when they open fire… game-changer, bro."

I would let them know what Kurtz, or Joe, wanted done, but they had the freedom to interact and handle anything magical that came at us from the enemy. In those situations, I had to figure out what they were doing and disseminate it to the Rangers in the assault platoon and the weapons team to make sure they didn't get in the way.

Did I tell you my heart was beating fast? And for some reason, my mouth was dry. I could use some…

… coffee. I remember thinking that. But I was trying so hard to nail my leadership position, I couldn't bring myself to hit it. Later, when we would be falling back, leaving four dead wizards behind us, I'd YOLO and pound a whole cold brew, one of the two I had on me, as a reward.

Get everyone through this and you can do that, Talker. I remember telling myself that. Like that was important to me.

Moon.

"Now?" she said to me breathlessly as we got the call to move from the garbage heap on the LZ to the overwatch at the breach as Second and First Teams watched the street leading into Market.

"Now, Moon. We move now. Heads down."

We'd taught her as much as possible and she'd done it all with a natural lightness and agility all the Shadow Elves possessed. Her face was serious, and we even put war paint on her as we did ourselves just to break up our outlines in the shadowy streets of the market. And also to scare the hell out of anyone thinking twice about engaging us as we made our moves to smoke the three minor juju blasters and finally the big bad.

In the morning light, as we pushed off from the garbage and ran, I saw her glance toward the fighting in Dockside where Sergeant McGuire was located with First. It was starting to get bad there, but not as bad as it would get. Our high-ex explosions to take the lighthouse and channelize the enemy were already going off around Dockside and the isthmus. And there was Sergeant Monroe's hit on the Saurian ground force commander. The Carl made a loud *crack* and *boom* when the area denial munition suddenly went off.

I saw her look at the explosions, but she kept running as we hustled to our position near the gate. When we were down, she looked at me with worry on her face and I couldn't understand why, because we weren't under fire yet.

Then, not psionics, but the part of me who was just some guy who'd once been in love too and worried about Autumn while trying to do my job as a Ranger, kicked in and told me why her brow was furrowed and her eyes were asking me for some answer she knew she wasn't supposed to ask because we had work to do now.

"He's okay," I told her. "No netcalls for wounded yet. I'll let you know if there are. He's fine, Moon. Let's do our jobs and everyone goes home tonight."

That was when Second engaged the first group of mercs to respond to the breach at the front door to Market. Gunfire erupted in short brutal blasts, ripping the mercenaries to shreds right there in the street in front of us.

Civilians were starting to come out to see what was going on.

"Talker, get on the horn and let them know to get down or get out," said Joe over the comm.

Which was another job I had.

"He'll be fine. He's a great Ranger. Don't worry, Moon," I said as I got the detachment's portable bullhorn off my assault pack and keyed the broadcast.

She looked down, testing in her mind to see if what I was saying was true. Can you know that the one you love is safe? And finding, like every soldier, and every loved one at home, that you can't know for sure. You don't know. But you must go on, get it done, at home or at war, and maybe, just maybe… there will come a day when…

In all the languages of the market, which were a mix of Arabic and Chinese and some Greek, Gray Speech even and a few others, I'd put together enough phrases to let the locals know to stay down, get behind cover, or head for the Gates of Mystery and clear the city.

Moon nodded to me that she would do her best when I finished making the announcement to the civvies. Then she was looking forward, watching the Rangers, her Rangers, for anyone who needed her help right now, just like we'd taught her. Waiting for the call that would summon her into action to do her job.

"*Medic!*"

She knew that word. And others. More words, our words, every day. Just like any Ranger, she was out here to do her job better than anyone else today. She had made up her mind that on this day she would do that and get to the other side of this. Just as McGuire was out there doing the same. Just as we all were.

Go, Moon, I thought. *You got this.*

And maybe, just maybe… there will come a day when this will be over, and we will be home. Wherever that is? Or maybe just in the arms of the ones we love. Which is a home, better than any home I can think of, right now.

One block later we got that call for "Medic." Magic missiles flying and other arcane sorceries in the air as the Rangers breached the first two dueling wizards on opposite sides of the street. Moon ran out into the battle and grabbed the downed Ranger, dragging him out of harm's way through magic outgoing fire.

Yeah…

Maybe there will come a day.

CHAPTER TWENTY-FOUR

WE were running this as a combat patrol with the lead wedge under Joe in Second Squad on point. It was a delicate situation with the civvies and dangerous wizards running loose around here, so normally the headquarters element for the patrol would actually be the weapons team, but in this case, Second was running the point in wedge formation as we moved up the street to our first hits as fast as we could while still moving tactically watching alleys, corners, and dark spaces.

Looks that kill.

As we moved up the street to the first hit, like I said, we had Second in front with the edge. Weapons team next and even though Joe was running the patrol, Kurtz was the sensei of all things two-forty and you would not want anyone else running the gun.

Side note… if Kurtz got killed it would be me as weapons team leader, though no one believed that, and me least of all. But everyone in the weapons team, because we'd worked together so much, could get it done with the gun. And if it was me, I was gonna get it done. *Soprano, un-live those bastards over there. A lot.* C'mon, how hard is that? Still, all acknowledged Kurtz as two-forty bravo grandmaster.

So it is known, so it is.

Sergeant Kang in First brought up the trail fire team that picked up the rear and would act as a flanking force should we find any resistance on the way to the first kill.

This is how it would work…

Second makes enemy contact. Weapons team establishes a base of fire. First flanks. Sergeant coordinates supporting fire and elevation of enemy contact, depending on which of the two squads can get it done better based on their position with respect to the enemy. In other words, someone's gonna pin the enemy. Then someone's gonna go in there and kill them. A lot. The rest of us shift fire when that happens and watch the flanks for bad guys number two.

There are always more bad guys that come out of the woodwork once the shooting starts. So we watch the flanks while we kill forward.

Which is what I'm supposed to be doing the entire time. Watching the flanks and coordinating everyone so Kurtz can direct the gun while two assault teams try to shoot, move, and communicate in order to kill wizards. But there are concerns and I'll go over what we knew they were, going in. And also let me say this, we knew new ones, concerns and problems we hadn't expected, would develop once we got in there and the situation began to unfold and get complicated like things tend to do.

We had plans for the unplanned too.

Rangers have plans for everything. Trust me. They even have a plan on how to rest. And before you think they just make this stuff up… it goes to battlefield lessons from as far back as World War 2. Though Vietnam is where Ranger culture and patrolling techniques really began to develop.

Where the Rangers became the ghosts in the jungle the enemy feared.

Since that time, Rangers haven't stopped refining and rehearsing everything so it all becomes second nature as they move through incredibly hostile environments like well-oiled machines where not just everyone knows their job, but leadership positions are ensuring everything is being done to Ranger standard. And leadership positions don't have much to do with rank. Or even time in the army. Young PFCs will regularly lead patrols and get peer-assessed by everyone on the patrol. Like me right now.

One of the Second Squad Rangers ran by as we bounded up the street and told me to watch the medic. She was exposed and trying to get a view of the street. Then he smiled and laughed.

"Spot-check peer review... major minus, Talker. Recycle due to Lack of Motivation."

Because I'm in taking-everything-super-serious mode, I didn't realize that guy was just messing with me. Keeping it light because you could feel the serious coming in the streets ahead like some fat guy getting up for another run at the all-you-can-fry.

Then the Ranger laughed and told me he was just messing with me and was gone up the street, his battle rattle barely making a sound.

I envied that. I could have done more with mine.

But he was right. I corrected her and put her where she needed to be. Then I began chanting my job skills holy litany to myself again, trying to get everything just right as we went along.

We were deep in enemy territory now and there were concerns. To our rear, the CCP, casualty collection point, was back at the Gates of Death. Which was a pretty fair hump.

Now that I write that, it occurs to me that the position didn't bode well for its job. The casualty collection point is staged at a place called the Gates of Death? Then again, Rangers would find that hilarious. See their dark senses of humor to understand.

So that was a concern going into this. We weren't owning this district though, we were just smoking the main dude and whacking three other wizards we couldn't leave on our back trail because we'd identified them as problem children to ingress and egress from the objective. And another concern: unlike Ranger standard operations, we were leaving the way we'd come in. Which is something they hate. We only had enough forces to punch one hole into the market and we didn't want to fight new battles taking another route out of Dodgeistan after actions on the objective.

So we'd leave as we came, considering a cleared avenue of approach safer than making a new hole through the enemy lines.

Also, no resupply. The CCP and the smaj were way back in the rear, which as ASL, I was monitoring the unit comm, was already sensing an impending attack by the desert orcs that would develop into an all-out battle right there in the sand until the Legion took the walls and pushed the orcs away from that section later in the day.

Once inside the walls, the 120mm mortars began to drop some serious judgment all over the orcs out there in the desert and coming for that side of the outer wall. Which, in hindsight, pushed the orcs for the Gates of Eter-

nity in the south and caused the breakout. Which had…
consequences.

Thoughts on the 120mm mortars to distract me for a
moment because I need to get this done and I'm not ready
to talk about the consequences. I will. But not yet. Soon.

First, the one-twenties and what they did when the
orcs tried to pincer the sergeant major holding the gate
practically alone with a few riflemen as he redeployed the
mortars behind the walls and into the necropolis of open
and ruined graves, crooked sinking tombs, and the genial
miasma of death on a hot morning just below the old Legion fort.

The Ranger mortar section, once set up, and with not a
lot of special munitions on hand because we needed more
resupply from the Forge way back in FOB Hawthorn, devastated a lot of orcs in seconds once they began to drop
the iron. In the morning, after I get off this wall tonight,
I'm going to go over and count all the dead out there the
mortars flat-out ruined once they got going. I should sleep,
but I've had too much coffee writing all this down and…
I can't stop thinking about Brumm and Kurtz at the Gates
of Eternity.

Which is ironic also.

It's almost as though the whole battlefield, and the ancient places here, were telling us what would happen to
us. The Gates of Death did indeed turn into a killing field
if the casualty reports regarding enemy dead are accurate.
And they aren't. Because that was done at the end of the
day and even with thermal optics, the orcs had been dead
and cooling to local temps for most of the day. Noon tomorrow, when the sun is right overhead and those dead

orcs smell as awful as it can possibly get, that's when they need to be counted.

Why?

Why, Talker, why do the dead need to be counted. And especially the enemy dead?

For a long moment after I wrote that I just sat there staring at this blank page wondering what any of it, everything I've written, means. Two brothers who wanted to be Rangers and served together, went down to the gates where the line wasn't just thin... it wasn't even a line. They made one and held. Not giving an inch until they paid the rent on the scroll with their lives.

So... I'll ask again... Why, Talker, why do the dead orcs out at the western gate, the Gates of Death, need to be counted. Why the enemy dead?

Thor and some Rangers want to burn them, Kurtz and Brumm, on a pyre. No one has said anything different should happen.

To be fair, it looks like all the orcs in the world are out there beyond the walls now. So the command team does have a lot on their plate at the moment.

Why count the dead?

The account, the numbers... those are the skulls that need to be stacked around them... the brothers, when the torches are set to the piles of wood we will lay them on.

I gotta stop for a second. That was too much for me.

If you look at the numbers of the 120mm high-explosive mortar round, it's about ninety percent as effective as a 155mm HE artillery round, which is huge, for the size of the blast radius. Basically, thirty meters versus thirty-five meters. This is way more effective than a 105mm howitzer HE round, which is just a fifteen-meter blast radius. Okay, deep dive and you probably don't care, but I will do the data dump anyway as my path to being a Ranger is to know as much as I can about killing systems, our tasks, and our purposes, so I can kill the enemy better.

That's blunt. But warts and all. Go look for some hero with better reasons to Ranger somewhere else. It's the same thing I did with languages. It's my approach to Rangering. It works for me. And right now… it's helping me cope as I contemplate the enemy dead as tribute for…

Mortar and artillery shells set for airburst, which means they detonate ten meters off the ground, have distinct patterns to their shrapnel sprays because of the angle on the round when it explodes. Mortars, on the other hand, fly in a high arc and tend to approach the ground nose-first as they drop down. They have a near-perfect circular shrapnel pattern once they detonate. Because artillery has a flatter trajectory and the rounds come in parallel to the ground when they explode, the shrapnel pattern looks more like a butterfly, meaning a little shrapnel ahead of or behind the round and most of the shrapnel flying off to both sides.

So, as the orcs came for the sergeant major at the Gates of Death, which must have really been something seeing a vast desert orc horde come sweeping out of the desert dunes like some old movie, you'd think you would have wanted cannons, or what we call in the modern military, *guns*. Artillery pieces. Infantrymen do not have guns. We have carbines, rifles, light and medium and sometimes heavy machine guns. But we do not have "guns." A gun is an artillery piece. And they're huge and they make *big booms* and if you get their attention they can ruin the grid square you're standing on.

Interesting to consider that the Ranger mortars have almost the same punch and a solid killing pattern when they launch almost vertically through their tubes and then come raining down as fast as the mortar teams can drop them.

And they can do it fast.

Indirect fire kills in three ways: shrapnel, blast pressure, and fire. For our purposes at the Gates of Death, the 120mm mortar system was perfect. It delivers a huge amount of anti-personnel destruction for the size and weight of the actual mortar system. A field piece, an artillery gun, needs a truck or tank to get hauled around. Think about it this way: a 120mm mortar platoon, which has four mortar systems shooting at a linear target with airburst HE, will have a ninety percent chance to kill everything in a rectangular box thirty meters wide by one hundred and twenty meters long. The sustained rate of fire for the 120mm is either fifteen or twenty seconds a round, with a max rate of fire of sixteen rounds for a danger-close type fire mission. The incoming orcs against the Gates of Death, with Ranger assault teams ruining forces inside the city and unable to contribute to the defense of the gates, got straight-up ruined by just one minute of fire by the mortar platoon. One minute and a mass wave charge out there in the sand, with no cover, covered a tremendous area in flying, fast-moving shrapnel, sheer force from overpressure, and even fire as camels and riders suddenly ignited in the blasts.

I need to go count the dead out there.

I need the brothers to know skulls were stacked.

CHAPTER TWENTY-FIVE

THERE were four wizards we needed to smoke. Three because they were on the way to the fourth. The fourth because he "ran Barter Town" or something.

Tanner had to explain that one to me. Someone had *Mad Max Beyond Thunderdome* on their device in the unit and I promised to watch it when I could.

Basically, that fourth wizard, Ur-Yag, was the head guy around here and putting him down went a long way to shutting down the district to support the Saur, and also making sure we were in full control of the city on the other side of this. The other wizards, who were supposedly a greedy and always-looking-for-some-advantage lot, would welcome whoever smoked the last head guy so they could become the new head guy.

"Please don't say we'll be welcomed as liberators," groaned Tanner around the sand table again.

Joe gave him a look, and that silenced Tanner. You don't mess with Joe. Even Tanner knew not to.

Kurtz also smoked him later. A lot.

But being dead, Tanner doesn't get tired. He just gets slower and slower and becomes more that dead... *otherwhere*... thing.

Even the side-of-the-mouth remarks stop when he gets too far down the well.

The first two wizards were known in the district as Kalifax and Su-Meen "the Green Wizard of Konga." And yeah, they really called him that. The Green Wizard of Konga. Everybody's gotta be something, I guess. Apparently, these two guys hated each other's guts and that may have been due to the fact that they'd both built pretty impressive towers opposite each other on the same narrow street inside Market. Both were just one block up from the gates we'd just breached and right along the yellow brick road to smoke Ur-Yag a few blocks later. Once that was done...

Then we'd beat feet.

Things started to go wrong when we hit the first two wizards' houses. Towers, I mean.

Tower One was a tall, leaning affair, and someone had carved strange dragons all over it. Torches and brass braziers burned from small windows and ledges accessed from the inside, all up along its length. That was the tower of the Green Wizard. He wasn't green. Never did get an explanation on that one. Sergeant Kang and First would do that guy.

Tower Two was dark and haunted-looking black. The stones were carved with gargoyles and the house smelled like sulfur. One of Joe's team noted the strong odor on approach to target.

We had to do these two dudes at once, so the gun team was watching the street when First kicked in the Green Wizard's door and started shooting the mercs inside at near point-blank range just after they flashbanged them. At the same time, one of Joe's door-kickers smashed in the front entrance of the other guy's tower with a battering ram and got rewarded with a concussive blast from a magical ward that hit him like the overpressure of a near-miss from a mortar round.

Or a ton of bricks.

That Ranger went flying end over end into the middle of the street, and Joe pushed in and started shooting whoever was inside. In that case, wizard one, Kalifax whose wizard color is unknown, was downstairs, and that guy threw up a magical shield, "blurring himself" as Joe described it later. Joe came in following the carbine's sights and started pulling the trigger, except he couldn't see the guy clearly once the wizard passed a long slender ring-filled hand over his own narrow and goateed face.

He was wearing red silk robes and he was bald, as described in our intel. Real sinister-looking.

We were hip to spellwork and so Joe just kept shooting the blur and hitting the guy anyway for all his arcane trickery. He shoulda been dead, and he probably was, but at the last second he fired a fireball as some kind of last chance to save himself from the Rangers.

Later I asked the guys with Joe what happened at that point when they were in there and the guy tried to det the fireball. They told me the wizard was down and Joe kept shooting him on the floor. Then this sudden ball of white-hot plasma began to form in the dying wizard's ring-laden hand.

Joe called, "Back out!" immediately because like I said, Vandahar has hipped us to how dangerous magic can be. Then Joe covered his squad while the Rangers fell back to the street. My guess, he knew it was a fireball and he was putting the whisky keg he calls a body in the way to absorb the blow if that would even work. But that's what NCOs do. Everyone knows the story of Alwyn Cashe and a burning fighting vehicle.

At the last second, Joe came flying through the door and ended up face-first in the street as the fireball shot right past him and exploded against the opposite tower higher up just as Kang and his team were dusting the Green Wizard. Since Joe's boots were in the air as he flung himself through the door, the fireball was so close it caught them on fire and melted the soles.

Shoes on fire at the moment, Joe rolls over, sits up in the middle of the street, and shouts, "Gimme a frag!" One of the Rangers tries to get him up because now there are magic missiles shooting out of the door he's just leapt out of. The wizard Joe had shot a bunch *still* wasn't quite dead. Yet.

That Ranger trying to get him on his feet hands Joe a grenade. Joe pulls the pin, pops the spoon, and chucks it into the wizard's tower as he shouts, "Fire in the hole!"

They confirmed the wizard dead, or alive in many parts if you prefer, spread all over the room beyond the door, moments after the blast sent debris flying out into the street.

Meanwhile Sergeant Kang and his squad flashbanged the mercenaries on the ground floor in the other tower and found the wizard coming down the stairs to meet them with most likely ill intentions due to the fact that both his fists were glowing blue—not green, go figure—and some type of ghost dragon was starting to form over his head. The Rangers shot him as he cast spells at them trying to make them think they were falling into the well of the universe… or something. It was real trippy to hear them describe it. Some of the Rangers got disoriented and stopped shooting for fear of hitting friendlies. Sergeant Kang was one of them. Heidenreich, who was a shooter, neverminded all the illusions and just shot the wizard twice in the chest, then once in the head once he was down on the stairs.

Then muttered, "Damn wizards."

Back on the street we had problems. The breacher for Sergeant Joe was down in the street and I was getting ready to lead Moon up now that they were calling for a medic, when suddenly mercenaries from all along the street began to fire crossbows at the Rangers.

Joe low-scrambled for cover and took a crossbow bolt right in the assault pack.

I hoped his wife's beef jerky was not injured. Because that's the kind of leader I am. Luckily, I acted cool and kept that fear to myself.

Once the Rangers were out of the way, Kurtz released Soprano to engage and keep the gun above the street from hitting the man who was down in the middle of it.

At the same moment Moon looked at me and said, "I go now?"

I held on to her gear to keep her from running into outgoing gunfire and incoming crossbow bolts.

"Sar'nt, we gotta get to that Ranger now!" I called out to Kurtz.

One of the Rangers forward and hugging wall in Joe's team was calling out, "Medic!" for the guy who was down. We had no idea if he was dead or alive and thankfully the mercenaries weren't shooting him with crossbow bolts as he lay there in the gutter.

Kurtz looked back at me and shot his knife hand at the wall on Kang's side of the street indicating what he wanted me to do. I got what he was saying and told Moon to follow me. Once in place, and it was clear we were gonna keep low and hug wall to go forward, Kurtz nodded and told Soprano to cease fire on the gun.

"Brumm! Move forward and suppress so we can pull that Ranger back to safety!"

Brumm hustled forward, moving past Joe, and began to engage mercenaries up the street with the SAW. Brass and linkage spat away from the light machine gun as he worked targets in short bursts. Moon left the wall, dashed for the Ranger, grabbed his drag handle, and pulled him back into a small alley, tugging and pulling with all her strength.

I fired at some mercenaries just to cover her and followed Moon back into the morning blue shadows between the towers.

And also, in a firefight, returning fire is first aid.

The Ranger, whose name was Case, was in real bad shape. Both his eyes were blackened. His orbital socket was fractured and his eyeballs were rolled back in his skull.

Severe concussion to me.

And he wasn't breathing.

Moon checked for a pulse as she'd been taught while the two-forty opened up again to suppress the street. Joe started to work the M320 and sent rounds into a few solid buildings the mercs up the street were using for cover.

Satisfied that Case had some kind of pulse, Moon checked for airway obstruction. Then, without me telling her what to do, she had a suction bulb out and was employing it to remove clotted blood and flesh from Case's throat. He began to cough and breathe unevenly. Then he began to babble nonsense.

Yup. Severe concussion.

I shouted to Kurtz, "He ain't dead, Sar'nt, but he's done. We gotta get him back to the CCP."

We had a plan for that.

Me was the plan. I would carry and Brumm would go as security.

As we stabilized Case and got him ready for me to fireman-carry him all the way back to the CCP, Brumm swapped a belt for a pouch on his SAW so we could move faster.

As we left, Sergeant Joe was getting the Rangers into the fight, and halfway to the gate I heard explosions as the Rangers began to dislodge and destroy the mercenaries.

Carrying the severely wounded man, I passed Vandahar and Kennedy. Vandahar looked grave as he stared at the death-white face of the kid on my back.

Case was the youngest Ranger in the detachment. He'd completed RASP a week before Area 51. As he hung life-lessly over my shoulder, barely murmuring, I began the hunched run to the CCP. I made up my mind he would live to be *not* so young. That he would have adventures, and maybe even half as good a life as I've had. That he would meet some elf girl like Moon and make babies and grow old. But knowing the Rangers, an orc chick with smoking glutes would do just fine.

I made up my mind that that would happen for Case.

He was just starting out. Kid needed a break. So I ran and ignored the pain like it was some prayer to whoever that the kid would get that break.

"Be safe and be quick, Talker," said Vandahar as I left. "The real danger lies ahead now. Ur-Yag knows we are coming for him now."

CHAPTER TWENTY-SIX

THE kid did catch a break even though it might not have seemed like it at the time. We were pinned down outside the gate. Trying to get across the trash heap to the old Legion fortress and then over to the Gates of Death.

I'll be honest, Case wasn't heavy, but I was smoked already. The morning was hot. I'd been racing around, physically and in my mind just to get everything right, and I was fading. Then the mercenaries had come out and were moving to secure the gate to Market that we'd blown wide open. Staging there in large groups possibly to go either see what was happening in Dockside or get involved in what was happening in Dockside.

Brumm had shot a bunch at the blasted gate exiting Market and as we made our way through the rubble, and over the bleeding and blasted corpses, me trying not to drop Case, the mercenaries out in the trash heap took control of the area between Market and the fortress.

"Down, down, down," hissed Brumm as they began to fire at us just as we entered the no-man's trash heap land. Covering behind some old marker stone that had once been the carving of something we'd never know, giving us some protection for the moment. Brumm popped over the broken rock and laid down a line of fire, shouting for the mercenaries to, "Get back!"

I doubted they understood his English. But I hoped so. I couldn't chance getting Case off my back for a rest because I was certain there'd be no way I was getting him back on again once we needed to move out.

Then, hearing myself think that, I told that negative part of my mind to *Lock it down*. A Ranger fights faster, longer, and harder than anyone else. I am one. That's what I'm gonna do.

"I ain't done," I muttered and tried not to shift the wounded Case because who knew how bad his injuries were.

I kept him over my shoulder anyway and apprised the sergeant major of our bleak situation.

That's when the kid caught a break.

Two choppers were already back from the refuel. One Little Bird and one Black Hawk with a medic onboard.

"Be advised, Rangers," said the Little Bird pilot as he streaked over the battlefield and not just a few of the mercenaries turned to watch this strange, small, armored bird in the sky. "I have your position and I have the tangos. Stay down. I'll clear the LZ for Intruder Four-Eight to pick up your wounded."

Intruder Four-Eight was the Black Hawk with the medic onboard.

"Brumm, get down," I shouted. "Gun run coming in."

"Can't, Talker. They're charging us. That pilot won't run that line fire this close to our position. Hang on, here they come. Get down and cover his airway."

I did.

At the same moment, the pilot came in steep and sharp, and his miniguns cut loose on the mass of strange and irregular mercenaries carrying all kinds of weapons, and outfitted in all kinds of strange armor from across the Ruin, all crossing the trash heap to attack our position. In the one last glance I had, Brumm had indeed been right. The mercenaries were that close and Brumm was dropping them with short bursts from the SAW.

Brass and linkage flew everywhere.

I didn't get hot brass burns from the Little Bird streaking overhead on the gun run, but I did from the Brumm's two-four-nine. The SAW gunner stayed up over the fractured stone rock carved with strange symbols long ago and kept engaging the warriors at near point-blank range. It was like they were being driven to kill us even as they were getting cut down.

The first gun run killed a lot of them.

That's when Al Haraq appeared.

The djinn from the bottle in my assault pack. He just materialized right there in the middle of the firefight for the LZ to get Case the help he needed.

Who knew.

The djinn was tall and massive, his immensely muscled arms crossed over his chest as he scanned the desperate situation. His dazzling white teeth and burning blue eyes shining like hot fires against his chocolate skin.

And his three succubi were there too, in all their curvy gossamer and revealed flesh. Beautiful dark hair, full red lips. Taut brown bellies and ample breasts. Wide hips. Dark eyes watching you as though commanding you to watch them.

Dammit!

They were gorgeous and looked like they'd just gotten out of hair and makeup for some movie.

In the middle of the battle. On a trash heap.

"Master!" exclaimed Al Haraq loudly and with much ill-placed goodwill. Ignoring the incoming crossbow fire. The Little Bird dosing the entire area in lead and mass death. Brass linkage flying everywhere. The dying kid on my back. The garbage field of the city getting ruined and exploding like sudden fountains of dust and trash at the worst casino in Vegas.

Fun, huh?

"I see you are in trouble, Master."

He looked around, his smile beaming. Like all of this was very new, and very amusing to him.

"Very serious trouble it seems, Master. Would you like to use a wish and have me do something amazing to rescue you from this?"

Meanwhile, the three beauties started their arching and stretching routines they always did around the legionnaires in order to drive the Italians, I mean Accadions, nuts. One time I saw one of Chuzzo's men bite his hand so hard he drew blood when they started doing this little flirty stretching routine. Sighing with feigned boredom as they did so. Even now, the demonic beauties were looking bored as mercenaries got torn to pieces just hundreds of meters away and Brumm blazed away with the two-four-nine at anyone daring to get closer. More mercenaries were coming from other directions and even with the Little Bird gun run I was in serious doubt whether we weren't about to get hacked to death right there around the rock we were covering behind.

"Oh, no," said Al Haraq, suddenly looking at dying Case. "This man is just minutes from death, Master. How could this be?"

The Black Hawk was getting close now, beating the wind with its blades as it came in for the LZ. Trash flying everywhere.

The MH-6 pilot came back over the comm.

"Stand by… one more pass should do it, coming around, Rangers. Hold on…"

"Ain't time for that," muttered Brumm and spat dip as he swapped for the belt of linked seven-six-two he had around his neck. "Switching to on, Talker. It's about to get real knife-and-gun show right here, right now. You boys wanna do this? All right. I been dead once… didn't take. Come get all you want!"

Al Haraq cleared his throat to get my attention.

"I could perhaps… if you use a wish, Master… make this dying man on your back… well again. Or I could, if you use a wish, slay your enemies with a wall of fire or a storm of knives. Or… I could transport you to the Flesh Pits of Hadiz and none of this would be important to you anymore, for the demandable pleasures of that palace of delights will take the cares of this waking life far from your mighty person, Master."

"Negative, Al Haraq…" I began. And then got some flying trash in my mouth. The taste was instantly foul. I know… Medal of Honor me. I coughed and gagged.

"Turn me loose on this world, Master, and I will make you its king within the turns of a few sand clocks. I can give you anything you want… Master. If… you just know the right words… to ask." He inclined his head respectfully. "Master."

I began to hurl as Al Haraq gave me that broad smile that tells me it's not really a smile, but more of a challenge.

The doe-eyed demon temptresses were watching me, and yes... they are hot. I understand why the legionnaires constantly debate the servitude of ten thousand years for just a moment of their time in pleasures imagined. I get that. They're incredible.

I gagged and vomited the trash in my mouth.

And kept Case on my back. Hero.

The trash heap exploded once more like one hundred fountains caused by high explosives as the Little Bird ran over the top of the battlefield, spraying death and turning the whole heap into the worst water show in the worst casino in Vegas.

Then the Black Hawk was coming in and we were running for it, leaving Al Haraq and the beauties staring at us as we tried to save Case's life. Struggling against the beat of the downdraft of the chopper just to get him close.

On board the bird, the medic and crew chief got hold of Case, and reaching out and taking him, they laid him out on the deck as the medic went to work. The chief gave us the thumbs-up and made ready to dust off from the LZ.

I'd done all I could. And it wasn't anything. Just carried a guy through a garbage heap. A kid. A kid who just needed a chance to get a little older.

Live, I thought as I ran from the chopper. *Live, Case. And stay away from hot demon girls.*

We cleared and ran back to the blown gate back into Market. Diving back into the fight once again when we linked up with Sergeant Joe and Second.

CHAPTER TWENTY-SEVEN

BY the time Brumm and I made it back to the others, or really, where the others had been and were no longer, we found ourselves looking over the destroyed remains of the third wizard's leaning old haunted house. A wizard's hovel if there ever was one. A real dump in other words. Multistoried and looking like it had been built and added on to for about three hundred of the past worst years. The bodies of strange monsters, they looked like large imps with bat wings, were burning in the street outside. The house was on fire and smoke, black and soot-grey, poured out through open windows high up. The old gnarled and warped wood, the parts that weren't on fire already, was dry and ancient and riddled with bullet holes. In fact, it was shot to hell everywhere.

The burning demons in the street smelled *bad*.

"Smells like a burn pit back in the box," muttered Brumm quietly as we stared at the damage Second had wrought. They'd done it exactly as Sergeant Joe had wanted it done. *Rolling thunder. Looks that kill.*

I mean, c'mon… there were dead demons in the street, man. The Rangers opened up a can of apocalyptically end-of-the-world beatdown on this place.

It would be minutes before the dead, dry place was consumed by the greedy flames.

And did I mention it smelled bad? Like someone lit a range latrine on fire after everyone had Mexican food.

"That wizard's dead in there," said Brumm finally as we watched the place burn. There were spent shell casings everywhere. Linkage too, meaning the two-forty had gotten involved, though from farther back and across the street, using an overturned cart filled with busted wine urns to stabilize the gun.

But I asked anyway how he knew that.

"How do you know that?"

If just to learn more. Brumm was exceptional, and quiet about it, at what he did as a skilled Ranger. He was a constant observer. And when he gave away some bit of hard-earned Ranger wisdom, you were dumb not to take it and make it yours.

"Sergeant Joe wouldn't roll on that Ur-Yag boy unless this guy was dead and burning in there somewhere. Second, also looks like someone in Second used the Carl. Fired an HEDP round right through that window. Musta seen the wizard and decided to get it done soon as he started… *summoning demons*. If that's what those bat-things are. That HEDP round is like firing a grenade wrapped in C4 wrapped in nails. Big bang, lotsa frag. That'd get it done on a structure like this pretty darn quick. Only better round we're carrying today is that single guided. That's boss, and I'm hopin' to see it go off."

Up the block we heard the Rangers getting into a firefight all at once. And we heard something else too, something titanic and raspy, calling out hoarsely over the cityscape, its sandpaper rasp echoing out over the baked red sun-bleached brick of the ancient desert port city. It sounded like some great war beast giving the cry to come out to battle on the hottest, driest day of ever.

For a moment it made my blood run cold. Like… this thing was from the neighborhood of the *otherwhere*. But on the wrong side of the tracks.

"It's going down, Talker. They'll need us. Let's get a hustle on."

CHAPTER TWENTY-EIGHT

THIS was the state of the battle ranging across Sûstagul at that moment. At around the same time as the death of the third wizard went down, the mortars were beginning to drop iron all over the north side of Dockside as the captain called in a danger-close fire mission. In fifteen minutes, the Legion would come ashore and push the Saur back into the streets, slaughtering them block by block, and the Saur would find the dwarves and Sergeant Monroe in their rear hacking and slashing their way to the creamy center.

The Saur were using an inn as a forward command post when the fierce dwarven QRF with the jacked minotaur tank found them. What followed was a no-holds-barred battle in which the dwarves and Sergeant Monroe defeated an entire platoon-strength element of Conan-Actual Saur praetorians, including the wizard protecting the command team. The Saur leaders escaped by falling back to the inn's cellar with spears and pikes. It was assessed that following them down there into the cellar was a sure way to get killed.

King Wulfhard was in a rage and wanted to go anyway. It was Max the Hammer who produced a brick of C4 and suggested another way to end the Saurian command structure.

Lessons from Sergeant Chris.

Five minutes later, watched by the minotaur to ensure they were getting it right, the dwarves placed the C4 on the inn's floor above the cellar and brought the whole structure down on the Saurian leaders below in the dark.

After that, block-to-block fighting devolved into mass slaughter as the legionnaires took no prisoners on what they called, "*Primo Passaggio*."

First Pass.

When the Accadion Legion passed over the battlefield in the first wave, they took no prisoners and made sure every corpse received at least one stab in the chest, minimum. If you survived *Primo Passaggio*, then you might live. But, as Corporal Chuzzo put it, "We no like-ah to take the *prigionieri*, Talk-ir."

Prigionieri. Prisoners.

"Too much work. *Sì?* Ah-sometimes we call it the *Angelo della Morte*. When the ah-*capitano* he say so. We do. *Sì? Comprende?*"

Angel of Death. No survivors.

But that would be hours later. Hours after the Gates of Eternity and what would happen there. Which explains why no one from Third could break through to hold the walls and keep the orc horde from entering the city. They were very busy. Even with the Legion, it was hard fighting for at least two more hours before the dwarves dropped the inn on top of the Saur leaders.

Meanwhile the smaj was holding the gate as the orcs began their first cav probes with mounted archers on camels, getting close to the walls. The mortars finished their fire mission to support Third on the isthmus, then shifted inside the city.

The 120mm mortars are great. But they are extremely heavy. Rangers got them inside the city and ready to fire in record time as the orcs pushed the gate. The massive horde came out of the dunes swinging scimitars and ululating war cries as they raced for the walls. They crossed open sand until the mortar teams dropped the hammer and it began to rain explosives out there on the desert floor. Then there was not so much waving of sharp metals and the orcish version of "For freedom!"

But that would happen as Brumm and I fought our way to the chopper, handed off Case, and ran back.

Whoever the orc commander was, he was smart. He kept pushing on the sergeant major's position at the Gates of Death, pinning those forces there. Massed arrow fire, expendable cannon fodder pushing on the walls with ladders. Light camel attacks to try and get close to the gates with shamans who we think were trying to cast some kind of spell that would have opened the gates, either with magical force or some other means like disappearing them or taking control of someone's mind to get it done.

We don't know that this was possible, but it has to be considered as they were clearly attempting something.

The result is that the Gates of Death held and the Legion made it in as the smaj and a few riflemen held the entrance until the Legion could take control, get the gates closed, and then get on the walls.

AAR time. That turned into a cluster. The Legion got disorganized inside the walls and started to take them slowly, capturing towers and working their way south. It was decided by the command team, with Captain Tyrus in attendance, that the Legion should have gone for the Gates of Eternity with a large force, and then closed forces with the Gates of Death. Basically, strangling any forces on the wall between those two points. Working south along the wall, like they did, left time for whoever thought this next move up to pull what they were gonna pull on us.

It was probably Ur-Yag.

He seemed like a real bastard.

The short story on Ur-Yag. Vandahar indicated this bastard was a minor wizard from the Wyrm Waystes. I've looked at that area on the map. It's way up beyond where we would have once placed Eastern Europe, the Caucasus Mountains. Then the Steppes.

Almost nothing is known about that area as mainly it lies on the other side of Umnoth, which is home to the Nether Sorcerer and the hordes of the Great Orcish Khan. A big no-go zone. That's the Ruin's Mordor. And everything I've heard indicates it's not a very nice place and, literally, according to some of the sages, Hell on Earth.

Regarding the Wyrm Waystes, Vandahar would only say this.

"It is a strange and quiet place. Vast in its silences and solitudes. I went there when I was a young wizard, among a company of heroes long gone now to slay a great foe. It is easy to believe nothing lives there that is good. Or anything at all for that matter. The dragons have ruined much of it. But there are fantastic hordes of magic, lost learning, and ancient gold there, and great beauty in the silences and solitudes of course. It is a much more different place there than the Ruin you have encountered so far. Dangerous, but beautiful too in its deadliness. If the dragons were gone, it would be better still as far as I am concerned. But yet, survival there is challenging in the extreme."

And what of Ur-Yag, Vandahar?

"A lowly hedge wizard from the barbarian tribes. A mean and dangerous gatherer of mean powers. He's a summoner. Learned that foul art in the east with the Orders of the Jade Mysteries. Few, mind you, survive the Mysteries. So he is not one easily trifled with when reckonings must be made. Why he came here... that's an easy question."

That question had been asked by the smaj during the intel dumps during the run-up.

"Access to the tombs of the Saur," the old wizard continued. "And the City of Thieves has an ancient power structure that would have nothing to do with him and his summonings. You see, summoning is... worse than necromancy. Deals with devils and the like. As they say in the trade, there are no old summoners. The devils usually get the better end of the bargain, eventually. In the end. But, having said that... Ur-Yag *is* an old summoner. Rules, exceptions... yes.

"The City of Thieves has its strange codes of honor, and if you want to plunder the tombs of the Saur then usually you hire out your expeditions there, on the other side of the gulf, and come at the Land of Black Sleep that way. But they don't take kindly to summoners in the streets, alleys, and pirate palaces of the City of Thieves. Already enough problems with ancient Saurian curses on stolen treasure and all that rot. No need to involve the Devils of Hadiz in your affairs when possible. They cause enough trouble. So instead he came here to gather his power. That's why."

Then the captain asked, "And what is summoning? What can my Rangers expect when they go for the hit on this target. Devils, demons?"

Vandahar nodded gravely.

"Among other things. And that is why I shall accompany the Rangers when confronting him. Your powers, formidable as they are, Rangers… will be little match for the foul summoner. Just think of me as one of your… Carl G's, as you call it. But a magical one."

That's when we knew this Ur-Yag is a real bastard. Even by Ruin standards. When a place called the City of Thieves won't have much to do with you, or anything at all, that says a lot about you.

So of course it was Ur-Yag who sent his mercenaries down to the southern entrance to the city, the Gates of Eternity, to throw open the gates and let the orcs in.

What did he have to lose?

By the time we'd smoked his three wizards, and there were others in the city in alliance with him as he was really the head mob boss among the wizards, but we'd smoked the three worst according to our intel, he'd figured out we were coming to *knock knock*—and it wasn't for tea.

I get that.

Open the gates and give you enemies something to get busy with while you make your next moves. He needed to figure out what we were and what we were capable of. He knew the orcs. They were a known factor to him. He could deceive or slay them later, as most of the city would have rallied around that cause because everyone hates orcs simply because they are orcs.

Orcs are horrible. Even Jabba says so.

"Only good orc… dead orc. Big bigga big say true all gobs."

So, as we pushed on his central tower, a tall structure that loomed over the market like some unclean bird, unknown to us the orcs were heading for the wide-open Gates of Eternity.

Unknown until halfway through the battle when the cute little ponytailed Air Force co-pilot flying the drones let us know we had company coming in from the south. Company-sized orc elements pushing away from the Gates of Death and heading for the Southern Gate.

Kurtz and Brumm had an hour left to live at that point.

This is the last time I can consciously remember… of them both.

When Brumm and I made the battle, Kurtz barked at both of us, giving us orders what to do. The medic was working on a downed Ranger. Kurtz ordered me forward to assist. Soprano was rocking the main gun trying to lay as much fire as he could on a massive sand demon clutching the wizard's tower and throwing bolts of lightning at the Rangers in the street below, who were tangling with more demons, smaller, in a massive street battle.

"Corporal Brumm!" Kurtz shouted at his brother.

Brumm had been promoted to corporal. He was really the assistant weapons team leader.

"Suppress those imps on the right!"

"Can do, Sar'nt!"

I saw Kurtz turn back to the two-forty, confident his little brother would get the job done. That's how they both were. They relied on each other.

I'll always remember them both in that moment.

Not the way Tanner would show me what happened later.

There's this line in a song by an old metal band called Poison. It's true.

Sometimes I think I wish I didn't know now the things I knew then.

But I had to know. I had to go see their last moments.

CHAPTER TWENTY-NINE

I don't remember much about the battle at the Tower of Ur-Yag now. I thought it would be important. Because of course, it was about me.

But… my perspective has changed a little since the events that followed. There were many heroes that day.

As Tanner says, "I'm just the guy next to the guy."

If that guy is a Ranger, or someone the Rangers trust with their lives, like Moon, then yeah, I'm happy to be the guy next to the guy.

Al Haraq… he came to me as I stood on this tower in the night after the battle, watching the orc horde out there spreading away in every direction on the sands. Legionnaires patrolling the walls. There's every chance those orcs are gonna rush the walls, and… we just finished one battle hours ago. A tough one.

Doesn't matter.

As the sergeant major put it a few hours ago, "Rangers move farther, faster, and fight harder than any other soldier. If those orcs wanna go to hell… then we'll get 'em on the Greyhound. We're gonna lead the way, Rangers."

The situation is desperate. But we hold the walls.

Al Haraq comes to me in the night and doesn't bring the girls. Thankfully.

"I am sorry for your loss, Master."

I stared at the sea of orcs out there in the desert. Drone reports that there are more forces—not orcs, legions of Saur—marching out of the deserts to the south. Chances they're on the same side… one hundred percent.

I am thinking about what Tanner showed me in the hours after the battle. When he was so beat down hard by the devils that almost killed all of us at the tower… that he went full *otherwhere.*

"I can see them, Talker. I can show them to you now. New power… I got. I don't know. Maybe it was always there."

In the night out there are thousands of fires. Torches, bonfires, smiths sharpening weapons. Orcs ready to do something wicked.

You can feel it in the late night as I get these words out.

Al Haraq whispers…

"You still have two wishes, Master. One will suffice to bring them both back. But I must warn you, for you are a good man, Master. Wishes… they are very dangerous. Even the ones that are not magical. Many who seek me, they get more than they bargained for. Just like the girls. You understand, Master? It is not easy. The wish… it must be… framed… just so. For I will, and I must, adhere exactly to what has been asked of me. You understand this, Master?"

I nodded.

"I shall wait in the bottle, Master."

He began to fade. But even as he vanishes, I hear his voice once more.

"I am so sorry, Master. They were great warriors. I am… sorry… for your loss. Master."

And then he is gone, and I am alone with all that has happened and all that must be written down.

The battle against Ur-Yag.

The Rangers are battling two separate elements when Brumm and I enter the battle.

First, there's a huge sand demon curled around the tower. Leering down at us with its triangular head, screeching and howling, casting lightning bolts at Rangers covering and firing at the summoned devils in the streets coming for them.

The devils.

They are grey-skinned. Fat but muscled. Horned heads. Bat wings they don't seem to use. They come from the tower, and the two-forty has already wasted several. The Rangers used grenades on them as they kept pushing on the street against us while our wizards dueled and supported.

Kennedy and Vandahar are casting spells at the sand demon wrapped around the tower high above.

The gunshot devils, they get knocked down by gunfire. But then they get up. Kennedy comes in and roasts them with the dragon-headed staff once they're down. That seems to do the job.

Note: you have to mag dump on a devil at close range just to get it down.

Sergeant Joe, who's running the battle, arrives at where Moon is trying to treat a downed Ranger. I'm shooting two devils getting close. The devils have flaming swords and black shields. The air is alive with hatred and fear. And you can tell it's coming straight from these laughing fiends.

I shoot them and they don't go down.

Joe is there next to me an instant later and he says, "Gotta jam 'em up good, Talker. Overwhelming firepower gets 'em on the ground. If Kennedy don't splash 'em with his magic nape, then we thermite 'em."

He drops one, the closest, and then hands me a thermite grenade. "I'll cover, you arm it and drop it on the corpse."

Then I'm running forward as Vandahar calls down what looks like a meteor strike on the sand demon. The strike hits the tower and suddenly half of the tall structure collapses into the street, splashing ancient brick and billowing dust everywhere.

If it ain't the end of the world, it feels like it.

The sand demon is still clinging to what remains of the high tower. Howling and screeching. Dark storm clouds swirling and forming overhead in the clear blue desert sky. It fires a lightning bolt on Vandahar's position just as I drop the thermite onto the body of the prone demon. The thing's eyes open and look at me suddenly, and my brain starts to hurt.

For a stupid hot second, I think about mentally engaging this thing with my psionics…

… but Vandahar warned me about that dumb move.

"Don't. Do not, Talker, ever allow a demon into your mind. They will stay and you will be lost."

"Talker!" shouts Joe. "Cover Sergeant Kang!"

Sergeant Kang is forward and emplacing some claymores. One demon has broken through the hate Brumm is laying down and going straight for the demo sergeant.

I bring my carbine up and start rocking the closing demon, firing short bursts and keeping the Vickers sling tight so I can control the weapon better.

Vandahar fired off a ton of magic meteors at that moment. Bright and dazzling, they streak overhead like artillery and savage the sand demon on the tower.

"Your time is at hand," thunders Vandahar to his foe. His voice echoes over the battlefield like Judgment Day itself. I advance through the incoming and outgoing fire. Did I mention the devils are casting small flaming darts from their black-nailed claws? Fun, huh? I keep shooting the demon until it goes down.

That's when we get the call about orcs pushing through the gates.

And that's when Sergeant Kurtz said he could handle the QRF and grabbed Brumm to handle it.

If we didn't at least check the orc advance into the city, all our lines and defenses meant nothing.

Joe released them to do their thing. I was busy. I didn't see them go.

"Kang!" I shouted. "Pull back! Gonna det this thing with my frag."

Kang sees me, nods, and fades, firing on more demons pushing our line. Burning brass on full auto.

I drop the grenade and move back, but not fast enough. The devil detonates, blowing pieces of gray flesh and midnight black horns everywhere.

I got knocked down by the blast.

When I came to, Moon was dragging me for cover.

"I… got… you…" she's gasping as I look up. Her face is covered with blood and one of the flaming darts is stuck in her armor. "I… got… you…."

Joe helps her a second later.

I try to get up but I'm… I'm dizzy.

Then a massive sharp thunderclap goes off and the battle is over.

The tower shatters from Vandahar's *doomsday bolt*, is what I call it. The wizard's spell hits the demon directly and then sucks it into a sudden black hole created right where the bolt struck. Slowly. Squeezing all the power of the demon-sorcerer into a tight ball that cannot be contained.

"Rangers… seek cover!" shouts Vandahar suddenly, in that Cloodmoor you-shall-not-pass voice we'd first heard him use.

The demon is being sucked down into the black hole of the doomsday bolt Vandahar has stuck it with. It howls in pain and fear as it realizes what's happening to it. The world seems to howl with it. Distantly, I'm watching the whole thing from my bell-rung brain.

Then Vandahar tells us to cover.

The last thing I see is the demon vibrating like it's a stuck video clip and the image is shifting back and forth between two frames. Violently and more so by the second.

I knew an explosion was coming. You could feel it in the air.

Then Moon threw herself over me when it felt like the energy of the exploding demon, which later Vandahar would tell us was Ur-Yag himself, transformed.

"His final summoning had been to surrender himself to one of the worst fiends of the pit. The sand demon Taargen of the Great Fall."

Moon threw herself over me as the demon exploded, ending the battle in one sudden violent moment.

Like a good medic does.

Telling me over and over as the very fabric of reality seemed to tear itself apart all around us in the street for one eternal second...

"I... got... you... Ranger..."

In the aftermath, an unreal quiet spread across the battle in front of what remained of the Tower of Ur-Yag.

I was on my knees by then, Moon helping me up in the surreal quiet and raining dust. Rangers were covered in sandy powder from the explosion of the tower and the blast that followed.

Joe smiled and said to the wizard, "Dayum, son. Get some."

Vandahar stood taller, more radiant than he had been before. In some subtle way that seemed to hint something more about him.

Then he simply said, "Unlike Carl G... I do care, Rangers."

EPILOGUE

THE First Battle of Sûstagul was over. That's right, First. It definitely looks like there's gonna be a second one if all these orcs don't find something else to do and go somewhere else.

But like the sergeant major said, they wanna go to hell, we'll buy the ticket.

That's tomorrow. Tomorrow's another day.

I won't quit tomorrow. I didn't quit today. No one did. Some even gave everything to rent the scroll today.

Gertz on the beach.

Brumm and Kurtz at the Gates of Eternity.

Rangers.

Someone else will pay the rent tomorrow. Maybe me.

I'm good with that.

The battle was over when Tanner came to me at the forward CCP. The battle with the devils had taken it all out of him. He was full otherwise. No one noticed but me. Everyone just figured we'd all been to hell and back that morning and it was just… coming down.

We marched back through the streets to the fortress. The Saur were finished in Dockside. The Legion was on the wall when the reports came in that the two Rangers were down at the southern gates.

Then the captain ordered in the two Reapers and they vaped that place, just outside the gates, off the map, eliminating all the orcs getting ready to enter the city, sending many others running off into the desert. Two companies of legionnaires moved into the gates, got them closed even though they were heavily damaged, and for a moment the orcs could not violate the city. Our stronghold.

Word spread quickly, Kurtz and Brumm were killed retaking the gate and pushing the orcs back. And mainly preventing the enemy from getting inside the city in any meaningful way.

They'd fought off a full company of desert orcs for fifteen minutes, alone, outnumbered, and low on ammo.

They picked a spot on the battle map and didn't move.

About a hundred and sixty orcs died trying to dislodge them, and that basically stalled the orc push right there. I guess their commanders were afraid they were being led into a trap, and this orc company seemed better than the cannon fodder hitting the Gates of Death, so they were cautious. And Kurtz and Brumm checked them.

It just cost them their lives to do so.

The Reapers handled the other companies of orcs running for the gates to support the company Kurtz and Brumm were engaging. Then were off station.

We got a break to grab some chow and get ready for whatever came next. But a stunned silence hung over everyone. The news was beginning to spread.

I… didn't want to believe… what had happened.

The sergeant major came by, took Tanner aside, and told him he was gun team leader for the moment.

Tanner came over and told me the bad news.

"They're dead."

Then he lowered his voice.

"Listen, man… I… ain't me. Didn't tell the smaj because he's got a lot on his plate right now. But if it don't get right in my head… I'll tell him quick. You can lie to the world, but you can't lie to the Rangers, man. I know that."

"What do you mean you're not… right… in the head?"

He took a deep breath, shucked a cigarette, and lit it in the desert heat. Our faces were covered in powdered brick from the explosion of the sand demon at Ur-Yag's tower.

"I'm seein' 'em, man. Kurtz and Brumm. How they died. I feel like…"

He stopped.

"You wanna see it, Talk? I can show you."

Otherwhere weirdness crept all around me.

At first, I was like… *hell no.* I mean, I could barely even wrap my mind around the fact that they were dead. I was still waiting for them to just walk into the forward CCP and say intel was wrong. That they Rangered and lived.

But guys were still wandering by, talking about it. And the more they did the more it made it true. Whether I wanted to believe that or not.

It happened.

"Talk… I need to go down there and see it. Like… they got some message, some… thing… they need to show me. Let's walk over to the gates, man."

"Can we?" I asked, feeling some weird excitement I'm still ashamed of.

Tanner looked around.

"Hell, I'm section sar'nt. Can do whatever we want. And… I got to see it, Talk. Don't know about you. I won't make you. But… I gotta."

So we did.

We crossed the necropolis and made the main road, lined with ancient columns all carved with the hieroglyphs of battles and glories past, carved and shaped marble to record deeds no one could remember anymore, and then we began to see the orc dead, and the spent shell casings in the dust of the desert.

"I'm seein' it, Talk," said Tanner in a trance, cigarette smoldering at his side. His hand bloody. Bones showing through. It was quiet there. In the distance I could see the legionnaires on the walls and at the gate. Guarding it now. Talking loudly and laughing. Nervous all the orcs in the world were on the other side, dying to come in and meet us.

Ready for another fight in their cheerily fatalistic Accadion way.

I remember thinking as Tanner began to tell me what happened, I remember thinking... I wish I were them. The legionnaires. I remember thinking, wishing, I was anyone but who I was right at that moment. The guy with the dead buddies.

Sucks to be that guy.

I hate that guy.

I began to want to leave, knowing this would be the worst day of my life. Revering Brumm and his quiet competence. His awe of his brother. Remembering Kurtz before dawn back on Bag-of-Death Island, showing me how to run my rifle. The two of us there in the quiet, not saying anything, and waiting for the enemy to try again by the river.

But I didn't leave the place where they died. And Tanner began to talk, telling me what had happened to them.

Like some grim play-by-play. But worse and ending in a loss.

A loss I would never not think about.

"They started here," he said. "Took opposite sides of the street and started working the orcs. These guys had swords and they put 'em down. One got close and stuck Kurtz with a dagger. I can see 'em, Talk. It's like watching it on replay."

His voice was dead.

Not like that time when Brumm had been killed beneath the fortress, holding our rear as orcs pushed up from the catacombs. Tanner had come out onto the street, crying and saying something.

Something about not wanting to Ranger anymore. And that Brumm was dead.

We'd won that day when it all began. The dragon had been driven off. Last of Autumn was alive when I thought the vampire SEAL had killed her. I shot McCluskey in the eye.

Then it was all snatched away. Brumm cut to death.

And then… for just a moment… we got him back. The chief did a miracle. He'd never done that again. I think he tried. But… who can know the way of things like that? Why people pray and what gets answered by who.

I know he's tried over every dead Ranger. But it hasn't happened again.

"Kurtz is bleeding bad and Brumm crosses the road, firing from the hip with the SAW," Tanner continues. "He says… he says…"

Tanner stops.

Otherwhere.

"He says, Talk... Brumm says... *Come on, Brother. You're okay. I'm here.*"

I felt ice-cold water stop my heart as it occurred to me I'd never heard Brumm ever call his brother that. Always *Sar'nt. Can do, Sar'nt.*

But you knew his brother was his hero.

"They fight here, but Kurtz is bleeding out. They kill a lot of them, Talker. Grenades. They work from the broken column over here where Kurtz can lean and work his rifle 'cause he's bleeding out. But the orcs are getting closer."

I go to that column, and I can see the dried blood all over it and in the dirt and on the stones of the road. The dead orcs, and there are a lot of them, lie everywhere around it. Gunshot to death.

To me, it looks like the orcs got around them and started firing arrows.

There are shattered arrows everywhere in the dust.

"They got hit by a lot of arrows, Talk. But they kept fighting. Brumm gets it through the throat. But he's still working the SAW. They're outta grenades."

I don't want to know any more but Tanner keeps telling me everything in that *otherwhere* dead voice.

"Brumm..."

He takes a breath.

"Brumm dies. Bleeds out and just falls over. Arrows are coming in from every direction and the orcs are close. Real close. By then."

"Where were *the damn helicopters?!*" I scream out suddenly in the graveyard silence of the place where they fell. Realizing they should have been there. Realizing they were not.

Tanner says quietly, simply, "Refuel. Birds were bone-dry."

I swore.

"Talk, I gotta tell you the last part now. There's someone here I... I can't tell you about. But he says you need to hear it."

I started to walk away. I was done. But I couldn't...

I turned toward the port and tried to smell the ocean out there beyond all this. If I could reach it, I would swim away and drown. Anything but... what came next.

"Kurtz sees Brumm go down and some big orc comes in with an axe and tries to take his head for a trophy. Kurtz fires his savage point blank because that's how close it is and blows the thing off its feet. Just before he does, he says..."

Not every battle ends with a win. Some stories end badly. It's almost dawn now. Tomorrow looks like a new battle for us. I've known this part, what happens next, since I began the account of the Battle of Sûstagul. The first battle. I told you I'd tell you then.

But I never wanted to. So I saved it for the last because it was the worst. I'm sorry. I wish... different... better. But it is... what it is.

Tanner says, "Just before he fires and kills the orc, Kurtz shouts, 'Stay away from my brother, you filthy bastard!' He does, Talk. Then he fires... and then he falls down over Brumm to protect him one last time because that's the last thing he can do for his brother now. And then the orcs come and... it's not pretty. It's a hard death, Talk. A very hard one."

The End

ALSO BY JASON ANSPACH & NICK COLE

Galaxy's Edge: Legionnaire
Galaxy's Edge: Savage Wars
Galaxy's Edge: Requiem For Medusa
Galaxy's Edge: Order of the Centurion

ALSO BY JASON ANSPACH

Wayward Galaxy
King's League
'til Death

ALSO BY NICK COLE

American Wasteland:
The Complete Wasteland Trilogy
SodaPop Soldier
Strange Company